THE GRAND

THE GRAND

A novelisation by
Katherine Hardy

POCKET
B O O K S

LONDON · SYDNEY · NEW YORK · TOKYO · SINGAPORE · TORONTO

First published in Great Britain by Pocket Books, 1997
An imprint of Simon & Schuster,
A Viacom Company

Simon & Schuster Ltd
West Garden Place
Kendal Street
London W2 2AQ

Simon & Schuster of Australia Pty Ltd
Sydney

A CIP catalogue record for this book is available
from the British Library

ISBN 0-671-00519-7

Typeset in Melior 10/11pt by
Palimpsest Book Production Limited, Polmont, Stirlingshire
Printed and bound in Great Britain by
Caledonian International Book Manufacturing, Glasgow

Chapter One

Leo Scarman looked every inch the man he wished to be perceived as by the world: a well-to-do, middle-aged, middle-class businessman – a doctor perhaps, or a bank manager or lawyer. The only question the patrons in the Manchester pub he walked into asked one another was why a toff like him had trespassed into their particularly grimy corner of the city.

The bar had a reputation for being rough, even among the tenement dwellers. The floor and walls were filthy, spattered with stains only the regulars found easy to ignore; the atmosphere was foul, redolent with unwashed bodies and clothes, cheap cigarettes and sour beer. There were worse dives in the back streets of the city, but not many.

A young man with an old man's cough that he'd caught in the waterlogged trenches in 1915, and hadn't managed to shake off in five years, spat into the brown mess of caked sawdust at his feet. Leo Scarman's nostrils twitched faintly in disgust as he picked up the brandy he'd ordered and carried it over to a bench seat set in the far corner of the room.

The barmaid eyed him boldly as she cleared glasses from his table. He opened his paper, and pretended he hadn't seen her. The whole point of choosing this place was its anonymity. Perhaps he should have suggested somewhere else. But where? He concentrated on the headlines, irritated by the editor's optimism for the coming year that heralded in a new decade. What made the man think the 1920s would be any different from, or better than, the last ten blood-soaked years?

He picked up his drink, tensing slightly as he recognised a man who was pushing his way through the crowded bar. He was very obviously an ex-soldier fallen on hard times. Just one of the hundreds of thousands returned from the war. Old before his years, down-at-heel, his suit baggy in all the wrong places, one of the returning heroes from what the government called the war to end all wars. Despite the hopeful editorial, Scarman couldn't help wondering how long it would be to the next.

The man didn't bother with a drink. Sliding along the bench seat, he pushed the long flat case he was holding ahead of him. When it nestled against the side of Leo's thigh, he flicked open the catch, lifting the lid just far enough for them both to see the gun nestling inside. Leo slipped his fingers into the inside pocket of his overcoat before shaking the young man's hand. The movement was so smooth, so swift, the barmaid hardly noticed the gesture.

Abandoning his brandy, Leo picked up the case and rose to his feet. His wallet was ten pounds lighter. Despite appearances, it was ten pounds he could ill afford, but then, if everything went according to plan, in a few hours money would be the least of his concerns.

He walked out of the pub, stood on the doorstep and looked up and down the alleyway. There were no cabs in sight, nor had he expected any. Few people had the money to pay for shoes, let alone any other kind of transport in the slums, but there was a tramstop around the corner. Tucking the box inside his coat, he turned his collar against the cold and started to walk.

Winter twilight as thick and dark as any night closed around him as he negotiated his way through the fetid lanes. People spilled out of their cold, comfortless rooms, shouting, fighting, hands outstretched, ready to beg as soon as they glimpsed his expensive trilby and cashmere overcoat.

Keeping his head down, he clutched the case closer to his chest and kept on walking. He saw people waiting for the tram, but, feeling the need for solitude, marched straight past them. Ten minutes later he reached a broader and better-lit thoroughfare; twenty minutes after that he found himself in the centre of Manchester with its imposing public buildings. Concealed behind the most majestic façade of all was his destination – the Grand Hotel.

He crossed the threshold out of the cold and into another world: one where everything was built on a grandiose, palatial scale that also managed to encompass a warmth, comfort and luxury the customers in the pub he had just left could only dream about.

Glittering chandeliers dispelled the darkness; lush, tropical greenery garnished the corners; an open fire blazed in the massive hearth that heated the hall; the deep rich glow of mahogany glowed dully in contrast to the burnished brass fittings on the reception desk. The marble floors and pillars gleamed with polish – freshly applied, he noted.

'Good evening, Mr Scarman.' Mr Collins, the grey-haired concierge, immaculately turned out, if a trifle elderly for his onerous post, greeted him as he walked to the desk. He nodded before turning to the young man supervising the reception area.

'Room eighty-seven.' Pocketing the key he headed for the stairs.

'Leo, ready for tonight?' A tall, well-built, fair-haired man dressed in an evening suit, starched shirt front and bow tie ran down the stairs towards him. Leo would rather not have faced John Bannerman, the owner of the Grand at that moment, but he managed another nod. Impervious to his guest's mood, John continued blithely, 'The party tonight should be quite an event, that's if we ever get this place ready on time. My father always used to say that the workings of a hotel should be invisible. As you can see' – he waved towards the footmen scurrying across the hall – 'we haven't quite managed it.'

'Everything will be fine,' Leo answered curtly, hunching his shoulders as he bunched his coat around the box. 'If you'll excuse me.' He ran on up the stairs.

John Bannerman was too preoccupied to notice his guest's brusqueness. He scrutinised the hall. Any large party, especially a New Year's party on the scale of the one he and his wife, Sarah, had organised, was nerve-racking, but this was doubly so. Lack of trade had forced them to close the Grand Hotel during the war, and it had taken every penny of his savings and an enormous bank loan he'd rather not think about to refurbish the place ready for its reopening tonight.

He stepped down into the foyer. As he passed the fireplace he automatically checked the hearth for dust, the pillars for polish, the reception desk for neatness. He was still examining the floor when a haggard young man walked through the door. He was vaguely aware of him dropping the kitbag he was carrying. He noticed the army greatcoat and hoped that the guest had more suitable clothes packed away if he intended to attend the party. Then he saw the man's face. There was a haunted expression in his eyes that belied his youthful features. An expression that chilled John's blood.

A porter crossed the foyer in front of him, blocking his view; he moved, his step quickening as the porter entered the service lift. But the moment he reached the young man he was beset by embarrassment. How did a man greet a son home from five long years of war? He hesitated, then held out his hand.

'Well, this is a surprise.'

'Hello, Dad.' Stephen Bannerman removed his hat and pushed back a shock of thick brown hair before shaking his father's hand. 'Nice job,' he complimented as he admired the hall.

'I think so, but it cost a bit.'

'I bet. Thought I'd come to the wrong place.'

'God, it's good to see you, Stephen.' Emotion finally overcame reserve as John hugged his son. 'But what are we doing standing down here?' he asked, disguising his feelings beneath a veneer of briskness. 'I'm not the only one who will be glad to see you. Come on, let me carry your bag upstairs.'

Sarah Bannerman stood in her living room and checked the list in her hand for the tenth time in as many minutes.

'Be sure to return all those ashtrays after they've been cleaned,' she ordered the maid who was carrying a fully laden tray out through the door, 'and when you come back dust the tables before you put them back into position.'

'Yes, Mrs Bannerman.' Mindful of the standards of service demanded from all the employees of the Grand, especially in front of the mistress, the girl balanced the tray precariously in one hand, in order to free the other to close the door quietly behind her.

'Adele,' Sarah addressed her daughter who was studying her reflection in the mirror that hung over the sideboard. 'Turn around and let me look at you, darling. The embroidery on that blouse is beautiful. It complements the rose pink of your skirt perfectly.'

'Thank you. What do you think of the headband?'

'Just right,' Sarah replied absently, frowning at her list again.

'Good.' Adele eyed her mother slyly, knowing full well her attention was elsewhere. 'Can I drink tonight?'

'Mmm?'

'Drink?' Adele repeated casually.

Sarah looked up. She'd heard the last word and knew her daughter well enough to realise what she was trying to do. 'I see no harm in a glass of wine. And while we're on the subject of tonight, the men from the bank will be there, so make sure you introduce yourself.'

'That's going to be fun.' Adele smiled mischievously.

'Adele.' Sarah adopted the lecturing tone she used to reprimand the hotel staff. 'Much as we'd all like to get drunk and chase the waiters, this isn't a party. It's work. Look at me. I haven't even changed yet, and I've a thousand and one things to do before the ball, including clearing and locking the office before people start arriving.'

'I thought Dad was taking care of that.' Adele pouted into the mirror, wondering if her lip colour was too pink.

'Exactly.'

Adele smiled conspiratorially at her mother in the glass. They both knew John Bannerman's failings better than he did himself.

'Is that someone taking my name in vain?' John asked as he walked in.

The Grand

'As if I would.' Sarah gave him a fond look that belied her words.

'I've heard from Stephen. There's been a bit of a mix-up.'

'What?' The list shook in Sarah's hand as she gripped it tighter.

'It's nothing serious – only the trains or something. I didn't get the whole message. But he won't be home on Saturday.'

'So when is he coming?' Sarah tried, and failed, to keep the disappointment from her voice.

John stepped to one side. 'Right now.'

Adele screamed as her brother walked into the room. Charging up to him, she hugged and kissed him so violently she bowled him into the sofa. 'Father, you liar.' Clutching Stephen with one hand as though he was about to run off, she punched her father with the other. 'You could have let us know,' she reproached Stephen.

'I'm sorry, who are you?' Stephen asked blankly. 'What's happened to my sister?'

'She's seventeen and grown up, that's what.'

'Since when has seventeen been grown up?' he teased. He turned to his mother. Sarah smiled and opened her arms to him. He returned her hug. When he stepped back there were tears in her eyes.

'Oh, she's off,' Adele mocked.

'All right' – Sarah pulled out a handkerchief and dried her tears – 'go ahead, laugh at me.' She gazed at Stephen, still unable to believe he was really there. 'And look at you. You haven't even shaved.'

'You'd better have some good stories.' Adele perched on the arm of the sofa beside him. 'Did you eat rats in the trenches? Jane's brother said they ate rats every day.'

'Adele!' her father cautioned, eyeing Stephen warily, wondering how he'd react to his sister's teasing about a war every returning soldier described briefly and succinctly, as 'hell'.

'They said you wouldn't be home until Saturday.' Sarah held on to her son's arm. 'How did you get here sooner?'

'Blackmail. We spent Christmas day in Berlin, and – I quote the colonel – "looking like the most miserable sinners on earth". After that we went from misery to downright depression. In the end they packed us off early so they wouldn't have to look at us any more. They're not so proud of us since the war ended,' he added softly.

John glanced at his watch in the awkward silence that followed Stephen's revelation.

'I'd best get downstairs. There's still a lot that needs sorting out. You've come home on the right night, Stephen. We've organised a big party to reopen the Grand and see in the coming year.'

'You go on, I've held you up long enough. And you,' he said, turning to his mother. 'If Dad's busy, you must be frantic.'

'Never mind New Year's Eve – it's your party now. A homecoming. The best we could have.' Sarah hugged Stephen again, and this time there was no stopping her tears.

The servants' corridor was a hive of activity. Maids and footmen darted in every direction, arms full, side-stepping swiftly to avoid collisions. Mrs Harvey, the thin-faced, sharp-featured housekeeper, who ruled as autocratically below stairs as Mr Collins ruled above, was sitting at the scrub-down table in the alcove where the staff took their breaks. Her voice resounded over the chaos as she sorted table napkins into piles: usable, ready to be folded for table, and reject, to be sent back to the laundry for bleaching and stain removal.

Kate, the most experienced of the chambermaids sat opposite her, rubbing a wax tablet of snowfire over her hands in the vain hope that it would soften the redness around her knuckles, the result of scrubbing out too many bathrooms.

'And you watch yourself, Kate Morris,' Mrs Harvey advised, as she tossed another napkin on to the reject pile. 'Any of those gentlemen take too much liquor and try to put an arm around your waist, you tell me. I'm having none of that jiggery-pokery with *my* staff.'

'Don't you worry, Mrs Harvey. One good slap usually stops them in their tracks.'

'Dear God, and you would!' Mrs Harvey gave her a look that bordered on admiration. 'Sometimes I think they should have sent us women off to war. We'd have ended it by 1915.'

'Sounds good to me.' A young barman who was all too aware of his good looks flashed his most devastating smile at Kate over Mrs Harvey's angular shoulder. 'If it happens again, Kate, you can ship out, and I'll stay at home cooking.'

'Don't you start with your tall tales of the trenches, Clive Evans,' Mrs Harvey scorned. 'Coming back without a scratch on you. I reckon you went off to Southport and hid in the sand dunes for three years.'

'It might have been quieter if I had. And it was just the thought of coming back to your smiling face that kept me going, Mrs Harvey.'

'That's enough of your cheek. What's there to smile about? I work ten fingers to the bone every week of the year, and what's my reward? More work. Mr Harvey says he has to look at my photograph to remember my face.' She shouted to a passing maid, 'You there. What's your name? Mary – Marian – something like that. Come here.'

The maid edged her way apprehensively towards the table.

'Kate, you take care of this one. She's new. Show her the ropes and make sure she knows how to use them.' The housekeeper bundled the pile of napkins she'd discarded into a linen bin at her feet. 'Look at us – you'd think we had a tea dance on. Time to get shifted.' She picked up the bin and the pile of napkins she'd folded and left the table. 'You there,' she called to another girl. 'Susan, Sally, whatever you are . . . you should be upstairs by now . . .'

Kate smiled at the newcomer. 'You'll get used to Mrs Harvey.'

'You better had,' Clive advised with mock seriousness, 'because if you don't, you'll be out on your ear.'

'So which one is it, Mary or Marian?' Kate asked, ignoring Clive's wink as he left them.

'Monica, Monica Jones.'

'Right, let's start by showing you those ropes, shall we?'

The refurbishment of the hotel hadn't been the only item that had stretched the Bannermans' budget to breaking point. Sarah was beset by pangs of conscience every time she thought of the bill for her ball gown. The extravagance would mean fewer new spring and summer frocks, but, as she studied her reflection in the cheval mirror in her bedroom, she decided the effect was worth every penny. A simple black, sleeveless, silk, tubular dress overlaid with a transparent, sequin-encrusted, silk-chiffon tunic clung to her still-girlish figure. Opening her jewellery case, she picked out the gold-beaded necklace John had given her for Christmas and slipped it around her neck. She was clipping on the matching earrings when John appeared in the doorway.

'Ready?'

'Just about.' She kissed his cheek as she took his arm. 'Of all the nights for Stephen to come home,' she murmured, scarcely daring to believe that her son was safe at last. 'I've hardly seen him, and the last thing he probably wants is a party.'

'A party is exactly what Stephen wants,' John insisted as he led her down the main staircase. 'After four years of war a celebration is long overdue, and as Stephen's going to be working here with us, it's also time for him to see the Grand at its finest. And' – he closed his hand over hers – 'it will be tonight.'

'If we ever get it ready.'

'Oh, it's ready. It's been waiting for this moment. Covered in dust and dustsheets, biding its time.' He squeezed her fingers lightly. 'Thank you, Sarah.'

'What have I done now?'

'Everything.'

'It's never enough though, is it? I dreamed of this, of all of us back together and the Grand restored. But it never quite happens the way you imagine. Stephen looked so tired . . . so . . . old.'

John knew exactly how much courage it had taken Sarah to voice her concern about their son. Taking her hand, he led her towards the empty ballroom. 'Dance with me?'

'Now?' She looked around at the tables covered with fine linens, the polished marble dance floor, the soft lighting, the new wallpaper . . .

'Now,' he urged, 'can't you hear the music?' He took her left hand in his right, rested his other lightly around her waist and led her on to the floor. Falling in with his mood, she dipped and swayed in time to the music only she and John could hear. A few hours . . . just a few more hours and they'd be back in business. Stephen home and the Grand reopened at the start of a brand-new decade. What more could she possibly ask for?

'God, what a crowd!'

'You were the one who picked tonight to come home,' Adele reminded Stephen, as she dragged him towards the packed ballroom.

'I didn't know all these people were going to be here.'

'Look at the buffet. The Grand's outshone itself.' She tactfully refrained from mentioning the way his dinner suit was hanging on his skeletal frame.

'And look who's at the family table,' he said.

Sitting bolt upright, more starched and dignified than Queen Victoria at her most majestic, was their grandmother, Mary Bannerman. A relic from another age, her upswept, grey hair, stiff, silk gown and jet accessories would have looked more in place at the long-gone queen's court than the present king's.

Adele stood back and straightened Stephen's bow tie. 'You definitely look much more respectable now that you've shaved in honour of the occasion.'

'I've done a lot more than shave, you little monkey.'

'Grandmother.' Adele dragged him forward. 'A late Christmas present.'

Mary Bannerman narrowed her eyes as she contemplated her grandson. 'Stephen.' She glowered disapprovingly at Adele. 'Why didn't you tell me he was home? You're as bad as your father for playing tricks.

Come here, so I can take a closer look,' she ordered Stephen. 'Good God, you look forty.'

'And so do you,' he responded, turning her criticism into an unexpected compliment directed at her.

She offered him her cheek to kiss. 'It is good to have you home,' she said sincerely. But she was glad that the band had chosen that moment to deafen everyone, and incidentally mask the tremor in her voice.

'That's Mr Bannerman's mother,' Kate whispered to Monica as they hid in the wings of the stage, peeping at the guests from behind the band. 'They call her the Duchess. She's best avoided. She thinks she's still in charge and isn't averse to giving the odd order or two, which can be difficult if it contradicts what you've been told to do by Mrs Harvey.'

'I'll remember that. Hey, think of all the leftover food.' Monica's mouth was already watering at the sight of the buffet. 'We'll be laughing tonight.'

'No we won't. They rehash it and put it on the breakfast menu as kedgeree. They don't waste money, the Bannermans.'

'Could have fooled me looking at this lot.'

'This might look posh, but it's done on a shoestring. They've called in favours and spent every last penny getting the place open again.' As Kate rose to her full height, she straightened her white cotton cap, cuffs and apron, and smoothed the long skirt of her pale-blue, striped maid's dress.

Monica followed suit, desperately trying not to contrast their drab uniform with the glittering evening frocks of the guests. One day, she promised herself fervently, she'd be dressed like a lady, just like young Mrs Bannerman.

*   *   *

A tall man pushed his way through the throng to the Bannermans' table. Tapping John on the shoulder, he held out his hand.

'Excellent stuff, first-class. I thought when your father died this hotel would go with him, but you've done a magnificent job of dressing up the old place for the new decade.'

'Thank you. Good of you to say so.' John left the table and deliberately led the guest away from his mother, who was beginning to hold forth on her family's failings.

'It's a shame you weren't here when your father first began to think about reopening the Grand, Stephen,' Mary rebuked her grandson as though he'd deliberately chosen to absent himself during the war years. 'If you'd been around you might have talked some sense into him. All this refurbishment. The place only needed a lick of paint.'

'I think the alterations work,' he contended mildly in his father's defence. 'It was like a museum before.'

'Oh really,' Mary Bannerman countered acidly. 'And what exactly does that make me? One of the exhibits?'

Stephen saw Adele stifling a giggle. It was too much: they both burst out laughing.

'I'm glad my grandchildren find me so amusing.'

'Do I get to dance with my son,' Sarah asked diplomatically, anxious to avoid the onset of one of her mother-in-law's moods.

'Of course.'

Sarah took the glass from Stephen's hand and set it on the table. 'And I think you should slow down a bit, don't you?' she whispered as she led him on to the floor.

*   *   *

14

The Grand

Clive Evans crept up behind Kate and Monica in the wings. 'What's happening? Any scandal?'

'No one's passed out yet,' Kate replied, 'but give it an hour.'

'I came to warn you. Mrs Harvey's looking for you two. She's on the warpath.'

'Come on, Monica. Time to go.'

'I'd rather go out there,' Monica sighed enviously.

'Would you? It's all show, that. It's not my idea of a good time. All of them strangers painting on a smile. And for what? That's what I'd like to know. I'd much rather get some wine from the kitchen and put my feet up.'

'Oh not me.' Monica was half drunk on the heady atmosphere of luxury, elegance and lavishness she'd only been able to speculate on until now. 'Out there. That's the place to be. And one day I'll be with them. You'll see.'

'Mother.' John led a red-faced, cheery man towards the family table. 'This is Mr Fairfax, from the bank.'

'Delighted to meet you, Mrs Bannerman.' Mr Fairfax held out his hand. 'I had the pleasure of doing business with your husband many times. You must be very proud tonight.'

'Yes I am.' She tapped him on the arm with her fan as she leaned towards him. 'Though don't tell my son. He'll get ideas above his station.'

'It's not often I get to meet Mr Fairfax, Mother,' John interrupted. 'Leo Scarman's been dealing with the bank for us. Sometimes I think he's been deliberately keeping us apart.'

'And where is old Leo?' Mr Fairfax looked around the room. 'It's not like him to miss a free bar.'

'He came up from London on Tuesday. He's staying

here. He'll be down soon.' John looked towards the door, wondering where Leo had got to. Fairfax was right: it wasn't like him to miss out on a party – or an opportunity to make new business contacts.

The orchestra was playing a modern waltz with just a hint of jazz resounding in the brass section. The melody echoed up the stairs, percolating along the corridors and through the walls of the guest rooms into Leo Scarman's bedroom. Accompanying the music he could hear faint, far-off laughter and the hum of conversation, but the sounds instilled no desire to join in the merriment.

He moved restlessly from the window to the bed, eyeing the plush surroundings as though he were seeing them for the first time. He fingered the rich, velvet drapes, ran his hands over the polished surface of the wood panelling, and recalled the money that had been spent on them.

Sitting on the bed, he lifted a silver framed photograph from the bedside cabinet. His wife and two daughters gazed back at him, innocent, trusting and, to his eyes, very beautiful. A family any man would be proud of.

His heart beat faster as he replaced the frame on the table. Pushing all thoughts of his daughters from his mind he tried to concentrate on the task at hand. If there was another way . . . he dismissed the thought as soon as it occurred. He had reflected on nothing else for days. There was no other way, and time was running out. Tomorrow the world would know, and he wouldn't be able to bear the expression of martyred reproach on his wife's face – not on her own account, never on her own account: always the girls'.

Slowly, with heavy, deliberate movements he reached

The Grand

for the case he had bought from the man in the pub. Sliding it over the satin counterpane he opened it and looked down at the revolver. It felt cold to the touch, unnaturally heavy for such a small object as he lifted it into his hands. The music continued to swirl around him. He even thought he could pick out the sound of Sarah's and John's laughter echoing above that of their guests. He closed his eyes, imagining Adele spinning around in some young man's arms. The music seemed to speed up . . . faster . . . faster . . . faster . . .

He had to move. Shake off the buzzing in his head. Stop thinking about anything other than what had to be done.

He laid the gun on the bed and walked over to the chair where he'd hung his jacket. He took a letter from the inside pocket and propped it on the mantelpiece. He traced the letters on the outside with his forefinger. 'John Bannerman'. Was there anything else?

He looked around the room. He had no more excuse for delay. He had procrastinated quite long enough as it was. Taking up the gun he sat in the chair next to the bed. He pulled back the safety catch as he looked to the photograph of his wife and daughters one last time. It was no use: he couldn't do it. Not with them looking on.

Turning slightly, he stared at the drapes, the wood panelling, again visualising the money they had cost. That made it easy. His finger closed over the trigger. He squeezed it, lightly, gently. The resulting explosion tore into his brain – killing the music, killing the light, killing everything except the deep red stain that flooded his consciousness and drowned out his existence.

Chapter Two

John Bannerman took a deep breath before climbing the steps that led up to the stage. He blanched as he looked out over the clapping, cheering crowd. Unlike his father and brother, he had never regarded making speeches as his forte. Tightening his hands into fists, he tensed his muscles in an effort to conceal his nervousness, cleared his throat and began.

'I'm only talking to you now, because you will all be too drunk at midnight to understand a word that's said to you.'

'Not on this beer, we won't,' a wag shouted.

John laughed along with everyone else. He waited for the noise to subside before continuing. 'Right, well . . .' he stammered, as his mind struggled to pick up the threads of what he'd intended to say. 'For months now, reopening the Grand has been the most important thing in my calendar, only to have it upstaged on the very day it happens by something far more momentous. I don't think all of you know my son Stephen.' He looked to the family table where Stephen was sitting, his head lowered in embarrassment. 'That's him over there, and he's back with us. We know we're luckier than most.' For the first time since he had begun he was conscious of the full attention of the crowd. 'Welcome home, son.'

The Grand

Sarah kissed Stephen on the cheek as all the glasses in the room were raised in their direction.

'And my thanks to all of you for coming. In fact, thanks to all the family.'

The double doors at the back burst open and the dark, satanic figure of his brother stood framed in the doorway. Although Marcus was two years younger than he was, he had always been the one to attract the limelight. Leaner, fitter, handsomer, and in John's eyes far more charismatic, he exuded the qualities John had always felt he lacked. Poise, assurance, self-confidence and an uncanny ability to make money. He wondered if Marcus had been endowed with both their shares of those characteristics.

His brother's fashionably tailored evening suit might have been considered an affectation on anyone else, but not Marcus. His clothes, like his personality, dazzled friends and acquaintances alike, and even those who had good cause to be wary of the younger Bannerman brother allowed a grudging respect for the way he could manipulate a crowd or a complex situation that would have confounded a lesser man. Marcus stepped forward, smiling and nodding as men and women forced their way through the throng to shake his hand.

Those who couldn't reach him called out greetings while John remained isolated on the stage, left with no choice but to wait for the excitement of his brother's entrance to subside. There was a woman at Marcus's side, dressed in a stunning gown of blue sequinned velvet, with a matching black feathered and sequinned cap that accentuated her exquisite features. She might have been considered beautiful if any warmth had been allowed to thaw the frosty expression on her face.

John smiled, and nodded to her. He knew that she had seen him, but there was no answering smile or hint of recognition in her dark eyes. As usual, he was left with the impression that Ruth Manning would have rather been elsewhere – anywhere – but in his or his family's company.

He waved to his brother and Marcus held up his hand to silence the crowd. A hush descended, and John found himself the centre of an attention he could never have commanded on his own account.

'It's strange seeing this place open without my father striding up and down shouting – usually at me.' John's attention remained riveted on Marcus as he recommenced his speech. 'He was devastated when we had to close the hotel during the war. As you all know, he died before the armistice. But the Grand waited, as I said to my wife earlier, covered in dust and dustsheets, biding its time. And it's taken a fair bit of time and a fair bit of money, but I think we've got it back just the way my father would have liked to see it. So' – he paused for a moment and lifted his glass – 'I'd like to dedicate this evening to him. My father, Charles Bannerman.'

'Oh . . .' The cry was inaudible, except to Stephen who was sitting next to Sarah.

'You all right, Mother?' he asked.

'Perfectly well. I'm sorry, I didn't mean to speak out loud.' She raised her glass, trying not to look too disappointed at John's toast, although she couldn't help but smile at the addition the man behind her made to John's salute:

'Charles Bannerman was a miserable old sod if ever there was one.'

'Right, that's enough from me,' John said as he sensed his audience's attention wavering. 'Get drunk, and enjoy yourselves.'

20

The Grand

Before he could step down from the dais, Marcus joined him.

'Hold on, just one minute.' He stood and waited for the jeers to subside.

'Dear Uncle Marcus – always has to be centre stage,' Adele sniped, *sotto voce*, to Stephen.

'I know you've heard enough speeches for one night,' Marcus proceeded coolly, as a man shouted, 'Bloody family, can't stop talking.'

Marcus pointed to the heckler. 'You can earn the right to scoff when you buy a drink, Jim, not before.' Revelling in the cheers that greeted his wisecrack, he stood back, working and controlling his audience with the expertise of a professional actor. 'This is the most extraordinary event. Resurrection! The Grand Hotel brought back to life by my brother's hard work and efforts. He asked me to join with him in reopening this place. I told him that we've had enough wars already this century.' He paused again for the laughter to subside. 'But John persevered. I've always said the man's practically a saint, and now he's proved it. But imagine having to live with a saint. His wife Sarah has to, every day and night of her life.' He smiled down at his sister-in-law, and for the first time since he had entered the room his smile touched his eyes. 'It must get cold, forever walking in a saint's shadow. Just for once, Sarah, you should be recognised, and it's my honour to do so. The toast is to both of them. Your hosts, John and Sarah Bannerman.'

John left the stage and went to Sarah as the toast 'John and Sarah' reverberated around them. Sarah glanced up at the stage. Marcus was still standing there, still smiling. She was suddenly beset by a disconcerting feeling that his smile was intended for her, and her alone.

*　　*　　*

21

Katherine Hardy

The dying echoes of the cheers that followed Marcus's toast resounded in the corridor outside Leo Scarman's bedroom as Mr Collins thumbed through a cumbersome ring of master keys.

'And I'm telling you, Mr Collins,' Kate urged. 'It was a gunshot. I should know: I used to work in the Red Lion, and the licensee was always firing guns out in the yard. He said it was to scare away the crows, but we all knew . . .' Her voice tailed as the concierge finally found the right key and pushed it into the lock. He turned it and opened the door. Kate peered warily over his shoulder before following him into the room.

'Oh bloody hell, and it was an' all.' She bit her lip as she stared at Leo's body, lolling over the arm of the chair in all its broken and bloody glory. 'I told you, Mr Collins. Who is it?'

'Mr Scarman. Leo Scarman.' Collins began to shake uncontrollably at the sight of the corpse.

'What should we do, Mr Collins?' She touched his arm, a familiarity she would never have dared under normal circumstances. 'Mr Collins?' she repeated, as he continued to stare, transfixed by the sight of the corpse. 'We'll call the police, that's what we'll do,' she decided for him, raising her voice in the hope of penetrating his trancelike state. 'And someone will have to tell Mr Bannerman. I'll call one of the footmen, and get them to do it.'

'No.' Mr Collins made a supreme effort to regain control of himself. 'It's my place to tell him, I'll do it.' He pushed past her and walked down the corridor. By the time he reached the lifts he was running. Kate watched him, more concerned about the concierge than the corpse. After all, there was nothing she could do now for Mr Leo Scarman, whoever he might have been.

*   *   *

The Grand

The orchestra was playing a modern, jazzy piece as Marcus wove his way through the crowd towards his brother.

'This place looks superb, John. Well done.'

'Come on, Marcus,' John chided. 'Every time you compliment me, it's with a double-edged tongue.'

'Not this time. I promise.'

'Wish you'd joined me?'

Marcus looked John coolly in the eye. 'Not for one single second.'

Sarah led a strikingly attractive woman to the family table. Her tall, slim figure was clad in an exquisite gown of scarlet silk and chiffon, adorned with the hallmark tassels and discreet beading that heralded it as a creation of one of the most exclusive French fashion houses. With her blonde hair curled and piled high on her head, and decorated with scarlet ostrich feathers, and her costly but tasteful jewellery, Esme Harkness was dazzling enough to turn half the men's heads in the room, although Sarah suspected that she was of the same age and era as her mother-in-law. But whereas Mary Bannerman clung to the rigid formality of Victorian dress and social conventions, Esme Harkness had moved on with the changing fashions and times.

Still beautiful, and knowing it, she flaunted attractions exceptional enough to attract attention in London's Bond Street, let alone the Grand Hotel in Manchester.

'Mother, this is Miss Harkness.' Sarah effected the introduction. 'Our first guest. We couldn't stop her from moving in, even before the Grand was ready.'

As Mary Bannerman shook Miss Harkness's hand, her eagle eye missed nothing: the elegant, couture clothes, the jet and diamond brooch that ornamented the simple silver ribbon at her throat, the matching earrings, bracelet and rings.

'I like to think of myself as a resident, not a guest.' Esme smiled gracefully as she shook Mary's hand.

'Guest, or resident, that must take some funds.'

'Mary!' Sarah reproached, shocked that her mother-in-law had dared to overstep the boundaries of courtesy by questioning the financial status of a guest.

'But it must,' Mary reiterated, unabashed. 'I'm sure you don't mind my asking, Miss Harkness. But I don't know of any estate in Manchester that bears your name.'

'The entire world doesn't revolve around Manchester, Mrs Bannerman. I'm from Kensington. You might have heard of it.'

'Your name is familiar,' Mary mused as though Esme hadn't spoken. 'I never forget a name, Miss Harkness, and I've heard yours somewhere before.'

Sarah glanced at the door and saw Mr Collins enter the room. Even from that distance it was obvious that he was upset. She watched as he discreetly signalled to John, who made his apologies to the couple he was taking to, before joining the concierge.

Tired of the old women's fencing, Sarah was glad of an excuse to leave their brittle conversation. She headed for the door, but Marcus intercepted her before she reached the centre of the room.

'You look wonderful tonight,' he flattered, taking her hand to delay her.

'Thank you, Marcus. But that remark makes me wonder what I usually look like.'

'Sensational.'

'Thank you for the speech.'

'Not at all. John's finest hour. I wouldn't have missed it for the world.'

'I see you've abandoned your friend.' She glanced at his companion, who was standing looking beautiful but a little lost and neglected in front of the buffet.

'She'll survive.'

'So, who is she?'

'No one.' He closed his fingers tightly over hers. As Sarah pulled them away she saw the woman staring at her; and, if looks could kill, she felt certain that they would be measuring her for her coffin within the hour.

Sheer panic sent the blood pounding headily through John's veins. Fighting a dizziness that threatened to overcome him at any moment, he leaned weakly against the mantelpiece in Leo Scarman's room. The smell of gunpowder, cordite and blood hung, acrid and metallic, in the air, but he no longer noticed its heavy taint. All of his attention was fixed on the contents of the note Leo had left him.

'Mr Scarman had a wife in London, sir,' Mr Collins ventured uneasily, trying to avoid looking at the corpse. 'I thought it might be appropriate for Mrs Bannerman to telephone her.'

John ignored him as he returned the note to the mantelpiece. He stared at the corpse thinking what he would like to have done to the man if he hadn't already killed himself. Even now, pushed to the absolute limits of desperation, his violent thoughts shocked him to the core.

'Dear God, Leo! You stupid, stupid man!' Going to a chest of drawers on the other side of the room he began opening them, one after another, frantically rifling through the clothes they contained in search of papers.

'He must have the certificates hidden here somewhere. They're not in the office. I would have seen them if they were there. For God's sake, I trusted him. He worked for my father.'

'Mr Bannerman,' Mr Collins reminded gently. 'The police will want the room undisturbed.'

John stopped and stared at the corpse again. 'Damn it! He promised. He promised!' Fighting back tears, he turned away from the body and Jacob Collins and left the room.

Head down, cheeks burning, Ruth Manning strode furiously from the ballroom. Marcus strolled after her, catching up with her in the foyer as she ordered a page to fetch her wrap.

'I don't know why you brought me, when you'd so obviously rather spend your time with *her*.'

'You know she's one of the family,' Marcus drawled.

'And very pretty, for a working woman,' she bit back viciously. 'Or hadn't you noticed? Perhaps I should take to the stage and make a speech to remind Mrs Bannerman just which Bannerman brother she's married to.'

'Unlike you, she observes the social conventions.' Marcus tapped a cigarette out of his gold case, and pushed it between his lips. He was amused by Ruth's display of jealousy, and made no effort to conceal his feelings in order to spare hers. 'Sarah was just being polite. She's not interested in me.'

'That's worse. Because disinterest is the only thing that excites you, Marcus.' Snatching her midnight-blue velvet wrap from the page, she turned on her heel and swept out through the foyer. Marcus didn't attempt to follow or stop her. Still smiling at her indignation, he watched as the door opened behind her. Two policemen walked in and went to the desk. Marcus wondered what could possibly have brought them to the Grand tonight, of all nights. Forgoing the party in the ballroom, he went to the office, and knocked on the door. He didn't wait for a reply to open it.

John was sitting behind his desk, a bottle of whisky and a half-empty glass in front of him. Sarah was standing behind him combing through a pile of papers heaped on a side table.

'Problem?' he asked.

'If you could possibly wait outside for a minute, Marcus,' Sarah replied abruptly.

'No, it's all right, Marcus. Come in.' John picked up the glass and drained it before facing his brother. 'Leo Scarman is dead. He's just shot himself in one of our bedrooms.'

'Perhaps he thought a suicide would be good for business.'

John only just managed to control his temper at the flippant remark. 'Leo raised the funds for the hotel's refurbishment. He was in charge. I put him in charge,' he reiterated firmly, shouldering the blame. 'He arranged a forty-thousand-pound loan. The builders have been paid off, every penny of the forty thousand the refurbishment cost, but from the hotel's operating capital, not the loan.'

'What happened to the loan?' Marcus asked.

John shrugged his shoulders, unable to answer.

Sarah looked Marcus in the eye. 'It's all gone.'

'Where?'

'Leo invested it. He played with the family's money and lost it.'

'As far as we can make out, he converted our war bonds into railway stock,' John disclosed bleakly.

'I see.'

'There's no way out, Marcus. The loan has to be repaid, and there's no capital left.'

'And you've no other savings?'

John swept his glass from the desk, in a burst of sudden, uncharacteristic anger. 'No. Tell me how to get out of this mess, Marcus. Tell me. You're the one who has always made money out of thin air.'

Sarah and Marcus watched in silence as he bent down and picked up the pieces of glass. 'This place eats money. There's the staff, the restaurant – all the overheads. We can't keep open without operating capital. I've lost the Grand. It's gone, Marcus.'

The chimes of midnight echoed into the office followed by a deafening burst of cheering. As the strains of 'Auld Lang Syne' closed in around them, John covered his face with his hands. Sarah went to him and cradled his head, wishing she could do more than simply be there for him.

Marcus reached for the whisky bottle. 'Happy New Year,' he toasted, lifting it into the air.

He continued to smile as Sarah glared angrily at him. Wishing he would leave, she turned away and buried her head in John's shoulder.

Stephen woke with a start and looked around his bedroom. For a split second he wondered where he was, then he remembered. Not only his homecoming and the party, but the nightmare. The recurring horror that had haunted his sleep ever since the armistice had been signed.

It was always the same. He was back in the quagmire of the trenches, ankle deep in blood and fragmented bodies, explosions rending the air and shattering his eardrums as he raced through the driving, torrential rain, alongside Edmund. Both of them running for dear life while the mud clutched and sucked at their boots, slowing them to a snail's pace.

Then another blast, fiercer, closer than the last, and Edmund lying, drowning in the soft, liquid mud that oozed over his body, threatening to engulf him. Him kneeling in that same cold, sinking, sticky mess, nursing Edmund's hurt and bloody head in his arms, screaming at the top of his voice in the vain hope that someone would hear him above the din of mortar and shell fire, screaming and screaming for stretcher bearers that never came.

Closing his eyes tightly against the horrendous images of death and destruction, he threw back the bedclothes, swung his legs out of bed and strode across to the washstand, where he poured water from the enormous jug into the china bowl. Plunging his hands into it, he bent his head and splashed his face.

The cold drove the last vestiges of sleep from his numbed mind, but when he looked at his face in the mirror, it was ashen with strain, the nightmare still etched in his eyes. And then he began to wonder. Would he ever really be rid of the war?

Monica and Clive eyed Kate over the rims of their cups as they sipped their tea.

'I tried not to think when I saw him,' Kate confessed as she continued to sketch the gory details of Leo Scarman's suicide. 'I just got busy doing what had to be done. But he was dead all right. Sitting there in the chair, stone dead, covered in blood and all this . . . this . . . stuff.'

'Chef says Scarman was the Bannermans' accountant,' Clive revealed authoritatively. 'He reckons the family's got money problems.'

'Do you think we'll have to clean the room?' Monica asked.

'Who else,' Kate replied practically, 'when cleaning up mess is what we're here to do? Tell you one thing though, Monica. I bet he didn't leave us a tip.' She looked across at Clive and they started to laugh. A discreet cough silenced their mirth. Kate dropped her cup back on to its saucer as Mr Collins loomed over her.

'A word, Kate.' He beckoned her away from the table.

Knowing she was in trouble, she followed him down the corridor into his private rooms. He sat behind the desk in his office, leaving her standing in front of it like a recalcitrant child sent to the headmaster's room for chastising.

'Close the door, Kate.'

Ashamed of her gossip, she did as he asked, keeping her head bowed even when she returned to her place before the desk.

'Mr Scarman was a guest, and a friend of the family. I don't think it is right that we mock him, do you?'

'No, Mr Collins. I'm very sorry.'

'Yes. Now that's said, I should thank you, Kate. You handled last night very well.' He coughed again to hide his embarrassment. 'I let you down. I don't think I could have managed if you hadn't been there. Seeing the body and the gun . . . well . . .'

She knew what he was about to say, but she didn't interrupt him. All the regular staff respected Mr Collins, and pitied him for the tragedy he'd rarely mentioned in the last five years.

'. . . I couldn't help thinking of my son. He'd have been thirty this year, Kate.'

'And he would have had the waiters working at twice the speed last night, Mr Collins.'

'He would have.' He pulled himself together. 'Right, I mustn't keep you. I'll only earn the wrath of Mrs Harvey if I tried.'

'You and me both.' Kate dared a brief smile before she left.

'So, we do the family's rooms as well as the hotel's?' Monica asked.

'Of course. Cleaning three times a week, but clean towels every day. This one's Mr Stephen's. You see to him.' Kate knocked on the door and walked on. Monica opened it and stepped inside, stopping and staring open-mouthed at the sight of Stephen standing naked next to the bed. He grinned at her, clearly amused by her mortification.

'Oh! Oh heck. Don't mind me, I'm just going.' She could feel her face burning as she darted back out into the corridor. Clapping her hand over her mouth she raced down to the linen trolley at the far end.

Arms full of dirty towels, Kate came out of a room and blocked her path. 'What's up?'

'Kate. Oh Kate . . .'

'What?'

'I saw him naked. I just walked in! That bloke, Mr Bannerman, the soldier who's just come back. He was stark naked.'

Kate stared at her for a moment, then began to laugh.

'Shut up!'

Despite her exclamation, Monica's laughter joined Kate's. Clutching one another they leaned against the wall, and carried on giggling until tears ran down their cheeks.

'What the hell's this noise?' John opened the door of his study.

Both girls fell quiet.

'Kate, what is this?' he demanded.

'Sorry, sir. It's all my fault.'

'If this is your behaviour in front of the family, then God help the guests, that's all I can say.' He marched back inside, slamming the door behind him.

The foyer of the Grand was crowded, just as John had hoped it would be the day after its reopening. House guests walked up and down the magnificent staircase. The cream of Manchester society sauntered in, ostensibly for morning coffee in the Reading Room, or a mid-morning drink in the bar, but Sarah knew it wouldn't take them long to inspect every public room in order to compare the new decor with the old.

She stood on the mezzanine and watched the scene, her heart breaking at the thought of the inevitable outcome of all John's hard work.

'You're still open then?' Marcus stood behind her, his arm resting on the rail next to hers.

'John's been telephoning all morning. I don't know what's happening.'

'Marcus?' They both looked around to see John coming towards them.

'Speak of an angel and he appears,' Marcus murmured into her ear, too low for John to hear. Raising his voice, he addressed his brother. 'Solved the problem?'

'Peter Fairfax has agreed to see me. At home. He supported the original loan, so he might look kindly on us now. After all he was a good friend of father's.'

'Don't go looking for friendship in business, John,' Marcus warned. 'The two never mix.'

'What will we do if he turns you down?' Sarah asked.

'I don't know. Try elsewhere, I suppose.' He glanced at Marcus.

'Oh no!' Marcus exclaimed, scotching that particular hope while it was still in the embryonic stage. 'I spent the war stripping businesses down. Why should I start building things up now?'

'Why indeed?' John asked lightly, hoping Marcus wouldn't see his disappointment. 'Anyway, Peter Fairfax is undoubtedly our man. Are you staying here?'

'Am I in the way?'

'I haven't told the family anything's wrong. I don't want Mother to find out, that's all. It's the last thing we need at the moment.'

'You won't be able to hide it from her when the bailiffs move in. She's bound to notice something's amiss when they start moving out her personal effects.'

'Thanks.' John had lived with Marcus's cutting edge long enough not to expect a more sympathetic response. 'I'd better be off.'

Sarah waylaid him. 'Good luck.' She kissed his cheek.

John squeezed her hand briefly before walking down the stairs.

'Coffee?' Marcus asked, once they were alone.

'The restaurant's open,' she informed him frigidly, following John down the stairs.

A thin, wintry sun shone down on the park, illuminating the iced bushes and gaunt, skeletal trees with a clear, white light that felt as though it had blasted directly from the Arctic. Despite the freezing temperature, the paths were crowded with families taking the air. Children darted over the bare, frozen flower beds and hoar-frosted lawns, calling to one another as they chased around, while their elders strolled along at a more sedate pace. The atmosphere was almost that of a holiday, as people wished one another a Happy New Year and a Happy New Decade. Stephen Bannerman listened to the polite exchanges, looked into the chilled, smiling faces of the children, and felt like an alien in a foreign land.

His grandmother's arm, rigid, cold, lay heavily on his, the Victorian train of her black walking gown sweeping the ground behind them as they sauntered down the central path.

Mary Bannerman bowed stiffly to her friends and acquaintances, accepting their good wishes for her continued health and happiness, but her attention remained fixed on her grandson. He looked almost as haggard and emaciated as the trees, but the introspective, tormented look in his eyes disturbed her far more than the lack of flesh on his bones.

Although they walked side by side, their arms touching, his coat brushing against hers, Mary felt as though his mind was still far away. More than anything, she regretted the distance the war years had put between them. She longed to reach out, say something that would touch his heart and make him look at her, really look at her, the way he used to before he had been conscripted. Instead she resorted to her usual disparaging conversation about her sons.

'Your father's always had the temperament of a rabbit. Last night was a splendid accomplishment, but look at him this morning. Hopping about right, left and centre.'

'It's the Grand.' Stephen tipped his hat to a man he remembered vaguely from his schooldays. 'That place will drive him mad before he's fifty. I only have to step into the foyer to feel the building weighing down on me. Forty years of Bannerman tradition. My inheritance.'

'You make it sound like a punishment.'

'More like a threat. It's been hanging over my head since the day I was born.'

'And you should be very grateful. You're lucky to have a legacy of that magnitude.'

'What if I don't want it?'

'Don't be ridiculous, child. I do hope going abroad hasn't filled your head with fanciful notions.'

'I wasn't on holiday,' he reminded her coolly.

'No, I know.' There was a certain amount of contrition in her voice and Stephen knew that was the closest he was likely to get to an apology from his grandmother.

'Sorry, I didn't mean that the way it came out. Maybe it was a mistake for me to go to the party last night. I felt as though I'd come back to an asinine world of music and chat.'

'At least we can agree on that. Ever since the armistice, the churches have been empty and the dance halls full. You'd think we fought the war for the right to be frivolous.'

'What did we fight for?'

'Stephen!' She stared at him in disbelief.

'I mean it,' he said sombrely. 'Tell me, what did we fight for?'

'You know full well.'

'Tell me it was for king and country, for honour and freedom, I'd like to think that is true. Because when I was there, with all the gun noises in my head, stepping on corpses so I could run and hide, I felt as though I was fighting for just one thing. To stay alive.'

Mary recoiled in anguish. Stephen had shown her

a glimpse of a world far removed from the patriotism and jingoism of the marching bands and recruiting posters. A world she neither knew nor wanted to know about. A grim, bleak place where young men spoke with all the cynicism and despair of the old. She hesitated for a moment, not quite knowing how to answer. When she finally did, her voice had none of its usual stridency.

'I can't know what it was like, Stephen. I can't even begin to imagine. But I can listen. Perhaps ladies of my age should listen.'

'I don't know where to begin.' Stephen stared down at the ground as he struggled to formulate his thoughts into words. 'It's almost as though I said so much out there, there's nothing left to tell the people back home. I . . . any soldier . . . would talk to a man – any man. It didn't matter who he was or where he'd come from, if he was an officer, a noncom or a private. Sitting in a trench, on a sandbag in the cold and the wet with rain soaking through your greatcoat and pouring down your neck, you'd tell him everything. Recount your whole life. Reveal things you'd never said before, secret things you'd never divulge to your family or your closest friend. Then, an hour later, you'd stumble across that man with a bullet through his brain, and you'd walk on. Turn to the next man, tell the story all over again. And then you come back here – home I suppose. And you talk to people you've known all your life, and the words are gone. It just becomes . . . chat.'

Mary tried, really tried, to understand what he was telling her, but even the brief scene he'd described was beyond her comprehension. 'Well, it's over now,' she consoled awkwardly. 'It's finished. And you're safe.'

The Grand

'But it isn't over. There are thousands of men out there who are still carrying the war with them, and will go on carrying the war until the day they die. Do you know why they didn't demob us all at once? They looked at us, these soldiers, these killers they'd created, and they were frightened. Frightened of what we'd become and what we'd do once we got back.'

She tensed her gloved fingers until they dug into Stephen's arm like a claw. She wanted to say more, as she sensed he did, but, just as he'd said, there didn't seem to be any words. They turned back, retracing their steps, making their way to the hotel as the silence closed in and consumed them.

Chapter Three

'Mr Collins, I'm expecting a guest this morning, a Mr Durham.' Esme Harkness lowered her voice as she moved closer to the concierge. 'He's a *very* old friend,' she whispered confidentially. 'We were in business together more years ago than I care to remember. Could you possibly telephone my room the minute he arrives?'

'Certainly, Miss Harkness.'

'And if you could show him to the Reading Room. He'll want Earl Grey tea, no milk of course, and a slice of toast. No matter what time of day he walks through the door, he'll want his slice of toast. Mr Durham is a man of very particular tastes.'

'I'll see to it, myself, Miss Harkness,' Mr Collins assured her, before she swept back up the staircase.

John sat in the book-lined, leather-upholstered comfort of Peter Fairfax's study. The coffee on the table in front of him grew cold as he perched on the edge of his chair and listened to the bank manager's verdict on his financial problems.

'There's one obvious solution to your predicament,' Fairfax advised. 'Sell off half the space. Convert it into offices. Quick sale, quick profit.'

'I can't do that. The Grand has to stay as it is.'

The Grand

'John, it would be foolish to cling to the hotel out of sentiment. Even your father would tell you that.'

'It's not sentiment,' John contradicted passionately. 'I absolutely believe it. The Grand is a huge monstrous building. It's an absolute nightmare to service and run, but for all of that, it's magnificent. Change it, cut it in half, and the whole thing tumbles down. You might as well turn it into a boarding house.'

'That's an interesting hypothesis, but your argument traps me. If the Grand can't change, then it must be paid for. I can't defer your payments, and the board would think me a fool for even trying to suggest it.'

'We can pay up to March the first,' John offered desperately.

'April the first I would have said, but then what? If you take my advice you'll close tomorrow before you lose even more money.' Fairfax closed the book on his desk. 'I wish you luck, John. I really do. And providence,' he added compassionately.

Esme Harkness stepped out of the lift and saw her guest talking to the concierge in the foyer. She stood back and viewed Mr Durham critically, almost assuming a stranger's eye. He appeared no different from any other fairly affluent, elderly, retired businessman. Perhaps, just a little hidebound? His clothes, like his mannerisms, were stuck in the Victorian age just as so many of his contemporaries were, including Mary Bannerman.

She hesitated, knowing she ought to greet him, but the weight of her years suddenly pressed down on her. She was too old and weary for any more games or pretence; but, once a businesswoman, always a businesswoman. Forcing a smile, she moved towards the two men, telling herself that long-standing contracts should always be honoured, even in retirement.

'Mr Durham.' She offered him her hand.

'Miss Harkness.' His face lit up when he saw her elegantly dressed figure. 'It's impossible – you're actually getting younger.' He lifted her hand to his lips, and kissed the tips of her fingers.

'Shame on you, Mr Collins,' she scolded lightly. 'I told you to give the gentleman tea.'

'It's not Mr Collins who countermanded your orders, Miss Harkness, but me. I don't think it proper to be seated before the lady arrives. Shall we go through?' He offered her his arm. She took it, and he led her into the Reading Room, where tea and coffee were being served by liveried footmen.

Comfortably upholstered chairs and sofas were clustered around polished mahogany tables, the luxurious effect of the deep carpets and elegant decor enhanced by soft electric lighting and the sedate demeanour of the staff, who waited discreetly in the shadows.

'This is a fine residence, Miss Harkness. It deserves you.'

Esme smiled graciously at the compliment. As Mr Durham took her to their table, a footman placed a tray of tea and toast before them.

'As you can see, I took the liberty of ordering in advance.'

'And there's toast, Mr Durham.'

'Our little ritual. Every New Year's day.' He took the seat opposite hers as the footman pulled out her chair.

'I came here once when I was maidservant to Lady Marchant.' She scrutinised the room, still recognisable from those far-off days, for all the modern improvements. 'But when I was in service I was expected to stand to the side and keep quiet. Not any more.' She picked up the teapot and filled the porcelain cups on the tray. 'Thank God for my investments.'

40

The Grand

'I wonder if you'd be interested in one final transaction, Miss Harkness. A special arrangement to celebrate the New Year. As always I can guarantee a profit.'

'I am listening.' She avoided meeting his steady gaze. Neither the ritual nor Mr Durham's language had changed in over forty years. He bit into his toast.

'But all in good time, Miss Harkness. All in good time.'

John Bannerman thrust the door open and strode across the foyer. He was in a wretched mood that had been honed to anger during his chilly walk across the city.

Monica Jones walked gingerly towards him, carrying a tray and a large jug of water. John saw her, stopped, swivelled round and stared.

'What do you think you're doing here?' he bellowed.

'They want the water changing at reception, s-sir,' Monica stammered, sensing she had infringed the rules, but unaware which ones. 'They telephoned through to the kitchens.'

'Maids are never to step into the foyer. Do you hear me? *Never*! That is a porter's job.'

'Sorry, sir.'

'You should have known that,' John raged, unleashing the full force of his anger now he finally had something to focus it on.

'How am I supposed to know if no one tells me?' she blurted out unthinkingly.

'What?'

'Nothing, sir.' She stepped back, terrified by the expression on his face.

'You said something to me. What was it?'

'How am I supposed to know if no one tells me?' she confessed miserably.

'Then let me ask you a question in return. How am I supposed to get respect in Manchester, if it can't be found in my own hotel?'

A hush descended over the foyer. Monica bit her bottom lip in an effort to contain sobs that threatened to erupt at any moment. 'I'll handle this, Mr Bannerman.' Mr Collins moved smoothly towards them.

'You do that, Mr Collins. Pay her for the week and get shot of her.' John ran up the stairs, leaving Monica staring open-mouthed in shock.

Sarah had witnessed the whole ugly scene from the mezzanine. Turning her back, she walked down the corridor. There was no point in asking John how he had fared with Mr Fairfax – his outburst had already told her everything she needed to know.

He caught her eye as he reached the top of the stairs. Shaking his head, he looked away and walked on quickly towards the office.

A fire blazed high in the hearth of the bedroom, spreading a warm, cosy glow over the piles of clothes and undergarments that lay strewn over the chairs and flowed out on to the carpeted floor. The air was perfumed with a seductive, heady fragrance that heightened the senses and soothed the mind. Mr Durham lay back languidly on the pillows of the double bed, lightly caressing the length of Esme's naked body with his own as his fingers slid sensuously over the satin coverlet.

'I think as transactions go, that was historic.' Lowering the sheet, he bared Esme's nipple and kissed it.

'I take good care of my investments.' She steeled herself to receive his touch without flinching.

42

'Indeed you do. It's the only exchange rate that's remained stable in sixty years.' He glanced around the room. 'This is all very nice, but I can't help missing the old days at Langham Court. It had the finest rooms, and you kept the finest girls in town.'

'You should see them now, Mr Durham. Ladies of society, every one of them. I dare not go to Ascot. I have more friends there than the king.'

'But they were just girls when you met them, Miss Harkness. Gauche and untutored. You transformed them into the ladies they became. And for all of that, you were always the best.' He uncovered her second breast. 'And worth every penny.' Pushing aside the sheet, he produced a plate of toast. 'Do you think they'd be shocked if I rang the bell for more?'

No matter what demands the running of the Grand made on her time and attention, every spare moment drew Sarah back to the mezzanine. She couldn't help herself. Mesmerised by the bustle and activity in the foyer, she was obsessed by John's need to hold on to the hotel. She had to help him, she simply had to. The question was, how?

She continued to stand there, as precious seconds ticked past into minutes, imagining the Grand closed again so soon after its reopening.

'When I was a boy, I'd wait until the foyer was empty late at night, or very early in the morning. Then, when no one was watching, I'd skate across the floor.' Marcus was standing behind her, but she neither moved nor acknowledged his presence. 'Now all it gets is one night of glory, then it's back on with the dustsheets, and I didn't even get to dance with you.'

'John thinks it's all his fault. He might blame Scarman, but he's even harder on himself.' She dared to ask the question that was uppermost in her mind. 'Is it his fault, Marcus?'

'It's bad luck. Though some would say that the luck you get is the luck you deserve.'

'But what's John done to deserve this? He's a good man.'

'It was good men who led us into the war, Sarah. And good men who died. Good men have no place in the world that's left. The rest of us saw what was coming and prepared for it. They didn't. That's the problem with good men: they are never ready for what fate throws at them.'

'Who could have been prepared for this?'

'I would have.'

'You could help now.'

'Tell me how.'

'You own property in Manchester. The theatre, the cinemas, and plenty more you keep quiet about. You could raise the forty thousand against them.' She forced herself to meet his scrutinising gaze. 'That is if you wanted to.'

'Why should I?'

'You grew up here. This was your home.'

'It's a hotel,' he countered dismissively.

'It's family, Marcus.'

'Even less important. And obviously father thought the same, since he saw fit to leave the Grand to John.'

'But now John's alone, and he can't save it. Help him, Marcus, please.'

'He's only my brother. When it comes to business that relationship is irrelevant.'

'Then for my children's sake. This is their home.'

'If you sold the Grand you could buy an estate in Cheshire. Your children would be fine.'

'If not for them, then for my sake,' she pleaded desperately.

'And if I gave you my money, Sarah, what would I get in return?'

'A share of the profit.'

'I don't need it. A good bargain needs something else, something special to make the investor bite. What more could you offer?' She clutched at the rail for support as dizziness took an insidious hold, blotting everything and everyone from view except Marcus. 'Sleep with me, Sarah, and I might consider it.' His voice was light, casual, as though he were inviting her to a tea dance instead of his bed.

'Don't be ridiculous,' she bit back sharply.

'That's what I like most about times of crisis. Matters are reduced to the most essential questions.' He moved closer to her, his lips hovering only a fraction of an inch above hers. 'The question being this time, how far will you go, Sarah Bannerman?'

'I love my husband very much.' It was a simple statement that enshrined all she believed and cherished, yet once spoken it sounded absurd.

'Why? Because he needs you?'

'It's far more than that.'

'Oh, I wouldn't underestimate being needed. It's the most comforting reason for existence.'

'How would you know?'

'Indeed. If one day I'm to find out, if I *am* fortunate enough ever to be needed, then it won't be for my money. I'll earn it. I swear to you, Sarah, I'll earn it.' He stepped away from her. 'Thank you for the offer.' He lifted her hand to his lips. 'And thank you for the dance.'

As she watched him walk down the stairs she called out after him, 'Think about it, Marcus, please.'

'I never think about business, Sarah, I make my decisions straight away.'

'Then what is your answer?'

He looked out over the foyer and uttered a single word. 'Dustsheets.'

The houses were large, solid and well cared for, the street upper-middle-class. Stephen halted at a gate and looked around. The surroundings reminded him of a life he hadn't dared allow himself to think about for four long years. Before the war youth had been allowed to be silly, girls had giggled uncontrollably and boys had laughed without cynicism, pranks had been stupid and pointless, and death hadn't yet intruded with its frigid, skeletal fingers.

Squaring his shoulders, he opened the gate, walked up the path and entered the porch of the comfortable villa. He pressed the bell quickly before he could change his mind and turn and run. To his surprise the door was opened by the lady of the house. A woman who might have been as handsome as his mother, if strain and exhaustion hadn't aged her well beyond her forty-five years.

'Stephen? Good Lord what a surprise.'

'Mrs Grange, how are you?'

She leaned forward and kissed his cheek. 'Happy New Year. You look marvellous.'

'I should have telephoned before calling.'

'Not at all.'

'Is Edmund home?'

'Yes.' There was a peculiar expression in her eyes that he couldn't fathom. 'Yes, he is.' She opened the door wider to admit him. 'He'll be delighted to see you.' She closed the door and led the way down the passage into the drawing room.

46

The Grand

A man sat alone in one of the deep, upholstered chairs that flanked the fireplace. He looked better than when Stephen had last seen him, well dressed, warm and cared for; but there was a vacant look in his eyes that troubled Stephen as much as the strain etched on Mrs Grange's face.

'Edmund, look who's here to see you.'

Stephen approached the chair. 'Hello, Edmund.'

Edmund looked up, but he made no attempt to leave his chair or shake Stephen's hand.

'When did you get back?' Edmund's voice was flat, oddly devoid of emotion.

'Late yesterday. We had a hell of a journey. It took us longer to get from London to Manchester than it did from France to England.'

'It's the strikes,' Mrs Grange intervened. 'The railways are still in a mess.'

'Well, sit down, don't just stand there,' Edmund ordered abruptly. Stephen took the chair opposite Edmund's. 'You're not finding me at my best,' Edmund apologised.

'Last time I saw you, we were both a lot worse off. At least we can sleep indoors now. I met George Clements in Dover. He sends his regards.'

'Would you like some tea, Stephen?' Mrs Grange offered.

'Yes, thank you. That would be nice.'

Edmund glared at his mother. 'We can't have tea yet, Mother. Tea's at half past four. It's not half past yet.'

'It's all right,' Stephen broke in quickly. 'I can wait.'

Edmund turned, greeting Stephen as though he'd only just seen him. 'Stephen? When did you get back?'

Stephen glanced across at Mrs Grange, who lowered her head in despair.

'Yesterday,' he answered slowly as comprehension dawned.

'Hell of a journey?'

'Yes.'

'It's the strikes. The railways are still in a mess.' Edmund smiled vacantly at his mother. 'Doesn't Stephen look well?'

Mrs Grange looked at Stephen, comparing him with her own son. 'Yes, very well indeed.' Her voice was clotted with misery.

Edmund nodded. 'Hell of a journey.'

It was as much as Stephen could do to stop the tears from falling from his eyes as they were falling from Mrs Grange's.

Kate and Mrs Harvey sat across the table from Monica in the alcove the staff used for breaks. The maid's face was buried in her arms and she was sobbing loudly enough to be heard in the guest bedrooms.

'He sacked me there and then on the spot,' she wailed between taking in great gulps of air.

'It's no good looking at me,' Mrs Harvey consoled clumsily, brusqueness negating any intended sympathy. 'I'll need your room cleared by six. That's the rules.'

'But she didn't know,' Kate protested. 'She was told to—'

'It's not a debate, Kate. Six o'clock. Come to my office when you're done, Monica, and I'll pay you what you're owed.' Unable to stand the sight of Monica's tears a moment longer, Mrs Harvey left the table and walked away.

With her audience halved, Monica quietened a little. 'I can't go back home, Kate. They don't want me. Me mam was glad to see the back of me as it was, and I can't go back to that filthy slum and that stinking bed. I just can't. There's water running down the walls. This is the first chance I've had in me life to wear dry clothes.'

Kate leaned towards her as a footman passed the table. 'Look, pack your stuff, but don't leave until I get back,' she whispered.

'Why?'

'Never mind why.'

Kate hurried off and Monica watched her go. Her tears soon dried without anyone to see them fall, but, truly terrified of the thought of being put out on the street, she couldn't stop shaking. Her outburst had got her what she wanted – an ally willing to try to help her get her job back. She crossed her fingers until they ached, hoping against hope that Kate's appeals on her behalf would be enough to induce Mr Bannerman to change his mind.

Kate broke into a run as she darted down the corridor. Having pushed her way through the huddle of maids and footmen milling around the servants' lift, she dived inside, pressed the button, looked up at the ceiling and silently rehearsed the speech she hoped Mr Bannerman would allow her to make. As the doors opened she began to tremble at her own audacity, but she held her head high as she walked towards John Bannerman's study. She knocked on the door and stood back, waiting for the 'come in' before turning the knob and stepping inside. Taking a deep breath, she faced her employer square on.

'I was in charge of Monica, sir. I didn't tell her the rules.' She blurted out the words, not knowing where the confession might take her, but suspecting that there might be two girls, not one, homeless by six o'clock.

'I doubt that, Kate,' John contradicted quietly.

'All right, sir, maybe I told her. But maybe I didn't make it sound all that important. I'll look after her from now on. She won't do it again, sir. I promise.' She locked her fingers behind her back, pressing her thumbnail into the palm of her hand to give herself the courage to add, 'I'm only asking, sir, because . . . because . . . it's not like you to dismiss a girl out of hand. You're the best of employers. Everyone in Manchester says so. All I'm asking is that she gets a second chance, sir.'

'Whatever happens, that girl will need supervision.'

'And she'll get it, sir. Every hour of every day. You can trust me.'

'Yes.' A smile hovered at the corners of John's mouth as he looked at Kate. 'I think I can. Tell the girl the incident's forgotten. And warn her to behave in future.'

'Yes, sir. Thank you, sir.' She paused before the door.

'What is it now?'

'It's Mrs Harvey, sir. She would skin me if she knew I'd been in here to see you.'

'I'll tell Mrs Harvey I changed my mind, without any help from anyone.'

'Thank you, sir. Very much, sir.' She closed the door quietly behind her.

'And tomorrow?' John asked wearily, turning to Sarah, who was sorting through files in the cabinet set behind the door. 'What happens tomorrow when I have to tell all of them they're out of work? Let's see them respect me then. I may be able to give a maidservant a second chance, but who is going to be that kind to me?'

Esme Harkness and Mr Durham descended slowly

in the panelled-mahogany guests' lift, which was a very different affair from the utility box the servants used to ferry themselves and their cleaning materials between floors.

'And of course, Miss Harkness, business must be closed.' Mr Durham pulled out his wallet and counted out four white five-pound notes.

'There's no need. Not any more.' A more sensitive man might have realised that Esme was insulted by the offer.

'Ah, but there is. If only for old times' sake. And this retirement of yours in such luxury.' He rolled his eyes upwards. 'It must cost a pretty penny.'

'Yes, it does cost a great deal,' she agreed. As the light flickered on to the large 'G' set below the first-floor symbol, she took the notes and pocketed them. The last thing she could afford to risk was someone in the hotel witnessing the transaction. Mary Bannerman was keeping far too close an eye on her as it was. The lift opened and they stepped outside.

Mr Durham lifted her hand to his lips. 'Goodbye, Miss Harkness.'

'Until the next time. New Year's day 1921?'

'I very much hope so. Though it's a new age, now. A new decade. Who knows where we'll be in a year's time?'

'I'll be here, Mr Durham, or somewhere very like this. There is nowhere else I can go. Nothing else I can do.'

'No.' There was genuine affection in the look he gave her. Both of them knew that, for all the pretence, Esme was trapped in the Grand. No more free than the lowest maidservant in the kitchen. He bowed one last time, turned and walked quickly to the door. As it closed behind him Esme realised someone was watching her.

51

She looked up. Mary Bannerman was standing at the top of the stairs looking down at her, but a frown on the old woman's face told her she still hadn't remembered exactly where she'd heard the name Harkness before.

Condensation trickled down the tiled walls of the Turkish baths, collecting in pools on the wooden benches. Two men wrapped in towels sat slightly apart from the other occupants, one of them suffering far more from the oppressive heat than the other.

'Of course the money's there, if you want it.' As Fairfax swabbed his face with a towel, he wondered how Marcus Bannerman could remain so unaffected by such a sweltering temperature. 'I could arrange a considerable sum on your behalf at extremely short notice.'

'Set against the sale of the Empire and its offices – and the *other* properties?'

'I take it they are not to be mentioned to the family?'

'Best not. They might not welcome a slum landlord at their table.'

'Like father like son,' Fairfax murmured.

'I think my sister-in-law has a notion of the way I make my money. Without a doubt she's the cleverest one in the hotel.'

'And a very attractive woman.'

'So I'm told.'

'And your brother has agreed to this?'

'No, but he will. He's a good man.' Marcus made the adjective sound like an insult.

'What interests you in the Grand?' Fairfax mused. 'Don't tell me middle age has made you sentimental.'

'There are certain aspects I find . . . shall we say attractive.' He mulled over the word as he rolled it off his tongue. 'Aspects I am confident that, given time, I could make my own.'

'I can't help but pity your brother, Marcus.' Fairfax shifted uncomfortably as he looked towards the door. 'You're a clever businessman, but as a partner? I'd sooner enter an alliance with the devil himself.' Unable to bear the temperature a moment longer, he left his seat and headed into the cool pool room.

Daylight was beginning to fade as Stephen walked down the passage of the Grange house and opened the front door.

'You'll come again?' Mrs Grange pleaded as she followed him.

'Of course.'

'You don't have to,' she qualified hastily, wondering if she'd been too forceful. 'You'll have things to do, starting your life all over again.' She offered him her hand. 'You're a lucky man, Stephen.'

Stephen shook it before turning abruptly on his heel and walking down the path. He didn't look back at the lone figure standing on the doorstep. He couldn't bear to.

'In *my* day people were *known*,' Mary complained, as she and Adele walked down the corridor towards the family's living room. 'That was the way society worked. And now this Miss Harkness moves in under our roof, and no one knows the first thing about her.'

'I like her,' Adele declared cheerfully. 'She sends out the porters to buy her cigarettes.' They entered the room where John and Sarah were sitting.

'You two are here early. We haven't seen you all day,' Adele complained. 'What's been going on?'

'One or two things,' John replied tersely. 'I thought we'd wait for Stephen.'

'And *I* thought I might go home,' said Mary.

'No, I'd like you to stay, Mother.' John pulled out a chair for her. 'We have some things to discuss.'

'What things?' Adele demanded impatiently.

'I'll tell you, if you stop and listen for a moment. There have been problems.'

The door opened again. John looked up. 'Yes?' he said irritably as Marcus strode into the room.

'There's no one employed out front to take charge of the cars. That will have to change. Good evening, Mother.' He kissed Mary on the cheek.

Sarah looked from Marcus to her husband, knowing that it would have been a painful ordeal for John to tell Mary and Adele the devastating news, without Marcus standing by to witness his humiliation.

'As you well know, that won't be a problem for long, thank you, Marcus,' John advised curtly.

Marcus held out his hand. 'Brother.'

Totally bemused, John stared at him. 'What?'

'Partners?'

'Since when?' Mary demanded, clearly horrified by the prospect.

'Of course, you haven't told them.' Marcus grinned at Mary and Adele. 'Leo Scarman's death left your father short of capital. To be precise, forty thousand pounds short. Money which I've raised and now possess.'

'Are you serious?' John sank weakly on to the chair behind him.

'It was Sarah's idea – she seduced me.' Marcus glanced slyly at his sister-in-law.

'What forty thousand pounds?' Adele queried, mystified by the conversation.

The Grand

'Marcus this is . . . wonderful. Do you really mean it?' The magnitude of his brother's announcement had only just penetrated John's consciousness.

'Would I lie to you, brother?'

'Come on through to the study. Let's talk about it.' John left his chair and opened the door.

'We can discuss it here. After all it involves the whole family, and what I'm suggesting is more than a straightforward loan.'

'Come on, I really think we should discuss it between ourselves first.'

Mary grasped her younger son's arm as he passed her. 'What have you done now, Marcus?'

'You'll soon see.' Kissing his mother on the cheek again, he looked to Sarah before following John out through the door.

Sarah tried to follow but Mary blocked her path.

'If the future of this hotel is in doubt, then I should be part of it,' she asserted imperiously.

'Just two minutes, Mother, please,' Sarah begged before entering the study.

'You've never wanted anything to do with the Grand before, Marcus.' John took the contract his brother handed him, spread it on the desk and began to read. 'So what changed your mind?'

'Your wife's bargain. Though the fine detail escapes me. What did we agree in the end, Sarah?'

Suddenly terrified of the events she had set in motion, Sarah went to John.

'Let me read that.' She took the paper from his hand.

'I warn you now: I'm not just lending you the money. If I gave you forty thousand all I'd get is a slow return. I am prepared to sell the theatre and the cinemas only in return for a full partnership, and I don't believe in

55

half measures. Now read the proposal. The last thing
I want is you accusing me later of rushing you into
anything.'

Sarah failed to meet John's eye as they both bent
their heads over the contract Marcus had drawn up.

Chapter Four

Setting himself a brisk pace, Stephen crossed the town and headed straight for the Grand. He ran up the short flight of steps and walked through the foyer, going directly to the bar. It was small considering the size of the hotel, and as luxurious as the rest of the public rooms, but with one marked difference. John Bannerman had set out to recreate the intimate atmosphere of a private gentlemen's club, and he had succeeded, judging by the number of men drinking there.

Stephen looked around. The customers were continuing their New Year celebrations with a fair amount of noise and enthusiasm. Most were young – too young, unmarked and unscathed to have fought in the war, he noted bitterly. And to be able to drink in the Grand, it went without saying that they were also more prosperous than the average veteran. Pulling a handful of silver from his pocket he ordered a Scotch.

'Clive, it is you, isn't it?' he asked the barman.

'It is, Mr Bannerman.' Clive smiled as he poured the drink and handed it over.

'When did you get back?'

'I was luckier than yourself, sir. I came here ten months ago. February last year.'

'How are you?'

'To be honest, Mr Bannerman, we weren't so bad off in the gunners. Safe at our posts, most of the time. And as your father kept my job open, ready and waiting, it's back to normal now.' He cleared a couple of empty glasses, setting them on the tray beneath the counter.

Stephen looked into Clive's face for something he could relate to. After all, gunners or infantry, it made little difference: they had been through the same war together. 'Is it really over for you?' he asked gravely.

'I think so.' Clive deliberately kept his side of the conversation light. 'Same old uniform, same old job. Just like the war never happened.'

Stephen clenched his fist around his glass, outraged that any soldier who had survived the trenches could say 'just like the war never happened'.

Clive knew he'd hit a raw nerve when he saw the look on Stephen's face. He wished his employer's son would appreciate the position he'd put him in. There couldn't be any old comradeship, not between employee and employer's son, no matter what experiences they had shared. The Grand demanded that the staff adopt a professional attitude at all times, particularly behind the bar, where drunkenness might encourage a familiarity that could lead to impropriety – or even worse: unsuitable friendship.

Stephen drained his glass and handed it back for a refill. 'But it happened,' he argued vehemently. 'And it's still happening now . . . Christ how can you . . . how can anyone who was there say things . . . can go on now as though it never happened?'

'Sorry, Mr Bannerman, I didn't mean—'

'It's *Stephen*,' he raged. 'My name is *Stephen*. All that we went through . . . all that we saw . . . the killing, the death, the foul, stinking stench of it. It was the same thing! We went through the same thing, and you can't even use my *name*!' His self-control finally snapped. He picked up the glass Clive had just filled and threw it across the room. It shattered against the wood panelling, the Scotch trickling down in a sticky mess on to the carpet. Conversation ceased, as the customers glanced uneasily at one another, the younger ones feigning amusement to cover their embarrassment at Stephen's outburst.

Clive wanted to help, but he wasn't sure how to. Emotional eruptions from returning soldiers were a common enough occurrence in Manchester – he had even seen one or two while he'd been serving – but he had no idea how to handle men who had gone over the edge. He was as relieved as the bar's patrons when his employer's son finally turned his back and walked out.

'Mr Bannerman?' Mr Collins tried to stop Stephen as he crossed his path. 'Miss Adele has been looking for you all afternoon. She wants to know whether you'd like to . . .' His voice trailed uneasily when he saw Stephen trembling. 'Mr Bannerman . . .'

Unable to endure compassion from Mr Collins, or anyone, Stephen pushed past and ran up the stairs.

Closing his bedroom door behind him, he wiped the tears from his eyes. They were cold. He was too far gone down the road of desperation for sorrow. War had been hell, but at least it had been a hell inhabited by people who had understood. He pulled out the top drawer of his bureau and scrabbled through his clothes. He found a photograph, crumpled, unframed, cracked across the corners. He stared at it, barely recognising his other, younger self. He was just one of half a dozen soldiers, all as fresh-faced, and innocent of what the future held in store for them, as himself. He traced the lines of their faces with his forefinger, halting when he reached Edmund. The only other survivor from the group.

Still holding the photograph, he dug deeper in the drawer and pulled out his service revolver. Unclipping the holster, he removed it, closing his fingers around the cool, hard, familiar weight. It had an oddly calming effect. He opened the chamber and checked that it was loaded, slammed it shut and eased back the safety catch.

He looked up to see Mr Collins watching him in the mirror. The concierge had crept in so quietly he hadn't even heard the door opening.

'I saw an old friend this afternoon,' he said casually as though they were in the middle of a conversation. 'I think you know him. Edmund Grange.' Mr Collins gave a small nod of recognition. 'We served together and we made a pact. We used to say . . . we used to laugh about it,' he added with a wintry smile, 'that if either of us was injured, the other would put him out of his misery. And now he's injured. He's destroyed, but the pact is useless. You see, I've lived with death for so long, Jacob, I can't take another man's life. Though my own doesn't seem so precious any more.'

The concierge stepped closer, closing the door behind him.

'Clive's got the right idea.' Stephen laughed sardonically. 'He's fine. Put it all behind him. Just as if none of it ever happened.'

'Clive's a good lad, Mr Bannerman, but he's not too bright. He never has looked into things very deeply.'

'And he's probably the better man for it.'

'No, Mr Bannerman, I don't think so,' he contradicted softly.

'Why did Leo Scarman do it?' Stephen asked suddenly.

'Mr Scarman killed himself over money. Just money.'

'Then I've got more reason than him.' He stared down at the gun in his hand. 'This thing seems out of place here, in this room. It used to be the nursery. Do you remember? It was full of toys. Now they've gone and all that's left is this. Such a small thing. Heavy, and simple. So easy to use. A child could pull the trigger.' The tension subsided as he slipped it back into the holster and returned it to the drawer. 'Perhaps too easy.' He paused for a moment before turning around to face Mr Collins. 'I keep getting told I'm a lucky man.'

'Yes, sir. You are.'

'I heard about your son. I'm sorry.'

'It was a long time ago now: 1915.' Jacob struggled to keep his voice calm, even. 'He was executed, sir. By the British Army. For desertion.'

Stephen paled. 'I didn't know.'

'That's the rules. It was war. I never thought him a coward, but then I wasn't there to see what he did.' The muscles in the old man's face trembled. 'I wasn't with him, so I can't know what happened.'

'Jacob, believe me, if he was trying to leave the battle, then he was wiser than me.'

'Perhaps. Whatever the truth of it, he's branded a coward. Even on his gravestone. The other graves read "Killed in action". Peter's epitaph is a single word: "Died". His disgrace carved out for all the world to see.'

Stephen stood up and put his hand on the old man's shoulder.

'Don't be ashamed of him, Jacob. Please, don't ever be ashamed.'

The concierge struggled to keep emotion from his voice. 'Oh I'm not, sir. I'm not,' he reiterated fervently. 'When I remember him, I think I'm lucky too.'

The hotel basement housed two dormitories and a row of identical, tiny cubicles. Barely large enough to swing a mouse in, let alone a cat, they were furnished in a drab, utility style that contrasted starkly with the extravagant environment on the upper floors. Each cubicle held twin, narrow iron bedsteads that sported thin mattresses, worn sheets and a single blanket. There were no satin bedspreads for the servants.

In the cubicle at the furthest end of the corridor, Kate was lying in her bed, daydreaming of a future more rosy than her past, when the door opened and Monica sneaked inside.

'Taa . . . raa! Look what I've got.' Throwing off the shawl that covered her nightgown, she stood at the bottom of Kate's bed and conjured two glasses from behind her back. 'Port and lemon. They were left at the bar.'

'You'll get me into trouble, you will.' Kate's caution didn't prevent her from sitting up and taking one of the glasses.

'This is just to say thanks. I'll pay you back, Kate. I swear I will.'

'Oh yes. When and what with?' Kate sipped the port. 'Diamonds would be nice,' she teased.

'I will, you'll see. First chance I get. Me mam says all the chances are up for grabs. Specially for us young girls now that half the men are buried in France. We don't have to be stuck below stairs like she was. We can take whatever we want.'

'Blimey, listen to you. Lady Astor move over.'

'We can, though. Just you watch me. I'm going places, you'll see.'

The enormity of Marcus's offer had totally overwhelmed John. He struggled to remain outwardly calm as he tried to assimilate the implications of the fine print in the contract, but both Sarah and his brother could see that his composure was wafer thin and likely to crack at any moment.

'You've asked me to come in with you often enough in the past,' Marcus reminded, 'though I suspect you never expected me to say yes. How do you feel about it now?'

'Fine. And father would be pleased seeing us together.'

'No, he wouldn't. He'd tell you to run as far and as fast from me as you could.' Marcus touched Sarah's arm. 'Just you remember, you were the one who asked me in. Whatever happens will be all your fault.'

'We should tell the family.' She moved the conversation on abruptly, wishing Marcus would refrain from attributing the credit for his involvement to her.

'Before we do, there's one condition we have to discuss that concerns no one except ourselves. If we're to own fifty per cent each, John, then it will be fire over the front line all over again. Disaster!'

'I couldn't accept less than fifty,' John warned.

'You will accept forty-nine per cent, and I will accept forty-nine per cent. The two-per-cent balance goes to Sarah.'

'We didn't discuss anything like this,' Sarah protested heatedly.

'You get the casting vote,' Marcus emphasised. 'And it's not an easy position: you'll be torn between us.'

'It will be a challenge, and if it means saving the Grand, I'll meet it.'

'John, doesn't it make sense to you? Sarah's always been a partner in all but name.'

'Yes. Of course, it's yes,' John concurred, astounded by Marcus's proposal. 'I'm just wondering if it's fair on you.' He laughed out of sheer relief. 'After all, Sarah's married to me, and that means she's more likely to vote with me.'

'You think so?' Marcus raised his eyebrows. 'Then let's find out, shall we?' He shook John's hand formally. 'It's a deal.'

'Thank you.'

'Good man, John.'

Sarah wondered if John had picked up on the hint of sarcasm in Marcus's voice. Marcus offered her his hand. She tried to shake it but he lifted it to his lips and kissed it instead.

'Now, what happened to dinner?' he said. 'I'm ready for the feast, and after all you've done today, you must be starving.'

He walked out ahead of them, knowing full well that Sarah was watching his back.

John and Sarah were in the foyer early the next morning. The reception area was crowded with guests. Porters bustled in and out of the doors and lifts, lugging suitcases, boxes and bundles that heralded departures and arrivals. Having picked their way through the chaos, they finally reached Mr Collins who was choreographing the proceedings.

'Tell me, how do we stand at the moment?' John asked the concierge.

'Very well, sir. We have seventy-one rooms occupied, fifteen of them departing today, but there are fourteen new arrivals expected. There's not a single absentee amongst the staff and I've been advised by the guests that last night's dinner menu was superb, both in quality and variety.'

'Excellent, thank you. I'm sure my brother will be delighted.'

'What time is he expected, sir?'

John glanced up as the doors opened. 'Right now.'

As Marcus strode in Sarah couldn't help comparing her brother-in-law's arrival to that of an invading army. He was accompanied by an entourage of six men in business suits, two women in plain black clerical outfits, and twelve clerks in shirtsleeves and bands.

'Good morning, all,' Marcus greeted expansively. 'This is unexpected: I assumed you'd still be asleep.' He looked to his staff. 'Mr Hopkins, take your men into the office and wait for me there. You know where it is?' He barely waited for the man to nod agreement before turning to the older of the two women. 'Mrs Sullivan, you see to the kitchens. Page?' He hailed a boy standing next to the desk. 'That's right, you there, escort Mrs Sullivan and her assistants to the kitchens. Mr Brady, you tackle the cellars, Mr Jackson, the kitchens with Mrs Sullivan, Miss Trefusis, the guest rooms . . .'

John and Sarah stared at him in bewilderment.

'What on earth are you doing?' John questioned.

'I believe the Americans call it a shakedown. As from today, I'm an equal partner in the Grand. I can check the books any time I want without giving prior warning.'

'If you're looking to find fault, you'll have to look very hard indeed,' Sarah broke in swiftly.

'Exactly, which is why I've brought my own staff.' He waved to the last remaining man. 'Mr O'Brien, you inspect the staff contracts and conditions, and look for savings there. Mr Collins, show him the way.'

'Very good, sir. This way.'

'Just one thing, Jacob, before you go. How old are you?'

'Fifty-three, sir,' Collins answered with a sinking heart.

John and Sarah didn't hear his reply. They were already following Mr O'Brien into the office.

Mrs Harvey burned with righteous indignation as she charged out of her office and down the servants' corridor.

'They've only just arrived, Mrs Harvey,' one of the maids prattled breathlessly as she struggled to keep up with the housekeeper. 'There's a Mrs Sullivan and two clerks. They're on their way to inspect us right now.'

'Inspection!' Mrs Harvey exclaimed at the top of her voice. 'Inspection of what? That's what I'd like to know. No one's said anything to me about an inspection.'

'Are you the housekeeper?' Mrs Sullivan blocked the corridor, looking Mrs Harvey up and down as though she couldn't believe someone of her appearance could occupy the position of housekeeper in an establishment like the Grand.

'And if I am?' Mrs Harvey crossed her arms and faced her belligerently.

'I'll need to see the kitchens, all the receipts and the staff rota.'

'You'll see the end of my boot, that's what you'll see. Who do you think you are?' Hearing the sound of tramping feet, Mrs Harvey looked up to see her employer accompanied by his brother, his wife and a cohort of clerks striding towards them.

The Grand

'Her name is Mrs Sullivan, Mrs Harvey,' Marcus informed her as he swept past. 'She's with me.'

Feeling a complete fool, Mrs Harvey watched helplessly as they carried on marching towards the staff offices.

'Mr Bannerman, Mrs Bannerman?' she called feebly after them, but her employers either didn't hear, or chose to ignore her. Turning to the maid, she vented her anger on the hapless girl. 'Where are the rest of the girls?'

'It's gone nine, Mrs Harvey. They're on break.'

'Get them shifted,' she ordered abruptly. 'And get them shifted *now*.'

The laundry occupied almost half the cellar area of the Grand. The air smelled clean, warm and steamy with a heady, eye-stinging, nose-tickling mixture of bleach, washing soda and carbolic soap. Wooden drying racks had been hauled close to the high ceilings, stretching from one side of the massive hall to the other, half of them filled with newly washed sheets. White-coated and aproned men and women swarmed around the sinks and tubs set near the taps at the sides of the room, sorting, sprinkling and immersing piles of soiled linen into boilers. As the Bannermans arrived they instinctively quickened their pace.

'This is the finest laundry you could wish to see,' John boasted. 'It could service half of Manchester if it had to.'

'Is that any reason to be proud of the place?' Marcus questioned. 'Look at the space it's taking up. This hall is large enough to house a second ballroom.'

The workers looked anxiously at one another as Marcus kept on walking.

* * *

The entire kitchens were buzzing in a state close to panic. Maids gulped down their breakfast while standing on their feet, grabbing piles of clean linen before they'd swallowed the last of their bread and jam.

'I've haven't had time to eat anything,' Monica whined to no one in particular.

'Complain to Mr Bannerman,' Kate suggested caustically. 'See how well that goes down.'

'Come on, shift!' Mrs Harvey had to shout to make herself heard above the din. 'I've seen bodies moving faster in the morgue.'

Girls started running in all directions.

'That sink's still blocked, Kate,' she yelled. 'I've asked you ten times over to see to it. You there, Edith, Evie what's your name . . . do you call those things on your feet shoes? They look more like Charlie Chaplin boats to me.'

'That's the list.' Kate pushed it into Monica's hand as she went to get a cart. 'Get cracking on the rooms and I'll be up in a minute.'

'But I've never done a room on my own before.'

'Well, now's your chance,' Kate retorted shortly before hurrying to the back of the kitchens.

'Bit of a laugh, eh?' Clive nudged her elbow, as they passed in the corridor.

'I'm glad to see someone's enjoying it,' Kate snapped back tartly, 'because I'm certainly not.'

Marcus and his attendants, who still included John and Sarah, finally reached the upper levels of the Grand, which housed the guest bedrooms. Maids fled from the sound of their footfalls, scurrying in all directions, their arms full of linen, dusters and polishing wax.

'It strikes me that for all the seventy-one beds we

have occupied, there are forty more in permanent use, that are not paid for.'

'You can't mean the staff quarters?' John whirled around to face his brother.

'Yes, I mean the staff quarters. Forty beds occupy a great deal of space. Wasted space.'

'Don't be ridiculous, the staff have to live in.'

'Why do they?' Marcus asked, his voice ominously soft. 'Is it written in some Bible I know nothing of? If you took out the staff dormitories you could build eight new guest suites. Eight more rooms that would give us cash in hand.'

As they moved on to continue their inspection, one of the maids grabbed the hand of the girl nearest her.

'Did you hear that? We're going to be thrown out on to the street. You mark my words, thrown out without so much as a "by your leave".'

Summoning all the strength she could muster, Kate lifted a huge jug of dirty water from the blocked sink and staggered out into the yard at the back of the hotel. Bending over, she steadied herself before beginning to pour the water down the nearest drain.

A girl with messy, uncombed hair, dressed in clothes that had seen better days, crept out of the shadow of the wall towards her. She clutched a torn and dirty waistcoat over her stomach in an ineffectual attempt to conceal her advanced state of pregnancy.

'Kate,' she whispered.

Startled, Kate cried, 'Oh bloody hell!' as she almost dropped the jug. Recovering her grasp on the handle, she turned and shook her head in despair. Everyone who had been part of the skeletal workforce that had manned the Grand during its closure had known and liked Janet. For all her ability to attract trouble, she had been that all too rare phenomenon Clive Evans referred to as 'a laugh'. But the last time Kate had seen her, she had been cleaner, tidier and, judging by the pinched look on her face, better fed.

Glancing warily over her shoulder to check no one was watching from any of the windows that overlooked over the yard, Kate stepped closer to the girl.

'Just look at you, Janet Brady.' She eyed her swollen figure. 'Both of you. And you're looking well.'

Janet's responding laugh was devoid of humour. 'Hardly.'

'You do. You look all right, really. What is it now? Six months?'

'Seven.'

'Seven? Has it really been that long?'

'Yes.'

'Look,' Kate warned, 'you've picked the worst morning ever to come round here. The whole place is being turned upside down for a spot inspection. Did you want to see someone . . . or . . .'

'I was just passing so I thought I'd call on my old friends seeing as how no one calls on me any more, and I thought, you know . . . well I thought . . . there might be a bit of food left over from breakfast.'

'I can't.' Kate was annoyed with Janet for even asking. 'You've worked here. You know how difficult it is to smuggle anything out of the kitchens.'

A clatter from the other end of the yard startled both girls. Kate turned anxiously to see Clive lugging a crate of empty bottles.

'Oh heck, she's back,' he shouted. 'Someone fetch the dogs.'

Janet winked at him. 'Clive Evans, haven't they had the sense to sack you yet?'

'Hey.' He looked at her stomach. 'Don't you go winking and pointing that thing in my direction.'

'Chance would be a fine thing for some fellows.' She sidestepped past Kate. 'I was just asking. There's nothing left over from breakfast is there?'

'Bit of liver, bit of fish. They'll only turn it into soup and give it a French name. Come on in and have some.'

'Clive!' Kate glared angrily at him. 'Have you seen what's happening in there?'

'Of course, but they've all panicked and gone upstairs.'

'Thanks, Clive.' Janet smiled reassuringly at Kate. 'I won't stop long. I'll be straight in and out – promise.'

'And why does breakfast stop at nine?' Marcus asked as he ran down the stairs into the foyer.

'Because it does,' John countered testily. 'It always has. The kitchens have to get ready for lunch.'

'But imagine it: breakfast at ten, at eleven, whenever you want. Absolute luxury. And a hotel thrives on luxury.'

'And if it's luxury, it's automatically double the price,' Sarah commented shrewdly.

'If making money is so distasteful to you, Sarah, there are plenty of charities who would welcome a woman with your business skills,' Marcus advised bluntly.

'Indeed.' Sarah moved away from him. 'Perhaps I should take you up on the suggestion. It certainly seems as though they aren't needed here.'

'We haven't finished yet.'

'I have,' Sarah answered coolly. 'I think you're enjoying this a little too much, Marcus. And depriving you of an audience might temper your appetite.'

As she walked away, Marcus turned to John. 'Show me the stables.'

Clive smuggled Janet into a tiny pantry behind the kitchens. An old table and two rickety chairs had been crammed into the back corner. An ashtray lay on the minute windowsill and yesterday's newspaper was folded on one of the chairs. Clive knew the cubbyhole well. It was one he and the other barmen frequently used to hide away from Jacob Collins's eagle eye.

Chivalrously, he allowed Kate and Janet to take the chairs. After begging an enamel mug of tea from one of the kitchen hands for Janet, he went in search of food.

'Of course people stare,' Janet confessed as she warmed her hands on the mug. 'But I stare back. Like this.' She made a ferocious face.

'You still got that room on Jericho Lane?'

'For what it's worth. Mind you, it's not so bad in summer, and there's a woman downstairs who looks out for me. Of course, the streets around there are full of Chinese.'

Clive returned with a piece of pie wrapped in a napkin. 'Here you go.' He slipped it into Janet's hand. 'It got dropped on the floor and kicked around a bit, but I cleaned off the worst of the dirt.'

'Thank you very much.' She abandoned it on the table.

'I was joking. Here.' He pushed it back into her hand. 'Have it.'

Janet started to eat slowly, nibbling at the edges, careful not to drop any crumbs.

'What are you going to do when this one's born?' Kate asked.

'I've got two months to go yet. My brother's sorting

out things. You remember my brother, Kate? You liked him a lot. He's a handsome lad, and with his help and a bit of luck I'll soon be out of Jericho Lane. And good riddance – that's what I say.'

'Two months isn't long.'

'It's time enough for him to sort things out,' Janet retorted irritably. 'I'll be fine.'

'He's got savings then?'

'You've not thought about me since you last saw me, Kate Morris, and now it's all questions.'

'Janet Brady? I though I heard your voice.'

Clive and Kate jumped to attention as Mrs Harvey appeared in the doorway.

'Sorry, Mrs Harvey,' Kate apologised. 'We just stopped for two minutes. We were going . . .'

'I'll bet you were. Now shift, both of you.'

'It's my fault, Mrs Harvey. I made them stop.' Janet tried to shoulder the blame.

'See you,' Kate murmured under her breath as she squeezed past on her way out. 'And mind you look after that one.' She brushed her hand over Janet's stomach.

Clive followed Kate, leaving Janet to face Mrs Harvey alone.

'I'll be off myself now, Mrs Harvey,' Janet said cheerfully, as though she'd just dropped in to pay a social call. 'I might even walk through reception. After all, I'm a member of the public now.'

'I'm not done with you yet my girl. You'll come to my office right now.'

Despite her show of bravado, Janet did as she was told and followed Mrs Harvey down the corridor into her office. The housekeeper moved behind her desk and sat down. Janet's defiance melted as she was forced to stand before her – just as she had done so many times when she'd been carpeted for minor misdemeanours when she had worked in the Grand.

'I've got girls of fourteen working here, Janet,' Mrs Harvey lectured. 'And I don't just pay their wages. Their families bring them to me so they can get brought up properly. Then you waltz in, proud as punch, showing them things they shouldn't know exist.'

'I don't need to hear this. I get it every day. If I'm not laughed at or spat on, then people look down on me like I'm a piece of dirt.'

'And do you know why? Do you?' Mrs Harvey repeated sternly. 'There's women out there, young girls left with children they're trying to bring up all alone because their husbands died in the war. Abandoned through no fault of their own. If there's no sympathy left for the likes of you, it's because you were just stupid. Stupid with a baker's boy who ran as fast as he could the moment you began to show.'

She was interrupted by a knock at the door. One of the older maids, Brenda, poked her head inside.

'Mrs Harvey, I thought someone should tell you that woman's in the wine cellar now, and she's not happy.'

'Good, that makes two of us.' Mrs Harvey left her chair. 'I'll be along now, girl.'

Brenda shot off down the corridor. Mrs Harvey ushered Janet out of the room.

'I won't see you again, Janet. I'm telling you now, you're not welcome here, and you're to leave those girls alone. They're not your friends any more.' She reached into her pocket, pulled out a couple of shillings and slipped them into Janet's hand. 'That's for the little one, not yourself. Get a good meal down you. Off you go.'

She looked down the corridor to see Mrs Sullivan walking towards her, Brenda at her side.

The Grand

'I can only account for half the stock,' Mrs Sullivan complained.

'Presumably because you've only *seen* half the stock, woman,' said Mrs Harvey brusquely. 'There are *two* cellars.'

'I said that. She wouldn't listen . . .' Brenda began.

'And I'll have your name, girl,' Mrs Sullivan intervened.

As the three women walked towards the cellars, Janet looked up and down the corridor. It was empty. Running as quickly as her swollen frame would allow, she darted back into the housekeeper's office. A ledger lay open on the desk. Quivering in fear lest someone walk in and catch her, she ran her finger down the list of occupied rooms. There was an empty space next to 53.

She turned to a wooden cabinet on the wall behind her and opened the door, her breath coming in quick, hard gasps as she broke into a cold sweat. Scanning the rows of key hooks, she searched frantically for 53. It seemed to take for ever, although it had been there all along, sandwiched between 52 and 54 just where it should be. She snatched the key from the hook and pocketed it, crept to the door and listened hard. Everything was silent. Opening it a crack, she checked the passageway before running out. She kept her head down as she scampered as fast as her legs would carry her along the corridor towards the back staircase.

Chapter Five

It took Sarah ten minutes to track down Stephen and, when she found him, she had no intention of letting him go until he'd agreed to help John.

'If you could just be at your father's side,' she pleaded. 'An extra voice, backing him up.'

'All right, if you really think I can help,' he conceded reluctantly. 'Only we haven't agreed a date for me to start work, let alone what duties I'm supposed to assume. I'm sure *you* would be more help to Dad than me.'

'Marcus likes showing off when I'm there. He can't talk to any woman without trying to impress her.'

'All right. You've persuaded me. I'll do what I can.' He headed off down the mezzanine before doubling back. 'I'll use the servants' passageway.' He pointed down the stairs into the foyer. Sarah followed his glance, saw her mother-in-law and darted back out of sight.

'Mr Collins.' Mary Bannerman's strident voice carried up the staircase to the back corridor where Sarah had already joined Stephen. 'Where are those sons of mine? Tell them I want to see them. At once!'

Half a dozen maids pushed trolleys loaded with clean linen, soaps, polishing wax and dusters down one of the corridors that housed the guest bedrooms. Marcus Bannerman's clerks stepped in between them, studiously examining one bedroom after another. Lynne watched them for a moment before sidling up to Monica and Kate.

'That's what he said, that Mr Marcus Bannerman,' she announced in a stage whisper. 'I heard him myself. Staff out! All our beds chopped into timber. We should complain to someone.'

'To who?' Kate asked.

'I don't know, someone.'

'Why don't you start a union? That should make you popular.'

'It's not just a rumour. I'm telling you it's true.'

'Oh aye. Like yesterday when you said the Germans started the war in 1912 when they sank the *Titanic*.'

'You'll see,' Lynne snapped peevishly. She waylaid another maid who was prepared to listen more sympathetically to her warnings.

'You've only done three rooms,' Kate scolded Monica.

'So?'

'That's terrible.'

'I've been on me own. I couldn't have worked any faster if I'd had a firework stuck up me bum.'

Kate caught the eye of one of the clerks as he left a room. 'Shh, lest you give him' – she nodded in his direction – 'any more ideas than he's already got.'

Janet skirted the side corridor where the maids were working. Treading softly, she tiptoed past just as Lynne shouted, 'This time tomorrow we'll be casual labour, you'll see! That's how much they care. That Mr Marcus Bannerman will have us in Carey Street. You mark my words.'

Janet hurried on down the corridor. She reached

number 53, slipped the key into the lock, turned it, and stepped inside. Leaning back against the door, she shuddered at the sheer audacity of what she'd done.

She looked around. The room was in semi-darkness, the curtains closed against the light as they always were in the unbooked rooms. But the bed was made up and fresh towels laid out, ready for the next guest.

Heart pounding, she moved from the door to the bed and sat on it. The springs were soft, far softer than anything she had ever lain on. From her pocket she pulled the remains of the pie Clive had given her. Sinking her teeth into the soft pastry, she devoured it greedily. She couldn't remember the last meal she had eaten, and she was glad no one was around to witness how close to starvation she really was.

Even after every crumb of the pie lay in her stomach she continued to smell and lick the paper napkin Clive had wrapped around it, trying to prolong the taste in the hope that it would stave off the worst of the hunger pangs that persisted in gnawing, even when she finally managed to sleep.

Marcus stood in the office with John and Stephen, watching as Mr Hopkins and his team of clerks combed through the ledgers stacked on the shelves. Papers were passed from one clerk to another, the expressions on their faces growing more sombre with every new revelation.

'I've made a thousand improvements,' John maintained defensively. 'When father opened this place it was more like a country house than a working hotel. It only had half the rooms we have now, and they were all twice the size of our present units. A guest couldn't even set foot over the door without a letter of introduction. Now it's a proper business, a growing business.'

'Of course it is,' Marcus agreed infuriatingly. 'Otherwise I wouldn't have invested my money in it.'

'Then is all this necessary?'

'Yes. Because I *have* invested my money, and I didn't find forty thousand pounds lying around in loose change. Even with the sale of my properties, the last ten thousand was a bridging loan. And given the emergency and short notice, the bank took great delight in imposing a severe rate of interest.'

'You know there's no fast return on an hotel. Things move slowly.'

'The interest payment on the loan is one hundred and ten pounds a month, John. That is one hundred and ten pounds above and beyond the Grand's standard monthly profit. I have to find it somewhere. My staff will have completed the audit by the end of tomorrow, and as soon as that's done, I want the money found.'

'Your suggestion that the staff live out is impossible.'

'Then find something else.'

'And if I can't? You know there's no way you can force a measure like that through. Sarah and I will outvote you.'

'But would you, John?' Marcus questioned. 'Would that be fair to me? I saved the Grand. I sold businesses that took me twenty years to build up, and all for you and your wife. I made a great sacrifice and you won't give me this one single favour?'

'Perhaps we can find another way,' Stephen suggested cautiously. 'There must be some other way of raising the cash.'

'How?' his uncle asked.

'I don't know . . . but there has to be some other way.'

'By all means try.' Marcus opened the door. 'You've

got plenty of time before tomorrow night. And then I'll be only too willing to hear your suggestions. Mr Hopkins, my solicitor, is expecting us.' He smiled at John and Stephen. 'Good luck.'

Stephen turned to his father. 'So, where do we start?'

John stared at him blankly and Stephen realised his father not only didn't know where to start, but he'd already begun to panic.

Mary Bannerman abandoned her tea and scones in the Reading Room, sailed into the crowded foyer and bore down on Mr Collins. Tapping him on the shoulder she barked, 'Tell my sons I won't tire of waiting no matter how long they try to avoid me. I've always said any partnership between them would end in disaster, but would they listen? Not them. My husband left this building to John and John alone for a very good reason. He knew those two could never work together.'

Uncertain how to respond to Mrs Bannerman's unsought and unwanted confidences, Mr Collins glanced around for someone he could use as an excuse to move away from his employer's mother. Seeing Esme Harkness enter the hotel, he greeted her.

'Miss Harkness, I trust you enjoyed your walk.'

'It's wonderfully cold out there, like fresh mint.' She nodded to Mary, who was openly staring at her. 'Mrs Bannerman,' she acknowledged coolly.

'Miss Harkness.' Mary Bannerman bowed stiffly.

Esme walked on, aware that Mary was still watching her. 'Is my nose bleeding?' she asked as she paused before the lifts. 'You appear to be mesmerised by me.'

'I was just wondering. Exactly which part of Kensington are you from, Miss Harkness?'

'The wealthy part.'

Mary didn't stop looking at her until she entered the lift and the doors closed.

Monica and Kate had scrubbed most of the bathroom in Esme Harkness's suite, when Monica started cleaning the washstand. She stopped working to investigate the enticing array of cosmetics, perfumes and make-up laid out on the marble surface.

'Look at this.' She held up a diminutive wickerwork basket. 'How can anyone need so many bottles of perfume? There's five in here. What does she do, drink them?'

'Stop prying,' Kate ordered briskly with all the authority of her senior status. 'It's the wrong day to lark about . . . Oh my lord! Smell this.'

Monica sniffed the soap in Kate's hand. 'It's gorgeous. It must have perfume in it.'

Seeing the door to her room open, Esme stole inside, taking the girls unawares. Her lips settled into a thin, disapproving line, but her eyes sparkled with amusement at their blatant envy.

'It's French and I rather like it,' she said suddenly, deliberately startling them.

Both girls reached for their baskets of cleaning materials.

'Sorry, miss,' Kate apologised. 'We didn't mean anything. We're almost done. Sorry.'

'I should think you are, but since my room is not my own at the moment, I believe tea is in order.'

'I'll call down for you, miss.' Kate left the bathroom, went to the bedside cabinet and picked up the house telephone.

'Make it three cups.' Esme dropped her severe expression and smiled. 'You can join me, if you're not too busy. In fact I demand it.'

Katherine Hardy

Kate glanced at Monica in alarm. This was one development she hadn't bargained for, and one she knew could get both of them the sack.

'Those girls,' Mrs Harvey complained to Mr Collins as they walked along the servants' corridor at the end of their break. 'They can't work for gossip. Have you heard the latest? Management's going to get rid of the staff accommodation and have them all live out.'

'I'm afraid that particular piece of hearsay might be true, Mrs Harvey. The gentlemen I escorted to the office were talking about it. Mr Marcus Bannerman has drawn up a money-saving proposal which would put an end to any of the staff living in.'

'But the family would never agree to it.'

'The family owe him, Mrs Harvey. They owe him a great deal. Don't you know, it was Mr Marcus who saved the Grand for them?'

Kate stood awkwardly in the centre of Esme Harkness's room, watching as Monica sat back in one of the easy chairs and played the lady for all she was worth. A footman laid a tea tray on the table. He straightened it before looking pointedly from the three cups to Kate as he retreated towards the door.

'And I still wake at six . . .' Esme Harkness revealed. 'The old habits of service die hard. They get in the blood and, no matter how much you try, you simply cannot shake them off.'

'If I had a bed that soft, you wouldn't see me until noon.' Monica gazed enviously at the thickness of Esme's satin-covered mattress. 'Ooh look, Kate, biscuits.'

'If there's nothing else, Miss Harkness?'

'Nothing.' Esme waved the footman away.

Kate opened the door for him. 'Thanks, Ted,' she murmured as he stepped into the corridor. Closing the door behind him, she turned to Esme. 'This is really very kind of you, Miss Harkness, but we can't stay.'

'I've told you to relax, Kate. Don't worry, I'll inform this Mrs Harvey of yours that I press-ganged you into drinking tea with me.'

'So how did you end up with all this?' Monica asked bluntly.

'Monica!' Kate exclaimed.

'I became that shocking and modern thing known as a businesswoman,' Esme divulged.

'Doing what? I bet it was clothing. I've seen those dresses of yours in the wardrobe. They're gorgeous.'

'I suppose it did involve clothing. In a small way.'

'I am grateful, Miss Harkness,' Kate asserted forcefully, determined to have her own way, 'and it's not the worry of Mrs Harvey, honest. But we have to go. We've a lot of work to do, and today's special. You see, we're in the middle of an inspection. Come on, Monica, we've wasted enough of the lady's time.'

'But the tea's here,' Monica protested.

'It's not our place to sit here and drink it. Come on. Thank you, Miss Harkness, you're very kind. *Monica*!' Kate opened the door, and left.

As Monica rose reluctantly from her chair she reached down and took a biscuit from the tray. 'Maybe another time, Miss Harkness?'

'I hope so. It's a splendid room but it does become an ivory tower. You'd be doing me a favour by visiting.'

'Great. I'd love to.'

'But only as long as your Kate approves. She is in charge of you, Monica.'

'She's in charge of my job, not me life,' Monica asserted as she followed Kate outside.

Esme sat back in her chair and smiled. In that one moment she had glimpsed something in Monica that she recognised from her younger self. Something of the same spirit and ambition, and she began to wonder just where it might lead the girl.

Monica caught up with Kate lower down the corridor. Still munching her biscuit, she dumped her dusters on the trolley.

'That Miss Harkness is just lonely.'

'She knew what she was doing. She said she'd been in service, didn't she? And a woman who's that reckless with the rules doesn't care much for anything if you ask me. Now find that footman, and tell him not to breathe a word of what happened in there, or I'll bash him. Go on!' She glared at Monica, who broke into a run. 'And don't you go talking to anyone about it, either.'

Kate waited for Monica to reach the lift before wheeling the trolley on down the corridor. A door closed inside number 53, but, preoccupied by Miss Harkness's behaviour, she carried on pushing the trolley. It was only when she heard the door close a second time that she stopped and pulled out her list to check it. There was a blank next to 53. It wasn't like Mrs Harvey to make a mistake, but certain of what she'd heard, she unhooked the keys from her belt, and pushed the trolley back to 53. She unlocked the door and glanced inside. The curtains were closed, just as they should be. She looked around and saw a shape sitting on the end of the bed. A woman, a young woman with a swollen body.

'Oh begging your pardon, miss. They didn't tell me someone had moved in here . . .' She hesitated. 'Janet?' she ventured.

The Grand

'Shut the door, Kate,' Janet whispered urgently.

'What the bloody hell do you think you're doing?' She stepped smartly into the room and closed the door behind her. 'This is one joke too far. Think what they'll do to you if they catch you in one of the guest rooms.'

Janet turned round and, even in the half-light, Kate could see that she was desperate.

'I've nowhere else to go, Kate. Don't tell them, please.'

Seeing how close Janet was to tears, Kate held out her arms.

'Jericho Lane's gone,' Janet sobbed brokenly, burying her head in Kate's shoulder. 'They're flattening it. One minute there was a knock at the door, the next all these men moved in up and down the street telling everyone that the landlord had sold the houses, and the whole lot was coming down.'

'But Janet, love, you can't stay here.'

'The room's not booked. I checked Mrs Harvey's ledger. It's here, it's empty, there's a bed and water going to waste. What's the harm?'

'Just listen to yourself. This goes way beyond the hotel rules: this is breaking the law. They'll call the police.'

'Oh yes? And when your home's taken away without a moment's notice, where's the police then? Please, Kate, just for the one night. I'll be up and gone tomorrow morning and no one will be any the wiser.'

'There's the workhouse. They've got proper wards now like a hospital and they'll give you food.'

'One night. Just one night in a proper bed, that's all I'm asking for. A good night's sleep for this one.' Janet patted her stomach. 'A bit of peace for one single night.'

Kate couldn't think straight with Janet's pleading ringing in her ears. Dizzy with fear and panic, she helped Janet back on to the bed.'I never saw you. If you're caught I didn't know a thing. And in the morning you're out. Promise me?'

'I promise. Thanks, Kate.'

'Don't thank me. This is nothing to do with me.' Kate walked to the door.

'Kate, do you think you could bring me a bit of food? It wouldn't have to be much. Just a bit to tide me over.'

Kate felt sick as she backed out through the door. If only the whole day was a nightmare she could wake from.

The onset of evening was Mr Collins's busiest time of the day. The reputation of the reopened restaurant had spread quickly, and a constant stream of would-be diners walked into the hotel, adding their demands to those of the guests. In addition, he still had to oversee the smooth running of the Gentlemen's Bar and the Reading Room, check that all the lamps had been lit and that no specks of overlooked dust or dirt were shown up by the electric lighting.

Despite all the claims on his time and attention, little went on that escaped his notice, including the arrival of a rather unpleasant-looking man with an extremely red face. He watched as the man handed a letter in at reception, giving his name as Mackenzie. It certainly wasn't a name he knew, and the man was a stranger, but Mr Collins filed both name and face away in his memory, just in case they were needed for future reference.

The duty clerk deposited the envelope in one of the

numbered cubbyholes that held the guests' mail, and the man walked into the Reading Room.

Mr Collins was in the bar when the man emerged moments later with a bottle of brandy and a glass. He wasn't there to see him read the number etched beneath the cubbyhole where his letter rested. Mr Mackenzie memorised it easily: 105. He'd never had any difficulty in finding someone in a hotel.

Mary Bannerman watched as he turned towards the lifts. She'd heard his name, seen his letter and the cubbyhole it had been deposited in. And she began to wonder.

Esme checked her reflection in the cheval mirror in her bedroom. Her new evening dress had been tailored by her usual dressmaker, but there was something in the flow of the skirt that she wasn't quite sure of. A knock at the door interrupted her musings. Before she could reply, Mr Mackenzie walked into the room.

'What are you doing here?' she cried, as shock gave way to indignation.

'Looking for you of course. Though I must say it would be quicker to get around the maze in Hampton Court than track down a specific room in this building.'

'How did you find me?'

'Word spreads, Miss Harkness, especially about women like you. They told me you'd retired. But I said, that one? Never! Wouldn't know what to do with herself.'

'You could have telephoned.'

'Oh, aren't we all refined all of a sudden?' He grabbed her face in his hand, squeezing her lips together. 'What colour's that?' He ran his finger along her mouth, smearing her lipstick. 'I don't like it.

Plain red suits you best.' He stared intently at her. 'A good proper red, like the colour *she* used to wear.'

There was a hard glint in his eyes that Esme knew only too well. A sinister glint that portended pain and humiliation, two things from her past that she'd hoped she'd finally put behind her.

Stephen rubbed his eyes as he spread the architect's drawings of the Grand out on his father's desk.

'If you took out the staff dormitories, the twin rooms and the staff washrooms you've got a space equivalent to eight guest suites.'

'That's exactly what Marcus said. Eight rooms. He knew. He knew from the start, even before he arrived this morning.'

'There has to be another way,' Stephen asserted wearily.

'If there is, I can't see it.' Grim-faced, John looked across at his son. 'I wish to God I could, but I can't.'

As the maids and footmen came off late duty they huddled together in tight knots in the corridors of the servants' quarters. Lynne's voice, harsh, abrasive, penetrated above the sounds of their whispered conversations.

'It's true,' she protested. 'We're all going to have to live out. I asked Mrs Harvey about it.'

'And she said it wasn't true at all, just a groundless rumour,' Clive broke in.

'She said it wasn't,' Lynne agreed, 'but her eyes went to one side, and everyone knows she only does that when she means the opposite. They're getting rid of our beds. We'll all have to live at home, and that means no home, no job.'

The Grand

'My home's a pit,' Monica declared flatly. 'That's the whole reason I wanted a job like this.'

'We'll have to tip up at the back door every morning like market girls,' Lynne moaned.

'Oy,' Brenda protested, 'my mother's a market girl.'

'I know. I've seen her,' Lynne acknowledged, 'which proves my point.'

'We should go to Mrs Harvey,' Monica suggested. 'Make a proper complaint. Put our side of it. We could send Kate. After all, Kate's been here so long she's almost her friend.'

'Kate's not here now though, is she? That one doesn't care about us. Thinks she's a cut above the common herd. I'd go, but old Harvey can't stand the sight of me.' Lynne neatly escaped the responsibility before it had even been suggested. 'You could do it though, Monica.'

Monica stared at her in amazement, taken aback by the suggestion.

'Yes you could,' Brenda concurred quickly before someone proposed that *she* tackle the housekeeper. 'You're new, you live in, you'd be perfect for the job.'

Kate closeted herself away in a small, but well-stocked pantry at the back of the kitchen. Pulling a damask table napkin out of her pocket she began heaping food on to the centre of it. When she couldn't get any more into it without risking spillage, she opened the door and looked around before stealing back down the corridor.

'Who's there?' Mrs Harvey called out from her office as Kate passed.

Kate hastily hid the bulging napkin in the folds of her skirt.

'Only me, Mrs Harvey, just clearing up.' She looked

through the open door of the housekeeper's office to see Mrs Harvey and Mr Collins sitting either side of the desk with drinks laid out in front of them.

'You get to bed, Kate Morris,' Mrs Harvey ordered kindly. 'It's been a long day for all of us, and there's more to come.'

'Yes, Mrs Harvey. Goodnight, Mr Collins.'

She ran on down the corridor, still hiding the napkin in her skirt.

'We won't hold on to girls like her,' Mrs Harvey sighed. 'If Marcus Bannerman has his way we'll end up with all sorts of riffraff off the street. Do you know what they're calling him?' She lowered her voice. 'The leprosy man. One touch and bits of the Grand start dropping off.' She smiled at the poor joke, but Jacob Collins didn't.

'He asked my age,' Jacob disclosed bleakly. 'He asked my age,' he reiterated as though he didn't want to believe it. 'And you know what that means.'

Sympathy etched in her eyes, Mrs Harvey reached for the bottle to replenish their glasses.

Room 53 was in darkness, but Kate knew exactly where Janet was sitting. She could hear her wolfing down the food she'd brought.

'He's a clever man, my brother.' Janet hiccuped in between mouthfuls. 'He was in service in Cheshire before the war, but he's been saving up. He's buying a little shop in Cheetham Hill. His own little business, a printer's.'

'So why can't you go to him now?'

'He's in London. Only for a few days setting things up, buying stuff for the shop and all that. When he's back he'll sort me out. "My little nightmare", he calls me. Once this one's born I can help in the shop.'

'Is he coming back tomorrow though? Because you can't stay here for more than one night.'

'Hadn't you better go before you're caught?' After she'd succeeded in worrying Kate into leaving, Janet filled her mouth with the last of the food to avoid answering her question.

John sat up in bed, his back propped against the pillows, ledgers spread out on the counterpane in front of him.

'I tightened every budget to breaking point before Marcus joined us. If we had a hundred and ten pounds going spare every month I'd know about it.'

'This is my fault, John,' Sarah mumbled from the depths of her pillow beside him. 'I was the one who asked him in.'

'Nonsense. I've asked him to join me in running the Grand often enough before. He just never paid me any attention.'

Sarah turned over and looked at her husband. She longed to confide in him, relate everything that Marcus had said and done since Leo Scarman had shot himself, but she held back, unable to think of a way to tell him that wouldn't cause him pain.

'Then why did he act on my word?' she asked lamely.

'Because you're prettier than me?' he suggested flippantly, his attention fixed on the ledger.

'John, whatever decisions are made tomorrow, I'll back you up. You do know that?'

'I should hope so,' he answered lightly.

'Marcus can't get past our vote.'

He finally laid down the account books and looked at her. 'It wouldn't be fair to block him at every turn, Sarah. We owe Marcus everything.'

'He certainly is clever,' she reflected acidly. 'How quickly a simple favour becomes a debt.'

'And debts must be paid.'

'It's my debt, not yours. Since I was the one to ask Marcus to save the Grand, I should be the one to pay his price, not you, or the staff.'

'And how are you going to do that?'

She didn't answer. He retrieved the ledger and carried on reading as she turned her back on him and curled up ready for sleep.

But her eyes were still open hours later – long after John had switched off the light and slipped into unconsciousness.

The decor in Marcus's bedroom was very different from that of his brother and sister-in-law's. An interior designer might have described it as hedonism carried to the extreme. The sheets and coverlet on the bed were silk; the fabric wallpaper, French; the lighting, soft, low, shedding a sensual glow over the room as Marcus twined his naked body around Ruth Manning's.

Fighting him, she rolled until she was on top. Locking his legs around hers, he forced her beneath him again, momentarily winning the battle. He stared down at her, smiling, victorious.

'You should have seen him. Poor John, he spent the whole day seething, but he's far too much the gentleman to explode. Sarah, on the other hand, was magnificent. Like ice, but beneath the ice you could see fire raging.'

'She looks like a woman grown dull with commerce and childbirth,' Ruth bitched.

'It's all buried away, hidden,' he continued, dismissing her opinion as jealousy. 'Everyday concerns have stifled the most fascinating woman I have ever met.'

'Perhaps her charms have been hidden so long they've died and rotted away.'

'They haven't rotted.' He smiled.

'You're not thinking of *living* in that place, Marcus?'

'What does it matter to you where I live?'

'It's a hotel. It's just—'

Marcus interrupted with her favourite contemptuous word. 'Common?'

Ruth laughed mirthlessly. 'All right, then, yes, common.'

'Won't I be good enough for you, if I move in there?' He continued to stare into her eyes. Lowering his head, he kissed her. A cruel, violent kiss that held passion but no tenderness. 'Sarah has no problems with a man of my background,' he mocked.

'Must her name even come to bed with us?'

'It's my duty to save her.'

'And just how would you do that?'

'By waiting. In the end she'll come to me.'

'Perhaps it's time I left you to your dreams of your brother's wife.'

'Then go.'

Pressing against his arms, she struggled to extricate herself from his grip. He pushed her back down on to the bed.

'Your dreams are all you've got, Marcus. She'll never submit to your will.'

'Well, she may put up more of a fight than you, but that's not difficult.'

Reaching up, she slapped him across the face with all the strength she could muster. Surprised, he stared at her for a moment, then slapped her back, using considerably more force than she had done. Holding her hands in his own, he used the weight of his body to pin her down, then kissed her again, hard, furiously, before rolling over and laughing.

'Envy becomes you, Ruth. I must remember that for future reference. I really must.'

Stark naked, his eyes wide, staring, Mr Mackenzie knelt before Esme Harkness. He looked up at her, cringing as she brought the flat of her palm full force down on to the side of his face. The blow sent him reeling.

'I'm sorry, Mother,' he pleaded in a high-pitched, childish voice. 'I'm sorry.'

She answered him with another slap, harder than the first.

'I'll be a good boy, Mother. Promise to God. Promise to God.'

Esme continued to stand over him in a long Victorian dress similar to the ones favoured by Mary Bannerman. Only her face was different. Her make-up was as thick as any music-hall artiste's, her skin milk-white, her lips painted a red so garish her mouth resembled an open wound.

'Mummy,' Mr Mackenzie begged as he gazed up at her.

She hit him again. The client she had loathed most during her working life had been Mr Mackenzie, but there had been one small satisfaction in servicing him: and that was his taste for masochism, which had enabled her to hurt him as much as she chose to.

'Mummy,' he continued to bleat. 'Mummy . . . Mummy . . . Mummy . . .'

Chapter Six

Every day began early in the Grand Hotel: no concessions were made to traditional days of rest, or winter darkness. The staff were up, washed, dressed and working hours before a cold dawn brought light into the sky. A full sixty minutes before the dining room began serving early breakfast to the guests, the servants' quarters were awash with footmen ferrying newly polished silverware to the pantries and maids stacking dusters, mops and beeswax furniture creams on to cleaning trolleys.

'Come on, girls,' Mrs Harvey chivvied as she walked towards her office with Sarah Bannerman. 'Move it. Your faces say it all. The lot of you look as though you've been up all night chatting instead of getting a good night's sleep. Well if you have, that's your fault, not mine. Now hurry up and get on with what needs to be done, while there's still time to do it.'

Sarah smiled at the girls as though she were attempting to redress Mrs Harvey's wrath. She followed the housekeeper into her office, just as Lynne and Monica passed the door.

'Mrs bloody Bannerman,' Lynne swore as soon as they were out of earshot. 'That one would have waltzed through the Somme with a smile on her face.'

'Well I can't very well go and see Mrs Harvey now,

can I? Not with her highness in there.' Monica failed
to keep the relief from her voice.

'When then?' Lynne asked. 'You promised that you'd
talk to Mrs Harvey for all of us, Monica. And the girls
are looking to you to do it.'

'And I will,' she promised irritably, annoyed by her
lowly trainee status which enabled the likes of Lynne
to put pressure on her. She was beginning to feel that
'last maid in' could soon become 'first maid out'.

Lynne gave her a sceptical look.

'All right, stop huffing. I said I would and I will.' She
pushed her trolley towards the lifts, panicking at the
thought of having to *face* Mrs Harvey, let alone make
any demands of her.

'I'm not worried for me, Mrs Bannerman.' Mrs Harvey
pulled a chair out from her desk so her employer could
sit down. 'I don't live in. I've got Mr Harvey at home,
and that's all well and good. But some of these girls and
the lads . . . they've got nowhere else to go.'

'I do realise that,' Sarah said awkwardly. 'We're
meeting at the end of the day. All I know is that we're
going to *talk* about the staff beds then. But after that –
I really don't know what is going to happen.'

'Staff living out means half my job gone. I look after
those girls, I give them standards. Some of them hate
me, but they listen. I make them listen and they learn.
That's what the Grand means to them: an education.
You can't just throw that away.'

'I do understand.'

Mrs Harvey looked to Sarah, knowing that she'd
meant what she said, but all too aware that the
decisions that were going to be made at the end of
the day weren't Sarah's to make.

*   *   *

The Grand

Shortly after the sun had risen somewhere above the cloudy January skies, women huddled in furs, cashmere and mufflers walked into the hotel, making a beeline for the Reading Room and morning coffee, Ruth Manning among them. She paused when she reached the middle of the foyer and looked around. Recalling her connection with Marcus Bannerman, Mr Collins approached her.

'Good morning, it's Miss Manning, isn't it? Can I help at all?'

'No,' she snapped brusquely, cutting him dead. Seeing Sarah, she pursed her lips and walked directly towards her.

'Mrs Bannerman. Ruth Manning.'

'Yes, of course. I saw you at the ball on New Year's Eve. Good morning. Are you looking for Marcus? I'd like to find him myself.'

'Marcus can wait. Do you have time for coffee?'

'I'm afraid you've caught me at a bad moment. It is rather a busy day.'

'For me as well,' Ruth concurred frigidly. 'And if I can make the time available, I'm sure you can.' She swept ahead into the Reading Room, leaving Sarah little choice but to follow.

Kate had cleaned two rooms when she chanced upon an abandoned meal trolley in the corridor. Lifting the lids on the chafing dishes she discovered cold chops in congealing gravy, dried-up bacon, stale toast and scrambled eggs. She took a pillowcase from her own trolley and began piling the leftovers into it. Every time she heard a board creak she started with guilt. Looking around to check that no one was watching her, she ran towards room 53. She had her hand on the doorknob when Lynne and Brenda rounded the corner.

Katherine Hardy

'There she is,' Lynne cried.

Kate whirled around, 'What?' She hastily dumped the pillowcase into a nearby linen basket.

'We want to know what you'd do if we went on strike. Would you come out on our side?' Lynne crossed her arms as she faced her.

'Who said we're striking?' Conscious of Janet behind the door, Kate moved further down the corridor.

'We're not yet, but we've got to make plans for when they try to take our beds off us. Monica's asking Mrs Harvey about it this morning, and as soon we get a straight answer as to what's happening, we'll make our minds up. All of us together. What we want to know is, are you with us or not, Kate Morris?'

Esme sat in a silk dressing gown, sipping the tea a footman had brought up for her, while she listened to Monica. The maid chattered non-stop as she crouched over the fireplace on her hands and knees polishing the tiles. Every few seconds Esme's attention wandered to the bathroom door. Any minute now the maid was going to get the shock of her life, and Esme felt a delicious sense of anticipation as she speculated just what her reaction was going to be.

'So Lynne says, "You do it, Monica," then everyone says, "You do it, Monica," till the whole world's saying, "You do it, Monica." And do you know what will happen, miss? Monica will do it, and then Monica will get booted out. What would you do, Miss Harkness? I bet no one's ever put on you.' She turned as the bathroom door opened and Mr Mackenzie stepped out wearing a towel and nothing else.

'What's all this chatter?' he bawled. 'It sounds like a bloody monkey house in here.'

Monica stared at him dumbfounded as colour flooded into her cheeks.

'And what do you think you're staring at, girl? Get on with what you're supposed to be doing.'

Monica turned back to the grate and scrubbed furiously at the tiles, unable to believe what she'd seen. Esme watched while Mackenzie divested himself of the towel and began to dress. Occasionally she glanced in Monica's direction, her mouth crinkling in amusement as she recalled the look on the girl's face when she had seen Mackenzie emerge from the bathroom.

'We're very grateful to Marcus,' Sarah assured Ruth as she looked around the Reading Room. It was gratifyingly full, not only with people drinking coffee and tea, but eating the expensive confections produced by the hotel's baker. 'He not only saved the Grand, but us as a family.'

Ruth picked up her coffee cup and sipped at it. 'Why do you think he did that?'

'Many reasons,' Sarah suggested vaguely. 'But he's just turned forty. He's made his mark on the world and now he probably thinks it's time to take stock. He hasn't really bothered with the family for years. Perhaps he regrets neglecting us.'

'The altruistic Marcus? I think not,' Ruth disputed. 'This hotel stands at the centre of Manchester and I think he believes a partnership in the Grand will give him a respectability which will redeem his otherwise rather dubious reputation.'

Sarah raised her eyebrows. 'Is it that bad?'

'You should know. After all, you are partners now, financially at least. That's why I thought we should spend some time in one another's company, seeing as how we both find ourselves . . . involved as it were.'

'Any advice you could give me on handling Marcus would be gratefully received,' Sarah said sincerely.

'You seem to handle him rather well on your own. I gather that you, and not your husband, enticed Marcus into the Grand. To be exact, you seduced him – or so Marcus says, and keeps on saying.'

'It was hardly a seduction, Ruth.'

'I wouldn't know, I wasn't there, and from what Marcus has told me, neither was your husband. I assume there were no witnesses to the transaction?'

'Did Marcus really say that I seduced him?'

'Yes.'

'But that isn't true. Surely you don't believe him?'

'He talks about you all the time, Mrs Bannerman. Incessantly. Even at the most intimate moments. Sometimes it feels as though the three of us are in my bed.'

'I can understand Marcus, or at least I think I can. He always has taken great delight in his malice. But I wonder that you put up with his behaviour. Why do you let him treat you the way he does?'

'I wonder at that myself, sometimes.'

'I am genuinely sorry if he's having fun at your expense.'

'There's no need to be sorry, no need at all, thank you,' Ruth snapped, angered by the unlooked-for compassion in Sarah's voice. Pity was the last thing she needed – or wanted – especially from Sarah Bannerman. 'I can cope with Marcus. But you, Sarah? You're a stranger yet suddenly you're very much a part of my life.'

'And we both seem to be the victims of Marcus's little games. If it needs saying, I'll say it. I'm happily married and I fully intend to stay that way. Besides, I can't think what on earth a man like Marcus would find attractive in a woman like me.'

'No,' Ruth agreed over-sweetly. 'That's a greater puzzle than the sphinx.' She looked towards the door as Marcus walked into the room.

'Well, well, well,' he murmured as he joined them at their table. 'The two most important women in my life sitting together. I can't tell you how often I've pictured this.'

'So I'm told,' Sarah broke in tersely.

'It's strange. I've only just arrived, yet I feel that I've been in this conversation from the start.'

'I've been warning your sister-in-law. Now that you'll be in close contact every single day she should watch you very carefully indeed. As should her husband.' Ruth turned from Marcus to Sarah. 'And if it's any reassurance, you can be certain that I'll be watching too, all the time.'

Marcus roared with laughter, attracting the attention of the entire room. 'Excellent, Ruth. *Excellent*!'

Ruth continued to sip her coffee, as cool and composed as ever, leaving Marcus to his amused laughter, and Sarah wondering exactly what she had got herself into.

Mr Mackenzie shrugged his ample shoulders into his jacket. Slipping his hand into his inside pocket, he pulled out his wallet, extracted a small wad of notes and handed them to Esme, who was still sitting in her dressing gown. She took the money, pocketed it, and smiled, very aware of Monica, who was obviously eavesdropping while ostensibly cleaning the bathroom.

'Thank you,' she replied graciously. 'And thank you for last night.'

'I am still one of your best, eh?' he leered.

'I'm thanking you for last night because it gave me the

confirmation I needed to reassure myself that I made the right decision to retire. If I want someone to slobber on my neck in future, I'll buy a dog.'

Mackenzie stood back, stunned by her choice of language. 'Well, that's an excellent attitude to present to a paying customer, I must say.'

'I can pick and choose now, Stanley, and I'd rather choose a man who wants an honest tart, not some parody of his own mother.'

'Fine words from a whore,' he spat furiously as he wrenched open the door.

'You're the one who goes whoring,' she reminded him coolly. 'Now run along before Mummy smacks you.'

Mackenzie's colour heightened to the point when Esme wondered if he was about to burst a blood vessel. He opened his mouth, but unable to think of a single thing to say he closed it and left.

Monica continued to work on the sink in the bathroom, scrubbing away with a rag and bar of scouring soap as though her life depended on its cleanliness. Esme left her chair and stood behind her.

'Oh, miss,' Monica cried, hardly daring to raise her eyes.

'Time for tea, Monica, don't you think?' Esme said as she took the rag from the girl's hand.

As soon as the lift doors opened, Mackenzie stormed out into the foyer. Mary Bannerman watched him leave.

'Did that man stay the night?' she asked Mr Collins.

'No, Mrs Bannerman. I believe the gentleman left last night and returned early this morning,' the concierge answered, utilising all the tact and diplomacy that forty years in the business had instilled in him.

Mary gave him a hard look, but she knew better than

to challenge Mr Collins. Holding her head high, she walked on into the Reading Room.

'I'll trust you to keep this as our little secret, Monica.' Esme poured out the tea and handed the maid a cup.

'Oh, I will, miss, I promise,' Monica gabbled, still shocked to the core by what she'd seen and heard. 'I don't know where you get the nerve, though. My heart's still thundering.'

'It's easily done. Stanley's all wind and bluster. There's never any real substance to a man like that.'

'Not just him, miss. I mean . . . you know . . . your . . . profession. Like you said to that man, you know' – she screwed her face against an image of Mr Mackenzie naked – 'slobbering.'

'There's something awful in every job. Even a vicar must loathe his parish sometimes.' Monica giggled at the comparison. 'But it's got me all the things you admire, Monica. Fine clothes, this room and a good meal whenever I want.'

'That's what I want, Miss Harkness.'

Esme leaned forward and whispered, 'But how much do you want it, Monica?'

'Oh, ever such a lot, miss. Me mam's done nothing but service all her life, and she's old before her time. I don't want that for me.'

'It's no good just wishing for the good things, Monica. It has to burn.'

'Oh it does. It really does, miss. You can go up on to the roof of this place and look down on the world. We go there sometimes, me and the girls, to see the guests arriving for the big functions, and it can be midnight, but there'll be all this light. Then you look across the city and it's all lights and people as far as the eye can see. You can even see the curve of the world and feel it turn. All those things, and all I've got is that small iron bed in the basement; and it's lights out by eleven and up at six and work, work, work. It's not fair. I know there's better things out there for me. I want to wear satin and silk so the light shines off me, so I'm part of the world. So you see, it does burn,' she contended solemnly.

'Then it's yours, Monica. You can take it.'

'I couldn't be like you.' Monica blushed again as she lowered her head. 'I couldn't do that.'

Esme laughed. 'Don't you dare. I wouldn't recommend it for any girl. But it's a different world now. The men are falling from their pedestals.'

'But what can I do? I'm just stupid.'

'No you're not. You're off to a good start already – the Grand. This isn't like the service of old. You're not trapped in the kitchen of some country house. A girl like you could end up running this hotel.'

'Me? I can't even get up the nerve to talk to Mrs Harvey.'

'Only because the other girls are telling you what to say. They're not in charge of your life, Monica – and it was you who said that to me, remember? When you speak, only speak for yourself. No one else cares, no one else matters.' Esme sat back in her chair, smiling smugly at the advice she'd given the girl, whom she was beginning to regard as her protégée. A girl she was confident could go a long way, given the right assistance – and perhaps she was just the person to do it.

Stephen walked into the office and dumped a pile of ledgers on to his father's desk.

'What time is it?' John asked without lifting his head from the account book he was studying.

'Midday.'

'And what time does Marcus want to meet us?'

The Grand

'Seven o'clock.'

'Only seven hours.' He looked despairingly at the column of figures he was working on.

Stephen picked up a sheaf of papers and joined him at the desk.

Kate left her trolley at the end of the guest corridor and sneaked back to room 53. She turned the key softly and crept inside. Janet was sitting on the bed with her back to her.

'It's time to go,' Kate reminded her.

Janet continued to sit with her back to her, remote and silent.

'You can get out through the kitchens. I'll go ahead of you to make sure the coast is clear.'

'Has anyone booked this room?' Janet asked as though she hadn't heard a word Kate had said.

'I don't know, and it doesn't matter.'

Janet jumped to her feet and snatched Kate's room list from her belt. 'It will say on this.'

'You can't stay, Janet. I won't let you.'

'It's still empty, see?' Janet hit the piece of paper with her fist. 'I've got to stay. Don't you understand? There's nowhere else I can go.'

'There's your brother. He's got a room. You told me so yourself.'

'He's gone.' Janet's voice wavered until it drifted faint and distant in the close atmosphere of the quiet room. 'He was injured in the war. He died before Christmas.'

'Janet, love, I'm sorry.' The trite words seemed pitifully inadequate.

'He was going to open a shop. He really was. He was a handsome lad, everyone said so. Now there's only the workhouse. And if I go there they'll take my child.'

Katherine Hardy

Knowing only too well how true that was, Kate searched her mind for something comforting to say.

'Have you tried the Salvation Army?' she suggested as a last resort. 'They've got that hospital on Broad Street. They'll take you in.'

'And they'll take my child when it's born.' Janet turned on Kate savagely for daring to make the suggestion. 'Even the army of God will take my baby. There's nothing else that can happen. She'll get taken away. I won't even see her.'

'Janet, I'm sorry.' Kate backed towards the door feeling impotent and totally inadequate.

'And even then they won't have finished,' Janet continued to rage. 'There's an asylum waiting for women like me. They lock you away, like being pregnant's being mad.'

'We wouldn't let that happen to you, none of us would.'

'Dear God, but you're simple, Kate. They'd lock me away because I'm filthy, shameful and diseased. Because I've dared to give birth. And how's my child going to grow up? I'll tell you how. She'll grow up in filth, thinking she's an orphan. Same life, same filth as me. Same useless life all over again,' she muttered, quietening a little. 'On . . . and on . . . and on . . .'

'There must be somewhere you can go,' Kate broke in. 'You must have some family?'

'Do you think I haven't already tried them? I want to stop her growing.' Janet clenched her fists around her stomach. 'I want to rip her out and stop her. But I can't. She's growing and she's taking my life with her. She's killing me, Kate. Killing me and no one seems to understand, or wants to help.'

'You seem to be feeding Ruth all manner of fictions,'

106

Sarah challenged Marcus as they walked from the Reading Room out into the foyer. 'As though you've invested in the Grand as part of a plan for an even greater conquest, with me as the prize.'

'That's absolutely true and you know it.'

'If I am so captivating, then please listen to what I have to say. This plan to remove the staff accommodation is disrupting the entire building. These people are not only employed by us, they respect us. They work hard, and we should be grateful to them, not wreck their lives.'

'Oh, I understand,' he mused, a wry smile turning up the corners of his mouth. 'You've come to speak on behalf of the common herd, is that it?'

'Since you wouldn't give them the time of day, yes.'

'And you care for them?' Marcus mocked sardonically. 'The unfortunate and the oppressed?'

'Evidently more than you do.'

'That's a lie. You didn't give a damn about them when you asked me to invest in the Grand.'

'What's your investment in the Grand got to do with the poor?'

'You knew that half my money lay in slum housing but you demanded it all the same. Now the slums are sold. People are out on the streets and it's all because of you, Sarah.'

'How many of them are out on the streets?' she asked, a cold claw of fear closing around her throat. 'How many are homeless?'

'Hundreds. The entire Baxter estate has been flattened. All the houses on Jericho Lane have gone, and it's your doing. You knew selling the slums was the only way I could raise the cash. So don't pretend the fate of poor innocent servants is keeping you awake at night. It won't wash.'

'I wouldn't deprive people of shelter,' she protested, 'not by choice.'

'Yes you would, and you have. And you'd do the same again. You only have a conscience when it's expedient, Sarah. You're exactly the same as me.'

'I'm nothing like you.'

'We're the same person. You'd act the same as me if you didn't have to wear the mask of dutiful, loving wife and mother, but' – he brought his face very close to hers – 'I can see what's underneath. I can set you free.'

'I wish you'd stop this ridiculous conceit. I'm John's wife and always will be.'

'The Grand was his once, remember.'

'You'll find it easier to move the hundred rooms of this building than me. Since your only experience of my sex is with deluded little rich girls, you wouldn't know that what I have with John and my children makes you, and everything you achieve, worth no more than a pan full of dust.'

She tried to walk away but Marcus gripped her arm, knowing that, with Mr Collins and the guests only feet away, she wouldn't risk creating a scene.

'John will always disappoint you, Sarah. Always. And the more that happens, the closer you will get to me. You and I are the same, and I need only wait, because slowly, surely, you'll come to think like me, act like me, and finally you'll come to me.'

She tried to stare him out but lost her composure, and wrenching her arm from his hand, she walked away. Marcus watched her go, his face dark, serious. He'd meant every word. It could only be a matter of time before she was his, he truly believed it, and he was certain that she did too.

Monica hovered outside Mrs Harvey's room. Although

she was flanked either side by Lynne and Brenda, not even their threats could galvanise her into summoning up the courage she needed to knock on the door.

'All right,' she burst out touchily. 'Stop bossing me.'

'I'll boss you all I like, Monica Jones,' Lynne retorted harshly. 'You're only a trainee housemaid. Now get in there.'

Monica looked from Lynne to the door, made her decision as to which was the lesser evil, took a deep breath and knocked.

Mrs Harvey opened it. 'Come in and be quick. You've caught me on my way out.'

As Monica walked through the door she sensed Lynne and Brenda retreating, and resented them for leaving her to it.

'What is it?' Mrs Harvey snapped.

'It's just that I wanted a word, Mrs Harvey,' Monica stammered nervously.

'Spit it out then, I'm listening.'

'You know these rumours about the beds—'

'For the last time I don't know what's going to happen. So don't bother me.'

Monica glanced towards the door, thinking of Lynne and Brenda's desertion. She stepped closer to the housekeeper, pitching her voice low, confidential. 'I realise that, and I just thought someone should say that whatever happens, we know it's not your fault, Mrs Harvey. You always do the best for us. I've seen that. And I know you're always shouting, but that's only because half the girls who work here are useless.'

'So you've come crawling. Is that it?'

'No, I felt someone had to tell you that some of the maids appreciate what you've done for us. The Bannermans can chuck us out, but we'll remember that it was you who gave us a home.'

'Well, thank you for that, I suppose. Now, haven't you got work to do?'

'Yes.' Monica opened the door. 'Thank you for hearing me out, Mrs Harvey.'

'Monica,' Mrs Harvey called. 'I need someone out there on my side. You hear any stories flying around, you come to me with them first, do you hear?'

'Yes, Mrs Harvey. I'll come straight to you.' She closed the door behind her and walked on up the corridor to where Brenda and Lynne were lying in wait.

'What did she say?' Lynne pounced on her as she rounded the corner.

'Is it true?' Brenda interrupted before she could answer.

'She wouldn't talk about it.' Monica did her best to look as though the housekeeper had given her a rough time. 'Bit my head off, then chucked me out of her office.'

Brenda and Lynne glanced triumphantly at one another as Monica walked away.

'See, they'll tell us nowt,' Lynne crowed. 'Lowest of the low, that's us.'

'I've got this, look.' Kate closed the door of room 53 behind her and handed Janet an old coat. 'I know it's not much, but it should help a bit.'

'If I don't go, what will you do?' Janet asked outright.

'I'm sorry, but I'd have to tell Mrs Harvey.'

'And I'll tell her an' all. I'll tell her that this was your idea. That you hid me away in this room.'

'Dear God, Janet, you always were one for wild stories, but this . . .' Kate fell silent, appalled by the enormity of Janet's threat.

'Why?' Janet begged. 'Why won't you help me?'

'Because I can't. I wish I could, but I can't. No one can. If you stay here and get caught, we'll all get the blame and what good would that do you? The management's taking our rooms away, never mind yours, and half the girls are talking of a strike. One more problem and the whole place will go up. Now, are you coming?'

'No.' Janet's voice was quiet, but firm.

'Then I've got no choice.'

'You won't do it,' Janet warned, as Kate turned the door knob.

'I've got no choice,' Kate repeated miserably.

'You won't do it. I've got a child. Don't you understand? A child . . .'

Unable to bear Janet's whining a minute longer, Kate fled. Safe in the staff quarters, she hesitated outside Mrs Harvey's office, but even as she lifted her hand to knock on the door, she knew she couldn't give Janet away. She walked on to the service cupboard and stepped inside. Relieved to find herself alone, she allowed the tears that had been building up all morning to finally fall. Frustrated and upset, she kicked a pile of blankets, buried her face in her hands and cried as though she was never going to stop.

Chapter Seven

'Monica, I told you to advance yourself. I didn't tell you to lie,' Esme reprimanded, as the maid filled her slipper bath with a huge jug of hot water.

'But it worked though, didn't it, Miss Harkness? Mrs Harvey thinks I'm on her side, and the girls think I'm on theirs – and it's all thanks to you. I reckon you could teach me lots.'

'Perhaps I could,' Esme murmured, surveying the maid critically. 'Just promise me one thing. That you'll do better than I have.'

'Better, miss? But you've got everything.'

'Everything and nothing. I'm an old woman seeing out my years far from home, and far from those who know me. And not entirely by choice. Sometimes I think my reputation is a marvellous thing, and at other times it seems too heavy to bear. You can do better than that, Monica. You can be proud of what you do with your life.'

Monica smiled, not really understanding what Esme was trying to tell her. Esme returned the smile as she reached for her bath salts. There were many ways in which she could help the girl. The only question was, which should be first?

'I can't find a thing that we can cut back on,' Stephen

complained as he went over the accounts for the tenth time in an hour.

'Nor me,' his father agreed. 'Marcus has this talent to look at a situation and see the potential other men would miss. If we could only view the Grand through his eyes . . .'

'Look at this,' Sarah suggested, pushing a sheet of paper towards them.

'We've tried everything,' John dismissed without even glancing in her direction.

'Please, just look at it,' she begged.

'What?' Stephen asked.

Sarah wished that either her husband or her son had recognised the potential for increasing the revenue in an existing institution in the Grand, before she had. It was staring them in the face. Why couldn't they see it? If they had suggested it before her, it would have proved that she wasn't the only other member of the family to think like Marcus. But as neither had, she pressed on.

'If I were Marcus – if I were the same as him,' she amended hastily, 'and thank God I'm nothing like . . . but if I were, I'd look to the laundry. You said yourself, John, that it could service half of Manchester. So let it. Open it up to all the restaurants, the smaller hotels, even the theatres; they all need their washing done. It's a separate business right under our roof. One we could extend for very little extra cost. It would easily generate a hundred and ten pounds a month.'

'Do you really think so?' John asked doubtfully.

'Of course it would,' Stephen enthused. 'That's an excellent idea, Mother. However did you think of it?'

'By trying to see things from Marcus's perspective. It was quite a sobering experience.'

'We'll need to check the figures,' John cautioned,

slightly piqued that he hadn't come up with the idea himself. 'Knowing Marcus, he'll want a proper financial plan. How long have we got?'

'Two hours.' Stephen scrabbled through the pile of ledgers on the desk searching for the laundry accounts.

'Then what are we waiting for?'

'Where are my brother and his wife?' Marcus asked Mr Hopkins as he met him and his clerks in the corridor that led from the foyer to the dining room.

'Slaving over account books, sir. They should be in the office a while yet.'

'Then let's do it now.' Marcus handed a letter to one of the clerks. 'Take this to Mr Collins.' He pulled another envelope from the inside pocket of his jacket. 'This one is for Mrs Harvey, and this' – he handed an identical missive to the third clerk – 'goes to the kitchens. Go now. As quick as you can.' As the clerks ran off, he winked conspiratorially at Mr Hopkins.

Mr Collins received his letter in the foyer. Recognising the clerk as one of Marcus's employees, he opened the envelope at once. His face paled and his lips tensed as he read the note it contained. He would have liked to be able to run and hide. But even if he could have thought of a place, there was no time.

The clerk who handed Mrs Harvey her letter couldn't resist waiting until she'd read it. He wasn't disappointed by her response.

'Oh my God!' she exclaimed as she jumped to her feet.

He smiled maliciously as she ran past him. Opening the door, she shouted to Brenda, who was in the service station, 'You there, get all the girls together. Quick sharp now.'

'All of us, Mrs Harvey said,' Lynne announced to her fellow maids as they wheeled their trolleys down the servants' corridor. 'In the Reading Room. It's the leprosy man,' she added knowingly, although she was only guessing, adding to the mood of panic that was rapidly escalating to fever pitch. 'He's gone and done it. You'll see. We'll go back to our rooms and find our stuff on the pavement. Well, he's going to get a gobful off me,' she threatened, as she followed Monica into the service room, where Kate was hiding her tear-stained face.

'Come on,' Monica urged. 'At once, Mrs Harvey said.' She peered at Kate. 'What's wrong with you?'

'I'm in trouble. We all are. It's that girl, Janet, I was telling you about. She's hiding in one of the guest bedrooms.'

'A guest bedroom? You've got to tell Mrs Harvey.'

'How can I, Monica? She was one of the skeleton staff during the war, and there weren't many of us. Mind you, she didn't last long. She was always in trouble.'

'And she's still there, now?'

'Room fifty-three.'

'Kate Morris, Monica Jones,' Mrs Harvey shouted from the doorway. 'Have I got to check every service area? Downstairs, now, this minute. If this is the end, then I want everyone to be there looking their best.'

'Sorry, Mrs Harvey,' Kate sniffed apologetically.

'And check the washrooms on the way, Kate,' Mrs Harvey shouted after them. 'Get all those girls downstairs. Run!' Kate charged down the corridor as though a bulldog was snapping at her heels, but Monica lingered until Kate was out of ear-shot.

'Mrs Harvey?' She glanced over her shoulder to make sure no one else was close enough to overhear what she was saying. 'There's something you should know.'

'Not now, girl.'

'It's important. Honest, it really is.' Monica lowered her voice to a whisper to emphasise the fact.

'Mr Marcus Bannerman has summoned the entire staff, sir,' Mr Collins informed John, Stephen and Sarah. 'They are gathering in the Reading Room now.'

'Marcus can't do that,' John protested.

'Have you got the figures?' Sarah asked.

'I haven't even started. All we have is an idea. Seven o'clock he said. Seven o'clock.' Scarcely knowing what he was doing, John gathered the papers and account books from his desk and led the way into the foyer. He was too flustered to notice that Marcus had left only a skeleton staff on duty, but nothing escaped Sarah.

As Mr Collins walked on ahead to open the door to the Reading Room, John snatched another pile of papers from Stephen's hands only to drop them.

'I didn't want these, Stephen,' he complained as he glanced at one of the sheets. 'I need the annual figures. Where are they?'

'We haven't got annual figures, Father.'

'I can't show Marcus this. Damn him! He knew it wouldn't be ready. He knew it!'

Sarah took John's arm, holding him back as Stephen went on ahead.

'Whatever Marcus is planning, John, stand up to him. Fight him.'

'Of course, I will,' he replied irritably. 'What do you think I'll do?'

116

The Grand

She stared at his back as he preceded her into the Reading Room. She was burning to tell him everything. But Marcus had already succeeded in one of his aims. He had driven a wedge between her and her husband, casting a cloud over the marriage she and John had worked so hard to make a happy one.

'I've got nowhere to go, no money saved,' Brenda wailed as the staff crowded into the room around her. She pulled a handkerchief from her sleeve in preparation for a good cry, but grief played second fiddle to curiosity and she, like the rest of the staff, fell still as Marcus strode in, climbed on to a table and called for silence.

'Sooner you're quiet, sooner this can end.' If anyone else had spoken as softly, their voice would never have carried across the assembly.

'I'll give him an ending,' Lynne countered belligerently. 'The end of my fist.' Unfortunately for her, everyone chose that moment to stop talking.

'If you've got something to say, say it out loud.' Marcus's cold stare had a greater effect on the maid than any display of anger would have. 'Now if I can continue.' Only a few murmurs of resentment greeted his request, and they soon died. 'No doubt this is a new experience for some, if not all of you, but it has to be done.'

John, Sarah and Stephen forced their way into the back of the room just in time to hear Marcus's last words. John looked up at his brother and shouted, 'Wait a minute.'

'No it can't wait.' Marcus turned to the crowd. 'I've spent the past two days familiarising myself with every aspect of the Grand, and I've reached a conclusion. If you don't like it, then so be it. I make no apologies.

117

Gentlemen.' He nodded to two teams of footmen waiting at the side doors. They marched in, Clive at their head, carrying huge silver trays loaded with glasses of ready-poured champagne.

'Champagne for all of you,' Marcus announced, smiling for the first time since he had entered the room.

Lynne looked around, totally confused by the turn of events. 'What's going on? Does he think he can buy us off?'

'The toast is to yourselves.' Marcus was clearly enjoying their bewilderment. '"The staff". The people who keep the Grand intact.'

Mrs Harvey turned her master key in the lock of room 53 and pushed the door open. The room was in darkness, but she spotted Janet's shadowy figure sitting on the edge of the bed. Her face settled into grim, fixed lines as Monica stole up behind her.

'I said I heard noises, didn't I? I said so,' Monica reiterated.

Janet turned towards them, her eyes huge, rounded pools of fear in her thin face. Stretching out her hands towards Mrs Harvey, she looked at her before breaking down. The housekeeper stood back and watched helplessly as tears of desperation coursed down the girl's thin cheeks.

Marcus waited for the commotion his toast had caused to die down before continuing his speech.

'I've heard rumours that you would all be thrown out, made homeless, but I can't imagine who would be stupid enough to suggest such a thing. You're the pulse of this building. Its life and its heart. Ladies and gentlemen, you *are* the Grand. It is true that we need to make more money. But with my contacts in the theatrical world, I've arranged for every artiste and musician appearing in Manchester to stay at this hotel. So, enjoy your champagne – you're going to need it. From now on every single room is going to be occupied.' Marcus raised the glass Clive handed him. 'The Grand has a glorious future and I know that thanks to your efforts, it will be a successful one. Here's to you, the staff. Congratulations.'

His toast was greeted by a stunned silence.

'You can clap if you want to,' he suggested drily.

A footman put his hands together, another followed. The sound escalated to a crescendo of shouting and cheering as Marcus stepped down from the table. He lifted his glass to his brother.

'Cheers.'

John looked on, dazed by the turn of events as the applauding crowd of staff dived for the champagne trays.

Janet backed away as Mrs Harvey approached her.

'Come with me.' Mrs Harvey concealed the compassion she felt for the girl by slipping into the role of unemotional, efficient housekeeper.

'I won't!' Janet looked to Monica who was standing behind the housekeeper. It didn't take her long to realise she'd get no sympathy from that quarter.

'Come with me,' Mrs Harvey repeated, taking Janet by the arm.

Janet pulled away roughly, sending the housekeeper reeling. She held out her hands. In them were the shillings Mrs Harvey had given her earlier.

'I'll pay. Look here's your bloody money. You gave it to me, have it back.'

She threw the coins at the housekeeper's face. They stung painfully as they hit her forehead. Rubbing

Katherine Hardy

her head to ease the soreness, Mrs Harvey let her expression settle into even sterner lines.

'Leave her, Mrs Harvey, she's mad,' Monica pleaded, horrified by the magnitude of the events she had set in motion.

'You'll come with me, right this minute, my girl.' The housekeeper grasped Janet's arm again. But the girl remained obdurate. She wrapped both her arms around the bedpost and stood, feet apart to brace herself, head bowed so her tears fell on to the satin bedcover.

'Please let me stay. Please let me . . .'

'You know you can't.'

The refusal was one too many. Janet swung round. Clinging tightly to the bedpost with one hand, she slapped the housekeeper soundly across the face with the other.

It took Mrs Harvey a few moments to recover from the blow. Outraged at the affront to her dignity, she retreated to the door, Monica backing out behind her.

'I had hoped we could sort this out between us and save you the shame,' Mrs Harvey stated bitterly. 'But stay in here if you want, Janet. Stay all you like, until I come back. And I won't be with a single slip of girl when I do.'

Retreating to the corridor, she slammed the door and locked it, leaving her key in the outside so Janet couldn't use hers on the other side of the door. The sound of Janet's sobs followed them down the corridor.

As Monica stepped into the staff lift behind Mrs Harvey she could still hear Janet crying, and even after the doors had closed behind them, the wail lingered on in her ears. It was then she realised that the sound had penetrated her mind. She could never escape it now.

120

'I did the right thing, didn't I, Mrs Harvey?' she ventured, needing approbation to counteract the shame that was rising like bile in her throat.

'Yes, you did,' Mrs Harvey replied shortly without much conviction. 'Good girl.'

The party atmosphere took a firmer hold on the staff assembled in the Reading Room as they began to knock back the champagne. The heady mixture of relief and the unaccustomed alcohol in the middle of the afternoon spurred the more intrepid among them into recklessness.

'Oy, give us a chance,' Clive shouted as he tried to ensure that everyone had one glass, and no more.

'I don't believe it,' Lynne gasped, swooping down on to Clive's tray. 'I'm taking it before I wake up. He called us ladies, proper ladies.'

'Oh blimey!' Brenda exclaimed, her hand shaking as she grabbed her share of the champagne.

'Look at her,' Lynne laughed, with a nod to Clive.

'It's gone up me nose,' Brenda giggled.

'It would,' Clive commented cynically. 'It's all bubbles this. Cheapest stuff we've got.' The sound of smashing glass echoed across the room. 'Behave!' Clive shouted in the direction of the crash. 'Anyone'd think you've never seen alcohol before.'

'You drink it like this,' Lynne advised the girls around her. Sticking her little finger out, she lifted the glass delicately to her lips.

Kate walked in behind them, but she made no attempt to join the rest of the maids, or take a glass of champagne. Standing apart from the others, she waited quietly for an opportunity to attract Clive's attention.

'And you can cheer up when you like, misery,'

Lynne snapped viciously when she saw her. 'What's the matter? Don't you like sharing the limelight with the rest of us? What do you want, a medal for not coming in with us when we asked you to?'

Kate ignored her as Mrs Harvey arrived at the door opposite and touched Mr Collins's shoulder to attract his attention. Pushing her way through the crowd towards them, Kate saw Mr Collins moving away from Mrs Harvey towards Clive.

'Clive put that glass down and come with me. You're needed.'

'Right away, Mr Collins.' He dutifully abandoned his glass on the nearest table. 'What's wrong?'

Mr Collins was too busy buttonholing the nearest porter to answer. 'And you, Paul. Quick now, both of you upstairs, fast as you can.'

As Mr Collins and the porters fought their way out of the room Kate tried to follow them. Monica stopped her.

'Leave them.'

'What's happened?' Kate asked, already suspecting the answer to her question.

'I kept your name out of it. Remember you did me that favour, by saving my job when I first arrived. Well, now I've paid you back.'

'Interesting manoeuvre, Marcus,' John criticised sourly. 'Start a rumour, then publicly denounce it, and incidentally make the staff adore you in the process.'

'They would have been thrown out when you lost the money. I saved them, so I believe I deserve a little adoration.' He looked to Sarah, not John, for confirmation.

'Excuse me, sir,' Mrs Harvey interrupted. 'There's something of a problem.'

'Really?' Marcus glanced down at her. 'My brother and I need to talk business, Mrs Harvey. I'm sure whatever it is, Mrs Bannerman can handle it.'

Sarah felt as though she'd walked in on a nightmare. Janet was fighting valiantly to retain her hold on the bedpost as Clive and the porter struggled to prise her hands free. As fast as they managed to loose one finger she tightened her hold with the others. Mrs Harvey and Mr Collins stood back watching the proceedings from the doorway, clearly hating every minute of it.

'Look at me,' Janet screamed at the men. 'Just look at me! For God's sake you can't do this. I've got a child.'

'Don't,' Clive pleaded as he struggled to keep her fingers away from the post.

'Please, Clive. *Please* . . .'

Clive and the porter finally succeeded in pulling her away from the bed. Clive held her left arm firmly while Paul gripped her right.

'I'm not doing any harm,' she murmured, pleading with the concierge and Mrs Harvey. 'I'm not. It's not as though this room was taken . . .'

'Janet. *Janet.*' Mr Collins repeated her name loudly to gain her attention. His voice had a strangely calming effect on the girl. 'Don't make this any worse than it already is. We won't call the police if you let Clive take you to the Institute. They'll take you in. It's better than prison.'

'Just let me go. I'll leave quietly. Just give me a chance.'

'A chance of what in that state?' Mrs Harvey asked practically.

'I'll get rid of her. That's what I'll do. She'll be better off dead.'

'Good God in heaven!' Mrs Harvey exclaimed, appalled by the suggestion. 'I'm sorry you had to hear this, Mrs Bannerman. You filthy child. You're talking about murder.'

'Is there really nowhere else you can go?' Sarah asked sympathetically.

'Would you take me in, miss? Bit of charity – is that too much to ask for?'

A horrible thought occurred to Sarah. 'You lived in Jericho Lane?'

'Yes.'

'The house you lodged in was sold off?'

'I was thrown out.' Sensing that Sarah wanted to help her, Janet turned all her attention towards her old mistress. 'I could work in the kitchens, miss. No one would see me there. Please, give me a room.'

Sarah glanced at Mrs Harvey and Mr Collins. One look at their faces was enough to tell her that she had no choice in the matter. There was no way she could risk compromising the hotel's reputation or its staff by employing an unmarried girl in Janet's condition.

'I'll write you a letter for the Institute explaining your circumstances,' she promised, hating herself for having to relinquish her charitable intent.

'A hundred rooms and you can't give me one?'

'I can't,' Sarah murmured despairingly. 'I just can't. It's not my fault. This is the Grand Hotel; it relies on its name and the prestige that brings.'

'They always said you were nice. That you knew every girl's name. You just pretend to care. You're a liar.' Janet spat out the words viciously. 'They'll throw me in with the lunatics and you won't care.'

'I do care about you, Janet.'

'Then *help* me.'

Sarah looked away, conscience-stricken.

'Clive,' Mr Collins prompted.

The moment Clive and Paul attempted to move Janet towards the door, she started fighting them. Kicking, struggling and screaming at the top of her voice.

'I'll not go. You can't make me . . .'

'Janet, you'll hurt the child,' Clive warned.

'*Good.*'

As they pulled her towards the corridor, Sarah stepped closer to her.

'I will write that letter.'

Janet spat in her face.

'Get her out,' Mrs Harvey ordered, shocked to the core.

They could hear Janet's screams and the thuds of her kicks on the carpeted floor of the corridor even after Clive and Paul had hauled her out through the door.

Slipping his hand into the top pocket of his jacket, Mr Collins pulled out an immaculately laundered handkerchief and offered it to Sarah. 'Mrs Bannerman?'

Sarah took the cloth and turned away, unable to bear kindness from anyone after what she had just done.

'It was her own fault,' Mrs Harvey pronounced decisively.

Mr Collins tapped the housekeeper on the shoulder and she followed him out through the door, leaving Sarah alone.

She went to the bed and leaned on it, fighting back her tears. Taking a deep breath, she only just managed to control herself. Then slowly she became aware that someone was watching her. She turned to see Marcus standing in the doorway.

'That girl lived in Jericho Lane. This is all your fault.'

'Yes,' Marcus replied coolly. 'And yours. We did this together, Sarah. And in future if something has to be

done, then we'll continue to do it together. The both
of us. And if it hurts, we can share the pain. Just as
we're doing now.'

He left as suddenly as he had arrived. Sarah stared
at the empty corridor and wondered exactly what she
had become. Just what kind of woman had Marcus
turned her into?

Chapter Eight

M r Collins noticed her as soon as she walked through the doors. Unaccompanied attractive young girls in their mid-twenties didn't often visit the Grand Hotel in the evening, and the few who dared usually displayed far more timidity and uncertainty than this confident young lady. She stood in the centre of the foyer, almost as though she were on stage, receiving the admiring glances of the men in the reception area as though she were accustomed to both masculine adulation and the opulent surroundings.

'I'm here to see Mr Stephen Bannerman,' she announced boldly as he approached her.

'And the name, miss?'

'Sutton. Miss Celia Sutton.'

'I'll inform Mr Bannerman that you're waiting. If you'd care to take a seat in the Reading Room.' He stood to one side, indicating the lounge, but she brushed past him and headed for the office, which was clearly visible through the glass panels set in the door and walls that separated it from the reception area. Stephen was sitting at the desk inside, his back turned towards them, apparently engrossed in a telephone conversation.

'Don't bother, I'll surprise him.'

Collins stepped alongside her. 'I'll have to inform Mr

Katherine Hardy

Bannerman for you, Miss Sutton. I'm afraid members of the public aren't allowed in the staff areas.'

Celia broadened her smile as she reached the door. 'But I'm not a member of the public. Never have been.' Ignoring his exasperation she went inside.

Oblivious of her presence, Stephen kept his back to her and continued his conversation.

'That's right,' he agreed, shouting down the mouthpiece in a bored voice. 'I'm sure we can do that. Yes . . . It's no trouble, sir . . .'

Celia clapped her hands over his eyes. He swung round and she removed them. He beamed, no longer knowing or caring what he gabbled down the phone.

'Fine . . . we'll get it done, thank you. Goodbye.' He dropped the receiver on to the cradle, reached out and pulled her close to him. 'Celia.'

'Hello,' she greeted him huskily, bending her head so he could kiss her.

Collins saw the kiss, and frowned. The family's affairs were none of his concern, not when he had a hotel to run and resident guests to take care of. He stepped towards the lift as the doors opened and Esme Harkness emerged.

'Where can I find the lad who carried my purchases this afternoon, Mr Collins?' she asked. 'He left before I could give him a tip.'

'Very kind of you, miss. It was Alfred. You'll find him in the Reading Room.' He lowered his voice discreetly. 'Oh and a Mr Napier called. He left a message for you at the reception desk.'

Esme modulated her voice to match his. 'Thank you.'

Collins watched her go. Still preoccupied with Stephen and Celia, he glanced towards the office again, and as a result didn't see Mary Bannerman until she stood in front of him.

'Collins, you're best positioned to keep an eye on our resident guest.'

'In what way, ma'am?' he questioned apprehensively.

'There's something about her name. I've heard it before, and I won't rest until I remember where. Keep an eye on the woman. Tell me her movements, who she meets and where she goes.'

'With respect, Mrs Bannerman,' he protested mildly, 'that's really not part of my job.'

'I want it done,' she charged imperiously. Tapping him on the shoulder with her fan, she added, 'And be discreet.'

Stephen remained stubbornly seated in his chair behind the desk while Celia tugged at his hands.

'I'm on duty until nine o'clock,' he remonstrated, his resolve beginning to crumble in the face of her coaxing.

'You're always working. I thought we could go to that new restaurant on Oxford Road.' She gave up trying to force him. Smiling beguilingly, she beckoned him forward with an elegantly manicured finger. Unable to resist her in that mood, he finally shut the ledger he'd been working on.

'Good boy,' she crowed, elated at her success.

'That restaurant in Oxford Road is rather expensive. How about we go to the White Swan instead?' he demurred.

She glanced into the foyer. 'Just look at this place. I don't honestly think you can plead poverty.'

'All the money's in the building, not my pocket.'

She continued to gaze at him. He reached for the box where the petty cash was kept. Taking a key from the chain clipped to his pocket watch he unlocked it.

'Just this once.' He removed a large white five-pound note. She crept closer to him, wriggling the tips of her fingers beneath his collar. 'And I suppose we could take in a show . . .' Trying not to think about what he was doing, he took another five-pound note from the box before relocking it. Leaving his chair, he offered her his arm. 'Miss Sutton?'

She linked her arm in his. 'Mr Bannerman.'

He escorted her out of the office. Releasing his hold on her, he turned to lock the door. Celia allowed herself a small smile of triumph as she glanced around the foyer, but the smile died on her lips when she saw Esme Harkness emerging from the Reading Room. She froze as a trickle of cold, naked fear crawled down her spine. Esme had clearly seen and recognised her and was already bearing down on her when Stephen turned around.

'Right that's done. Good evening, Miss Harkness,' he politely acknowledged the hotel's senior resident.

'Mr Bannerman, Miss Sutton.'

'You know one another?' He looked from Esme Harkness to Celia, confused by the acquaintance.

'I'm afraid you have the advantage, Miss . . . Harkness.' Celia struggled to keep her emotions under control.

'London, three years ago,' Esme reminded frostily.

'Of course,' Celia answered with the same hint of ice in her voice. 'How are you?'

'Unchanged.'

'Good.'

'And yourself?'

'Oh the passing of three years has brought about many changes. All of them for the better.'

'Perhaps,' Esme cautioned heavily.

'If you'll excuse us.' Needing reassurance, Celia took Stephen's arm.

The Grand

'I'm sure we'll meet again and catch up on old times,' Esme said as she stepped back to allow the young couple to pass.

'I'd like that,' Celia replied insincerely.

'Miss Harkness.' Stephen nodded as he led Celia away. Esme remained in the foyer, straining her ears to listen to their conversation as they walked towards the doors.

'You never told me you lived in London,' Stephen remarked as they passed Collins.

'You didn't ask,' Celia dismissed lightly, controlling a shiver as she caught a glimpse of the dark, foreboding expression on Esme's face before the door closed behind them.

Sarah Bannerman had always thought of her private sitting room as a haven after a hard day's work, and it had never looked more comfortable or welcoming than the present. Sunk into a sofa beside John, she picked up the drink he had poured for her and looked across at Marcus and Ruth, who sat opposite them. But hotel affairs even managed to intrude into this peaceful moment. John pulled an envelope from his pocket and handed Marcus a docket to sign.

'I thought the whole point of having separate rooms above the hotel was to get away from work,' Ruth commented tartly.

'It never stops,' John confessed wryly. 'I just need your signature on the bottom of that, Marcus.'

Marcus took the paper, glanced at it and scribbled his signature. 'Waste of time,' he declared flatly as he handed it back.

'Thank you, but you voiced your objections at the meeting and you were outvoted. So the staff get new equipment, just as we planned.'

'Indeed, I can hardly complain, seeing as how the voting system was my invention. I thought Sarah deserved some authority in the Grand after working here for all these years, but it shows my ignorance of married couples. They act as one, joined at the hip. Siamese twins. Thank God I'm not married. I couldn't bear the dependence.'

'I don't vote with John just because I'm his wife,' Sarah contended warmly. 'I vote on each resolution according to its merits.'

'If I tried to force Sarah's hand, I'd get my own bitten off.' John took the docket from Marcus and pushed it into the inside pocket of his jacket as he left his seat. 'I'd better get this into the post right away. Thank you, Marcus. I'm sure the staff will be delighted.'

Marcus looked to Sarah as John left. 'So it is possible? One day you could actually vote with me?'

'I agree with Ruth. We've talked enough business.'

'Actually, for once I'm interested,' Ruth purred smoothly.

'So?' Marcus pressed.

'For me to vote with you, you'd have to be right.'

'And your husband would have to be wrong. But given John's character we all know that's impossible, don't we, Sarah?' He stared his sister-in-law coolly in the eye. She tried to meet his steady gaze, but she was the first to break and look away. Just as Ruth knew she would be.

The staff quarters were in even more chaos than usual. Working under Mrs Harvey's supervision, Clive and a contingent of porters were hauling in a consignment of tall, heavy boxes from a commercial van parked in the yard.

'Bit of a weight on this,' Clive complained as he struggled with one of the boxes single-handedly.

'You be careful with that. It's cost the Bannermans good money,' Mrs Harvey warned.

'What is it?' Kate left the trolley she was setting up for the following morning's chambermaiding. 'What's going on?'

'It's all questions with you lot,' Mrs Harvey dismissed irritably. 'I'm already late with Mr Harvey's tea so you can wait until tomorrow. You've seen the notice. All the girls in room six, nine o'clock sharp. You there, what's your name, I said be careful.' Mrs Harvey followed one of the porters, who was shoving a box into the storeroom with his foot.

'Staff meetings on a Sunday. What happened to the day of rest?' Kate asked no one in particular.

'Oh she does what she likes,' Lynne said airily. 'Mrs Harvey thinks she's God.'

'That's blasphemy, that is,' Brenda rebuked.

'Oh, hark at her and her big words.' Lynne picked up a pile of aprons. 'Oy, this is Monica's stuff. Why should I skivvy for that lazy piece? Where is she anyway?'

'Don't look at me. I'm not her mother,' Kate retorted testily as she returned to her own trolley.

Monica sat at the table in Esme Harkness's bedroom, revelling in the luxury of the deep-pile carpet that lapped around her feet, and the shining, silk-brocade drapes drawn against the winter night. The table was laid for a meal but there was no sign of food.

'I'm all right on cutlery.' She studied the place setting in front of her. 'Start on the outside and work in. Mrs Harvey taught us that. It's the wine glasses I get lost on. And me hair's going to get in the way. I'm not used to wearing it down.' She picked up a strand

and examined it thoughtfully. 'I don't know – we go to all this bother to look pretty when all the men want is to get their hands on us and mess us up.'

'Is that what you think this is? Instruction on bedding a man?' Esme enquired frigidly. 'I'm teaching you how to attract a gentleman. There is a difference.' She left her chair and paced restlessly to the window. 'If you want education in the sexual act, go to a doctor.'

'What have I said?' Monica asked, alarmed at the thought that she'd upset her benefactress.

'You're not the first girl I've taught.' Esme was thinking more of Celia than the maid sitting before her. 'And you wouldn't be the first to disappoint me.'

'I wouldn't,' Monica breathed apologetically. 'I promise.'

Esme stared into space, her thoughts busy with the past – past disappointments, past treachery . . .

'I could name dozens like you,' she muttered. 'Begging for my help, desperate to better themselves. So desperate they became greedy and fed off me. I won't allow it to happen again. I simply won't.'

Stephen carried the drinks he'd put on his account at the bar to the secluded corner where Celia was sitting, waiting for him. She took the wineglass he handed her, and sipped delicately at its contents.

'Sorry we had to end up back here,' he apologised. 'Shows I've been out of circulation. Before I went away ten pounds used to pay for a whole night out. God, I sound like my own grandfather. Sorry.'

'We could go upstairs,' Celia whispered as she slipped her glass on to the table in front of her.

'My parents will be there.'

'There's always your bedroom,' she suggested boldly.

Stephen laughed to conceal his embarrassment. 'Right.' He made no attempt to move.

'I've shocked you, haven't I?'

'No,' he lied.

'We can stay here.'

'I'd rather we did.'

She looked away lest he see in her face the amusement she knew would upset him. No man had ever fallen for her quite so hard or quite as quickly as Stephen Bannerman, or had been so nervous in her company.

'It's not that I'm shocked,' he explained hesitantly. 'It's just that you're the first girl I've really . . . you know, since I came back. And it's different. I want you to be different.' He paused for a moment. 'There have been girls. In France,' he blurted out suddenly. 'In the war. We'd stop at a village, we'd stay a few days, a few weeks sometimes . . . and . . . there would be girls.'

'And you'd pay for them?' she asked with a candour that took his breath away.

'Yes.' He coloured, ashamed of himself. 'We all did. We had to. None of us knew how much longer . . . whether it would be the last time.'

Celia took his hand into her own, stilling the trembling in his fingers. 'I understand.'

The silence closed in on them crushing in its intensity.

'Now I've really shocked you.' He picked up his drink.

'You haven't.'

'Then you don't mind if we stay here?'

She smiled, appreciating a respect and concern for her reputation she had never known before.

'I'm perfectly happy, sitting here with you.'

He dared to look at her. 'Thank you.'

*   *   *

Katherine Hardy

As Kate and Monica retreated to their cold, comfortless bedroom for the night, Monica looked around and contrasted the plain iron bedsteads and bare floorboards with the luxurious surroundings of Esme Harkness's bedroom. Clutching her mug of tea to her chest, she glanced across at Kate.

'You've had boyfriends, haven't you?'

'Waste of time, all of them,' Kate pronounced dismissively.

'Proper boyfriends, though?'

'Not since last November. Frederick Blythe, he was all freckles. He worked at the Lamb and Flag. He shared a bath with his mother. I was straight out through the door when I realised what was going on.'

'So what did you actually do?'

'What do you mean, do?' Kate asked, indignant at the implication.

'Men and women,' Monica persisted naively. 'What do they do?

'Oy, what makes you think I'm an expert? I'm having a wedding ring before any man drops his trousers in front of me, thank you very much.'

'I know you get a bloke, and then . . . you know. The sexual act. But what actually *happens*?'

Uncertain whether Monica was having her on, or genuinely ignorant and curious, Kate gave her roommate a sideways look. Deciding the question had been prompted by the latter, she deigned to answer.

'Blimey where do I start? I warn you Monica, it's not pleasant . . . but . . .' She looked at the door, lowered her voice, and began to explain.

Clive dragged a crate of empties through from the bar to the yard. Dusting off his hands he walked back into the servants' quarters to see Mr Collins helping himself to his usual end-of-shift glass of wine.

'Evening, Mr Collins. It's all quiet up there. I'll be done by half past eleven.' He looked at the concierge carefully. He knew his immediate superior well enough to realise he wasn't happy. 'Nothing wrong is there, sir?' he ventured.

'No. It's a new world, Clive, that's what we're told. But the old world's still there, still giving instructions. It's hard sometimes to know quite where you stand.'

'At your post, sir, same as always. Mrs Harvey calls you the foundations of the Grand Hotel.'

'And, as we all know, foundations are built over and forgotten, Clive.' His sombre mood was broken by the sound of hysterical laughter hooting down from the corridor that housed the maids' bedrooms. Storming down the passageway, he hammered on Kate and Monica's door.

'Kate Morris, what is this noise?' he demanded furiously.

At the other side of the door, Kate stuffed a corner of a sheet into her mouth in an attempt to stifle her hysterics. Turning away from Monica, who was rolling around on the bed burying her face in the sheets, she succeeded in muffling her giggles enough to answer.

'Sorry, sir.'

'Have you seen the time? Now get to sleep.'

Kate lay silent as he walked away, then burst out laughing again, only this time she managed to keep it quiet.

'Shush,' she ordered Monica, as she pushed her fist into her mouth.

'That is *so* disgusting,' Monica pronounced decisively. 'Do you mean me mam and dad did that?'

'As you've got two brothers, it means they must have done it at least three times.'

The idea was too much for both of them. They both erupted again, burying their heads in their pillows, hoping this time the sound of their laughter wouldn't carry outside the room.

Stephen rose late the next morning. He didn't need a clock to tell him he should have begun work half an hour ago. The foyer was already busy with porters bringing in the luggage of new arrivals and carrying out the boxes and trunks of the guests who had checked out. Ignoring the bustle, he walked briskly towards the office to find his parents already hard at work.

'Morning.' He opened the door and headed for his desk, ignoring his father's noticeable black mood.

'You were on duty last night,' John barked. 'Did anyone use the office?'

'The clerks from reception, Mr Collins. The usual.' Stephen lowered his head as he felt his cheeks burning.

'We're ten pounds down. I counted the takings at six o'clock, and locked the petty cash myself. Ten pounds is missing.'

'Perhaps you got the figures wrong,' Stephen suggested guiltily.

'I've checked and rechecked.'

'It's only ten pounds.'

John walked to the door. 'If we lost ten pounds every day. . . Collins was on duty you say?' Stephen nodded. 'I'll see him about it right away.'

'He's not happy unless there's a problem,' Sarah sighed. 'Are you coming to church with us, Stephen?'

'No.'

'It's your grandmother's birthday,' she reminded him gently. 'She expects us all to be there.'

'I don't go to church any more.'

Sarah tried to conceal her disquiet. The last thing she wanted to do was make a fuss and risk upsetting Stephen, but she was worried about him. His decision to reject the church and all it stood for was just one more indication of how much he'd changed, how much they'd drifted apart during the years he'd spent fighting in France, and yet another reminder of all the things – important things – that they hadn't talked about. Stephen smiled at her, but the gesture was an empty one, and she knew it.

'But I was going to ask about the meal tonight,' he said as he sat back in his chair and looked at her.

'Don't. That's what I'm doing now: working out which of the staff we can take away from manning the restaurant. This birthday becomes more of an epic every year. When your grandmother reaches seventy, she'll want a brass band and a twenty-one-gun salute.'

'I thought I might bring a guest.'

'Oh.'

Stephen's smile broadened, and this time it touched his eyes. 'Her name's Celia.'

John found Collins at his post in the foyer; buttonholing him, he drew him to one side.

'I'll need a list of everyone who was on duty in the foyer last night. Especially those allowed inside the office.'

'I'm sure I would have noticed anything untoward, sir,' Collins demurred.

'I'm not saying money's been stolen, but it's best to check all the same.'

Collins glanced uneasily at Stephen through the glass panels that walled off the office.

'Very good, sir. But your son was in the office most of the evening. May I suggest that he'd be more help?'

'Just get me the list,' John ordered, barely listening to him, before he walked off.

'Then you switch it on here.' Mrs Harvey contemplated the group of maids assembled in the unoccupied bedroom to make sure she had their full attention, before touching the button set in the handle of the vacuum cleaner. The lead she'd plugged into the overhead electric light fitting tightened as she manoeuvred the unwieldy machine over the carpet. The girls stepped back, some terrified, all of them deafened by the noise.

Mrs Harvey raised her voice in an effort to make herself heard above the din. 'Then it's to and fro, to and fro.' She demonstrated the action as she shouted out the words. 'Try to finish each piece of carpet with individual sweeps in the same direction, or the pile will end up striped.' She finally turned the machine off, to the girls' relief. 'Then disconnect it from the light when you're done. First thing tomorrow morning, start of the week, there's one on each floor. The Bannermans have been very kind, so you take care of them. I warn you now, damage these and it'll come straight off your wages. Any questions?'

The girls glanced doubtfully at one another, but it was Brenda who raised her hand.

'Brenda?' Mrs Harvey peered shortsightedly at the maid.

'Please, Mrs Harvey, do we have to use them?'

Clive and half a dozen other porters were hard at work

140

stacking rubbish ready for removal in the downstairs area when Mr Collins walked in on them.

'Clive, Robert, Alfred,' he ordered abruptly. 'Mr Bannerman wants a word.'

'What about?' Clive kicked an empty crate aside.

'You'll find out. Come along.'

Trailing behind the concierge, they passed the maids returning from their lesson.

'There's a girl in the Midlands who died using a vacuum cleaner,' Brenda announced in an awed whisper.

'She did not. She fell into a cesspit,' Kate contradicted.

'It kills you, electricity,' Brenda continued unabashed. 'Me mam said. You know that big sign that's lit up outside the Empire? Me mam was walking past that and she fell down in a dead faint.'

'It was four o'clock in the morning and she was blind drunk,' Lynne taunted.

'But you can't see it, can you?' Brenda persisted. 'Electricity is invisible, like poison. I mean what happens when you unplug the cleaner from the light. Where does the electricity go then? It doesn't just stop: it keeps oozing out, gets inside your head, addles your brains.'

'Bit late for that in your case,' Kate snapped cuttingly as she walked into the rest area.

'We tilled up at midnight, then I put the money in the safe, Mr Bannerman.' Clive looked down at John, who was sitting behind his desk.

'Did anyone else have access to the key?'

'No, sir. I kept it with me as instructed.'

'That's all for the moment. Thank you, Clive.' Clive left the office and joined Robert and Alfred in the corridor outside. Mr Collins was with them, frowning, as he monitored the stern expression on John's face through the window.

'In you go, Robert,' Collins ordered.

Clive looked at the concierge. Collins patted him reassuringly on the shoulder, but he sensed that his trust was of little consolation to the boy, who was clearly fuming at being accused of theft.

The lamps had been lit in the Reading Room and the drapes pulled, bathing the room in a soft, red glow. Celia was sitting at a table waiting for Stephen. Her clothes were new, and she had selected them carefully with a view to impress. With some degree of success, she noted with a smile as a young man eyed her from across the room. She turned her smiling face to his before looking away. When she looked back, he was still watching her. It was an old game, and one she enjoyed playing.

A porter interrupted the flirting, by bringing her a drink on a tray.

'Excuse me, miss – with the compliments of a friend.'

'Give the gentleman my thanks.' She fluttered her eyelashes as she took the glass.

'No, miss. It's the lady.' He pointed to the other side of the room. Celia paled when she saw Esme sitting there with a polite smile and eyes as cold as ice.

'Good Lord.' Stephen gazed at the table in the private dining room of his parents' apartment above the hotel. A magnificent centrepiece of flowers set off the glittering crystal, silverware and porcelain.

'They didn't make this much fuss when they laid out

Queen Victoria,' his mother acknowledged ruefully. 'Still, what your grandmother wants . . .'

'Should impress Celia. You'll like her, I know you will. She's wonderful,' he enthused as his mother picked up the loose ends of his bow tie.

'She must be. She's got you smiling again.'

Stephen hesitated for a moment. 'I think I love her.'

Flustered, Sarah struggled to hide her concern. 'I see. You've only known her a week.'

'Dad says he fell in love with you straight away, soon as he saw you. I never believed him. Now it's happened to me.' A note of impatience crept into his voice as Sarah fussed with the bow she'd fastened around his collar. 'She'll be waiting downstairs. Thanks.' He kissed Sarah on the cheek before rushing out through the door.

Sarah watched him go, wishing with all her heart that she could still protect him, the way she had when he had been a child.

Chapter Nine

Celia resented the presence of the other guests and porters in the Reading Room more with every passing minute. She sat next to Esme, conversing with the old woman in the muted, polite tones expected of ladies in refined society, when all the time she longed to scream and shout and tell the old witch exactly what she thought of her.

'You threw me out of London,' she murmured, not bothering to soften the edge of her voice. 'It's hardly my fault you've followed me here.'

'And how do you make a living now?' Esme questioned caustically. 'Someone must be paying for these clothes.'

'His name's Henry Docherty,' Celia retorted proudly. 'It's said he'll stand for Parliament at the next election.'

'And meanwhile he keeps you in splendour?'

'In a far better place than this. My own apartments, in the centre of town.'

'And what does his wife say to this arrangement of yours?'

Celia smiled wryly. It had been foolish of her to try to dupe Esme Harkness into thinking that her 'arrangement' with Henry Docherty was anything other than what it was. 'As a matter of fact I think she knows. The arrangement suits her.'

'And while Mr Henry Docherty is out of town, his mistress finds an amusing diversion.'

'I'm not sleeping with Stephen Bannerman – we're friends.'

'Dishonest whores can always invent a new phrase for their gentlemen friends – companions – escorts – it amounts to the same thing in the end. I taught you, Celia. I taught you my trade and its honour and you corrupt it. You stole my clients, pretending to be their lover instead of their whore.'

'I keep Henry very happy.'

'By telling him that you love him? By chirping with delight at his every little gift, then asking for more before moving on to the next idiot? You're a parasite, Celia Sutton. Prostitution is an honest profession, the most honest of all, but you've twisted and corrupted it. I won't allow it.'

'Then what? You'll have me thrown out of Manchester the way you hounded me out of London? I think you forget, Esme, you're not in charge any more.' She looked up to see Stephen standing in the doorway. She waved as he walked towards their table.

'Good evening, Celia, Miss Harkness. I'm sorry to deprive you of your companion, Miss Harkness, but they're ready for us upstairs. Celia?'

Celia looked down at Esme as she rose from her seat. 'I'm meeting the family. It's a shame so much time has passed and we have so little in common now.' She took Stephen's arm without a backward glance.

More courteous than his companion, Stephen offered a polite, 'Good evening, Miss Harkness', before leading Celia away.

Esme watched Stephen's arm slip around Celia's waist as they crossed the foyer and walked towards the lifts. Drumming her fingers impatiently on the table she summoned a waiter. There had to be something she could do to protect the boy. The question was, what?

The stiff, formal atmosphere in the Bannermans' dining room had clouded the meal, stifling conversation while the plates were being handed; but once the serious business of eating was done and coffee and liqueurs had been served by the waiters prior to their leaving, John turned his attention to his son's new girlfriend.

'And where do you live, Celia?' he asked. 'Are your parents in Manchester?'

'No they passed away some years ago. I have apartments here, in Baveystock House.'

'Baveystock House,' Ruth repeated, as though she were waking from a trance. 'That's a wonderful location. So central, yet surrounded by greenery.'

'Isn't it?' Celia agreed enthusiastically.

'Absolutely. And that dress is remarkable. You certainly didn't find it in the North.'

'New York,' Celia revealed smugly.

'Indeed, Miss Sutton, I'm not surprised.'

'Perhaps the gentlemen should retire for more brandy and cigars while you discuss the latest fashions,' Marcus drawled in bored tones.

'You should listen more closely, Marcus,' Ruth reproached. 'You'd find this fascinating.'

'If I could go to New York I'd die,' Adele announced dramatically.

'Might I ask where you met my grandson?' Mary enquired sternly, steering the conversation into her control.

'I'm sure it's none of our business,' Sarah interposed swiftly, concerned at what the answer might be.

'We met in town,' Stephen responded vaguely.

The Grand

'In a pub,' Celia confessed, with a sly glance at Mary. 'Not the best of locations. I do apologise.'

'No need, since it's none of my business.' Mary glared at Sarah.

'I only meant that we shouldn't pry,' Sarah asserted defensively.

'You see, Celia, nothing's my business any more.' Mary assumed the martyr's mantle. 'And I have to accept that. I don't complain. The Lord God made us old folk that way. He stiffened our legs and slowed us down so we wouldn't get in the way.'

'Ah, the birthday speech. I wondered when it was coming,' Marcus muttered.

'Though mankind plays its part in excluding us,' Mary continued, pretending that she hadn't heard her younger son. 'When I was a child, we were taught the Bible, and honoured every word. Then, when we grow old we're told we're descended from chimps. I'm glad I won't be living for very much longer.'

'Oh don't say that,' Adele protested, chilled by the thought of death.

'Your grandmother's only joking,' John intervened smoothly.

'Take this place, Celia,' Mary carried on as though no one had spoken. 'Changed beyond all recognition. Suddenly it takes three people to run the Grand.'

'We do have three times the number of guests, now,' John reminded her.

'If you can call them guests. I think the word is "itinerants".'

'It is rather . . . *open* nowadays. It has lost a certain something. Anyone could walk in here off the streets provided they had the money,' Ruth agreed.

'If that offends you, then by all means leave.' Marcus bent his head to a candle to light his cigar.

'And these guests just relax, treat the place like their own homes,' Mary said, picking up her brandy glass. 'Miss Harkness for example. She presides over the foyer as if she owned it. And she's no more than a stranger.'

'Celia knows Miss Harkness,' Stephen revealed in the hope of lightening the conversation.

'Really?' Mary swooped down on Celia like a hawk.

'In passing,' Celia admitted reluctantly, wishing Stephen hadn't mentioned the connection.

'What do you know of her? Her background?'

'We met once at a party. Why? Is it important?'

'The name's an irritation. I've read it somewhere and I can't think where or in what. Where was this party?'

'Clarence House.'

The expression on Mary's face grew more fixed and imperious as everyone at the table tried to stifle their laughter.

Stephen used the interruption in the conversation to catch Celia's eye. Glancing at his watch, he rose from the table.

'I'm sorry to break up your party, Grandmother, but I promised to get Celia home by eleven.'

'But don't let me spoil the party. Please, stay where you are,' Celia insisted as she followed suit. She nodded to Mary. 'Thank you for allowing me to come, Mrs Bannerman, and many happy returns.'

'No doubt I'll see you again?'

'Oh, you will. I can vouch for that.' Stephen ushered Celia from the room and down the corridor. They only just made it to the end before they both burst out laughing.

'God, if I was bored, what must you have thought?' he apologised. 'But that's what this place is like – the family, and the business – ad nauseam.'

'It's still early.' Celia linked her arm into his. 'Where shall we go?'

'Anywhere,' he answered recklessly.

'The Regent's Club?'

He thought of the expense and faltered, but only for an instant. 'Fine.'

'You go downstairs and get a taxi cab. I just need to powder my nose.'

'I'll see you down there.'

Celia waited until he'd left, before tiptoeing cautiously back down the corridor. She tried one door after another, poking her head tentatively into the rooms until she found what she wanted – a study. Slipping inside, she closed the door softly behind her and nipped smartly over to the desk, took a pen and a pad of hotel stationery and started to write, rushing the words in fear of being caught. As soon as she had finished, she blotted the page and scanned the letter.

Dear Mrs Bannerman,

For your information, Esme Harkness was the most notorious prostitute in London. For twenty years she ran the infamous brothel at Langham Court, Knightsbridge, and has been arrested many times, the last in the spring of 1913. She intends to make the Grand a similar establishment.

Regards,
A Friend.

She folded the sheet and wrote 'Mrs Mary Bannerman' on the outside before pushing it beneath the cuff of her evening glove.

*   *   *

Katherine Hardy

Stephen crossed the foyer and went into the office. He held on to his keys as he walked to the desk and opened the petty-cash box. Trying not to think about what he was doing, he helped himself to twenty pounds before slamming the box shut, relocking it and stowing it back in the desk.

Stepping outside, he remembered to lock the door before crossing the lifts to wait for Celia. Collins was on duty, and as he approached, Stephen was beset by the uncomfortable feeling that the concierge knew exactly what he had done, not only now, but also the night before.

'Jacob, I'll need a car.' He reached for his cigarettes to conceal his agitation.

'Very good, sir.' If Collins was suspicious, he didn't reveal his misgivings by either look or gesture as he called to the porter on outside duty.

Celia left the lift when Stephen's back was turned. Concealing herself behind one of the pillars in the foyer, she waited. The minute the clerk manning the reception desk turned to check the vacant rooms for an incoming guest, she stepped out, slipping the note she had written on to the counter.

'The car's waiting.'

'Good.' She took Stephen's arm and hugged it close to her chest. 'I must think of some way to thank your grandmother for the party.'

'I'm sure you will.' He smiled as he held the door open for her.

'That's me done for the day.' Kate pushed her trolley into the service bay. 'Come on, Monica, school time.'

'School?' Lynne looked up quizzically from the pile of sheets she was folding.

'I'm teaching her the facts of life.'

150

Mortified, Monica looked from Kate to the porters crating the empty bottles next to the back door.

'Shut up!' she hissed.

'I know all about the facts of life,' Brenda bragged. 'My mother paid a nun two bob to come to the house and tell us. I felt sick for a week.'

Laughter echoed mockingly towards them, Clive's louder than that of the rest of the boys.

'You can laugh, you lot,' Kate shouted at them. 'It's all your fault. Waving it about.'

Lynne crept up behind Monica and pushed her towards Clive. 'Go on, ask him,' she goaded. 'He'll show you.'

'Get off . . .' Monica elbowed her in the stomach.

'I'll give you a demonstration,' Clive offered suggestively.

'And he would.' Brenda giggled.

'What are you waiting for, Monica?' Lynne taunted, her stomach still aching from Monica's blow. 'Best lesson you'll ever get.'

'Listen to you lot!' Monica exclaimed furiously. 'A girl would end up stupid as a pig if she stayed down here with you. Stupid people breed more stupid people – that's the facts of life.'

'Ooo, pardon me, modom,' Lynne jeered as she stormed off. 'That's you, that is, Kate Morris, filling her head with notions.'

'It's nothing I've said,' Kate asserted.

Monica continued to tear down the corridor, neither knowing nor caring where she was headed as long as it was away from the laughter of the rest of the staff. When she could no longer hear them, she ripped off her apron, threw it to the ground and kicked it savagely, imagining that it was Kate Morris's grinning face.

* * *

Marcus left the lift and signalled across the foyer to Collins to fetch Ruth's coat.

'Well, to think I've been dreading that all week,' said Ruth. 'I didn't expect such entertainment. Thank God for Celia.'

'So you've found another friend?' Marcus queried uninterestedly.

'Come on, Marcus.' Ruth looked at him as though he'd lost his senses.

'Come on what?' He took Ruth's coat from the porter and helped her on with it.

'The girl lives at Baveystock House. Miss *Sutton*?' She stressed the name. 'She's Henry Docherty's girl. Don't you realise she charges by the hour?'

'*No*! You've got to be joking.' When he saw that she was serious, Marcus howled with laughter. 'That was Henry's girl? That's priceless. Ruth, you're absolutely brilliant.'

'Thank you.' Ruth was gratified by his unaccustomed praise.

'And she sat with my mother – on her birthday of all days. That has to be the best evening in history. Do you think Stephen knows?'

'Of course he knows. He must be paying her.'

'This is superb. But John doesn't know. He couldn't possibly?'

'I presumed that was the joke.'

'Good old Stephen.'

The lift clanged open behind them and Mary emerged.

'Good night, Mother,' Marcus shouted. 'That was the best evening. *Ever*.'

Ruth slapped him lightly on the wrist. 'Marcus!' she chided, but she could no more control her laughter than he could his.

Mary watched with a jaded eye as her younger son

and Ruth left, and wondered why she always felt that she was the butt of their jokes. As Mr Collins walked towards her, the clerk from reception left his desk.

'If my son is such a clever man why does he always act the idiot in front of me?' she demanded of the concierge.

'Your car is waiting, ma'am,' the clerk informed her before Collins had a chance to reply. 'And this was left at the desk for you.'

Mary took the sheet of paper he handed her, flicked it open and began to read.

'The car, ma'am,' Collins reminded.

'Tell it to wait. What room is Miss Harkness in? Never mind, I remember.' She turned sharply on her heel and returned to the lift.

Holding on to the letter as though it were a talisman, Mary rode up to the first floor. She strode purposefully down the corridor and rapped hard on the end door. Esme didn't keep her waiting long.

'Esme Harkness.' Mary spat out the name contemptuously. 'I knew your name had significance.'

'Mrs Bannerman.' Esme opened the door wider. 'Won't you come in?'

'I read about you in the newspaper: 1913, the arrests at Langham Court. The shame of London. When a certain woman was arrested for keeping a house of ill repute. Miss Harkness, you're nothing but a common whore.'

'I object to the word common, Mrs Bannerman. And it was 1912. The police were charming, the judge an old friend.'

'I thought there was something indecent about you from the start. I could smell it. Well, I won't allow you to bring your filth into this hotel.'

Katherine Hardy

'I suit the Grand very well, Mrs Bannerman. Let's be honest, we're in the same trade.'

'We are not!'

'My business and your family's business is that of hiring out bedrooms. Though guests are made to feel rather more welcome in mine.'

'If you'd compare the Grand with prostitution, you're even more godless than I thought.'

'We both accept money for services rendered, and it's made both of us rich. There's no difference between sex and business. You should know that. After all, you're a Bannerman.'

'I'll have you removed from here tonight.'

'Then it will be a noisy departure. I can guarantee you that. Your husband built this hotel's reputation – it would be a shame to have it sullied. The late Mr Bannerman would never approve. I know he wouldn't.'

'What are you implying, you disgusting woman?'

'I miss him very much, old Charlie. I have such fond memories. He spent many nights on business in London. Many nights away from his wife. Threaten me, Mrs Bannerman, and I'll recall those nights in loving, and loud, detail.'

Mary opened her mouth, but for once words failed her. Esme's revelation had rendered her speechless.

'It's been lovely talking to you. We must do this again sometime.' Esme closed the door, leaving Mary standing staring at the wooden panelling. As Mary turned back and began what seemed like a very long walk to the lift, she imagined Esme sitting, gloating over her triumph. Ensconced in a bedroom her son had lovingly restored and furnished, a bedroom in the hotel she and Charles had built up from nothing.

Mary's imaginings couldn't have been further from

the truth. Far from gloating, Esme was leaning against the door desperately trying to control the trembling in her limbs. Sick to the pit of her stomach, she was every bit as shaken by the confrontation as Mary Bannerman, but, unlike Mary, she was far more adept at concealing her emotions in public.

Mr Collins was alone in the foyer when Mary Bannerman returned. Her footsteps echoed hollowly over the marble tiles as she left the lift and crossed to the door. The distance had never seemed so great, or the air so cold.

'The car's still waiting, ma'am,' Collins prompted.

She looked around as though she'd only just seen him.

'You must have known,' she reproached balefully. 'Men like you always know.'

Collins was bewildered by her accusation, but his bewilderment didn't stop him from feeling guilty. He hadn't worked for the Bannermans all his adult life without discovering that Mary Bannerman was not one to lay blame lightly.

Holding the door open for her, he watched her glide towards the car, slowly, with dignity just as she always did, but she seemed smaller somehow, and more alone than he had ever seen her before.

Mrs Harvey began supervising the maids in the guest corridors early the next morning. She waited until the girls had stripped and remade all the beds before giving permission for the new hoovers to be brought out, and although she allocated two girls to the task, she still found it necessary to superintend them as they carried the machine from the store cupboard to the first bedroom.

'Rosie can start with the vacuum this end,' she directed, 'then it will work its way down, finishing with you, Kate. Got that?'

'Yes, Mrs Harvey.'

'And you're in charge of locking it up for the day, Kate, and mind you take care. There's burglars would pay good money for one of these.' Thinking of the hundred and one other pressing tasks that demanded her attention, she finally left them to it.

'Burglar wouldn't get far if he tried stuffing that up his jumper,' Kate observed as Rosie propelled the machine clumsily into the first bedroom.

'Are you grizzling again?' Lynne asked Brenda, who was snivelling behind her.

'It's like the grim reaper working its way down the corridor towards me.'

'If I don't get you first,' Kate threatened. 'Where's bloody Monica got to now? She's on half time that girl.'

Monica had sneaked away to Esme's room. She was more on edge than usual, not only because she was playing truant at the busiest time of day, but also because of what Esme had just told her.

'But you can't go, Miss Harkness,' she pleaded, as though her begging would be enough to induce Esme to change her mind.

'I might have no choice if word of the argument I had with Mrs Bannerman reaches the management.'

'But what am I going to do?' she whimpered selfishly. 'Who's going to teach me? I'll end up stuck in this job for ever.' A sudden thought momentarily lifted her despondency. 'I could come with you. We could travel together. A lady and her maid?'

'Would you do that?' Esme asked, touched by the offer.

The Grand

'I'd do anything for you, Miss Harkness.'

Esme reached out and stroked the girl's face. 'We'll see, and thank you. But for now you'd better get back to work. If I am to be evicted I have things to do, and' – her lips settled into a thin, determined line – 'people I must see.'

'Another twenty pounds.' Despite the outward lack of emotion Collins knew that John was furious. 'That is thirty pounds in total. Gone!'

'No one entered the office, sir. No one except your son,' Collins hinted heavily.

John didn't pick up on the insinuation. 'Until we sort this out, there's only one thing to do. I'll have to call in all the office keys, and that means taking them off the staff.'

'Very good, sir, if you think that will help.' Collins removed his own key from the breast pocket of his jacket.

'Jacob, I didn't mean you.'

'I'm staff, sir. Please take it.' He slapped the key down on to the desk in front of John, turned and left.

'Now you've met her, you can see what I mean. How could I not love Celia?' Stephen asked his mother as they descended the stairs into the foyer.

'But surely you can see that you've got all the time in the world. You don't have to rush into anything.'

Marcus climbed towards them, his arms full of files. 'Very good last night.' He winked at Stephen. 'Very funny.'

'Right,' Stephen agreed, mystified by Marcus's approval.

Marcus aimed a grin at Sarah as he passed.

'Go on, you should have started at nine,' Sarah

reprimanded Stephen before walking on through the foyer. She smiled at Adele, who was standing waiting, and scurried all the faster into the Reading Room when she caught sight of her mother-in-law on the steps outside.

'Morning,' Adele greeted her grandmother as she entered the hotel. 'As you can see I'm all ready for town.' She twirled round so Mary could inspect her new walking-out outfit, but to her amazement her grandmother passed by without a word, and went into the lift.

'I thought we were going to do some shopping?' Adele called after her.

'I've some things to collect,' Mary said coldly. 'Then I'll be done with this place.'

'I don't want to be dead,' Brenda moaned as Kate climbed on to a chair to plug the lead of the hoover into the light fitting.

'You'll stay there, Brenda Potter. You think I'm doing all the work,' Lynne warned swiftly.

'Look, it's simple. You just go like this.' Kate switched on the machine. As it thundered into action Brenda jumped back against the wall, absolutely terrified by the sudden burst of noise.

'Hey, look at me,' Kate shouted, astounded at her success with the new gadget. 'It's posh, this. Just push it to and fro, like a lady of leisure. I'll have muscles after a week.'

'It's not just the electric,' Brenda shrieked nervously. 'What if that thing sucks up your foot? You could lose a whole leg.'

'Oh shut up, you big balloon,' Lynne bellowed, masking her own anxiety by attacking Brenda.

'Look it's working fine.' Kate demonstrated. 'It's

about as dangerous as a little boy with a hoop. We'll be done in half the time. Look, it even reaches the bathroom.' She waltzed across the carpet pulling the lead as tight as it would go. 'It could even clean the bath, as well as get the whole floor finished in ten minutes.' As she pulled harder the entire light fitting broke free from the ceiling and crashed down on to the bed in a welter of plaster lumps and clouds of dust.

Brenda screamed as a film of chalk-white powder settled over all their faces.

'I told you,' she whispered into the awed silence that followed. 'We're dead.'

Celia entered the foyer and found Stephen already waiting for her.

'I wasn't expecting you to telephone today. I thought you'd be up to your eyes in your precious work.'

'To hell with this place.' He dismissed the Grand with a wave of his hand. 'I told Father I had to drum up some business in Hale. We can be gone all day.'

'The very person.' Esme walked across from the Reading Room with a gleam in her eye that sent shivers of guilt rolling down Celia's spine. 'Mr Bannerman, I'm sure you don't mind,' Esme purred. 'I need a word with Miss Sutton.'

'I'm sorry, we were just leaving,' Celia said rudely.

'Yes I'm sure, but this won't take a moment.' Esme grasped Celia's arm in a clawlike grip and steered her away from Stephen.

'I'll wait here.' Stephen glanced up as Collins approached. 'I've got a meeting in Cheshire, so I thought I'd take Miss Sutton with me and make a day of it,' he explained unnecessarily.

'Yes, sir. But could I discuss something with you, sir, before you go?'

Katherine Hardy

'If it won't take long.'

'It's this situation. About the missing money.'

Stephen studied his fingernails intently before answering. 'Yes?'

'The staff are getting the blame, sir. At least, we're all under suspicion.'

'Including yourself?'

'All of us. I won't pretend each of those boys is a saint, but I've always been careful with front-of-house staff. They're the best you can get. Then money goes missing and all that good work counts for nothing. And that's simply not fair.'

'No, of course not. But what can I do?'

Collins stared him in the eye.

'I don't know, sir. I just thought you ought to know about it.' He gave Stephen one final damning look before walking away.

A small table littered with teacups, milk and hot-water jugs and sugar bowls separated Celia from Esme as they sat in the Reading Room.

'On the day you arrive, Mary Bannerman discovers the truth,' Esme charged caustically. 'In my book that's too much of a coincidence.'

'Esme, there's no friendship lost between us. But if I were to reveal your secret I'd risk my own. And besides, if I'd wanted revenge, I'd have had your name printed in the *Manchester News*. You said yourself the old woman's been nagging at you since you first arrived here. It had to be only a matter of time before she remembered where she'd heard it.'

'I suppose that's true,' Esme allowed grudgingly.

'Then, if you'll excuse me, Stephen and I are going out.'

'Mary Bannerman wasn't the only reason I needed

160

to talk to you. I've been moved on before – I'm used to it. My real concern is for Stephen Bannerman. It's my last chance to appeal to your honour.'

'What could Stephen possibly mean to you?' Celia asked curiously.

'He was a soldier.'

'So were a lot of men.'

'In our profession we had a wonderful war. We stayed in our comfortable beds while the children were sent out to fight. Now they're back among us, we should look after them. We owe them that much.'

'Stephen's enjoying himself in my company.'

'I'm sure he is. But I've watched him, and I've heard talk of the old Stephen before the war. Happy and proud, and perhaps a touch arrogant. I can see precious little of that left.'

'Esme, please try to believe me, I truly like the man.'

'Then why use him? A soldier of all people.'

'He treats me with respect. A few evenings of respect, that's all I'm taking. I wouldn't hurt him,' she added quietly.

'But you haven't told him what you are?'

'No.' Celia stared down at the table napkin.

'Would it hurt him if you did?'

'I don't know.' Celia was acutely aware of the probing glances Esme was sending in her direction. 'Yes . . . maybe,' she conceded at last, wishing it could be otherwise.

Mary swept into Sarah and John's private sitting room and gazed at the row of family photographs set out on the mantelpiece. Removing one of her husband, she slipped it reverently into her handbag.

'I think that's all. Now there's nothing to remind you that I ever lived here.'

'But why?' Adele asked, baffled by her grandmother's behaviour. 'What have we done? You enjoyed yourself last night. We all did.'

'What's the matter?' Sarah asked from the doorway.

'I don't know,' Adele answered. 'Grandmother's taking all her things.'

'I should have done it long ago. You were quick enough to move me out of the Grand when you took over. I'm merely completing the move.'

'You wanted a separate house,' Sarah reminded. 'It was entirely your own idea.'

'I'm not welcome in the Grand Hotel, I know that. And you, Sarah, you delight in all these changes. I never interfered in the men's work. I never demanded a vote. The whole city is laughing at you, and your pretensions.'

'Adele.' Sarah turned to her daughter. 'Could you leave us alone?'

'But I want to know what's happened.'

'Please.'

Realising that nothing more would be said while she remained in the room, Adele reluctantly left.

'If I've offended you, I'm sorry,' Sarah apologised to Mary. 'But you're very much a part of the Grand. You and Charles created this hotel together.'

'And Esme Harkness maintains that Charles was her client,' Mary disclosed bitterly. 'My husband with her . . . a common prostitute.'

Astounded by the revelation, Sarah sank into the nearest chair. 'When did she say this?'

'And you let her stay!' Mary charged accusingly. 'In my hotel.'

'We had no idea.'

'She's lying of course. Contaminating the place with her lies.'

'We'll get rid of her, I promise.'

'But we can't ever know the truth. That's what makes the lie so clever. It infects my marriage, every single memory I have of Charles.' Mary paused for a moment. 'Perhaps it makes sense. Perhaps we are descended from animals. Especially the men.'

It was only when she turned to walk out through the door that Sarah saw the tears in the old woman's eyes.

Chapter Ten

Sarah burst into the office to find John sitting behind the desk staring at a ledger.

'John . . .'

'Is there a problem, Sarah?' Marcus asked as he followed her into the room.

'No – I just need a word with John.'

'Does it concern the hotel?'

'Yes.'

'Then it concerns me,' he said firmly.

'I suppose it does,' she murmured, forced to accede to his logic. 'And in that case, Marcus, would you mind closing the door?'

Mrs Harvey shook her head in despair as she stood beside Mr Collins in the wrecked guest bedroom, watching the maids scrape lumps of plaster from the carpet.

'And you, Monica Jones,' the housekeeper scolded, pouncing on the trainee as soon as she entered the room. 'I want this room tidy.'

'But I didn't make the mess,' Monica protested.

'Clean it up,' Mrs Harvey ordered sternly.

Resigned to her fate, Monica got down on her knees with the others.

'But I didn't do it,' Lynne mimicked, careful to keep

her voice too low for either Mrs Harvey or Mr Collins to hear.

'We'll have to get this guest moved out into another room, wash the walls down, clean the curtains, and God help the mattress!' Mrs Harvey exclaimed as she surveyed the damage. 'And to top it all, we're one vacuum cleaner down on the first day.'

'I don't think you can take the blame for that, Kate,' Mr Collins said kindly, seeing the subdued expression on the maid's face. 'The ceiling must have been rotten.'

'Yes, sir, that's what I thought.'

'It's an old building.' He smiled to himself as he left the room. 'Still, the foundations are strong.'

Mrs Harvey dogged his steps. 'I hope you don't find this amusing, Mr Collins. The cost will come off my budget.'

Kate stared at the broken hoover after they had left. 'The march of progress,' she said scornfully. '"Wonderful machine, does the work in half the time." And look at us now, back on our hands and knees, just like before.'

Lynne and Brenda sniggered. Only Monica remained grim-faced.

'Probably for the rest of me life,' she said sourly.

'We have no choice,' John declared, after Sarah had related Mary's version of the confrontation between herself and Esme Harkness. 'Miss Harkness leaves the Grand this morning.'

'Do you want me to tell her?' Sarah asked.

'I'll do it.' John left his chair.

'Has either of you considered that Miss Harkness might be telling the truth?' Marcus mused thoughtfully, stopping John in his tracks. 'I don't think this

Katherine Hardy

family is in a position to condemn prostitution. Father might well have used her – and even if he didn't, there's Stephen.'

'What's Stephen got to do with this?' John queried testily.

Marcus was amused by his brother's bewilderment. He had difficulty keeping to himself the knowledge that Celia was a whore, but he had a feeling that there'd be a better time to tell John and Sarah the truth, so he contented himself with generalities. 'Stephen was in the army. How do you think soldiers pass the night?'

'Marcus!' Sarah rebuked primly, more embarrassed for John than herself.

'Indeed, I shouldn't involve family. This is business. Look . . .' He strode out through the door, leaving them little option but to follow. He walked down the stairs into the foyer and pointed to the reception desk. 'The Grand Hotel. One hundred rooms. Do we investigate the history of every single guest who walks through these doors, and then pass judgement on them?'

'Miss Harkness is proud of her reputation,' John reminded his brother quietly, conscious of the presence of guests around them. 'She threw it in Mother's face. If we sit back and accept that, what sort of men are we?'

'Businessmen?' Marcus pronounced bluntly as he turned and pointed to the other side of the foyer. 'And there in the bar, what do you think happens? Girls ply their trade, just as they do in every hotel in the land.'

'Mr Collins turfs them out,' Sarah remonstrated.

'Only the amateurs. And, Sarah, are you saying that you'd condemn the women, not the men who buy them? Every single businessman turns his mind to those girls. That's why business trips exist. And do we

166

turn those men away? Do we? No, we take their money. Every day, we take their money. It's what keeps the Grand going. Like it or not, we're part of the process. Stop it happening and the Grand will be empty. And then you can shout your principles to thin air.'

'No one's suggesting that we try to reform the entire world . . .' John began hesitantly.

'Neither can we afford to take half measures. If we evict Miss Harkness, where do we stop? Tell me, John, would you allow Germans into this hotel?'

'I don't know. It hasn't happened.'

'But it will. London hotels let them stay already. They have to take their reservations to make money.'

'Then I would let them stay, yes. I can't blame an individual for the actions of his country.'

'Two years ago they were slaughtering us. They would have killed your own son. Now they are welcome guests. But a prostitute? Someone who just has sex? She's worse?'

'In this case. In the particular case of Esme Harkness, the answer has to be yes,' John maintained fiercely.

'And you, Sarah. You're independent of your husband, or so you claim, what do you think?' He led them back towards the office. 'Well?' He opened the door and walked in ahead of them. 'You came running back here to tell us what Mary wants, so you've done your duty as her daughter-in-law. But now you're one of the owners of the Grand. And bear in mind, if you don't want to cause my mother any further offence, you'll stop working in this hotel right away.'

'I suppose I would,' Sarah acknowledged ruefully. 'Marcus does have a point, John. We've always known girls come in and out of this place. We've talked about it, we've even laughed.'

'So if we put this issue to a vote, then what? You'll

side with me, Sarah?' Marcus held the silence, using it the way an actor would, to heighten the tension in the atmosphere, all the while staring at Sarah, sensing that he was finally on the point of driving a wedge between her and his brother.

Terrified by the thought that she might actually be compelled to vote against her husband's wishes, Sarah looked to John, but he was avoiding both her own and Marcus's gaze.

She didn't understand that at that moment, John didn't give a damn whether prostitutes were admitted to the hotel as guests or not, only about the gulf Marcus had engineered between them.

'Perhaps you're right, Marcus,' he conceded, finally breaking the silence. 'We have to adopt double standards. That's business, but nothing can alter the fact that Miss Harkness has attacked one of the family.'

'She's just our mother,' Marcus commented pragmatically. 'She's nothing to do with the Grand.'

'But that's not true,' John challenged. 'The day that becomes true is the day *I* want nothing more to do with this place. I simply won't let it happen. I don't care how much money we lose.'

'This from the man who's been chasing thirty pounds all day?' Marcus sneered.

'I know the difference between thirty pounds and my mother's honour.'

Marcus fell silent, suddenly realising that for all his machinations, there was no way he was going to coerce his brother into abandoning his principles.

'As Miss Harkness started this, perhaps she can end it,' John said decisively. 'I will give her the option of apologising to Mother. But if Mother and Miss Harkness can't settle the situation between them, I will intervene. And you can vote against me. Both of you. You can do what you like. But I won't have my own mother too scared to enter this place. If that happens, then all the business, all the profit, all the money means nothing. It's worthless.' John stalked out of the office with a dignity Marcus knew he could never hope to emulate. Sarah tried to go after him, but Marcus called her back.

'Would you have voted with me?'

'There is no vote,' she answered, avoiding the issue. 'John's just told you. All that effort, Marcus, and you couldn't turn him.'

Marcus dropped the charm as he stepped closer to her. 'I meant what I said. The Grand is important to me. I need to know. Would you have taken my side?'

Sarah's 'Yes' seemed to be torn from her throat.

The triumphant look of victory in his eyes brought home to her the enormity of her defection. Marcus's intervention may have saved the Grand, but at what price?

'I'm sorry this has reached you, Mr Bannerman,' Esme apologised, sitting bolt upright in the chair in her room, as John stood before her. 'And if any story about your father has—'

'Thank you, but I remember my father very well, and with pride. Your voice isn't part of that memory.'

'Then you want me to leave?'

'If Mrs Bannerman chooses to involve me, then yes, and I'll take you to court for slander. But at the moment this is an argument between the two of you, and I hope it can be kept on that scale. I've been told I shouldn't judge you, but you've caused my mother a great deal of pain, Miss Harkness. If you want to make

amends, you have until tomorrow morning. Good day.'
Controlling his anger and his guilt, he closed the door
softly behind him.

Celia was sitting in the Reading Room, listening to
Adele, who was narrating the story of her grandmother's peculiar behaviour.

'. . . and of course just as it was getting interesting,
just at the point when Grandmother was about to say
what was wrong, I was sent out of the room. As usual.
I warn you now, Celia, if you become part of this
family, everything interesting goes on behind closed
doors. They don't tell you a thing.' She turned to see
her brother standing behind her. 'Must go. See you
two later.'

'Sorry about that.' Stephen slid into the chair
opposite Celia's.

'What?'

'Adele's mention of you as one of the family. Bit
presumptuous.' He laughed nervously. 'Not that I'd
object to the idea.'

Her laughter joined his, but he couldn't help noticing
that hers was shriller, harsher, as though she had seen
through his dreams and was mocking them.

Clive dumped the broken hoover in the middle of the
service bay where the maids were scrubbing out their
trolleys, pans and brushes.

'Well done, Kate. It's buggered. I wouldn't take you
on in a fight.'

Lynne grinned as she studied the broken machine.
'Look at it now, Brenda. How could you think that
dangerous? It's all wires and bits. It's a toy.'

'Go on laugh at me,' Brenda sniffed touchily.

'I don't need permission.'

'I was right though, it was nowt but trouble. They'll get rid of them now, you'll see.'

'Don't be stupid.' Kate kicked the machine into the corner. 'The first time someone got run down in the road they didn't stop making cars. It's just the first of many, that thing. They'll soon have machines that polish, machines that scrub, no end of them, you'll see. And then they won't need us any more. Happen you were right. I'd call that dangerous.'

The maids continued to work on in silence. Even Lynne glanced across at the ruined hoover and shivered, chilled by a cold draught of a mechanised future that threatened to take away their livelihoods, and the only security she had ever known.

Mary Bannerman arranged herself carefully on one of the sofas in her son and daughter-in-law's private sitting room. Shouting 'Come' at the expected knock, she watched the door open and Esme walk into the room.

'Have we anything more to say to one another?' Mary asked coldly, stiffening her back as she faced Esme.

'Nothing, except perhaps farewell.'

Silence ticked past, hot and oppressive.

'I never even met your husband,' Esme murmured. 'Living these months at the Grand, I've become steeped in his name, that's all. It was convenient ammunition.'

'I knew you were lying,' Mary crowed triumphantly.

'Part of my job. And stupid. You could never have believed me.'

'Indeed not.'

'But the lie's become something of a trap. I wouldn't hurt you, Mrs Bannerman, but if I leave the Grand Hotel now, it might give the nonsense I said some

171

Katherine Hardy

credibility. I'd hate that.' She paused for a moment to allow the scenario she'd painted to sink into Mary's mind. 'But of course if you want me to go . . .'

'The words of a whore can't affect me. I wouldn't give them such weight.'

'Then you're not angry?'

'Last night was my birthday. An emotional day. It might have appeared that your words hurt me, when I can assure you that's not the case.'

'Honestly? I'd hate one of us to deceive the other.'

'I don't lie, Miss Harkness.'

'Then, I might stay?'

'If you like,' Mary declared indifferently. 'It is of no consequence to me one way or another.'

Esme smiled at her small victory, but having won she felt the need to be totally honest on at least one point, with Mary as well as herself.

'I like the Grand Hotel. I'm happy here. And the Bannermans are a great part of my liking. A proper family, a good family. I've never had that. I can only admire from a distance.'

'Then I pity you.' Mary, raised her eyes, but there was no hint of warmth or compassion in her dismissive look, only exultation.

Stephen moved closer to Celia on one of the leather-upholstered sofas in the bar. Sensing that she'd retreated into some other, private world that left no room for him, he spoke quickly, and a little too loudly, in an attempt to gain and hold her attention.

'You should meet George. We served together. He lives out in Cheshire. We could visit him tomorrow—'

'I'm busy tomorrow,' she cut in abruptly. 'In fact I have to go now. Look at the time.'

'But I've booked a table for dinner.'

'Stephen, I like you very much . . .' she faltered, as the realisation came that there was no way she could end their relationship without hurting him.

'Oh God, I'm sorry,' he said. 'Listen to me gabbling. You must be fed up with me. I can't stop talking.' He left the sofa and held out his hand to her. 'I'll make it all right.'

'Where are we going?' she asked suspiciously.

'I'll make it all right,' he repeated.

'I promised to meet a friend.'

'Please.' His deep-blue eyes had never seemed so vulnerable, or so appealing. He reminded her of a small child begging for a treat. There was no way she could refuse him, not with that look tugging at her heartstrings. Taking his hand, she allowed him to lead her out of the room.

'Then you're staying?' Monica asked as Esme bustled into her bedroom.

'Having made myself out a liar to do so.' Esme went to the mirror and pretended to straighten the low-cut neckline on her dress, although it was already perfect. 'My honesty was my only virtue. But it's useless: the world prefers me to lie.'

'You don't have to lie to me,' Monica said shyly.

'And I won't.' Esme smiled, addressing Monica's reflection in the mirror. 'I thought I'd teach you some manners, a little etiquette and flirtation. But it's not enough. You won't make my mistakes. I'll teach you the whole lot, Monica. I'll teach you survival.' She saw Monica's eyes reflected in the glass, glittering hard in anticipation of advancement. She hadn't underestimated the girl. She had more ambition than most her age. But did she also possess the ruthlessness to match

Katherine Hardy

that ambition? Because without that one quality, there could be no success.

Stephen didn't say a word as he and Celia rode up to the top floor of the hotel in the lift. As the doors opened on the corridor that housed the Bannermans' private apartments his silence could no longer mask his agitation – or his intentions.

'No, Stephen,' Celia protested as he led her towards his bedroom.

'It's what you wanted.'

'It's not.'

'It'll be all right.'

'Stephen, I don't want to,' she asserted as gently as she knew how.

'Then we can just sit in here . . . together.' He opened the door and pulled her in behind him.

'I don't want to be with you.' The words came out more brutal than she'd intended.

'What have I done wrong?'

'Nothing.'

'I must have done something.'

'It's me. It's my fault. I lied to you.' Summoning all her courage she faced him. 'There's a man. I'm with another man.'

'Who is he?' The anguish in his voice set her teeth on edge.

'It doesn't matter. I should have told you before now.'

'Does he love you?' He waited for her to answer. When she didn't, he murmured, 'I love you.'

'You can't possibly.'

'And I don't care about the other man,' he blurted out recklessly. 'You can see him, you can see both of us. It happens all the time. Just spend time with me,

174

The Grand

that's all I ask. Then you'll see that I mean it. He could never love you as much as I do. You've no idea . . .'

'He keeps me,' Celia confessed in an effort to silence his protestations. 'Don't you understand? He pays for me. You shouldn't love me. I'm not worth it. I'm a whore,' she added so there'd be no mistaking her situation in life. 'When I was with you, I thought I could be someone different, not his property, just for a little while.'

'But if you're not happy with him, you could be with me,' he persisted.

'But I am happy with him. I'm happy with the things he gives me. I love them too much to give them up.' She walked to the door. 'I'm sorry, Stephen.' She laid her hand on the knob and turned it.

'I'll pay!'

She turned her face to his but he was too distressed at the thought of losing her to register the pain in her eyes. Taking out his wallet, he pulled all the notes from the back.

'I will, look.' Clutching the bundle of money, he held it out to her. 'I don't mind. You can spend time with me, and I'll pay, and you'll get to see that I'm different. You could love me, Celia. I know you could. Here.' He thrust the wad at her.

'No!'

'One night then. Just one night.' He was shivering in a frenzy of grief and rejection. 'What's wrong with me? Can't I even be a client?'

'There's nothing wrong with you, that's why I can't.'

'Once. That's all I'm asking. Just once.'

Celia released her hold on the door and closed it.

'All right,' she assented, suddenly realising that this was the only favour that she could grant him.

She brushed his hand aside. 'You don't need to pay.'

He took her handbag from her hand, opened it and shoved the money inside.

'There, now you're mine.' He held out his arms and she moved towards him.

He kissed her, his mouth hard, passionate against hers, but there was no love or tenderness in his embrace, only a violent, brutal savagery that instilled a fear she had never known before – with any man.

He pushed her down on to his bed. Standing back, he stared at her as he tore off his jacket. She hated what he was doing to her, although she couldn't have explained why. It wasn't as though he was hurting her – not physically the way some clients had.

Without any further preliminaries or finesse he climbed on top of her, kissing her again while his fingers fought with the fastenings on her clothes.

'Slow down, Stephen,' she begged.

He continued to kiss her, lifting her skirt and fumbling with her underclothes, all the while keeping his lips pressed to hers, as though the force of his embrace would be enough in itself to make her love him. He kissed her neck, then buried his face in her soft white breasts, breathing in her perfume as he whispered, 'I love you . . . I love you . . . I love you . . .'

He repeated the words over and over again, his voice breaking into sobs as he realised it was no good. That he could neither coerce nor caress her into loving him. And as the kissing stopped, so the crying took hold.

Close to tears herself, Celia pushed him away. He rolled off her, and curled up as far from her as the bed would allow. She swung her legs to the floor, straightened her clothes and looked down on him.

The Grand

He was whimpering like a child, and she couldn't escape the fact that it was all her fault.

She took the money from her bag and laid it on the bedside table. He saw neither the gesture nor her move towards the door. She wrenched it open and walked away, silently cursing fate – and Esme. But most of all herself.

Traffic had slowed to a trickle in the foyer, and Collins was looking forward to going off duty when the lift opened and Celia stepped out. Despite her immaculate appearance he realised something was wrong. Her eyes were puffy beneath the coat of freshly applied make-up, and although there wasn't a seam, a button or a hair on her head in disarray, she looked as though she'd been through an emotional storm.

He called out, 'Good evening, Miss Sutton,' as she passed, expecting her to walk on, but she turned back.

'Is Miss Harkness still in residence?'

'Yes, Miss Sutton.'

'Would you give her a message from me?'

'Of course.'

'Tell her . . .' She faltered for a moment before regaining her composure. 'Tell her she was right.'

Monica did her best to ignore Kate as she undressed, donned her nightgown and slipped between the cold sheets of her bed, but it wasn't easy given the confined space of the cell they shared.

'Go on then,' Kate goaded snidely, 'what do you want to know tonight? The mysteries of men?'

'Nothing,' Monica snapped haughtily.

'Oh, think you know it all, now?'

'No but I will soon. You'll see if I'm not right.'

*   *   *

The foyer was empty, the lights dimmed, as Collins led John and Sarah across the floor towards the office.

Stephen was sitting behind the desk. His face was blotched, there were tear stains on his cheeks; but Sarah could see that he'd moved into a realm of wretchedness far beyond weeping. When he looked up at them, his eyes were wild, almost frantic, yet she could still see something of the child he'd been, mirrored in their depths.

'I'm putting it back,' he announced in a singsong voice as they opened the door. 'Look, I took it, and I'm putting it back.'

John stood back, appalled at the sight of the petty-cash box open and its contents strewn across the desk. Stephen picked up a handful of coins and let them drop from his fingers. They rolled over the surface of the desk. He scooped them up before they fell from the edge, then he dropped them again . . . and again . . . and again.

'What's happened?' Sarah asked. 'Is it Celia?'

'It's me,' he said in a cold, dead voice that froze her blood. 'I went too fast. You meet, fall in love, then she's gone – all in a day. It was so fast out there and it's still going fast in my head. It won't stop. I can't make it stop. It goes on and on and on – and it never stops. Slow down . . . slow down . . .' he repeated, unconsciously reiterating Celia's words.

Sarah tried to hold him, but he shrugged off her touch. She looked helplessly at John, who was standing with his back to the wall behind the door.

'Son. What we can do?' he asked doubtfully, feeling the need to say something.

'Don't give me that.' Stephen turned the full force of his anger on his father. 'You care about this hotel and nothing else.'

'That's simply not true.'

'Sod the family. Business, all the time. Business! Money! that's all you care about. You just want me stuck behind this desk. A carbon copy of yourself. It doesn't matter what I want.'

'Stephen, that's not fair,' Sarah reproached, torn between her love for her husband and her son.

Stephen glared at John as he pointed to Collins. '*He* knew. He knew it was me. He was watching, he could tell.'

Collins was horrified by the revelation, John shattered.

'I don't want your job,' Stephen said firmly.

'Then leave it,' Sarah pleaded. 'Your father doesn't mind. He only wants—' She broke off, too upset to continue.

Stephen reached for her hand. 'Don't cry. Please, don't.'

She hugged him, and this time he allowed her to embrace him. She rocked him as she had done when he was a baby.

'Make it slow down,' he implored.

'Whatever you want. You don't have to do anything. We got you back alive, that's enough.'

He continued to cling to her, while John remained standing next to the door. He had never felt so impotent or less a part of his own family. Hearing the sound of footsteps echoing across the empty foyer, he looked up to see Collins, head bowed, walking away.

Chapter Eleven

Cold, dark winter had given way to a spring that was on the brink of bursting into warm, luscious summer. It was a summer Stephen intended to make the most of. A summer he hadn't thought he would survive to see, and one he felt the need to live to the hilt, not only for his own sake, but for all those who weren't there to appreciate it with him. So he had given himself entirely over to a life of idleness and pleasure, cultivating friends who were of like mind and had the funds to indulge their every whim.

Freshly shaved, sprinkled with cologne, dressed in a new suit that had taken almost three months of the yearly allowance his father paid into his bank account, Stephen left his bedroom, and ran down the stairs.

Collins, as always, was immersed in the early-morning bustle in the foyer: directing incoming guests to the reception desk, ladies to the Reading Room for coffee, businessmen to John, who was discussing room occupancy with the desk clerk. Behind him, Stephen saw three of his companions, waiting impatiently for his arrival.

'Right what's the plan, George? Where do we start?' Stephen deliberately ignored his father's watchful eye.

'The bar's over there,' George suggested with a wink.

The Grand

'Oh no. We're not staying in this place. It's too much like drinking at home.'

'That's a shame. I was going to put the drinks on your account.'

'Ten o'clock's a bit early in the day, isn't it, George?' John tried not to sound too concerned as he left the clerk to join them.

'We've hired a coach, Mr Bannerman, for a day at the races. Then we're moving on to Charlie Palmer's. There'll be one hell of a party there tonight.'

'Don't expect me back,' Stephen warned, as he steered his friends outside.

'If I tell him to calm down, he'll only go the other way.' John felt the need to explain his lax attitude towards his son to Collins, as one of the porters closed the door behind Stephen.

'Don't worry, he'll find his way home, sir.' The concierge eyed two men who had walked through the door. Neither of them was dressed quite up to the standard he expected of the Grand's clientele. 'Can I help you?' he enquired politely.

John glanced at the men, muttered his excuses and headed for the office.

'Mr Jacob Collins? Is that right?' the older of the two asked.

'Yes, sir.'

'Could we have a word? My name's Simon Carlyle, and this is Thomas Jordan. We were in the Fifth Regiment. We served with your son Peter and we wondered if we could talk to you about what happened.'

For once Collins found it difficult to keep his composure. 'It's very good to meet you, but I am rather busy. As you can see I'm on duty.'

'We were with him at the end,' Jordan revealed in the hope of inducing the concierge to change his mind.

'As I said, I'm on duty.' Collins paused for a moment. 'But I have got a break in fifteen minutes. If you'd care to wait, perhaps I could see you then.'

The servants' quarters were as hectic as they were every morning, but there was far more horseplay and chatter than either Mrs Harvey or Mr Collins would have tolerated if they had been present. Running across the service bay to avoid a porter who was chasing her, Lynne picked up a pile of sheets and held them aloft.

'Oy, Monica, did you fold this lot?'

'Yes.'

'That's a pity.' She threw them across the row of trolleys to the accompaniment of gales of laughter from the other girls.

'Get off,' Monica shouted angrily.

'Lynne, don't start!' Kate warned.

'Oh, shut up, you. Monica put them on my trolley, and they shouldn't have been there. Not mixed up with my things.'

'Mrs Harvey hasn't gone,' Kate cautioned. 'She's got a cold, that's all. She could be back any minute and then look at the mess she'll find.'

'It might be the flu. She might die and I'm not wasting any hankies on her.'

'Thank you, Lynne.'

Lynne whirled around to see Sarah standing behind her.

'I'll be sure to pass on your sympathies to Mrs Harvey.'

'Sorry,' Lynne mumbled shamefacedly into the sudden silence. 'It's all your fault,' she hissed illogically at Brenda.

'Do you need something, Mrs Bannerman?' Kate asked.

'No, just carry on. But while Mrs Harvey's ill, someone needs to stand in.'

'What you?' The shock caused Lynne to forget both her embarrassment and her manners.

'Any objections to that, Lynne?'

'No . . . it's just I didn't think you'd work . . . with us I mean. You don't normally.'

'You know that I'd rather be upstairs drinking cocktails in the lap of luxury. But once a year – just once mark you – I don't mind getting my hands dirty. Now come along. And pick those up.' She pointed at the sheets. 'And someone could break their neck tripping over that . . . that' – she stared at a mop that lay in the corridor – 'what's it called again?' she appealed, with a sly glance at Kate.

'Mop,' Lynne answered eagerly, trying to make amends for her earlier comments about Mrs Harvey.

Sarah clicked her fingers. 'That's it. Mop.' She disappeared into the housekeeper's office. All the girls except Lynne burst into laughter. Lynne glared at them furiously.

'Do you mind telling me just what's so funny?'

Mr Collins's room was as immaculate, formal and decorous as the professional image he projected when overseeing the foyer, but it was also impersonal. The only private possession in evidence was a framed photograph of his son, that stood on a side table. He showed Carlyle and Jordan to the hard, upright chairs set before his desk, and took his customary seat behind it.

'He was well liked, Mr Collins.' Jordan opened the conversation without any further preliminaries. 'I often think of him. He liked nothing better than a good laugh, did Peter.'

'Yes, that's true.' Collins's forehead creased in pain

at some half-forgotten memory that had surfaced with Jordan's reminder of his son's personality.

'Always laughing,' Carlyle reiterated, echoing his companion.

'Have you told anyone how he died?' Jordan asked.

'Just once. Another soldier.'

'Do you think he was a coward, Mr Collins?'

'He must have been.' The concierge had to exercise every ounce of willpower to keep his emotions – still raw and bleeding – under control.

'Have you asked anyone who was with him?'

'No.'

'Then how can you judge him? Your son wasn't a coward, Mr Collins. Neither was he a deserter.'

'But he must have been, Mr Jordan,' Collins persisted, stubbornly clinging to the official line because the alternative was too horrible to contemplate.

'Mr Collins,' Carlyle interrupted, 'I presume you've heard of the Whittaker case?'

'I've read about it.'

Carlyle lifted his briefcase on to his lap, opened it and removed a copy of *The Times*. He handed it to the concierge.

'Jack Whittaker was found guilty of cowardice and he was executed in July, 1917, but his parents have sworn testimony from a dozen men that Whittaker had severe concussion. He couldn't have followed orders. He was incapable.'

'The point is, sir,' Jordan said, picking up the story from his companion, 'that the Whittaker family aren't willing to accept the verdict. They are fighting to get their son's name cleared in the High Court.'

'I've read the details,' Mr Collins admitted, 'but they aren't expected to succeed, and I don't see how any of this can possibly involve me.'

'The Whittakers own a jeweller's shop in Nottingham. They've got a fair bit of money, but the costs are mounting up. Mr Collins, we've come for money,' Carlyle petitioned candidly.

'The Whittakers *need* our support,' Jordan added in more persuasive tones. 'There's a number of us. All ex-soldiers. Men who saw what happened out there. We're raising money to pay the Whittakers' costs and, if they win, it will set a precedent. More names can be cleared, including Peter's.'

'Then you're activists?'

'If you like,' Jordan conceded.

'I see. I really don't think I can help you.' Mr Collins had learned to live with Peter's shame – after a fashion – but the thought that any innocent man, let alone his son, had been executed by an inept and vengeful army was more than he could bear. 'I must get back to work.'

'Just a small donation would help,' Carlyle pleaded.

'This is where I live Mr Carlyle.' He glanced around the austere room. 'This is all I've got. Do you imagine I have much money?'

'We've started a petition.' Carlyle opened his briefcase again. 'Just your name would help and contributions—'

'I'm sorry but I have to say no.'

'Why?'

Carlyle looked to his friend. 'Come on. Thank you for your time, Mr Collins.'

'I'd like to know why,' Jordan persisted after Carlyle had risen to his feet. 'Your son was innocent. So was Jack Whittaker. Why won't you fight to clear their names?'

'They can't have been innocent,' Collins contended. 'Innocent men don't get sentenced to death.'

'You weren't there. I was with Peter—'

'Peter was in the army. He was subject to His Majesty's Regulations. Gentlemen, I work here, in this hotel, and if something goes wrong, if someone does something and it's considered to be wrong, then it's dealt with according to the rules laid down by the management. And in the army, High Command lays down the rules. That's the way it works. Especially during wartime. No quarter can be given, or expected. It has to be that way.' He spoke as someone who needed to believe in a higher authority and order. 'Peter knew the rules and he did the wrong thing.' His voice softened with emotions he could no longer suppress. 'God help the boy, but he did.'

'Mr Collins.' Jordan projected his voice as though he were addressing a political rally in a crowded hall, instead of one lonely man in a tiny room. 'If you've such respect for the army, then remember that we were soldiers and a part of that army. Our version of events deserves at least the same amount of respect as that of the authorities. I looked Peter in the face. I saw the state he was in—'

'I don't think anything will be served by us talking about this any further,' Collins said firmly, too upset to continue with the conversation.

'How much do you know about his death?'

'I know what his commanding officer told me.'

'One letter,' Jordan dismissed scornfully. 'Is that enough? One single letter. Don't you want to know the rest? I can tell you. I—'

'I know all that I need to know,' Collins broke in fiercely.

'I can tell you everything – exactly what happened – the last words he spoke—'

'Mr Jordan, I'm very busy. I'll have to ask you to leave

now.' Collins opened the door, in the hope that they'd go before the tears that were pricking at the back of his eyes spilled down his face.

'He talked about you.' Jordan's words stabbed, bitter and painful, into the old man's heart. 'That's how we found you. All the time he'd speak of his father. The man he held in such esteem, the man he loved. Did you love him, sir?'

'Of course I did,' Collins retorted, furious that anyone could even suggest otherwise.

'But not enough,' Jordan said acidly.

'Thomas!' Carlyle laid a restraining hand on Jordan's arm.

'You're ashamed of him.' Jordan finally rose from his chair. 'You're scared to have his name spoken out loud, isn't that right? The army took his life, but what you're doing is even worse, Mr Collins. Denying his memory as though he never even existed.'

'That's enough, Thomas.' Carlyle walked out through the door. 'I think we should be going. I am sorry, Mr Collins.'

Jordan clutched the back of his chair tightly in an effort to calm himself before joining Carlyle. Unable to look either of them in the eye, Collins walked behind them.

When Jordan took his leave, his voice was muted, but the concierge could still hear anger simmering in his carefully modulated tones. 'I didn't mean to press you the way I did, sir, but we have other families to see. Families like the Whittakers, who are proud of their sons and willing to fight for them. Good day, sir, and thank you for your time.'

Kate unlocked the door to Esme's room, and stood back so Monica could carry the bucket of coal in ahead of her.

Sarah marched down the corridor behind them, her face red, her usually immaculately coiffed hair frizzed at her temples.

'This floor should have been cleared by eleven, so hurry up. Kate, where does Mrs Harvey keep the afternoon roster?'

'Top left-hand drawer of the desk in her office, ma'am.'

As Sarah strode off, Monica kicked the door of Esme's room shut behind them, so there was no chance of anyone overhearing their conversation.

'See, it happens all the time,' Monica declared as they knelt before the fireplace. 'Mrs Bannerman can step down to be housekeeper, so why shouldn't I step up? Look at that princess, the one that just died, the crown princess of Sweden. She was British; she was no one; she bettered herself.'

'She was born a duke's daughter for goodness' sake,' Kate informed her tartly. 'You were born and bred in Salford. There's a bit of a difference.'

'Miss Harkness doesn't think so. Next Saturday she said she'd take me out. For a proper dinner.'

'Tiger nuts and pop?' Kate baited.

'You can stop taking the rise, you. Miss Harkness says I could be a proper lady. She says I've got the bones.'

'Bones make soup and glue, not ladies.'

'You know what's wrong with you, Kate Morris?' Monica stopped brushing the hearth and stared at her. 'You don't think, that's your trouble.'

'I'm thinking a lot right now, but you don't want to hear it.' Kate sensed that the argument between them was escalating from the usual banter to a more serious level, but she had no idea how to put a stop to it.

'You don't think though,' Monica pronounced

decisively. 'Anyone can better themselves. Anyone, not just me, but you wouldn't even think of it. If someone offered you a throne, you'd set about polishing the legs.'

'They had an act like you at the Empire,' Kate retaliated crossly. 'Wee Georgie Porter and his talking doll. A little dummy that sat on his lap going yap yap yap. You open your gob and all I can hear is Miss Harkness, yap yap yap.'

'Good morning, Monica, Kate.' The door had opened and Miss Harkness was walking into the room.

'Good morning, Miss Harkness,' they echoed in unison.

Esme glided through to the bathroom and closed the door. Monica turned to Kate.

'Tell her what you just said,' she whispered fiercely.

Kate shook her head.

'See, you wouldn't dare. You wouldn't even *think* of daring. It must get awfully quiet in there.' She knocked on Kate's forehead with her fist.

Kate sat back on her heels and watched Monica as she polished the hearth tiles. She was angry but she was also considering her criticism, wondering if any of it could possibly be justified.

Marcus paced the foyer impatiently, waiting for Collins to return. 'At last,' he breathed irritably as the concierge appeared.

'I do apologise, sir. I've been on my break.'

'Which finished at ten thirty.' He frowned at the concierge. 'Am I right?'

'Sir.'

'So where have you been until now?'

'I do apologise, sir.'

'No doubt you were sitting in the kitchens waiting for

one of the maids to hoist up her skirts. You're slipping, Jacob. Now tell me, where's Mrs Bannerman?'

'In Mrs Harvey's office, sir.' Composing himself, Collins moved into his customary place in the centre of the foyer, but no matter how he tried to immerse himself in the demands the hotel made on him, all he could think of, all he could picture, was the corpse of the son he had nurtured through childhood and boyhood, destroyed by an executioner.

'Mrs Harvey told you that the meat was bad,' Sarah stated flatly, conscious that, for once, the staff were creeping quietly around the servants' quarters, presumably straining their ears in order to listen in on her argument with the butcher. 'She also warned you that if you continued to pester her for money, she'd blacklist your name in every Manchester newspaper. So what do you expect me to add?'

'She's a witch, that Mrs Harvey. She never did like me,' he whined. 'I had hoped that a lady like yourself would see reason.'

Sarah was suddenly aware of Marcus, leaning nonchalantly against the doorframe behind her. She turned to see a smile of pure amusement on his lips. His presence only served to infuriate her even further.

'I see only that Mrs Harvey's a woman of exceptional patience, and if I'd known of this harassment, I'd have called the police. Our business is closed, Mr Williams. Permanently. Goodbye.'

'You owe me money . . .' he blustered.

'Out!' She opened the door and pushed him into the yard. Slamming it shut, she saw the staff staring at her. 'Come on — the fun's over.' Looking to Marcus, she barked, 'Yes?'

'I'm going, I'm going!' He held up his hands in

mock horror as if to protect himself from her temper.

Ignoring him, Sarah picked up the bundle of files she'd left on a chair outside the office, and headed down the corridor.

'Sarah . . .'

'We've got nine girls off with this cold. The kitchen's lost an oven. That Mr Howard has insisted on moving rooms three times today and even Mr Collins seems to be working at half speed. We should pay Mrs Harvey double . . .'

'Or sack her,' Marcus suggested. 'You take her place very well. Anything I can do to help?'

'I don't think so. You see, this is where the real work is done, Marcus. There's no time for brandy and cigars down here.'

'Then show me the real work. I've always refused the budget for an assistant housekeeper, so you can have one for free.'

'Right.' She smiled maliciously. 'You're on.'

The windows in Mrs Harvey's office overlooked the high-walled back yard, so the sun's warmth rarely filtered into the room, even at the height of summer. The atmosphere remained chill as a young girl stood before the desk, facing Sarah and Marcus who sat side by side behind it, interviewing her.

'Um . . .' Florence bit her lips and rolled her eyes to the ceiling. 'I done three weeks work at the Connaught . . . that was nice . . . then I done some work behind the bar at the Lamb and Flag . . . that was nice, and . . . that's it. Sorry.'

'And why do you want to work at the Grand?' Sarah asked, already suspecting that she was wasting her time.

'Dunno . . . sounds nice.'

'What do you mean by nice?' Sarah pressed.

'Dunno . . .' Florence gave a vacant smile. 'Posh?' she suggested vaguely.

Marcus sat forward. Leaning his elbows on the desk, he took over the questioning.

'Florence, I want you to think hard before you answer this. What do you want out of life? Where do you see yourself in ten years' time?'

'Dunno.'

'You must have some idea.'

'Dunno . . . here would be nice,' she added almost as an afterthought.

'As a housemaid?'

'Yes, please.' She demonstrated the first signs of animation she'd shown since entering the room.

'In ten years' time, nineteen hundred and thirty, still doing the same job, still scrubbing floors? Is that all? When you lie in bed at night, when you think of all the things you could do, all the places you could go, all those secret little dreams, where do you see yourself then?'

'If we could move on,' Sarah intervened.

'No, go on, tell me, Florence. I want to know your ambition.'

'Dunno. No . . . I suppose . . .'

'What?' he pounced eagerly.

'I mean if I'm lucky . . .'

'Yes, tell me?'

'Married,' she announced with a dreamy smile.

Marcus slumped back in his chair, disappointed by her response. 'Married? Is that all?'

'Nice to be married,' Florence repeated, broadening her smile.

'You're like a little boy pulling the wings off a fly,' Sarah

The Grand

scolded after they had dismissed Florence. 'That girl might have waited her whole life for an interview at the Grand. Then you go and ruin it.' Picking up her folders, she stepped out into the corridor.

'She was just stupid. I tried to make her *think*, and I failed, miserably,' he added, as he walked alongside her.

'Marcus, she was terrified. Just because someone wears a uniform, it doesn't mean that they just service the hotel and think of nothing else. They get nervous, they get upset, just like the rest of us. You're in charge of these people – you should realise that much about them.'

'If you're that girl's champion does she get the job?'

'No.' Sarah caught his eye and they both burst out laughing. 'But that's not the point,' she argued, angry with herself for ridiculing the girl. 'Not the point at all.'

As John walked into the foyer after a long and indigestible Chamber of Commerce lunch, he saw Sarah and Marcus leaving the office.

'And how's our new housekeeper?' he asked.

'Exhausted,' Sarah complained, 'and Marcus hasn't been any help. He's been following me round all day. It's just like having a demanding pet.'

'What? You downstairs, Marcus? I'm amazed you can even find the place.'

'It was down the stairs,' Marcus drawled superciliously.

'Well, some of us have been busy. I am delighted to announce that we are hosting a reception for the Lord Mayor, right here in the Grand Hotel.'

'You did it.' Sarah kissed him on the cheek. 'You see,

Marcus? You just play while the rest of us get on with it. Well done, John.'

'It's nothing huge, but it should be special. Just the one problem. It's tomorrow night.'

'Oh my God!' Sarah covered her mouth with her hands.

'They're giving him a reception at the Midland Hotel next week and we have to get in first.'

'Oh my God!' she repeated.

'Does the housekeeper think we can manage it?'

'Oh my God!'

The three of them were walking away laughing, when Collins left the staff lift. He looked more careworn and drained after his afternoon break than he had when he'd finished his morning duty. Since Jordan and Carlyle's visit he hadn't been able to think of anything other than Peter, and what his death must have been like. Slow, bureaucratic, every preparation for the final moment pure mental torture. The last man he wanted to see was Jordan, but he was standing waiting for him as he walked out into the foyer.

Studiously ignoring him, Collins went to the desk and spoke to the clerk, but even while he patiently listened to answers to questions he had absolutely no interest in, he monitored Jordan's movements, wishing that the man would leave. Just as he'd run out of topics to discuss with the clerk, Clive appeared, and – prepared to use any excuse – Collins waylaid him.

'Did you sort out the arrangements for the Lancaster Suite?' he asked officiously.

'Yes, sir, all done.'

'I'd better check.' He walked alongside Clive.

'It's all laid out. I checked myself, sir,' Clive stressed, resenting the concierge's sudden lack of trust.

Collins dragged out his inspection of the suite as

long as he dared, but after he left Clive in the bar and
returned to duty Jordan was still waiting, and this time
there was no way he could avoid him.

'Mr Collins?'

'Mr Jordan,' he addressed him formally. 'I don't think
we have anything more to say to one another.'

'I have. I'm sorry.'

For the first time Collins saw that the man was
genuinely upset. He recalled what he had said, about
being with Peter at the end. Reaching out, he finally
offered him his hand.

Kate quickened her step as she hurried along a badly
lit backstreet. The shadows closed in around her as
she strained her senses to their utmost, listening for a
footfall behind her, watching for a shadow that moved.
She'd heard many stories about men lurking to do no
good to young girls these days, and all of them were
flashing through her mind.

A figure swayed in the gutter, slumping down on to
the pavement ahead of her. As she ran across the road,
she heard a voice. She turned.

'Mr Bannerman?' she asked hesitantly.

Stephen peered through the gloom, stupefied more
by drink than the darkness.

'Mr Bannerman?' she repeated, more sure of his
identity this time. 'Are you all right, sir? Well, no,
you're not, are you? Maybe it's time you got home.'

'I'm all right,' he slurred, swaying forwards until his
head was almost jammed between his knees.

'Course you are. Come on, you.' She walked back
to him, hooked her arms beneath his shoulders and
helped him to his feet. 'Up you get.'

'I'm all right,' he protested, almost dragging her
down with him.

'You walk me back, and I'll walk you back, then that's both of us safe and sound. Now come on, sir. If I'm not in by ten thirty they'll dock my pay. Off we go.'

He swayed on his feet clinging to her as she tottered unsteadily beneath his weight. 'Hello, Kate,' he grinned as though they'd only just met.

'Hello.' She laughed as she steered him forward. 'Not that way, this. That's the job, Mr Bannerman. We'll be home before you know it.'

Collins waited until his break, before taking Jordan back to his comfortless room.

'I'm my own worst enemy, Mr Collins,' Jordan said ruefully as he took the chair the concierge offered him. 'I try to help but I always end up offending the very man I want to serve. I'm sorry.'

'There's no need to apologise.' Collins took the hard chair next to his.

'Since we came back, there's been nothing – nothing to hold on to, and I'm luckier than most. I got myself a job. But it felt like a waste of time. Then the Whittaker family got in touch and for the first time I felt . . . I don't know . . . I suppose I felt there was something worth doing, Mr Collins.'

'And it must take courage. I admire you for that.'

'Don't.' Jordan gave a deprecating smile.

'And I should thank you. You've offered me something precious and I refused it. Now you've given me a second chance.' Collins steeled himself for the anguish he wanted to face for the first time since he'd received notification of his son's death. 'Tell me about Peter.'

'There's no need.'

'There's every need.'

'Perhaps it would be better for you to remember him as he was.'

'Please, tell me.'

Jordan closed his eyes as though the effort of remembering was almost too much to endure. 'I was with him from the first day. Ten months we spent together. So I know for a fact he wasn't a coward.'

'But how can that be true?' Collins wanted to believe Jordan, but he could recall every word, every damning phrase, of the official letter that had informed him of his son's death.

'Mr Collins, the man at the end wasn't Peter. Peter was gone. All the laughing, all the talking, it had all gone. They call it shock, but it was beyond that. He just sat there for days, rocking to and fro. He was lost. God knows, we *all* were, but Peter needed help. He should have been in a hospital. They shouted at him and he didn't move. They kept on shouting and he still didn't move.'

'It was war and he was a soldier. If you're told to do something, you do it!'

'As I said, they tried to make him move. They picked him up and told him to march. And he was crying, crying like a little kid. But they kept on shouting and pushing and screaming. And then he was running, but he wasn't running away. He was just running, running across a field. He didn't know where he was going. He was like a child running for home.'

Something crawled down Collins's cheek. He reached up to brush it away, starting in surprise when he saw it was a tear. 'Oh good Lord, look at me.'

'They arrested him. Two weeks later he was executed.'

Collins took a handkerchief from his pocket and dried his face. 'Could I ask . . . you see I've never known. Was it . . . ? I presume it was a firing squad.'

'Yes.'

'Was he blindfolded?'

Katherine Hardy

'Yes, he would have been,' Jordan answered abruptly.

Collins nodded sagely. He had visualised his son's death correctly after all.

'Peter did nothing wrong, Mr Collins. He was scared. We all were. Still am.' Jordan was close to breaking point. 'And I did nothing. I could have spoken up and helped him but I did nothing.'

'What could you have done?' Collins asked realistically.

'I let them kill him.' Jordan buried his face in his hands so the concierge couldn't see him cry. Slowly, hesitantly, Collins reached out and touched him.

'It's not your fault,' he murmured. 'It's really not.'

Chapter Twelve

S tephen stumbled as Kate guided him through the unfamiliar darkness of the hotel's back yard. She propped him against a wall as she unlocked the door that led into the servants' quarters. Following the pale gleam of her scarf as it bobbed down a passageway, he staggered unsteadily after her, stopping and blinking as she lit a lamp and led him to a huge, stone Belfast sink.

Having turned on the tap, he ducked his head beneath a stream of cold water in an effort to sober up before facing his parents. As he reached for a linen tea towel, Kate reappeared with two steaming mugs of coffee.

'Here you are. It's the posh coffee, the one the chef keeps hidden.'

'You saved my life, Kate,' he slurred. 'The last time I got drunk, I came back through the foyer. You should have seen the look Dad gave me.'

'You've been out a lot lately.'

'Talk of the kitchens, am I?'

'We don't miss a trick down here.'

'And what do they call me? A drunkard?' he asked with false jocularity.

'No they don't. Everyone knows you were a soldier, sir. They all think "He's done his bit, so good for him."'

'My father's just biding his time. Waiting for me to return to the fold. In the meantime he continues to give me *that* look.'

'Do you think you will do the job again, sir?'

'I don't know. To be honest I don't care. I had years of instructions and orders in the army. Now I just want . . . nothing.'

'That must be nice. I get orders all day long – hot water, bleach, and coal in the grate, that's me. Maybe I should wish for better. But then, I like my job, and what else could I do?'

'Anything you like.'

'Oh, you should talk to Monica. She thinks I'm incapable of thought and imaginings. She told me only today that I don't think.' She smiled at him. 'I don't think, and you don't *want* to think. Proper little pair, aren't we?'

He laughed as Mr Collins and Jordan passed the washroom on their way to the back door.

'Mr Bannerman?' Collins looked at him in surprise. 'Excuse me, sir. I didn't expect to see you here.'

'Jacob.' Stephen made an effort to steady his voice.

'I'll get out of your way.' Jordan opened the door. 'Thank you, Mr Collins.' He shook the concierge's hand.

'Thank you, and my apologies.'

'There's no need.' Jordan smiled at Kate, before stepping out into the darkness.

'A guest of mine, sir,' Collins explained awkwardly. He eyed Kate sternly. 'What time is this to come in? Have you signed the book?'

'No, sir.'

'It's my fault,' Stephen interrupted.

'You'll have to sign in late,' Collins continued to lecture Kate. 'You know the rules, no exceptions.'

'Yes, sir. Sorry. Goodnight.' She gave Stephen one last smile before running off down the corridor.

'Jacob,' Stephen protested. 'That's not fair. If she gets in trouble, I'll say it was my fault.'

'We have to follow the rules, sir.'

'Are you all right?' Stephen asked, noticing that the old man didn't seem quite himself.

'Yes, sir. It's just been a long night, that's all.'

'Yes, and for me. Another night gone. I survive the war, then I waste the time that I've been given. What would the dead think if they could see me now? Peter, would he forgive me?'

'We can't know, sir,' Collins answered clumsily. 'It's more a question of can we forgive them . . . him . . . ?'

'I'm sorry,' Stephen apologised, realising how tactless he'd been. 'It's me. I'm drunk. I shouldn't have mentioned Peter.'

'We shouldn't be sorry to mention him, sir,' Collins said staunchly. 'Not at all.'

Collins went to his sitting room early the next morning, but Jordan and Carlyle were already outside the door waiting for him. He handed Jordan a bulging envelope as they went inside. 'A hundred and twenty pounds, Mr Jordan. It's my savings. Use it well.'

'We'll keep in touch,' Jordan promised. 'We're going to write to all the families every week so you'll know what's happening.'

Collins smiled and nodded, but he hadn't heard a word they'd said. His thoughts were centred on Peter, not Jordan and Carlyle's crusade. 'I want to forgive him, but I can't,' he murmured. 'But then, if the courts can pardon the Whittaker boy, perhaps they can show me the way. Perhaps I can be led to forgiveness. Perhaps then, I will finally be able to sleep.'

John handed Sarah a series of lists, scribbled on pages torn from a notebook, as they hurried down the stairs. 'There's the table plan, wine list, guest list, staff list . . .'

'People haven't had time to reply to the invitations. What if no one turns up?' she asked.

'Marcus,' he called down to his brother, 'you can use that Masonic Lodge of yours to put together a guest list guaranteed to impress, can't you?'

'Consider it done.'

'We're still short-staffed. Those girls hear there's a cold going round and use it to get a day off,' Sarah complained.

'The assistant housekeeper can deal with them.' Marcus met them as they reached the ground floor.

'Don't sack them, Marcus. Not today.'

'Right, we'll reconvene at six,' John said as he headed for the office. 'We can see how the land lies then.'

'Yes, sir,' Sarah snapped smartly.

Marcus looked after his brother, but followed Sarah. She turned and barked, 'Heel, boy.'

Clive knocked on the door and waited. At Marcus's brisk 'Come', he opened it and entered Mrs Harvey's office. Two waiters followed and stood nervously behind him.

'Yes?' Marcus pressed his fingertips together, sat back in his chair and faced them.

'The thing is, sir,' Clive said, having decided to broach their grievance head on, 'we're not in charge of tables. That's the porters' responsibility, and Mrs Harvey says we should never cross jobs.'

'Am I Mrs Harvey?'

'No, sir.'

'Then get it done.'

'We'll need the key to the storeroom, sir. Mr Collins always keeps it.'

'Then where is he?'

'I don't know, sir,' Clive answered anxiously, not wanting to get his immediate superior into trouble.

'What do you mean you don't know?'

Clive lowered his head. The gesture told Marcus everything he needed to know, and more.

John opened the door to the office to find Collins using the telephone.

'But they gave me this number.' Collins's voice escalated as panic set in. 'They wrote it down . . . are you sure that you have no resident by the name of Jordan? Thomas Jordan? Or a Mr Carlyle?' he pleaded, clutching at straws. 'But they wrote it down only this morning . . . They told me this was their number . . . No . . . No thank you. I'm sorry, thank you.' His face was ashen as he turned to John. 'I'm sorry, sir. Mrs Bannerman gave me permission to use the telephone.'

'That's all right, Collins. I think they need you downstairs. I heard my brother asking for you.' He looked at him closely. 'Is there a problem?'

'No, sir.' Collins went to the door.

'You can use the telephone any time you want to. Don't leave on my account.'

'No, sir, it's nothing. A petition. I didn't sign the petition. Didn't commit my name.' He straightened

Katherine Hardy

his back. 'Excuse me, Mr Bannerman, I must go downstairs.'

Sarah stood in the centre of the guest corridor handing out lists to the maids.

'Brenda, your team clears out the reception room at six o'clock, not a minute later.'

'Yes, ma'am.'

'Lynne, your lot give it a final check at half past seven.'

'Yes, ma'am.'

Marcus walked towards them. 'So be quick about it,' he ordered. 'Run,' he shouted as they darted off. 'I said *run*!'

'They work much faster if you don't shout,' Sarah advised, as he followed her down the corridor. 'They are just toys to you, aren't they?'

'Good afternoon, Mrs Bannerman, Marcus,' Esme Harkness greeted them as she left the lift with Monica. Sarah stared at the maid, who was out of uniform and carrying a dress box.

'Miss Harkness. Monica isn't it?'

'Miss,' Monica replied hesitantly.

'I didn't realise we hired out staff to fetch and carry,' Marcus commented.

'It's mine, sir.' Monica looked at him, more defiant than scared. 'Miss Harkness bought me a proper dress. And very nice it is, too.'

'Good, then enjoy it,' he said, respecting her for daring to answer back.

'Yes, sir.' Monica beamed.

'As soon as your break is over, get back to work, Monica,' Sarah warned. 'We need everyone on duty. We're hosting the Lord Mayor's reception tonight,' she informed Esme.

204

'I've had a reception with him. No doubt not quite on the same scale,' Esme added. 'Good day.'

Marcus laughed as Esme and Monica walked down the corridor to Esme's room.

'That woman simply doesn't care,' Sarah complained, 'and you're cut from the same cloth.'

'But that's the sort of girl we should be employing. What was her name?'

'Monica Jones. And she'd rather court the guests than do her job. If they were all like her, nothing would ever get done.'

'Oh, I like that. You criticise me for not respecting the staff, then you want to put the first girl who shows a bit of fire back in her place.'

'But look at her: she chose today of all days to walk around town.'

'That's hypocrisy, Sarah. First you tell me to treat the staff like people, and have some regard for their feelings. Then one girl sticks her head above the parapet and you slap her right back down.'

'That's not true.'

'I just saw it happen.'

'All right,' Sarah retorted, angry because she knew he was right. 'I'll do the same to the assistant housekeeper. You're sacked.'

Marcus's laughter followed her all the way to the lift.

'Forget Mrs Bannerman, Monica,' Esme counselled as they walked into her room. 'If ever you meet proper ladies, titled ladies, you'll discover that they treat prostitutes and archbishops with the same respect.'

Monica laid the dress box on the table. 'I dare not keep this in my locker, Miss Harkness. The other girls will be jealous. Janey Birdsall had a frock for her birthday. The next morning someone slashed it with scissors.'

'Then keep it here,' Esme offered. 'And we should give it a debut. We could go to the theatre.'

'Ooh, we could do the Ice Palace in Cheetham Hill. They've got a man from Paris there who does trick skating.'

'I thought the opera.'

'Oh.' Monica failed to keep the disappointment from her voice. 'Aren't they all a bit glum? Don't all the women have horrible deaths at the end?'

'Only because they're written by men.' Esme smiled.

Collins waited until the office was deserted before returning to make his second telephone call. He dialled the operator, who took only a few moments to connect him to the number he wanted.

'I'm very sorry to disturb you, Mr Whittaker. But I was contacted by a Mr Jordan acting on your behalf. He was collecting money for your family. For the court case . . . a Mr Thomas Jordan and a Mr Simon Carlyle . . . Jordan . . . I see . . . there's no such fund . . . They did say they were acting on your behalf . . . No . . . no I understand. My mistake, sir. My mistake . . . No . . . I'm sorry . . . I'm very grateful.' Collins replaced the receiver and sank down on the nearest chair, his worst fears confirmed.

'Mr Collins, where have you been?' He looked up to see Clive standing in the doorway. 'It's started, sir, the reception. They're waiting for you.'

'Yes, I'll be there.'

Unable to wait any longer, Clive left. Collins rose slowly to his feet, tugged down his jacket, and straightened his tie. Duty called. Composing his features into a suitably bland expression to greet the guests, he walked out of the office and into the crowded reception room.

'Chin up, it *is* the Lord Mayor,' Marcus murmured to Ruth as he escorted her across the room.

'He's not a proper lord. It's only a council post.'

'Good evening, Ruth.' Sarah smiled as she shook her hand.

'Don't be taken in by that smile,' Marcus warned. 'This woman sacked me on the spot this afternoon.'

'Is that a euphemism?' Ruth enquired frostily.

'Some champagne I think.' Marcus stopped a passing waiter. 'And a little vinegar for my companion.' He saw Collins standing in the doorway. 'Mr Collins, you made it.'

'Sir.'

John took Sarah's arm and led her away from Marcus and Ruth. 'Ruth looks delighted to be here,' he observed sarcastically.

'If I can handle the butcher, I can handle her.'

'You'd better wear gloves. She gives me frostbite.'

Collins stepped to the side of John and Sarah to gain a better view of a waiter on the far side of the room. The lad said something to another waiter and laughed, a fraction too loud for the concierge's liking.

'Clive,' Collins called. 'Tell that boy to stop his antics. He can go back to the kitchens.'

'He'll be all right, sir. I'll tell him to calm down.'

'Get rid of him right now,' Collins ordered, with a flash of uncharacteristic anger.

Clive looked at him closely, but he did as he'd been told.

Seeing Collins alone, Adele took the opportunity to speak to him.

'Mr Collins, there's only so much orange juice I can

drink. I don't suppose there's any chance of a gin and tonic?'

'Perhaps you'd better ask your parents, miss,' he suggested politely.

'Oh, really?' She glanced over to where her father and mother had joined Marcus and Ruth in greeting the guest of honour. The Lord Mayor's voice carried towards them.

'Miss Manning, I'm delighted to see you again. Tell me, when's Marcus going to make an honest woman of you?'

'That would take some doing,' Marcus muttered loudly enough for everyone to hear.

'It's a lovely evening, Your Worship,' Ruth said, flashing her dark eyes angrily at Marcus. 'Please don't spoil it by invoking my worst nightmare.'

'Oh I don't know, though,' Marcus broke in. He looked to Sarah as he mimicked the girl they'd interviewed. 'Nice to be married.'

Sarah burst out laughing.

'I do apologise.' Ruth took the Mayor's arm. 'These two spent all day together, and in no time at all they've developed their own private little jokes.' She looked to John. 'I warn you, it's an exclusive club. No one else is welcome.'

Collins watched the room with an increasing sense of frustration that had little to do with the behaviour of the staff or guests.

'We'll need an extra pair of hands,' Clive warned as he approached the concierge. 'I've sent to the kitchens but they're all busy.'

'A staff of sixty and you can't find one man?'

'I could go and look myself, sir, but then we'd be another man down.'

'Oh for heaven's sake!' Collins took the tray of drinks

The Grand

Clive was carrying and set about doing the job himself. Stephen walked through the door just as he began to circulate.

'Good timing, Jacob. Quick, before my father tells me to slow down.' He snatched two drinks from the tray, downed one and abandoned the glass on a nearby table.

'Very good, sir,' Collins replied automatically, before moving on. He wove in and out of the crowd, the conversation and laughter growing harsher and louder in his ears as the guests removed drinks from his tray and replaced their empty glasses without acknowledging his presence.

Clive watched Mr Collins's progress anxiously from the doorway, wondering if it was his imagination or if the concierge was at breaking point. He was moving with the jerky gestures of an automaton, reminding him of a clockwork figure that had been too tightly wound and was likely to explode at any moment.

'Mr Collins? Mr Collins?' Adele had to address him three times before gaining his attention. 'Mr Collins, if we made it a gin and orange, my parents wouldn't be able to tell the difference.'

'Yes, sorry, miss. Just one moment.' He looked around in bewilderment, as though he had woken from a trance.

'Oh, then I can?' Adele asked in amazement. 'Are you sure?'

'Whatever you want, miss.'

He turned abruptly and collided with a guest. The tray and glasses went spinning, crashing to the ground in a welter of splintering shards and noise.

'Watch what you are doing, man!' the guest exclaimed furiously.

'Yes, sir. I'm very sorry, sir.' Collins stooped to pick up the mess.

'I can do that.' Adele crouched beside him.

'No, miss, please don't. I can manage.'

Clive moved in to help, giving Collins a worried look as John approached.

'Never mind, soon cleared up,' John said smoothly.

'I'll get your drink, miss.' Leaving the mess, Collins stumbled off towards the door.

'I was only joking. Please leave it,' Adele called after him.

'Are you all right, Mr Collins?' Clive asked, stopping him at the door.

'The wine's not that bad, Jacob,' Stephen joked before he saw the concierge's face. 'What's the matter?'

'My fault . . . the mess . . .'

'Maybe you should take a break, Mr Collins,' Clive suggested.

'I'm perfectly all right,' he snapped.

'Clive can take over, can't you?' John asked.

'Yes, sir.'

Collins tried to walk through the door, but Stephen stepped in front of him. 'Jacob? You're crying.'

'No.'

'What's wrong?' Stephen pressed.

'Nothing.'

'I'll take over, Mr Collins,' Clive offered. 'You go downstairs.'

'I can manage. Don't you hear me? Or do you think I can't cope?' Collins scowled at the porter. 'Would you rather I turned my back and ran away? Is that what you want? Do you want me to run away?' he shouted. The guests nearest the door stared at him. Mortified, he looked from the disgusted expressions on their faces to the concerned expressions of the Bannermans.

The Grand

'I'm sorry, sir,' he apologised quietly to John. 'I'm very sorry, sir. I've let you down.'

Kate closed the door of Mr Collins's bedroom behind her as she stepped into the corridor.

'Clive's sitting with him for the moment, sir,' she whispered to Stephen. 'He says he has a head cold. He shouldn't have gone on duty, but you know him: he never stops.'

'Just tell us if he needs anything.'

'I will, sir.'

He looked at her for a moment. 'Right, I'd better get back.'

'Goodnight, Mr Bannerman.'

'Please, it's Stephen.'

'Goodnight, Stephen . . . sir,' she added as he walked towards the lift.

Sarah returned to the reception and sought out Marcus and Ruth.

'He'll be fine. Apparently it's just a cold.'

'I assumed that you'd get rid of him. After all, his head has gone above that parapet. He brought a little piece of himself to the party, and we can't have that, not with a servant, now can we?'

'You wouldn't recognise the man out of uniform, Marcus,' Sarah said icily.

'Be honest, Sarah, you were embarrassed. You prefer Collins the craven soul. Practically a slave.'

'The Mayor wants to see the changes to the Lancaster Suite,' John announced as he joined them. 'You can head upstairs if you want, Sarah. I can take over.'

'Are you trying to get rid of me?'

'Not at all, but you were in the kitchens at five o'clock this morning.'

'I'm just getting started.'

'Well you can take me home soon, Marcus,' Ruth broke in. 'I'm quite worn out.'

'Oh? And what have you been doing all day?'

'I've been busy.'

'Shopping?'

'And other things,' she countered, sensing John and Sarah's amusement.

'Such as?'

'Plenty of things.'

'Name them.'

Please, excuse us.' Sarah took John's arm and led him away to save Ruth any further embarrassment.

'I'm very glad that the Grand Hotel has become your court, Marcus. With me as your fool,' Ruth snapped bitterly.

'Sorry.' He took her hand, making an effort to sound as though he meant it. She looked at him, accepting his poor apology.

'Do you think . . . ? I mean, one day. Do you ever see yourself married?'

'No.' There was a tenderness in his voice she had rarely heard before.

'No. Nor me.' She smiled at him, a tight, brittle smile, and in that one moment she sensed all the wistful 'might have beens' crowding in on both of them.

The distant sounds of chatter and laughter from the party echoed through the servants' quarters to Collins's room. He sat alone on his bed, still dressed for duty, holding a scarf that he'd taken from his drawer.

Leaving the bed, he laid the scarf over his eyes, and tied it behind his head. Standing stiffly to attention, he continued to stand blindfolded, trying to imagine just what it had been like for Peter.

He tried to remain still, but tears soaked the cloth, burning his eyelids. He imagined the sound of rifles loading, safety catches being removed, the brusque orders being shouted . . .

'Take aim . . . *fire* . . .'

The final report. Shaking, he fell to his knees, sobbing because unlike Peter, he could still think, hear – and feel – enough to make his heart break.

'We did it,' Sarah crowed triumphantly as they bade farewell to the last guests in the foyer.

'You did,' John congratulated, as Clive burst in. Pushing aside a porter, he ran towards them.

'Excuse me, Mr Bannerman, sir. It's Mr Collins.'

'Stop it, Mr Collins,' Kate pleaded frantically as she ran alongside the concierge in her nightgown. She laid a hand on the box he was dragging down the corridor towards the boiler room. 'Just slow down a minute, please.'

'I can manage. Leave me alone,' he ordered, closing the lid on the contents of the box, which were threatening to spill out every time he heaved it forwards. 'Out of my way,' he repeated to the maids and footmen who had crowded into the corridor in their nightclothes to see what was going on. 'This has to be done.'

'Mr Collins . . .'

He almost knocked Kate over as he dropped the box.

'This is my business. Leave me alone,' he cried savagely.

Terrified by the stranger he'd become, Kate finally retreated.

'I don't need anyone's help. This has to be done.' As he swept the overflow that had fallen from the box into his arms, Lynne pulled Kate back.

'Leave him.'

'He's mad, he is,' Brenda chanted.

'How can I leave him?' Kate asked, pushing past Lynne to follow him.

Monica inserted the key she had appropriated from Mrs Harvey's office into the back door. Trembling at the sheer audaciousness of what she was doing, she crept inside and breathed a sigh of relief. Almost there! All she had to do now was replace the key, remove her make-up, hide her new dress and theatre programme and no one would be any the wiser. Then she heard Kate shout, 'Mr Collins?'

'Oh God!' She panicked, dropping the key as she tried to conceal it in her purse.

'Mr Collins, just tell me what's wrong.' Kate followed the concierge into the back corridor, where Monica was standing open-mouthed in horror at being caught.

'All of you just leave me alone,' he roared as he disappeared into the boiler room.

Kate stopped, transfixed at the sight of her room-mate.

'What the hell . . . what time is this to be coming in?'

'I was . . . I was . . .'

Remembering Mr Collins, Kate gave Monica a hard look before running on, but Lynne, Brenda and the other maids didn't go after her.

'Oh bloody hell, girls.' Lynne tugged at Monica's sleeve. 'What have we got here? Lady Muck?'

'You can shut up. I was invited out.'

'She's wearing powder! Look at her!'

'It's a frock, a proper frock.' Brenda couldn't keep the envy from her voice.

Lynne snatched at the skirt of Monica's dress.

'Don't you touch it,' Monica warned.

'Oh, la di da. Isn't she fine? Smell her, go on smell her. That's perfume that is.'

'She smells like a tart!' Brenda condemned the trappings of a wealth she knew she could never aspire to. 'A bloody tart.'

'And what's this, lady?' Lynne snatched the programme Monica was holding.

'Give me that,' Monica cried, as Lynne held it tantalisingly out of reach.

'Opera. She's been to the opera! Her!'

'I said give it—' Monica had closed her hand into a fist ready to sock Lynne in the eye, when she saw the Bannermans walking down the corridor with Clive.

'That's enough,' John commanded. 'Where's Mr Collins?'

'Through there, sir,' Lynne answered, more quickly than the others.

'Get back to your rooms.' Sarah noticed Monica's dress and make-up but decided the scolding the maid deserved could wait until a more opportune moment. 'And you, Monica,' she added, following John before the maids dispersed.

Mr Collins had opened the door of the incinerator, allowing the temperature in the boiler room to climb to an unbearable level. The armful of things he had taken from the box lay in the middle of the cellar. He stood before them, throwing them into the flames, one after another.

'Don't, Mr Collins,' Kate pleaded, distraught by the change in the concierge. 'They belonged to Peter . . .'

'Peter's dead.' He tossed in a book, watching the cover shrivel over the coals, shrouding them with a layer of charring paper before sparking into a blaze.

'You've kept them all these years,' she entreated as he tossed in a small wooden box.

'They should burn.'

'Please, let me have them . . .'

'You think you knew him?' The concierge held up a photograph of his son. 'You think that you knew Peter Collins? You didn't, Kate. None of us did. My own son and I didn't know him.' He hurled the photograph, frame and all, into the fire.

John, Sarah and Clive reached the doorway.

'All right, Kate,' John reassured. 'Mr Collins?'

Collins dropped the book he was holding to the floor.

'I'm sorry, sir,' he murmured without turning his head. 'Very sorry, but this is my business. It's private, sir.'

'What are you doing?' John asked quietly.

'Everyone back to bed,' Sarah said, turning to face the staff who had begun to crowd in the doorway to get a closer look at what was going on. 'Clive, get them back, there's a good lad.'

Clive tried to do as she asked, but he only succeeded in moving a couple of the maids out of the corridor.

'Jacob, let's go back to your room,' Sarah suggested.

'Sorry, ma'am. But the sooner this is done, the sooner it will be finished. I have to be rid of Peter. I have to—'

'Those are Peter's things?' She was horrified by the thought that he was destroying all the tangible mementoes of his only son.

'He wouldn't stop, Mrs Bannerman,' Kate explained tearfully.

'All of you, please,' said Collins as he picked up the book again. 'Just leave me alone. Peter's dead, and now he's dead for good. He deserves to burn.'

'He does not.' Kate tugged at his arm. 'Don't say that.'

'It was right that he died,' Collins said calmly. 'It was justice. Peter didn't die in action. No soldier's grave for him. He lied to us all.'

Stephen pushed his way through the crowd in the doorway. Touching Kate's shoulder, he steered her towards his mother.

'Don't, Jacob.' He removed the book gently from the old man's hands. 'You don't have to say anything. Come with me.'

'I have to stay. I have to be finally rid of him.'

'No you don't,' Stephen asserted compassionately. 'Come with me.'

'This is his fault. Don't you see, sir? He's brought me down to this. It's his fault. Weakness breeds weakness. He was a coward and that cowardice brought those men to me. They lied, they stole from me. My life savings. And that's my punishment.'

'What happened, Jacob?'

Collins fell to his knees. Stephen crouched beside him, watching as the concierge scooped the remainder of Peter's things into his arms. Collins looked up and addressed the crowd in the doorway.

'My son didn't die a soldier. He was a coward. He ran away. He was a traitor to his country. To me . . .'

'No . . .' Kate sobbed.

'He was executed by the British Army on the fifth of October 1915. They shot him dead. Stone dead. And he deserved it.'

Shocked into silence, the Bannermans and the staff continued to watch as tears fell from his eyes.

'All I've got left is his shame.' Collins turned to Stephen. 'If only he'd never been born, sir. Never been born. Then I'd be at peace.'

Katherine Hardy

The roar of the furnace filled the silence. Only Stephen found the courage to reach out and hold the concierge while he continued to mourn his shame and his loss.

Chapter Thirteen

Kate sat alone at the table in the alcove where the staff took their breaks. It was past midnight, but she was loath to go to the cell she shared with Monica. She couldn't bear the thought of confronting the trainee for taking the key from Mrs Harvey's office and staying out past curfew; neither could she face the thought of tossing and turning on her bed. She knew she wouldn't sleep. Not after the traumatic events of the evening.

She opened the book she was holding, the only one of Peter Collins's that had escaped the inferno in the boiler room. Tears fell from her eyes, obscuring the print, as she tried to read. She dried them hastily as Stephen walked in and sat across the table from her.

'Mr Collins is asleep?' he asked.

She nodded bleakly, staring at Peter's signature on the title page. It brought back memories of all the dockets and orders that he had signed before the war had changed so many lives, including everyone's at the Grand.

She closed the book carefully. 'He was a nice lad, Peter. He always had a joke. In fact more than half the time he was here, he was getting told off for joking. Just goes to show, you can't tell. I never would have taken him for a coward.'

Katherine Hardy

Stephen watched her while she continued to stare down at the book.

'What do you mean?' he asked when he could no longer bear the silence that had fallen between them.

'You know. Peter was always one for helping out, working late, doing a bit extra to make it easier for the rest of us. Who'd have thought he'd turn his back on a battle and run.'

'And you think that is wrong?'

'Of course it is.' She looked at him, astounded that he should even ask such a question.

'Jesus Christ, girl!' he exclaimed harshly. 'You were right. You don't think, do you?'

'Sorry . . .' she stammered not even sure what she was apologising for.

'Tell me, did Peter Collins deserve to die?'

'All right,' she conceded, frightened by the venom in his voice. 'Perhaps not die, but he should be in prison. After all, he did run away.'

'And if it had been a German bullet that killed him, that would have been all right? That would have been an honourable death? Mr Collins would be in his room now, laughing and singing because his son had died a *proper* death?'

'I don't like it any more than you,' she protested heatedly. 'But Peter Collins was guilty. He had to be.'

'You weren't there, Kate. You have no idea what you're talking about. If you'd try to think for just once in your life, you'd realise that it's people like you who drove Jacob Collins into that state.'

'You didn't run,' Kate countered, angry with him for accusing her of not thinking. 'You didn't. And Peter's not the only man I knew. Jim Crawford, remember him? Tom Brookes? Dan Miller? They stayed on the lines. They died soldiers. Tell me, if Peter's not a coward, what does that make them? Stupid? Idiots for throwing their lives away? You'll dishonour them all, Mr Bannerman.'

'It's not as . . .' He tried to think of a way to tell her about the war. The blood, the death, the sheer agonising hell of it. But once again he couldn't find the words. 'It's not as simple as that,' he finished lamely.

'Then maybe I'm the simple one,' Kate retorted, hurt by his reply.

'If you'd been there—'

'I didn't see it. All right, I couldn't,' she interrupted. 'But if you call them all good men, even the cowards, then what have the good men got left?'

'We were reduced to animals, Kate. And animals don't think what they're doing. They just run.'

'I am sorry for him. I am, truly.'

'I was like you,' he said slowly, making another effort to explain events that now seemed inexplicable. 'I despised them at first, when the battle seemed so . . . so fine. But that was before we all wanted to run. I hated those men then. I'd take them food and spit on them. Call them . . .' He lowered his head and Kate realised he was on the verge of tears.

'I'm sorry.'

'Maybe you're right,' he conceded, fighting to keep control of his emotions.

'No.' She reached across the table and held his hand. It was cold. As cold as the deserts the chef kept on ice.

'But the Peter you knew?' he asked, looking into her eyes. 'He wouldn't run?'

'No.'

'Then think what must have happened to make him run.'

'I know. I will. I'll just have to think for once in my life, won't I?' she joked feebly.

He managed to laugh.

'You've seen so much more than me. France . . . Berlin. I've seen nothing. Just this place. I was fifteen years old before I even saw the ocean. It scared me rigid.'

His laughter lost its cynical edge.

'It did,' she insisted in mock indignation, cheered by the sincerity in his smile. 'It scared me out of me wits on Blackpool's prom.'

'I've never been there.'

'What? Blackpool?'

'Nope. So, you see, I haven't seen everything, Kate.'

'I'll take you.'

'All right.'

'I will, though,' she promised. 'One day.' She shook her head at the thought. 'Now that would be a sight. You and me walking out.' She shivered as the chill in the room and the silence of the night settled around them once again. 'I am sorry I didn't understand. But I will try. For Peter's sake,' she added as Stephen left the table.

Lynne and Brenda crept out of their bedrooms early the next morning, but they didn't go straight down to the staff kitchen for breakfast as they usually did. Instead they stole back up the corridor to the section of the basement that housed the single rooms where the senior live-in staff boarded.

'Go on, do it.' Brenda nudged Lynne's elbow as they stopped outside Mr Collins's room.

'I am,' Lynne hissed, 'so stop pushing.' She looked around, checking again to make sure no one was watching them, before dropping a book outside Mr Collins's door. Hammering loudly, she ran off, closely followed by Brenda.

They halted around the corner, stifling their giggles and peeping around the wall, as they waited for the concierge to open his door.

Mr Collins emerged, and looked up and down the corridor before seeing the Bible. Mystified, he stooped down, picked it up and opened it. A white feather fluttered from its pages. It drifted slowly downwards before landing at his feet.

Esme was still in her dressing gown when a knock at her door disturbed her. She opened it to find Sarah standing outside.

'Miss Harkness, it was drawn to my attention last night that I've neglected my staff, but that is now in the past. Which brings me to why I'm here.'

'I take it we're talking about Monica?' Esme asked, deliberately keeping Sarah waiting in the corridor.

'Do you mind telling me exactly what your friendship with that girl entails?'

'All I want is to show her one or two things she wouldn't otherwise see. Open her eyes a little. I like the girl, she's my friend.'

'You've had many friends over the years, Miss Harkness, and all of them have paid for the pleasure. What is Monica's price? Is she the latest in a long line of girls?'

'Mrs Bannerman,' Esme protested. 'Must everything I do come down to prostitution?'

'Actually, as you've mentioned it, yes,' Sarah rejoined bluntly.

'Very well,' Esme rallied, stung by Sarah's frankness. 'And I understand that you'd use the same tricks yourself on your husband's brother.'

'What on earth do you mean?'

'Marcus said so himself when he was in the bar

regaling guests with the story of how you seduced him to get money for the Grand behind your husband's back.'

'That's a lie.'

'You expect me to take your word when you ignore mine?' Esme questioned in dulcet tones.

'Yes. I'll ignore malicious gossip, whether it comes from you or Marcus. And as much as that man would like to give the impression that he owns this place, I hold equal power in the Grand. So take it from me, Miss Harkness, you're here under sufferance and while you remain under this roof, you'll follow my rules.' Turning on her heel, she swept away before Esme could close the door in her face.

Kate launched straight into Monica the moment she appeared in the service bay to collect her trolley.

'You came here, a scrap of a girl, that pleased to have a job. Now you're sneaking out at night, stealing the back door key, and all thanks to Miss Harkness. You're to leave her alone. Do you hear?'

'Oh, so what happens in Kate's world then?' Monica sneered. 'Stay below stairs, don't voice an opinion. Don't dare look up.'

'If we want to keep our jobs, yes.'

'So what about you and that Mr Bannerman?'

'What!'

'I've heard, and you were seen last night, making eyes, flirting your way into bed with him. We're all laughing at you. So don't tell *me* how to behave.'

'I've not looked at him once.'

'Then you *should*, Kate Morris. Stay where you are, and you'll end up like Mr Collins, driven mad by service.'

'I'm nothing to Mr Bannerman, nothing.' Kate was

more upset by the allegations than she was prepared to allow Monica to see. 'And it's you everyone is laughing at,' she railed furiously. 'A Salford girl painted out in make-up, wearing silk, using her fingers in restaurants. And once Miss Harkness has finished laughing, she'll cast you aside, and we won't be there to pick you up. We'll be too busy laughing. Laughing at the stupid housemaid and her stupid dreams.'

Covering her mouth with her hand to stifle her sobs, Monica abandoned her trolley and ran headlong down the corridor. Kate watched her go, regretting her outburst, but knowing it was already too late to try to make amends.

Monica didn't stop running until she stood outside Miss Harkness's door. Bursting in without knocking, she confronted Esme.

'Where's the dress? Where is it?' she asked, needing to reassure herself that not only the dress, but also Miss Harkness, was still there for her.

'It's here.' Esme held out the box. After her altercation with Sarah, she felt that she needed the maid's friendship as much as Monica needed hers. Monica opened the box and carefully removed the gown. Holding it in front of her she stared at her reflection in the cheval mirror.

'I don't care what they say, it does suit me. Don't you think so, Miss Harkness?'

'Those people, the people who mock and taunt, they like everything to stay in its place, Monica. But we can walk the world, you and I. Walk above them together.' Esme rose from her chair and kissed Monica on the forehead. Monica barely registered the touch. Her eyes shone, glittering back at her reflection in the glass as she built exquisite castles in the air and into her future.

*   *   *

Katherine Hardy

'But, Mr Collins,' Clive entreated, 'you've got to rest.
And that's an order from Mr Bannerman.'

'There's work to be done, Clive.'

'They've put Mr Douglas on duty. Everything's fine.
They don't want you in the foyer.'

'I see. Then I'm an embarrassment.' The concierge
turned away so Clive wouldn't see the pain of rejection
in his eyes.

'That's not what I meant, sir.'

'But if I don't go on duty, Clive, what else can I do?'
he appealed bleakly.

Marcus strode into the foyer from the street and stared
at the strange man uniformed in concierge's livery who
stood in Mr Collins's customary place.

'Who are you? Where's Mr Collins?'

'Perhaps Mr Bannerman can answer those questions,
sir,' Mr Douglas replied politely. 'You'll find him in the
office.'

Furious, Marcus ran up the stairs and burst in on
John and Sarah.

'Why didn't you tell me about Collins?'

'You know now,' John pointed out.

'But you didn't think to tell me before I saw his
replacement on duty?'

'Frankly, Jacob's ashamed enough without the story
being spread across town.'

'So what are we going to do about it?' Marcus looked
to his brother.

Stephen tapped on the door before opening it. 'Mr
Collins is back in his room. I've told him he's due a
holiday, but he's just sitting there.'

'So, what are we going to do?' Marcus reiterated.

'What can we do?' John replied.

'Something, anything, other than just sit here bleating.'

226

'Any course of action we take means relating the story of Peter Collins all over again,' John reminded his brother. 'If we went to the police we'd have to tell them everything. Jacob's in a bad enough state now — that would just about destroy him. I'm telling you to leave him alone, Marcus.'

'And that's precisely what those men, whoever they are, depend on. All of us keeping quiet.'

'God knows how many families they've cheated,' Stephen murmured.

'Jacob Collins is family,' Marcus said firmly. 'At least, that's what you say about the staff until they need your help, Sarah. I told you it was hypocrisy. But can't you see this is wrong? Doing nothing will play right into those men's hands, leaving them free to play their filthy tricks on the next poor, gullible sod.'

Sarah remembered Esme's allegations, and looked her brother-in-law coolly in the eye. 'Everyone's talking about Mr Collins as it is, Marcus. You'd only use him as a good story at the bar to regale your friends with yet another anecdote at someone else's expense.'

'I would not.'

'You've a great talent for taking a joke too far. Anyone who gets involved with you becomes your victim in the end.'

'Where's this come from, Sarah?' he asked directly, ignoring Stephen and John's presence.

'You know full well. You've played at housekeeper, but that's finished, so leave it. We can look after Mr Collins.' She moved closer to her husband.

'Fine! I can see you don't need me. I'd obviously only make things worse.' He slammed the door behind him as he left.

*　　*　　*

Marcus controlled his temper only as long as it took him to reach the end of the corridor. He lashed out, punching the wall and bruising his knuckles painfully in the process. Hearing a door close behind him, he turned to see Stephen standing next to him. Marcus looked at him, sensing that his nephew had seen, and understood, his anger.

'I saw him – Jordan,' Stephen explained, reading the confusion on his uncle's face. 'And I'd recognise him again.'

The men Marcus employed wasted no time in tracking Jordan and Carlyle down to a backstreet pub. Ordering a man to watch them, Marcus arranged for a car to pick him up at the Grand as soon as it was dark. Stephen went with him. They drove into the slums and parked behind another car in front of the pub. From their vantage point, they could see both the doorway of the pub and Marcus's man waiting in the shadows opposite.

After half an hour it began to rain. A fine drizzle that clung to the cap and coat of the watcher, thoroughly soaking him. Jordan and Carlyle emerged at closing time in a cloud of cigarette smoke and whisky fumes. Carlyle was laughing. Marcus pushed back the window of the car so they could hear what he was saying.

'The 25 Club's still open. We could go there, what do you say?' he shouted to Jordan as they stumbled from the pavement on to the road.

'Fine by me if you're paying,' Jordan agreed.

Marcus nodded. Four men left the car in front of them, moved forward swiftly and grabbed Jordan and Carlyle's arms, pinning them behind their backs. They dragged the men to the top end of the alleyway.

The Grand

The pub's regulars, who saw what was happening, pulled their caps lower and their collars higher to conceal their faces from view. It wasn't the kind of area where men got involved in someone else's trouble. Besides, Jordan and Carlyle were strangers in that part of the city, a fact Marcus had been quick to establish.

Marcus nodded again. The leading bruiser punched Carlyle in the stomach. Jordan struggled to free himself as his companion doubled up in agony. It was difficult to know whether he intended to help his friend or flee, but all he got for his trouble was a throbbing skull as another of Marcus's men grabbed his hair and smashed his head against a wall.

The bruisers dragged their quarry towards a street light. They stopped, holding Carlyle and Jordan by their necks as Marcus left the car. He stood there quietly, studying both men as though they were specimens of livestock being held for his inspection.

'Michael Redman and Paul Swain, better known as Jordan and Carlyle?' Marcus's voice was ominously soft. Stephen had never seen his uncle in such total command, or look quite so terrifying.

Mouths gaping open, eyes creased in pain, both men gazed at Marcus, too petrified to make a sound.

'I'm a friend of Jacob Collins and his son Peter. They're family.'

'You can have the money,' Carlyle babbled. He would have fallen to his knees if one of the men hadn't yanked up his chin.

'Shut up,' Jordan yelled.

'We've still got most of it,' Carlyle said, ignoring his companion's directive. 'You can have it. We had to . . . we couldn't . . . You try coming back from the front, no jobs, no nothing . . .'

Katherine Hardy

'If all you've got to offer are tales of hardship, you had better shut up right now,' Marcus warned coldly.

Carlyle fell silent. Stephen had seen men paralysed by fear, in the trenches, but this was something more, a fate more inexorable and inescapable.

'It's obvious you didn't pick on Collins alone.' Marcus pushed a cigarette into his mouth. 'You had to be working the area to make it worth your while. I've got contacts in Manchester. Men who know things the police could never discover. Have you got the money on you?'

'No,' Carlyle whispered hoarsely, half strangled by the hold on his throat.

'Then I can't kill you – yet.'

'I'm sorry . . .' He cringed. 'I'm sorry . . .'

'You knew Peter Collins?' Jordan clenched his teeth against the pain Marcus's men were inflicting on him.

'Yes.'

'Then tell his father that he was a coward.' More cunning than Carlyle, Jordan knew he had nothing to lose, and possibly something to gain if he succeeded in aggravating Marcus. 'Peter didn't panic. He planned it. Crept away and left the rest of us to die in his place. He knew what he was doing all right. He was a treacherous little bastard. We stayed. We stayed. Tell your Mr Collins that.'

Jordan's words had the desired effect. They touched Marcus. But Marcus's anger was cold, calculated and restrained. He walked up to Jordan and gazed into his eyes.

'Were you there, at his execution?'

'Wish I had been. He deserved it,' he spat viciously.

'Then you missed it. Missed seeing his face. How did he look? Like this?' In one easy movement Marcus slipped a gun from his pocket and pressed it to Jordan's forehead. The men holding Jordan stepped aside as he fell to his knees, pleading and begging for his life. 'Yes, like that,' Marcus murmured. 'He was guilty, and so are you.' He eased off the safety catch. 'That's the verdict, and this is justice.'

'Marcus!' Stephen shouted.

Marcus heard his nephew but he didn't turn his head.

'At least it ended for Peter Collins. But not for you.' He lowered the gun. 'Because I'll come back. For the rest of your life, watch out for me.' Still holding the gun, he motioned his men forward with the barrel as he retreated towards the car. The bruisers charged in. The nauseating thud of fists pulverising flesh filled the air. Stephen turned aside, sickened by the transformation of both men's faces into bloody, unrecognisable pulp.

'That's enough,' he cried, unable to take any more. Marcus's men ignored his command. And all the while Marcus kept on staring at the two men as the beating continued. He didn't call a halt until Jordan and Carlyle lay, two broken, bloodied, unconscious heaps of flesh on the pavement. But by then Stephen had begun the long walk back to the Grand.

'It was left with the porter this morning,' said Stephen. 'There wasn't a message, Jacob. Perhaps the Whittakers refused Jordan and Carlyle's help, or perhaps the army put the fear of God into them.'

Jacob stood in the doorway of his room and took the envelope Stephen handed him. He opened it and saw that it contained his money. He nodded briefly as Stephen walked back down the corridor.

Kate and Monica saw him as they folded sheets in

a service bay. Preoccupied with his own thoughts, Stephen didn't pick up on the frosty silence between them.

'Keep an eye on Mr Collins, Kate,' he said as he passed.

'Course I will, sir.'

He stopped and turned back.

'Kate, what time's your break? I thought – I don't know, we could go for a walk, get you out of this place for an hour or two. Blackpool's a bit far, but we could go to Victoria Park.'

Kate was conscious of Monica listening to every word.

'No,' she answered briefly.

'Or anywhere?' he suggested easily.

'Sorry, I can't.'

'Tomorrow?'

'No, I don't think . . . It's very kind of you, sir, but I'd rather not. Thanks all the same.'

Hurt by her refusal, Stephen walked on.

Ignoring Monica's pitying look, Kate lifted another sheet from the basket and handed her the corners.

'Now we have to dine here,' Ruth complained as she entered the foyer with Marcus. 'You'll have me working in the kitchens next.'

'You might scrub up well at that,' he baited.

Sarah and Stephen approached them as the pageboy took Ruth's wrap.

'Marcus, Ruth,' Sarah acknowledged coldly. 'I take it you've heard about Mr Collins?'

'Very good news,' Marcus agreed. 'Stephen told me.'

'We should thank God that you didn't go blundering in, causing more trouble. I hope that's a lesson learnt,' she lectured.

The Grand

'Indeed it is.'

Ruth waved to a fashionably dressed couple in the Reading Room. 'Do excuse us,' she apologised to Sarah, 'but as you can see we're meeting friends.'

'Sarah, Stephen,' Marcus murmured before leading Ruth away.

'What a shame, just as you and Marcus were becoming such good companions,' Sarah said to her son.

'There was no need for that,' Stephen complained irritably.

'You've never liked Marcus. What's this sudden conversion?' When her son didn't answer, she adopted a warning tone. 'Don't start thinking of Marcus as a friend, Stephen. He does nothing without profit.'

'That's not true.'

'I know him better than you.'

'Who do you think got Collins his money back?' he blurted out.

'It was handed in.'

'It was Marcus,' he divulged angrily. 'He found those men. He . . . he spoke to them and stopped them. The rest of us just sat around making the right noises, even Dad, but Marcus did something.'

Sarah was astonished by the sudden glimpse of another side to Marcus's character. 'Then why didn't he say?'

'Because he doesn't want the credit. He did it for Collins.'

'That I don't believe.' But she did, already seeing Marcus in a new light.

'I know his reputation. Call him a bastard if you like. But Peter Collins is down as a coward on official papers, and we know it's not that simple.'

They were interrupted by Stephen's friend George,

who walked through the door with a crowd of young men.

'Don't say anything. No one's supposed to know,' Stephen warned, as he went to meet them.

'Ready for the off, Stephen?' George winked.

'Sorry lads, not tonight. You're on your own.'

Sarah looked from Stephen to the doorway of the Reading Room. Marcus was standing there with Ruth and another couple. Perturbed by a totally new perception of him, she stared at him, starting in embarrassment when she realised he was staring back.

For once there was no hostility in their eyes. Smiling, Marcus nodded to Sarah before taking Ruth's arm and leading her into the dining room.

An hour later Stephen saw Mr Collins, dressed smartly and correctly in his uniform, walking down the corridor towards the foyer. Abandoning his drink on the desk, Stephen opened the office door and called to the concierge, 'You really should take that holiday, Jacob.'

'At the end of the week, sir, when it's due. Mr Douglas isn't available for duty this evening, so I'll take my post now if you don't mind.' He paused for a moment. 'Mr Bannerman, I am sorry for the trouble I caused . . .'

'Don't—'

'No, sir. It has to be said. For one night I lost sight of God, but he didn't abandon me. And he teaches forgiveness above all else. We'll never know the truth of what happened to Peter, but forgiveness can't be conditional, I've learnt that much.'

'Then you do forgive Peter?'

'It's a journey, sir. A journey.' He opened the door that led to the foyer, took a deep breath, smiled briefly at Stephen, and marched out.

The Grand

Stephen stood back, watching as the concierge took his customary place at the very heart of the Grand. He understood why the old man felt that he had to return to work, and he admired his bravery. The same bravery that had driven soldiers to venture valiant, and sometimes pointless, deeds in battle.

Clive approached the concierge as soon as he took his place in the foyer.

'Mr Collins, did the Evans party confirm numbers for tonight?'

'Yes they did, Clive. It's a party of six at eight o'clock. I'll greet them and show them to the bar.'

'Thank you, sir.'

As Clive returned to his domain, Esme Harkness walked out of the lift.

'Good evening, Mr Collins.'

'Good evening, Miss Harkness.'

Stephen turned his back. The Grand Hotel was functioning at its best, as it always did when Jacob Collins was in control. The concierge's voice followed him back down the corridor and into the office.

'Yes, sir. If you take the stairs first on the right . . . Yes, ma'am, just follow the corridor to the left . . . Not at all, sir, it's not a problem, the porters can help you . . . Yes, sir, of course not, sir . . .'

Chapter Fourteen

K ate pushed open the door that closed off the servants' corridor from the foyer and glanced around the proscribed, front-of-house territory. Seeing Mr Collins standing next to the desk, she stepped hesitantly on to the marble floor.

'I'm allowed, sir,' she explained swiftly, when the concierge saw her. 'Mrs Harvey sent me up. She said it was special duty.'

He beckoned her forward. 'The young lady you've been sent to assist is coming in now, Kate. But mind you get straight back to your work once you've done what you have to.'

Puzzled by Mr Collins's brusqueness, she went to the door. A weary, middle-aged man was helping a young woman up the steps. The girl – who looked to be in her late teens – was walking slowly, her face creased in pain as though every step was agony, but to Kate's surprise, neither Mr Collins, nor John or Sarah Bannerman, who were standing next to the concierge, offered to assist them.

'Kate.' John smiled in relief when he saw her. 'This is Miss Rigby. Could you show her to room ten?'

'Yes, sir.'

'I don't need escorting,' Maggie Rigby snapped

ungraciously, shrugging off her father's helping hand. 'It's all right, Father. Please stop fussing. Really.'

Disconcerted by a rudeness he wouldn't have tolerated in his own daughter, John turned from the Rigbys and called for a porter. 'Alfred, room ten. Could you take the luggage straight up?'

'You've got everything you need?' Mr Rigby asked. 'I'll see you on Thursday,' he muttered, when his daughter didn't answer. 'Take care of yourself, there's a good girl.' He stood awkwardly beside John, unsure whether to embrace his daughter, or not. She made the decision for him, by walking away without a backward glance.

'It's this way, miss.' Kate pointed to the lift.

'I'm not blind.' All too aware of the effect of her impoliteness, Maggie stepped in ahead of the maid.

Adele glanced up from the copy of *The Times* she was reading aloud to her grandmother in the Reading Room, just in time to see Maggie cross the foyer with Kate.

'That must be Miss Rigby. I heard father talking, all in whispers, when he thought I wasn't listening. She's been in hospital or something.'

'I wouldn't know,' Mary commented cuttingly. 'Your parents seem determined to keep events at the Grand a secret from me.'

'She must be about my age.'

'Adele, stop gawping at the guests and read the obituaries,' Mary commanded. 'They make more sense than the headlines these days. At least I know the people involved.'

Adele reluctantly turned the page, but she couldn't resist taking another peep at Maggie before the doors closed on the lift.

*   *   *

Katherine Hardy

'You can reach me on this number, John.' Mr Rigby handed over a business card. 'Of course, I'd stay if I could, but we're having trouble with the Liverpool office. There's always something amiss there that needs my personal attention. I'll see you on Thursday.'

'We'll look after her, Lawrence.' John wished his friend would leave so he could put the whole unpleasant business of Maggie Rigby's arrival behind him, and get on with his day.

'I'm grateful, John. I really am.' There was nothing to keep Lawrence Rigby in the Grand, yet he continued to stand next to John and Sarah in the foyer. John finally held out his hand. Rigby shook it, turned to the door, and walked down the steps.

'I doubt he's needed at work,' Sarah contended sceptically. 'He should be with her.'

Unwilling to criticise an old friend, even to Sarah, John left her and walked over to Mr Collins.

'Miss Rigby will be staying in her room for the duration, so anything she needs will have to be delivered by room service. Make sure there's someone standing by.'

'Sir.' Collins made no effort to hide his disapproval.

'What could I do, Jacob?' John asked. 'He's an old friend. We were at school together.'

'Strictly speaking, sir, we could be breaking the law.'

'Hardly,' John retorted, surprised at the concierge's attitude.

'A law has been broken, sir. And nothing can alter the fact that we're giving her shelter.'

Alfred opened the door to room ten, dropped the suitcases next to the bed and left as Kate walked in with Maggie.

238

'Shall I unpack your things, miss?' Kate offered.

'If you would. Then you can get me some provisions.'

'I'll bring you the menu, miss.'

'You can get me some whisky and brandy. One bottle of each. Charge it to my father's account.' She smiled maliciously before adding, 'It's medicinal.'

'Yes, miss,' Kate answered, wondering what had happened to Maggie Rigby to make her so uncivil and unpleasant to everyone, including her own father. Whatever it was, she guessed it to be a tragedy of some magnitude. Nothing less could make a young woman with Maggie Rigby's looks and money so obviously and thoroughly miserable.

No sooner had John and Sarah left the foyer than Ruth swept through the doors. As no one else was around, she cornered Mr Collins.

'Where's Mrs Bannerman? I want to see her.'

'She's in the study upstairs, Miss Manning. But I'm afraid she doesn't want to be disturbed. She's doing the monthly accounts.'

Ignoring his directive, Ruth went straight to the lift. Stephen saw her as he came out of the bar and muttered, 'Oh my God!' loud enough for the concierge to hear before running after her. He caught up as Ruth entered the elevator. He shouted to the lift boy to wait, but she hit the boy's hand away from the button. Staring at Stephen, she cut him dead as the doors closed.

Doubling back across the foyer, Stephen charged up the stairs as fast as he could run. He reached the floor that housed the family accommodation just as the lift doors were opening. Ruth emerged, looked back, saw him and walked down towards the study.

'Ruth!' he shouted, utilising what little breath he had left. 'Ruth!' he croaked. 'I'm sorry.'

'Easily said after the event.' She turned to face him.

'I really am,' he panted, propping his back against the wall in an effort to regain his breath. 'I was going to come and see you. I didn't mean to cause you any offence. I'd had too much to drink . . .'

'Oh, I realised that,' she interrupted acidly.

'Stephen?' Sarah opened the study door and looked at her son and Ruth. 'Good afternoon, Ruth. Is anything the matter?'

'Indeed there is. Shall we go into the drawing room and discuss it?'

'I'm busy—'

'And I'm here to complain about the behaviour of your son.' Ruth led the way into the living room. 'And believe me, I'm not the only one with cause for grievance. Stephen is gaining notoriety throughout Manchester, both as a drunk and a fool. It was only seven o'clock in the evening, a decent enough hour I would have thought, but he was insensible. And he took great delight in introducing me to his companions as his uncle's concubine.'

'I am very sorry,' Sarah apologised, looking to Stephen who was standing, sheepish and silent in the doorway.

'I was in company. While his little gang laughed at me – I won't dignify their comments by repeating them to you—'

'It won't happen again,' Stephen broke in quietly. 'And I'm not a child. I'm practically the same age as you, so you've no need to involve my mother in this.'

Ruth continued to look to Sarah. 'He lives under your roof. He spends your money, so you're involved,

Sarah. I know that you're obsessed with this precious hotel, but I think it's time you concerned yourself with matters a little closer to home.'

'And I think the childless are quick to find fault in other people's children.'

'I beg your pardon.' Ruth stared at Sarah, wondering if she'd heard her correctly.

'No matter what Stephen's done, you have no right to criticise the way I lead my life.'

'I can see where he gets his manners.'

'I imagine you expect children to sit silently in their place, because in the world you come from, parents have nothing more onerous to do than manage their estates. But the rest of us have to work, and if that means I can't keep an eye on Stephen every hour of every day, then I can only apologise, because the situation isn't going to change. Now is that all? Because if it is, I have work to do. Good day.'

'She's only nineteen, Mrs Harvey,' Kate said, as she faced the housekeeper and the concierge in the housekeeper's office. 'And she's lying in bed all on her own. If she wants someone to sit with her, I could read her a book—'

'You are not to concern yourself with Miss Rigby, Kate,' Mr Collins intervened sharply. 'And you are not to go into her room unless you receive specific instructions from either Mrs Harvey or myself. Is that understood?'

'I'm only offering. I don't want to be paid for it, sir,' Kate explained, anxious that her motives shouldn't be misunderstood.

'The matter is closed. She is to be left alone.'

'Yes, sir.' Kate opened the door and walked out into the corridor.

Katherine Hardy

'That was a bit severe, Mr Collins,' Mrs Harvey reproached.

'But necessary.'

'Why's that?'

'I'm sorry, it's not for discussion.' He went to the door. 'And it's only my opinion. Which counts for little in the running of this establishment.'

Maggie was lying in bed, listlessly flicking through the pages of a magazine she was too idle to read, when she was disturbed by a timorous knock at the door. It inched open.

'Excuse me, am I bothering you?'

'I don't know. Are you?' she enquired flippantly.

'I'm Adele Bannerman.'

'Ah, one of the Bannermans. Or is it Bannermen?' Maggie swung her legs out of bed. 'As you're here you can make yourself useful. Pass my dressing gown.'

'Shouldn't you stay in bed?'

'My mother went to bed. Two weeks later she was dead. Have you been told what's wrong with me?'

'No.'

'I'm supposed to say it was my appendix. But it's not. They've locked me away because I've committed murder.' She stared solemnly into Adele's awestruck face, before bursting into mirthless laughter. 'Look at you, Adele Bannerman! I'd swear you'd believe me if I said the world was flat. You can stay.'

Adele had never heard anyone talk like Maggie before. She handed her the dressing gown and waited for more evidence of what she took to be sophisticated conversation. She wasn't disappointed.

'As my father's in the habit of saying, the sun's past the yardarm.' Maggie slipped on her gown and reached for the bottle of whisky and glasses Kate had brought her. She set a glass in front of Adele. 'Why don't you send a porter upstairs and tell your mother that you've gone out for supper, or whatever it is that Manchester folk do.'

'I'll tell them that I'm here, in your room.'

'No. Tell them a lie because that's much more fun. That's what parents are for. Besides, they wouldn't approve of you spending time with me.'

'I can do what I like,' Adele protested, with all the assurance of her seventeen years.

'No, they'd see me as a bad influence, and they'd be right. I am rotten to the core.'

'You're no such thing.'

'That's what my father thinks. He wants to sell the house in Oxford, and move to London where no one will know us.'

'Why would he want to do that?'

Maggie narrowed her eyes as she studied Adele. 'Do you like me?'

'Yes.'

Maggie dropped her smile. 'Then I won't say.' She filled both glasses almost to the brim and raised hers. 'Chin-chin.'

Adele took a sip, enduring the foul taste as the price that had to be paid for experiencing the prohibited pleasure of grown-up drinking. But much as she relished her initiation into the adult world, she delighted even more in the companionship of her new friend. She hadn't yet realised the implication of her sudden rejection of the values her parents had tried to instil into her, but Maggie had. Adele was hovering at the beginning of a path Maggie had already followed to a wretched and painful end.

Marcus sat at his desk in the office trying to add up a

Katherine Hardy

column of figures. It wasn't proving an easy task, given
that Ruth was pacing up and down in front of him.

'She attacked me,' Ruth added to her list of com-
plaints about Sarah. 'All but told me to leave the room.
As if *her* children are beyond criticism . . .'

'Your timing could have been better.'

'Of course. I should have known. In your eyes,
Sarah's beyond reproach.'

'Tomorrow's the fifth. It's the anniversary of
Catherine's death. Her firstborn child,' he explained, in
response to her quizzical look. 'She died of pneumonia
when she was five years old.'

'I've never heard mention of this. I've seen no
photographs, nothing.'

'It's hardly remarkable. Look across the foyer. I doubt
that there's a family in Manchester that hasn't suffered
a similar tragedy.'

'But John and Sarah are such wonderful liberals.
So proud of their bleeding hearts. And now you
tell me that they've kept a secret like that. That's
not the sort of behaviour I expect in the perfect
marriage.'

'I think it stems from John,' Marcus murmured
thoughtfully. 'But perhaps you're right. Perhaps John
and Sarah do have an imperfect marriage.'

'You should have seen them,' Lynne cackled as she
and the other maids congregated in a service bay in
one of the guest corridors before starting their shift. 'I
was dying to laugh. Alfred and the others, they have
to stand there like statues. I wanted to go up and pinch
their bums.'

'I'm not impressed. We've all been in the foyer at
some time or other.' Brenda reached for her apron.

'Yes, scrubbing it clean at dawn,' Kate agreed.

244

The Grand

'My mother's been in there in the middle of the day,' Brenda boasted.

'She was selling pegs and they chucked her out,' Lynne joked. The smile died on her lips. 'Oh bloody hell, look at her. She's gone and done it again.'

They all looked up to see Esme and Monica walking towards them. Monica was out of uniform, her arms full of dressmakers' boxes and drapers' packages.

'Good afternoon, girls,' Esme greeted them as they passed.

'Miss Harkness,' Kate acknowledged. 'Monica, you've got five minutes till the shift starts,' she warned.

'I know. But I'm not late.' She couldn't resist lording it over her workmates. 'We've been to the Harrods of Manchester,' she revealed, her eyes still shining with the excitement of the experience. 'You should see it. There's a doorman, and you say which department you want, and he walks you to it.'

'Monica?' Esme called.

'Don't tell me she walks through the foyer looking like that?' Brenda queried as Monica ran off. 'Old Collins would have a pink fit if she tried.'

'That Miss Harkness is too clever to make a mistake.' Kate checked that her trolley had the full complement of dusters and polishes. 'They use the side entrance.'

'If Harvey ever found out . . .' Lynne muttered darkly, 'I'd like to see Monica Jones smiling then.'

'It's not worth the bother of telling her.' Kate pushed her trolley out into the corridor, leaving Lynne scheming behind her.

Monica darted into Esme's room and dumped the parcels she was carrying on to the bed. 'I'd better dash, Miss Harkness. I've got to change.'

'Where were you born, Monica?'

'I've told you, Salford.'

'And those other girls?'

'Kate's from Oldham, Lynne's from Ancoats. I don't know where Brenda's from, but I wouldn't like to go there.'

'You'd think from your tone of voice that you are from better stock. Which is not the case. They are your friends. You shouldn't forget that.'

'I'm not friends with that Lynne Milligan. She's always giving me looks.'

'I've taken great care with your lessons, Monica. I do hope I'm not breeding a snob. You're no better than them. You're just lucky, that's all. Lucky in finding my friendship. A friendship which wouldn't exist if *I* thought myself superior, as you now seem to do. I don't want to hear you talking like that again.'

'Sorry, Miss Harkness,' Monica apologised, stung by the truth in Esme's rebuke.

'Lesson learnt.' Esme smiled. 'Now run along.'

At the end of a long day, John left the bustle of the Grand's public rooms for the marginally more peaceful atmosphere of the family's private quarters. As he poured out the pre-dinner drinks, he was amazed to see his son join them.

'This is a rare occasion, Stephen. Are you staying in for the night?'

'No money,' Stephen explained wryly.

'And I thought it was the pleasure of our company.'

'That as well.'

'I don't want to talk shop, but the three of us should meet up tomorrow, first thing,' John suggested to Marcus and Sarah. 'We need to discuss O'Neill's account. The man's getting away with murder.'

The Grand

'It will have to wait until the afternoon.' Sarah laid her drink on the table.'

'Why's that?' Marcus asked.

'It will have to wait,' Sarah repeated.

'It's the fifth,' Stephen reminded quietly.

'Of course. Sarah, I'm sorry, I completely forgot,' Marcus lied. 'You two go to the cemetery. I can manage on my own.'

'I'll be here.' John finished handing round the drinks and took a chair near the door.

Mary frowned at Sarah. 'You'll pardon my saying, but I've always found this particular anniversary strange. A birthday, I can understand, but the day of her death? It's morbid. Still, perhaps it's one of these modern ways you've so enthusiastically adopted.'

'I don't visit her grave to dwell on her death. I go to remember her.'

'Nonetheless it's unhealthy. The Lord God's taken her, we have to accept that and move on. I've no such fixation and I lost two children.'

'Three,' Marcus interposed.

'Two. The third was stillborn,' Mary corrected. 'The midwife took it away. I imagine she burnt it.'

Sarah turned away, too angry at her mother-in-law's insensitivity to trust herself to reply.

'Do you know? I think of Catherine often,' Stephen began diffidently, sensing his mother's pain. 'I was only little when she died, but I can still see her face, and I always see it upside down. Do you remember that time I bit the edge off a wineglass?' He looked at his mother. 'You don't mind me talking about her?' he asked uneasily.

'Of course I don't mind.'

'Someone grabbed me by the heels, in case I swallowed it.'

'Your grandfather. The rest of us were too busy screaming.'

'I could see the whole room, the wrong way round, bouncing up and down. Catherine just stared at me and she was smiling . . .'

John moved restlessly on his chair. He had never found it easy to listen to anyone talking about Catherine. 'Excuse me, I'd better check . . .' He left the sentence unfinished. Striding resolutely to the door, he walked out.

'I think she *wanted* me to swallow it,' Stephen continued. 'To see what would happen, like I was an experiment. This great, big, upside-down smile. I wonder what I looked like to her?'

Sarah smiled faintly, fighting the pain and sense of loss evoked by the memory. When she looked up, Marcus was staring intently at her, the way she would have liked John to do – if he'd had the courage to remain in the room.

The back entrance was in darkness when Monica returned to the Grand after her evening out, a full half an hour before the staff curfew. She was dressed in what had been her 'best' walking-out outfit when she had come to work in the hotel, ordinary clothes that owed nothing to Miss Harkness's money, or influence.

No sooner had she closed the door, than Lynne jumped on her and grabbed her hair. Dragging her to her knees, Lynne called out to someone who flicked on the light further down the passageway. Through a haze of pain and humiliation, Monica caught a glimpse of Brenda and two other maids hovering in the shadows. She screamed.

'You just keep quiet,' Lynne hissed.

'Let go of me.'

'Been out with your lady friend, have you?'

'I've not. I've been having a drink.'

'You just listen.' Lynne yanked her hair all the harder.

'We've all had enough of little Miss Monica Jones. You might think that you're a cut above the rest of us, but you're nothing. Do you hear me? What are you?'

'Let me go!'

Lynne tugged at her hair again, pulling out a handful. 'What are you?'

'Don't—' The rest of Monica's protest was swallowed by a moan as Lynne banged her head against the doorframe.

'What are you?'

'Lynne, keep it down,' Brenda begged, terrified that they'd be caught.

'Say it, what are you?'

'Nothing . . .' Monica gasped, momentarily blinded by the pain in her head.

'You keep at it girl. You keep parading around and looking at us like we're dirt and I'll get you. Understand?'

'I'll tell Kate.'

'You'll not say a thing, or there'll be more of this.' Clenching her fist she punched Monica savagely in the kidneys before rising to her feet. 'Fat lot of good you were,' she taunted Brenda and the others, before walking away. They ran after her, leaving Monica crying on the floor.

Adele giggled as Maggie refilled their glasses. Between them they'd finished off three-quarters of the bottle of whisky, and the taste that had seemed so foul at the beginning of the evening didn't seem quite so bad now.

Katherine Hardy

'I can't go back upstairs.' The words rolled sluggishly off Adele's tongue. 'I'll have to sleep on the floor. Imagine me, sleeping on the floor in my own hotel.'

'This should sober you up.' Maggie lifted her pillow and produced a small silver box. She opened it and showed Adele the fine white powder inside.

'What is it?' Adele almost fell from her chair as she peered into it.

'A tonic. You take it like snuff.' Maggie pinched a few grains between her thumb and forefinger and inhaled them. 'Have some?' Adele looked down at it doubtfully. 'It won't kill you.'

Adele reached out, took a pinch and emulated Maggie. She continued to sit, wide-eyed, staring, waiting for something momentous to happen.

'My friend Ellen went to a dinner party in Hampstead. They had cocaine in silver salt cellars. Everyone passed it around with the port.'

'Is that cocaine?' Adele asked innocently.

'Adele Bannerman, you really don't know a thing.' Maggie leaned towards her. 'Why do you think I'm ill?' she whispered confidentially.

'Your appendix?'

'An abortion. Do you know what that is?'

Struck dumb by the revelation, Adele nodded.

'Go on then,' Maggie goaded, 'tell me what it is?'

'It's – it's a baby.'

'My father paid them one hundred guineas. They pulled it out of me with hooks. Little dead thing. They didn't show it to me, but I think it must have looked like a newborn puppy, all curled up and blind. I tried to get rid of it myself. Took bitter apples, and that's when Father found out. He was furious. Then he packed me off up north so no one would find out about it. We're moving house now in case anyone suspects.'

'Who was it. Who was the—'

'Clive Jeffries, the boy next door. Can you believe that? The boy next door? I don't see him any more, and I'll never see him again. There now, Adele Bannerman, you're the last to find out the truth about me. You must think I'm shameful.'

'Oh no.' Adele continued to sit, mesmerised by the worldliness of her new friend. 'I think you're wonderful.'

Kate was half asleep when Monica crept into the bedroom they shared. She stumbled around, undressing in the dark before finally climbing into bed. Kate heard her mattress creak, then another sound propelled her abruptly out of drowsiness.

'Are you crying?'

When Monica didn't answer, she grabbed her shawl, threw it over her nightdress, and left the warmth of her bed to sit on Monica's.

'What's wrong?' Kate persisted, as her roommate turned over, curling away from her.

'Nothing,' came the muffled answer.

'It *looks* like nothing an' all. What's happened?'

'You don't care. You're the same as them, always telling me off. Leave me alone.'

Monica kept her face turned to the wall, but Kate didn't move. She continued to sit next to the girl, stroking her hair, and murmuring inadequate words of comfort.

John dimmed the lights in the foyer, but he couldn't resist checking everything one last time. Satisfied that there was no more to do at reception, he went into the bar, where Clive was setting out clean ashtrays ready for the morning.

'All done?' John asked.

'Just about, sir.'

'You head off, Clive, I'll finish that.'

'Thank you, sir. Goodnight.'

Marcus passed the barman as he walked through the door. 'Still hiding?' he asked his brother.

John managed to ignore the gibe. 'Maybe I should go with her to the cemetery,' he suggested as Marcus helped himself to a drink.

'I wouldn't. It's probably best to leave her.'

'Do you think so?'

'Trust me. I'm the expert in women. You married the first girl you went out with.'

'I did not.'

'Name the others.'

'Judith Connolly.'

'You were fifteen. You held hands. Once.' They looked into each other's eyes and laughed. 'If Sarah's made the day her own, then let her keep it,' Marcus advised. 'That's how women do things. God knows, they get little enough opportunity in the world, so they make their own space. Like tomorrow. It's hers. We shouldn't intrude.' He climbed on to a stool. 'And, be honest, you don't want to go, do you?'

John shook his head.

'It wasn't your fault,' Marcus said quietly, referring to another conversation that neither of them had forgotten.

'I wish I could be sure.' The lines around John's mouth tightened. 'She'll be wondering where I am. Goodnight, Marcus.'

'Goodnight.' Marcus finished his drink and poured another.

Ten minutes later he saw Collins leave the Reading Room and signalled to him.

'Jacob, I made an appointment with Mr O'Neill in the morning. Could you cancel it please? My brother's on duty, but don't bother him with it, he'll be busy with other things.'

'Certainly, sir. And if Mr O'Neill needs to talk to you?'

'Tell him he can't. I'll be out all morning. On a personal matter.'

Chapter Fifteen

'Wouldn't you rather stay in bed,' Sarah asked solicitously as Adele appeared, white-faced and red-eyed at the breakfast table.

'I'm all right,' she mumbled as she took her seat. 'It's just a headache.'

'It must have been quite a supper.' Stephen poured his sister a coffee, strong and black, to match his own.

'What do you mean?'

'Looks more like a hangover than a headache to me.'

'You should know.'

'Thank you, both, for a peaceful breakfast.' John folded the newspaper he'd been reading.

'You'll feel better if you eat something.' Sarah pushed the toast rack towards her.

'Don't have the boiled eggs,' Stephen warned. 'They'll only make you worse.'

'Why on earth should they do that?'

'Don't you remember? When you were a kid you were scared of boiled eggs. You used to burst into tears at the sight of them.'

'Don't be ridiculous.'

'You used to say, what if I break it open and there's a dead chick trapped inside? Boiled alive.'

'That's just silly. Kitchen eggs aren't alive, there's no sperm inside. They haven't been fertilised.'

Stephen burst out laughing. Sarah was amused, but one glance at the thunderous expression on John's face froze the smile on her face.

'Well it's true,' Adele countered irritably.

'Thank you Adele. That's enough,' John reprimanded.

'She obviously knows what she's talking about.'

'Don't talk about me as if I'm not here, Mother,' Adele asserted primly.

'You could show a little respect considering what day it is,' John reproved.

'John, Adele didn't mean anything.'

'I see, Sarah. It's all my fault. I've got it wrong again. If you'll excuse me.' Pushing back his chair he left the table and the room. Stephen went to his mother, she patted his hand to acknowledge his sympathy, but her gaze remained fixed on the empty doorway.

'That's enough of that talking back, Monica Jones,' Mrs Harvey lectured. 'I've been told on good authority.'

'Who told you?' Monica shifted uneasily from one foot to another as she stood before the housekeeper's desk.

'Never you mind. You know the rules. You don't consort with the guests.'

'I'm sorry, Mrs Harvey, and I'm glad you've had a word, because I'm stuck. It also says in the rules that we have to do whatever the guests want of us, and Miss Harkness asks me to go with her.'

'That's all well and good—'

'And the Bannermans know,' Monica said, playing her trump card. 'They've seen us, so it's all above board. I am really sorry, Mrs Harvey, but I've done nothing wrong. If anyone's at fault it's Miss Harkness. It's her you should be telling, not me.' She looked the housekeeper squarely in the eye. 'But I don't suppose that's allowed, is it?'

The first task the maids tackled after their morning break was the reloading of their trolleys in the service bay closest to the storerooms and Mrs Harvey's office. Lynne was working at half speed. Having manoeuvred her trolley until she had a better view of the office door than access to the stores of polishes, soaps and clean dusters, she waited impatiently for Monica to emerge.

'Oy, you?' Kate shouted cheekily as Clive walked past in a waiter's livery, 'where's Clive Evans gone? I've not seen him all morning, he's vanished.'

'Very funny,' Clive retorted.

'What's all this then?'

'That bloody Roy's gone sick, so I'm waiter for the day. Poxy job. Serving tea. Everyone knows that tea isn't a proper drink.'

'Don't knock it.' Kate nudged him with her elbow. 'I could almost fancy you dressed like that.'

'Get off!'

'You're blushing.' She pulled at the sleeve of the nearest girl. 'Look at him, Rosie, he's blushing.'

The office door finally opened. Lynne turned away from Clive and Kate to stare at Monica. The spiteful smile on her face confirmed the trainee's suspicions. She knew exactly who had told Mrs Harvey about her and Miss Harkness.

Pushing her half-empty trolley out into the corridor, Lynne walked away. Monica followed.

'Milligan, it was you who told Mrs Harvey about me and Miss Harkness, wasn't it? Well, you wasted your time. There's nothing she can do to stop it, and I told her so.'

Lynne whirled around, jamming Monica against the wall with her trolley. 'There's plenty I can do,' she spat viciously. 'So watch it.'

'Oh aye. You're nothing without your mates round you,' Monica jeered.

Grabbing her by the hair, Lynne slammed her against the wall. 'You think so? I've not started.'

'Get off,' Monica shouted, loud enough to be heard above Kate and Clive's laughter.

'Say please. Go on, say please. "Please, miss" like I'm one of your lady friends. Say it!'

Tearing off Monica's cap, she'd wound her fingers into her hair and yanked her head away from the wall ready to bang it, when Clive and Kate walked around the corner.

'Oy, oy, oy! What are you doing?' Clive pushed the trolley aside and forced his way between the two girls.

'She started it,' Lynne snarled, twining her fingers even more tightly.

'Lynne, stop it for God's sake,' urged Kate. 'You'll get us all in trouble.'

'You can shove off, Kate Morris.'

'I said stop it.'

Taken aback by a new authority in the older girl's voice, Lynne finally released her hold on Monica's hair.

'All right, girls, playtime's over.' Clive carried on down the corridor.

'Next time,' Lynne said, glowering at Monica. 'You just wait until next time.'

'Lynne, get back to work.' Kate pushed what little influence she had to the limit.

'You can't tell me what to do. I've been a chamber-maid just as long as you, Kate. She's the one who needs telling.' She poked her finger into Monica's stomach. 'We're sick of her, all of us. She's got it coming.'

She grabbed her trolley and stalked off down the corridor. By the time Kate turned to Monica, the trainee had run off in the opposite direction. Kate stared after her, her sympathy rapidly evaporating in a welter of exasperation.

Furious that Marcus had broken yet another engagement with her, Ruth crumpled the note he had left and tossed it on to the reception desk. Irritated by the sight of the clerk clearing it away, she walked to the centre of the foyer and glanced at her watch.

'Ruth, are you doing anything?' Adele called from the Reading Room. 'If you're not, come and sit with us.'

Ruth forced a smile as she crossed over to their table.

'It's good to know someone's glad to see me,' she murmured caustically.

'Uncle Marcus?'

'He's manufactured yet another excuse to avoid my company.' Ruth held out her hand to the girl sitting with Adele. 'How do you do?'

'And how do you do?' asked the girl, turning the conventional phrase back on her.

'Maggie Rigby, Ruth Manning.' Adele effected the introductions. 'Maggie's one of the guests. Ruth's . . . with my uncle Marcus. I mean she's his lady friend. I'm never sure what to call you,' she whispered coyly.

'Girlfriend sounds too young for someone of your age,' Maggie broke in knowingly. 'But lady friend sounds like a dowager aunt. Partner? That's too clinical. I suppose you're his lover. That's the most honest.'

Ruth's smile stiffened. 'Well, Maggie, you're quite a lexicon. Where are you from?'

'Oxford.'

'Oh, the seat of learning. You must live on the outskirts.'

The barb wasn't lost on either of the girls.

Adele made another attempt at conversation as Clive brought a pot of coffee to their table.

'Ruth's been everywhere. Haven't you?' she appealed to the older woman. 'She's even been to India. She's got all sorts of stories. Thank you, Clive.' She smiled at him as he laid out the sugar and milk. 'It's another Clive. I'm afraid you can't escape them, Maggie.'

'So you're a Clive are you?' Maggie surveyed him coolly.

'Yes, miss.' He stepped away from the table.

Maggie lifted her cup and saucer. 'Then come along, Clive, do your duty.'

'Miss.' Realising he was being set up as the butt of a joke, he picked up the coffee pot and began to fill her cup, stopping half an inch from the top.

'Clive, I didn't tell you to stop.'

'Sorry, miss.' He filled it almost to the brim.

'Did I say stop?'

'It's full, miss.'

'Clive, what's your job? Pouring coffee. So pour the coffee until I tell you to stop.'

'I'm sorry, miss, I don't want it to spill.'

'Pour the coffee, Clive.'

'Adele, what's the point of this?' Ruth interceded.

'Clive,' Maggie prompted coldly.

'I can't, miss.'

'And why not?' she demanded petulantly.

'In case it spills.'

'Like this?' Picking up the pot he'd replaced on the

table, she continued to fill her cup until the coffee flooded out, soaking the cloth.

'Oh, for goodness' sake!' Ruth exclaimed, before walking off in disgust.

'Don't they do things like this in India?' Maggie shouted after her.

'I'll get a cloth, miss,' Clive muttered, anxious to be anywhere except at their table.

'You do that, Clive,' Maggie sneered.

He backed away from the table into Mr Collins.

'Miss Rigby.' The concierge frowned. 'I understood you were to stay in your room.'

'Who's this, Adele?'

'Mr Collins,' Adele replied, subdued by the look in Mr Collins's eye.

'Well, Dr Collins, thank you for your concern, but look what your servants have done. The boy's name was Clive – blame him. I do.'

'Miss Bannerman? Your father might have something to say about this behaviour.'

'Adele, if he's not going to help, tell him to go away. The man's a pest.'

'Miss Bannerman, if I could have a word in private?'

'It's your hotel. You pay these people, tell him to go away.' Maggie waved her hand in the direction of the concierge.

Adele couldn't look at the concierge, but she murmured, 'Please leave us alone.'

'Very good, miss.' He walked away, outwardly his usual, implacable self, but inwardly seething. Maggie's laughter, harsh, brittle, followed him into the foyer. He looked into the office. Stephen was arguing with John. Turning his back on them, he faced the door, composing himself ready to greet the next guest who walked in.

*   *   *

'She's upstairs now, ready to go, like it's some sort of bloody vigil,' Stephen shouted angrily. 'You should go with her.'

'Stephen,' John reasoned patiently, unconsciously utilising Marcus's logic. 'It's your mother's day. I'd only be intruding. I've never gone with her on the fifth before, you know that.'

'Yes, and I never questioned it before. Maybe that's the advantage of spending all those years away. I don't have to accept things the way I used to.'

'She doesn't want me to go with her.'

'You've asked her, have you?' He glared at his father, who remained stubbornly silent. 'No, of course you haven't. That's not the done thing is it? It's a good thing I fought to keep this bloody world so intact.'

'I've never told the staff what to do before,' Adele confessed as she accompanied Maggie back to her room.

'Why ever not? It must be the only compensation in living here.' Maggie spotted Monica walking down the corridor towards them. 'You there? What's your name?'

'Monica, miss.'

'Well, Monica miss,' she mocked. 'Come with me, Monica miss.' Unlocking the door to her room, she beckoned the maid inside. Monica followed, standing at the door, watching, while Maggie walked to the wardrobe and opened it. 'Do you like clothes? Pretty thing like you must do. And I bet you like these?' She pulled out the skirt of one gown after another. The colours and fabric alone brought an envious glow to the maid's cheek that Maggie recognised only too well. 'Have them,' she said carelessly.

'How do you mean, miss?'

261

'God, they're slow in this place. Where do you get them from? The farm?' Maggie appealed to Adele as though the maid was invisible. 'I mean have them,' she mouthed slowly to Monica. 'They're yours.'

'Maggie, you can't throw them out. They're beautiful.'

'I don't want them, Adele. They belong to the Maggie Rigby that everyone knows, and she's gone. She's moving to London and leaving all this behind.'

'I'm ever so grateful, miss,' Monica enthused.

'But there's a price put on that one.' She pulled out the prettiest dress.

'I haven't got any money, miss.'

'Put it on. Then you can sit and have a drink with us. That's the price.'

Monica smiled warily as Maggie reached for the bottle of brandy. If she could have turned and run, she would have. But what if Miss Rigby complained about her? The last thing she could afford to do was give Mrs Harvey another excuse to carpet her.

'I won't be long.'

'Right.' John dropped his pen on the desk and looked up at Sarah. She was already dressed in her coat and hat. 'I could come with you?'

'If you want.'

'Marcus hasn't turned up. I don't know where he's gone. I can't really leave the office unattended . . .'

'No, that would never do,' she interrupted frostily. 'I'll be back by midday.' She walked out into the foyer. Stephen raced down the stairs to meet her.

'Give her my love,' he called out, as though Catherine was alive and well. Sarah kissed his cheek before walking to the door. She looked back just once. John had been watching her, she was sure of it, but the moment she turned her head he looked away.

Dressed in Maggie's frock, Monica sat back in an upholstered chair, sipping a glass of brandy while Maggie combed out her hair. Torturing the long strands into tight curls, Maggie piled them on to the crown of the maid's head and fastened them into place with the steel pins Adele handed her. Standing back to survey her handiwork, she realised that Monica had barely touched the brandy.

'Drink it in one,' she ordered briskly.

'I've had enough, miss. If Mrs Harvey knew that I'd been drinking—'

'I'm one of the guests, and how do you behave when a guest tells you to do something?'

'Do as I'm told, miss,' Monica chanted automatically, her voice wavering through tides of nausea.

'Exactly! So drink it in one.'

She lifted the glass to Monica's lips, forcing the maid to open her mouth and drink the brandy, or risk spilling it down the front of the dress.

'There, that's how I used to wear my hair.' Maggie turned Monica's head towards Adele as though she were a rag doll. 'She's the very image. Look in the bathroom, Adele?'

'What for?'

'Fetch my make-up, we're going to paint her. Monica, fill your glass.'

'I don't want to, miss.' Monica closed her eyes, steeling herself against the sickening after-effects of her last drink.

'That's a shame, because that's an order.' When Monica swayed precariously on the chair, Maggie took the glass from the maid's fingers and refilled it herself.

*　　*　　*

'Half an hour she's been,' Lynne grumbled to Kate and Brenda as she pitched her trolley into the service bay. 'Well, I'm not covering for Monica Jones. If she's skiving, I'm going straight to Harvey.'

'I told her to clean the service,' Kate lied. 'Now stop nagging.'

'Half an hour? It doesn't take half an hour to clean the service. We're not having it! Are we, Brenda?'

'Oh, stop your noise. I'll get her.' Kate dropped the jar of polish she was holding back on to her trolley, and headed straight for Esme Harkness's room.

'I'm sorry to bother you, Miss Harkness,' she apologised when Esme opened the door. 'But I'm looking for Monica.'

'She's not here.'

'Sorry.'

'Kate,' Esme said, laying a delaying hand on Kate's arm, 'I know you don't approve of my friendship with Monica, but I'm only helping her, just as you are. We're both her friends.'

'Maybe so, miss.'

Esme smiled drily. 'You've a remarkable little face, Kate. You're an open book, and a disapproving one at that. I was in service too, you know. A long time ago when things were a good deal worse than they are now. We were forced to wear uniforms made of hessian. I'd have given the world then for someone to come along to warn me about the mistakes, and guide me through the experience, but I had to find my own way.'

'Begging your pardon, miss, and I don't mean to be rude, but if you don't mind me saying . . .' Kate waited for Esme to nod assent before continuing. 'I hope you're not intending Monica to . . . you know . . . turn out like yourself?'

The Grand

'Kate, I'm a prostitute. I wouldn't wish that on anyone. I hope that one day Monica will put me to shame. She can teach me. Show me what I could have been. So you see, you shouldn't resent my friendship. I'm the only piece of luck ever to come her way.'

'I don't know about that.'

'But I am. She's come from a terrible home.'

'Excuse me, Miss Harkness, but she's from Regent Road. They're poor little houses, I'll give you that, but they're two up, two down. She's not from a hovel. She does tend to make things up.'

'Well, so did I at seventeen.'

'And you can tell a story now.' Kate stared up at Esme defiantly, waiting for a scolding that didn't materialise.

'I haven't seen her.' There was a cold glint in Esme's eye as she dismissed the maid.

'Very good, miss.'

Brenda was waiting at the end of the corridor.

'Kate, you're needed in room ten. They asked for you by name.'

Monica was slumped, insensible, in the chair, her face covered in garish make-up. Large rouge circles had been painted on to her cheeks, half-moons of bright blue powder shadowed her eyelids, oversized crimson bows were etched around her lips, the whole contrasting bizarrely with the clownlike pallor of her face.

'I used to look like that,' Maggie announced contemptuously as she eyed her handiwork. 'Look at me, Miss Margaret Rigby, decked out and painted up. Like a china doll, or so Father used to say.'

'I feel sick,' Monica babbled.

'Poor Margaret, she's sick. Does it hurt, Margaret? I bet it hurts, and it's all your own fault. That's what Father says. Come in,' Maggie shouted to a knock at the door.

Kate walked in. 'I got your message, miss . . . Oh my God!' She stared horrified at Monica.

'Take her away,' Maggie commanded.

'What's she done?'

'Take her out. I don't want to look at her. I want to forget that Margaret Rigby. I'm moving on. I don't want to look at her one second more!' she exclaimed, her voice rising hysterically. 'Go on, take her!'

'Miss Bannerman?' Kate appealed to Adele. 'Did you do this?'

'The staff in this place!' Maggie exclaimed. 'Adele, tell her, will you?'

'Kate, do as you're told,' Adele directed uneasily. 'Take her and clean her up.'

Kate walked over to the chair. Picking up Monica's hand, she rubbed it in an effort to bring her round. 'Monica? It's me. Are you all right?' Putting her shoulder beneath Monica's arm she helped her to her feet.

'Kate?' Monica mumbled, unable to focus on her fellow maid's face. 'I feel sick.'

'She's been drinking.' Kate glowered at Maggie and Adele. 'What the bloody hell have you done?'

'Do as you're told,' Adele repeated, guilt reddening her cheeks until they were almost the same shade as Monica's.

'Or what?' Kate contended.

'Or . . . or I'll report you.'

'Go on then, do it,' Kate challenged. 'And we'll both have a fine story to tell your parents.'

'Who do you think you are?' Maggie drawled.

266

'Someone who's a damn sight more sensible than you, that's who. You should be ashamed.' She turned her attention to Monica. 'Come on, you're coming with me. That's it.' She coaxed the girl to put one foot in front of another. 'God, you're stinking,' she complained as she caught a whiff of brandy-laden breath.

It seemed to take an age to get Monica to the door. The trainee moved like a sleepwalker, meandering all over the room in every direction except the one Kate wanted her to take.

'Tell her . . . tell her she can have the afternoon off,' Adele offered in an unsteady voice. 'She has my permission.'

'That's very kind of you, miss,' Kate snapped back caustically. 'It's good to know you've got such Christian hearts. Both of you.'

Adele closed the door as soon as Kate managed to get Monica into the corridor.

'There, she's gone, I'm rid of her,' Maggie said brightly, desperately trying to pretend that everything was fine. Her blithe cheerfulness didn't fool Adele for an instant.

Burning with remorse, Adele looked at Maggie. She watched as the older girl's wide-eyed, brittle confidence slipped inexorably away.

'But she's still here,' Maggie sobbed.

Adele crossed the room and hugged her. Maggie clung to her, digging her nails into Adele's arm as though she were her only hope of escape and survival.

A cold wind blew through the exposed section of the cemetery where Catherine was buried. Sarah shivered as she stood beside the headstone.

Katherine Hardy

Catherine Mary Bannerman,
beloved daughter of John and Sarah.
Sister of Stephen,
granddaughter of Charles and Mary

Stooping low, she replaced the vase she had filled with fresh flowers, before stepping back.

That was how Marcus found her. Standing, dry-eyed and pensive, beside Catherine's grave. She looked up when she heard his footsteps on the gravel path, but he knew from the expression on her face that she had expected to see John, not him.

He hesitated, waiting for her to tell him to go away, but she only smiled, a cold, distant smile that failed to touch her eyes, before turning back to the grave. He walked over to her and stood at her side.

John was sitting at his desk staring into space when Collins knocked on the door.

'Mr Bannerman, there was something of a problem earlier . . .'

'Can it wait?'

'Of course it can, sir. I shouldn't have bothered you. This is a difficult day.'

'You would remember.'

'Indeed, sir.' Collins hesitated wondering whether he should leave John alone or not. 'I remember Catherine with great joy,' he ventured. 'If it's any consolation, sir, don't think of her as a life interrupted, but a life completed. I try to think of my son in that way too. It doesn't always work, but sometimes it helps.'

The silence bore down on John, weighing heavily, just like his guilt.

'It was my fault, Collins,' he confessed wretchedly. 'My fault that she died.'

268

The Grand

'Oh no, sir . . .'

John didn't even hear the concierge. He was lost in the infinitely painful world that returned to haunt him, not only on the anniversaries, but every single day and night of his life.

'"Leave it," I said, "leave it",' he disclosed abruptly. 'Catherine had started that cold and we'd called the doctor. He'd seen her. Then she got worse and I said, "Leave it." She was still full of noise, wouldn't stay in bed a minute. You know what she was like? Always a little actress. I thought she was making a fuss. So I said, "Leave it. Give her the weekend. See if she'll be better by Monday." So we waited. Sarah didn't want to, but she did as I said. The Grand was a different place then. My father was still in charge. His own kingdom, and he expected the women to keep to their place. And then the cold became pneumonia. If we hadn't waited. Two days . . . I made her wait . . .'

'That doesn't make it your fault, sir,' Collins sympathised awkwardly. 'I'm sure Mrs Bannerman doesn't think so.'

'I don't know. I've never spoken to her about it. I made her wait, but I've never dared to ask her if she blames me for Catherine's death. I'm not at all sure I could bear the certainty that she does.'

'Does John know that you're here?' Sarah asked Marcus as she finally turned away from the grave.

'No, and I'd rather you didn't tell him. I don't want to intrude. He should be with you, not me.'

'He comes on her birthday and Christmas. With Stephen, Adele and your mother. He can lose himself in the crowd. Does he talk to you about Catherine?'

'No.'

'Nor to me. He's too much like your father in that

269

respect. "Don't dwell on the past." That's your father's voice, I can still hear him. "What's done is done, move on." It's as though—' The breath caught in her throat as she struggled to formulate her thoughts into words. 'It's as though Catherine failed us in dying. As though we should be ashamed of her.' She dabbed at her eyes with a handkerchief. 'I promised myself that I wouldn't do this.'

Marcus stepped forward, wanting to hold her, but something in her eyes prevented him from touching her.

'Do you remember the Grand in those days?' Sarah pushed the handkerchief determinedly back into her pocket and forced a smile. 'All that dark wood panelling. It was so austere and forbidding, just like a gentleman's club. I felt I'd broken the rules just by stepping inside.'

'Why do you think I left?'

'But Catherine just charged around, chattering away, all of it nonsense.'

'And you were scandalous, taking an interest in the business. We had that useless woman, what was her name? The housekeeper. I always wondered why father kept her on. It must have been her ample charms rather than her book-keeping.'

'Marcus!' There was amusement, not shock in her voice.

'You took on her duties. Someone had to. In no time at all you were practically in charge of the staff. Father thought you should have been looking after the children.'

'He told you that?' Sarah questioned intently.

'No, not directly. We hardly used to speak. But from what John says . . .'

'What?'

'I'm sorry, I shouldn't have said anything.'

'They thought I was at fault?' There was a tremor in her voice.

'John's never said that.'

'But he thinks the same as his father. Always did, always will. Perhaps they're right. Perhaps it *was* my fault.'

'Sarah, you couldn't have stopped her catching a cold.'

'We'll never know. If I hadn't been so busy downstairs . . .' She looked into his eyes. 'John *has* talked to you about Catherine, hasn't he?'

'No.'

'Tell me what he said,' she pressed, refusing to believe him.

'There's nothing to tell.'

'Does he blame me? Does John blame me?'

'No.'

'Tell me . . .' Her tears came again, and this time she couldn't control them. 'Perhaps he's right. I could have saved her.'

'Don't torture yourself, Sarah.'

'I'd have done anything.'

He opened his arms and she went to him.

'He can't help it,' he murmured as he stroked the back of her neck. 'He's his father's son. Poor John.'

Chapter Sixteen

'I couldn't think where else to take her, Miss Harkness,' Kate prattled nervously, as she laid Monica on Esme's bed. 'Brandy, she said, and some sort of powder. That was all I could get out of her before she passed out. White powder.'

'Cocaine?' Esme asked, as she pulled off Monica's shoes.

'I think so, miss. She will be all right, won't she?'

'She certainly will. It's Adele Bannerman who should be worried when I tell her parents.'

'Please don't, miss. It doesn't matter what we say, Monica will get the blame, and then they'll sack her. What am I going to do? She's bound to be missed.'

'Say she's with me.'

'I'm sorry, Miss Harkness, but that will only make things worse.' She ran to the door, glancing back at Monica as she opened it. 'I'll think of something.'

'Don't worry, I'll look after her.'

'I can't stop. There'll be murder if both of us go missing.' Kate paused as she opened the door. 'Thank you, Miss Harkness.'

'Go and do what you have to, Kate.' Esme smiled.

'I wanted to know if it was a boy or girl, but I didn't ask. Maybe they can't tell when it's that small.' Maggie pushed the brandy and cocaine on to the wardrobe shelf and closed the door on them. 'You are my friend, aren't you?'

'Yes,' Adele answered staunchly.

'My best friend?'

'Yes.'

'I don't see my friends in Oxford. Not any more. Father won't allow them into the house in case they find out about me. So no one calls, not like they used to.'

'You can start again in London.'

'What am I supposed to do then? Get married to some old man to make myself respectable? I'd have a different name, no more Maggie Rigby.'

'I like Maggie Rigby.'

'Who'd marry me? They'd know what I've done. Father would tell them. He'd have to. Maybe I could marry one of the invalids back from the war. They were killers once, too, so we'd be the same. We could look after one another. James Rayburn had his jaw blown off. They brought him home and he's locked away. No one calls. That's the sort of husband I'll have.'

'You'll find someone,' Adele said clumsily, in an attempt to console her.

'*You* will.' Maggie couldn't keep envy and just a touch of bitterness from her voice. 'You're nice and pretty. You've never done anything wrong in your whole life. There'll be plenty of men to love you.'

'I could come to London. I'll be old enough soon.'

'Would you call on me?'

'All the time. We could find a place together. I'd look after you.' She reached out and touched Maggie's hand. 'My family don't want me here. I wouldn't be missed. You see, I'm just a replacement. My sister died, so they replaced her with me.'

'But you'd soon get tired of me being the pathetic invalid. You'd find some man, then you'd be off.'

'I wouldn't.'

'You should.'

'I'd stay with you. You're my best friend. I love you. You don't need Clive Jeffries, or injured soldiers or anyone. You've got me.'

'I really would be safe with you, wouldn't I?' Maggie said eagerly. 'Promise you'd do that? Keep me safe. No men, no danger, just you and me?' She leaned forward and stroked Adele's cheek before kissing her on the lips. As she moved away she read the expression in Adele's eyes. 'But it wouldn't work,' she cried softly. 'It wouldn't work.'

'Can I ask a favour, sir?' Kate asked as Stephen opened his bedroom door to her knock.

'You'd better come in.' He opened the door wider.

'If anyone asks for Monica, will you say she's with you? Say you've asked her to do some special duty, like cleaning the attic, or something. Just make it up if you have to.'

'Well, I'm not so sure.' Stephen didn't bother to conceal his amusement. 'I could be getting involved in something underhand. How do I know Monica isn't robbing the guest rooms while you give her an alibi?'

'I *can't* tell you why. I know I should, but then you'll *have* to do something, and then there'll be murder. I can't risk that happening.'

'It all sounds dodgy to me.'

'One favour, that's all I want,' she shouted in exasperation. 'I've done enough for you. Covering up when you stagger in drunk and throw up in your room. Who do you think cleans it up?'

'Hey.' Stephen held up his hands up as though to ward off her blows. 'All right.'

'Never mind. It was stupid of me to come here, expecting favours in return. It's obviously too much trouble.' She wrenched open the door. 'I'll manage on my own, sir.'

He put his arm around her shoulders.

'All right, Kate, I'll do it.'

'I'll manage,' she snapped, shrugging off his hand.

'I will. I'm sorry. Friends again?'

Fighting her pride, she managed a small smile of assent before running off back to the service bay.

Sarah glanced up at the office as she entered the hotel. John was on the phone. He waved to her. She didn't bother to wave back.

Collins called after her as she climbed the stairs, but she carried on as though she hadn't heard him. All too aware of her grief, he didn't take offence. As he resumed his place, Marcus breezed in, his gaze fixed on the staircase and Sarah. Collins turned his head. Although he was sure Sarah had seen her brother-in-law, she made no move to acknowledge his presence.

Handing his overcoat to a page, Marcus went straight into the office. Collins had seen enough to know exactly what had happened between Sarah and Marcus Bannerman, and his heart bled for John.

'Sarah's back, I've just seen her,' Marcus announced casually, as John replaced the receiver on the telephone.

'Has she gone upstairs?'

'She looked fine, don't worry. Now what's been happening here?'

'Nothing important. I've managed very well without you.'

Marcus smiled as he took the chair opposite John's. 'And I've managed very well without you too, brother.'

'Monica's with Mr Stephen Bannerman, Mrs Harvey,' Kate explained breathlessly, as she joined the housekeeper and the rest of the maids in the service area. 'I said she was needed, but he grabbed her and took her off.'

'Oooh, chance would be a fine thing,' Brenda shrieked enviously.

'Brenda Potter, wash your mouth out,' Mrs Harvey commanded.

'He's going through all his army things, chucking them out,' Kate elaborated, crossing her fingers behind her back.

'In his bedroom?' Brenda hinted suggestively.

'Brenda!'

'I'm just asking, Mrs Harvey.'

'He could have asked me,' the housekeeper complained. 'I'm the last to know anything in this place. The last to know,' she echoed as she bustled down the corridor.

'I took a tray of tea up to Mrs Bannerman,' Lynne chipped in, 'and that Stephen was with her.'

'Well then, Lynne, he must have left Monica in his bedroom,' Kate bit back.

'I'd stay there an' all.' Brenda giggled.

Lynne clouted Brenda across the ear. Ignoring her yelp, she carried on grumbling to Kate.

'She's missed a whole afternoon's work. I had to shift the coal on me own. Look at me, hands like a nigger because Lady Monica wasn't around. I think something's going on.'

'When are you going to leave her alone?'

'When she's gone. You can protect her all you like, Kate Morris, but I'll get her sooner or later, you'll see.'

Monica swam reluctantly into consciousness. Her eyes were burning behind throbbing eyelids, and her head ached so much, she was dreading the moment when she would have to lift it off the pillow. Uncomfortably hot, she threw back the blankets that covered her.

'How are you feeling?'

She sank down into the bed as a cool, damp cloth was pressed against her temples. She opened one eye to see Esme sitting next to her.

'There's nothing I'd love more than to give those two girls a piece of my mind, and tell the righteous Mrs Bannerman about her daughter.'

'Don't, miss,' Monica pleaded, surprised to find herself in Esme Harkness's room, and even more amazed to see that someone had stripped her down to her underclothes. She had no recollection of anything after drinking the brandy and sniffing the white powder in room ten. 'It would all come down on me. It always does.'

'Did they do this?' Esme questioned, noticing the bruises on Monica's arm.

'That was Lynne Milligan.'

'The maid?'

'They all hate me. You're my only friend,' Monica cried pathetically, suffering from a combination of hangover and self-pity. 'Everything I do turns out wrong.'

'Hush,' Esme soothed. She folded her arms around the maid and rocked her like a baby. 'I'll protect you, my little girl. I'll protect you.'

*　　*　　*

'Two nights in a row?' Sarah queried as Stephen poured himself a drink and sat next to her on the sofa in the living room. 'Don't tell me your friends have deserted you?'

'I don't think it's safe to go out while Ruth's in town. Next time she'll call the police.'

'Might do you some good.'

Adele walked in. Engrossed in conversation, her mother and Stephen barely acknowledged her presence. Aggrieved by their indifference, and feeling ignored and neglected, Adele went to the sideboard, picked up the decanter and poured herself a large whisky.

'Adele?' Sarah stared at her, bemused by her behaviour.

'The sun's past the yardarm.' Revelling in being the centre of attention for once, she lifted the glass and downed half the contents.

Stephen burst out laughing. Sarah caught his eye and followed suit.

'I'm sure it is.' Sarah struggled to regain her composure. 'You can have a glass of wine.'

'I like whisky. I've developed quite a taste for it.'

'That's my influence,' said Stephen.

'It's nothing to do with you, Stephen. I'm quite capable of doing things on my own,' Adele disputed.

'All the same, I think you'd better put that down,' Sarah advised swiftly, as she heard John's step outside the door.

'What a day!' John exclaimed as he walked into the room. 'That Mr O'Neill's still sending letters about his account. I don't think he's ever going to pay.' Uncertain of his reception, he kissed Sarah tentatively on the cheek. 'How are you?'

'Fine,' Sarah replied in a brittle tone.

'Good. Adele what's in the glass?'

'Whisky. Do you want one?'

'You can stop that right now.' Adele stared at him as she took a defiant sip. 'That's quite enough. Give me that.'

'Stephen's got a drink. Tell him.'

'I won't ask again.'

'Adele, is there something wrong?' Sarah asked quietly.

'It's a wonder you can remember my name. This makes a change. Everyone looking at me, and listening for once.'

'Oh, act your age,' Stephen snapped impatiently.

'It's all right for you.' Adele rounded on him. 'The great soldier. No one ever worries about me. I sat at home all the years you were away, and I may as well have been invisible. You'd come home on leave and we all had to leap around, then you'd go, and we'd continue to sit here in silence. Everyone continuing to ignore me, just like I didn't exist.'

'I'm sorry.' Stephen was startled by the realisation that she felt that way about him.

'And now you're back, and it's just the same, everyone dancing around you and no one caring about me.'

'I've had enough of this, Adele,' John said sternly. 'You know perfectly well that it isn't true.'

'What are you going to do? Lock me in my room like you've done with Maggie.'

'Maggie Rigby?' John asked, horrified by the thought of Adele spending time with the girl.

'She's my friend. She listens to me.'

'How long has this been going on? You're to leave her alone.'

'You can't stop me having friends.'

'Good evening.' Marcus and Ruth walked in.

'Marcus, could you leave us for a moment, please?' Sarah asked.

'Trouble?' He lifted one eyebrow.

'Adele, we can discuss this in your room.' Sarah left her seat.

'Exactly, and shove me out of the way. Maggie's father treats her properly. He looks after her. She's allowed to drink and everything. She can do what she wants.'

'You are not to associate with that girl.'

'As a matter of fact, John,' Ruth contributed, 'I found myself in Miss Rigby's company, and it has to be said she's not a suitable friend for Adele.'

'Adele, what's been going on between you two?'

'They were in the Reading Room, John,' Ruth continued, 'behaving like infants.'

'I've been looking after her. She's ill.'

'What's she told you, Adele?' Sarah asked in alarm.

'That she's had an abortion, and yes I know what that is. It's not her fault, and you've locked her away.'

'She told you,' John said weakly. 'Dear God in heaven, I'm phoning her father right now. I'm not having you making friends with a girl like that. I only let her stay on the condition that she kept to herself.'

'And that's exactly what you want from me, isn't it?' Adele taunted. 'All nice and quiet. Catherine's been dead for nineteen years and she gets more attention than me. Maybe I should die, then you'd sit up and take notice.'

John wrenched the glass from Adele's hand. 'How dare you!' he raged. '*How dare you?*'

'John.' Sarah took his arm. 'Please, John, calm down.'

The Grand

Adele walked towards the door.

'Where are you going?' John shouted.

'Maggie's room.'

'You are not.'

'John,' Sarah remonstrated.

'She's my friend,' Adele retorted fiercely, '*she* loves me.' Pushing past Ruth, she ran out into the corridor. John followed. Grabbing her arm, he thrust her against the wall.

'Just stop right there,' he ordered as Sarah came towards them.

'Leave me alone!'

'I don't know what Maggie Rigby's been teaching you, but she's leaving this hotel.'

Adele pulled free. Without thinking John slapped her across the face.

Stunned by the first blow her father had ever given her, Adele charged headlong down the corridor into her room, slamming the door behind her.

Sarah gave John a look that froze his blood. She walked quickly to Adele's room, knocked on her door and went in, consciously shutting out her husband. Wishing that he could turn the clock back just five minutes, John looked up to see Ruth and Marcus standing in the living room doorway. Marcus looked away as though he was ashamed and embarrassed by the ugly scene.

'Excuse me.' Ruth pushed past both of them.

Adele's screams resounded through the walls.

'I hate him. I really hate him . . .'

Sarah's voice, soft, muted, murmured soothing words that hurt John even more than his daughter's.

Ruth knocked the door of Maggie's room and opened it.

'Am I expected to apologise?' Maggie demanded aggressively as Ruth walked in.

'I just wanted to say that you will get better.'

'How would you know?' Maggie asked flippantly, swinging her legs down from the bed.

Ruth didn't answer, but neither did she leave until the hostility on Maggie's face had faded.

Lynne tipped the final jug of hot water into the slipper bath in Esme's room.

'There you go, miss,' she informed Esme, who was sitting before the mirrored dressing table. 'Give it five minutes, it's boiling.'

'Thank you.' With one, quick, fluid movement, Esme grabbed one of Lynne's arms and twisted it high behind her back. She pulled off the maid's cap with the other, and tossed it aside. Holding her by her hair she forced her over the bath, until her face was barely an inch away from the steaming hot water.

'Leave her alone.'

'Who?' Lynne whimpered, terrified that Esme was about to scald her.

'You know my history. And you'll know that I've faced girls far more dangerous than you. Not one of them survived me. Now leave her alone.'

'Let me go,' Lynne screamed as Esme pushed her even closer to the water.

'Leave that girl alone?'

'Yes, miss . . .'

'Say it!'

'I'll leave her alone.'

Esme finally released her. Lynne staggered back against the door. Esme smiled sweetly as though nothing had happened between them.

'You're mad.' Lynne retrieved her cap, and rubbed

the back of her head where Esme had pulled her hair.

'Probably, but who'd believe you? Now run along, lesson learnt.'

Quaking in her boots, and clutching her cap, Lynne backed out of the door.

'I want all of this spick and span before the shift's done,' Mrs Harvey ordered the assembled maids as she ran her fingers along the shelves in the service bay in the servants' corridor. 'Just look at this dust.' She held up her blackened forefinger. 'And look at the time. If Mr Harvey leaves me for another woman it will be your fault.'

'I wouldn't blame him,' Brenda muttered as the housekeeper turned her back.

'I heard that,' Mrs Harvey's voice echoed back down the corridor.

Kate glanced across at Monica, who was as white as a sheet. 'How's your head?' she whispered.

'Thumping!' She turned her back on Lynne, who came in carrying a set of water jugs.

'Lynne,' Brenda crowed, 'I've just been saying, Monica's left all those sheets again. It's her job. We shouldn't be cleaning up after her.'

'I'll do it.'

'Blimey, you feeling sick, Lynne?' Kate asked.

'Shut up.'

'Wonders will never cease,' Kate said, and smiled at Monica.

Monica gave Lynne a sly glance. Miss Harkness had told her she'd sort Lynne Milligan out for her, but she never thought she would do it so quickly.

*   *   *

'If there's anything I can do,' Marcus offered as he sat alone with Sarah in the family's living room.

'It's all right. Adele's in her room.'

'I meant about John. Such a temper. He's even more like father than we thought.' He looked up as John walked in on them.

'I've telephoned Lawrence Rigby,' said John. 'He's coming for Maggie tomorrow morning.'

'I'll leave you two alone.' Glancing at Sarah, Marcus left the room.

'I am sorry,' John apologised. 'I'll talk to Adele. She was right. She is my own daughter and I have neglected her for too many years. I've never said this, but it's my fault.' He looked to her, hoping for consolation. 'Then you agree . . .'

'It's certainly not my fault,' Sarah retorted heatedly.

He stepped closer but she turned away. More than Adele's outburst lay between them, but he didn't know how to even begin to bridge the gulf he sensed widening with every passing minute.

Marcus ran down the stairs into the foyer, where he found Ruth waiting for him.

'Who'd have thought it possible?' he said. 'Trouble in the paradise of the perfect marriage. Where are you going?'

'For a drink.'

'The table's booked for seven.'

Ignoring his reminder she went into the bar.

'Red wine,' she ordered. 'Trouble in paradise,' she mused as Marcus stood beside her. 'And with such timing. I consulted Mr Collins about your sudden absence this morning, and he was happy to tell me – indeed he took a certain amount of pleasure in telling me – that you ordered a car. To a particular destination.

284

You've surprised even me this time, Marcus. What sort of a man would use a dead child to advance his cause? What sort of a bastard?'

Clive handed her the glass of wine. She took it and tossed the contents full into Marcus's face.

Marcus was conscious of the attention of the entire bar fixed on him and his wine-drenched suit, as he stood and watched Ruth walk away. Clive manfully stifled a laugh as a few of the patrons chuckled. Marcus took a handkerchief from his pocket and wiped his face. Ruth might have humiliated him in front of the clientele, but he couldn't deny that he'd deserved it.

He saw Collins standing in the foyer. From his vantage point the concierge must have seen everything, but he made no attempt to come to his assistance. Marcus nodded to indicate that he understood exactly why.

Kate swept into Maggie's room early the next morning. Ignoring the huddled figure beneath the bedclothes, she made no attempt to move quietly as she opened the curtains. Daylight flooded into the room, warm, blinding.

'I'll pack your things. Your father is waiting downstairs. It's nice for some, being looked after,' she added contemptuously.

'Mr Bannerman sends his regards, sir,' Mr Collins informed Mr Rigby formally, as the man waited self-consciously in reception for his daughter to appear. 'As he's rather busy at the moment, he can't be here.'

'I see.' Rigby knew only too well that John didn't want to face him. 'Give him my apologies.'

The lift doors opened and Maggie, accompanied by Kate and a luggage-laden porter, stepped into the foyer.

'There you are.' Rigby nodded to his daughter before looking to the door. 'All ready? And I'll have one or two things to say about your antics once we're out of this place,' he added for the benefit of the hotel staff.

Relieved to see the back of Maggie Rigby, Kate opened the door to the servants' corridor.

'Maggie!' Adele charged down the stairs towards her. 'I couldn't stay in my room. I don't care what father says—'

'You should listen to him,' Maggie interrupted coldly.

'I won't. I hate him. I wish I had a father like yours. You will send your address won't you? As soon as you move to London. I can come and stay, and look after you.'

'I've got my father. Ever since Mother died it's just been the two of us. He doesn't need anyone else.'

'But I've got to come. I can't stay here.'

'Adele Bannerman, you don't know how lucky you are,' Maggie said earnestly.

Shocked by the serious expression on Maggie's face Adele appealed to Rigby. 'Mr Rigby, please tell Maggie that I can come and visit her in London. My name's Adele. I'm John Bannerman's daughter. You can trust me.'

'Maggie needs time on her own,' he replied brusquely.

'But she's told me.' Adele lowered her voice as she stole closer to him. 'She's told me everything,' she repeated. 'It's not a secret.'

'What do you mean?' He whirled around furiously, glaring at his daughter.

'The baby. I *know*.'

'Maggie, what have you *said*?' he demanded, panic-stricken. 'We're leaving, now, this minute.'

286

'But it's all right,' Adele reassured. 'Don't go. I don't blame her. It was Clive Jeffries's fault.'

'Who?' Mr Rigby was confused by the mention of the name.

'Clive Jeffries? The boy next door?'

'Clive . . . ? I'm sorry Miss Bannerman. We have to go. Boy?' he shouted to Alfred. 'Take these.' He handed him Maggie's hatbox and jewellery case, before following him out through the door.

'Clive Jeffries was six years older than me,' Maggie confided to Adele. 'He was killed on the Somme. He's been dead for five years. I never even spoke to him.'

'Then who . . . ?'

'Maggie!' Rigby's voice echoed towards them.

In one dreadful moment Adele understood. Maggie glanced through the door at her father, then back to Adele. She didn't have to look hard to see that her new friend was disgusted by the revelation.

Maggie kissed her on the cheek. She looked back at Adele one last time before climbing into the car. Adele watched as Rigby put his arm around Maggie. She saw fear mirrored in her friend's eyes, but all she could do was stand helplessly, watching while he drove her away.

Chapter Seventeen

'This trip has been all work,' James Cornell complained to Kate and Monica as they bustled around his bedroom, stripping and remaking his bed with clean sheets. 'Five nights in Manchester, and all I've seen is the office and the inside of this place.'

'Oh, you should go out, sir,' Monica broke in eagerly, braving Kate's disapproval at her familiarity with a guest. She glanced at him as he sorted through his briefcase. He was young and attractive. Two qualities that were rare in single men well-heeled enough to afford a room in the Grand Hotel. 'There's all sorts of restaurants in the city centre,' she added, defying Kate's warning look.

'I was told people up north eat nothing but tripe.'

'Londoners, you're all cheek.'

'I didn't say it,' James protested. 'I was told.'

'There's one place by St Anne's Square, the Bohemian. It's French. You get bread on a plate. You'd love it.'

'You must be well paid, Monica.'

'I've got this lady friend who takes me there.'

Kate checked the bed and smoothed over the counterpane. 'Monica,' she called abruptly as she opened the door.

'It's by the Town Hall. You should try it,' Monica continued unabashed.

The Grand

'Don't know if there's much point. Table for one. It always looks rather sad, businessmen on their own, eating off expenses.'

She gave him a shy smile as she finally followed Kate out into the corridor.

'How many times?' Kate scolded. 'How many times? I give you every chance, and you let me down.'

'He started the talking.'

'Oh, it's talking is it? That's all it is? Save yourself time, Monica. Go back in there and undress him.'

She fell silent as the door opened behind them and James appeared. He smiled at both of them before heading for the lift. As soon as he was out of sight, Kate propelled Monica around the corner into the service bay.

'You're making a fool of me. Do it again and I'll go straight to Mrs Harvey. I'll have to.' She took a chamberpot from their trolley. 'And if you're so fond of Mr Cornell, he left you a souvenir. Clear it away.'

'Signed the deal?' Marcus asked as James appeared in the foyer.

'All done, very successful.'

'James has come up on behalf of Imperial Shipping,' Marcus explained to John. 'They're investing in the canals. Manchester to Liverpool.'

'All these years they've been saying that the railways will kill us dead, but it's the opposite,' James informed them seriously. 'Bringing more trade for everyone.'

'And more trade for the Grand,' Marcus observed. 'Is Jackson Tyler on his way?'

'Try stopping him. Though I'm afraid we won't be staying here, Marcus.'

'Anything we've done wrong?'

'Not at all. It's simply a matter of money. There's

ten of us, all the architects and engineers, and we'll
be staying for at least a month, so it will be cheaper
to rent a house.'

'Half price?' Marcus offered impulsively. 'You can
have ten rooms at half the price.'

'Really?'

'That should impress Jackson. Tell him you twisted
my arm.'

'Marcus,' John interrupted. 'Could I have a word?'

'In a moment, John.' Marcus held out his hand.
'Agreed?'

'Well, yes.' James shook Marcus's hand vigorously.
'That's excellent. Thank you very much.'

'Mr Collins?' Marcus called.

'Sir?'

'Mr Cornell wants to make a booking. Could you sort
it out?'

'Certainly, sir.'

As Collins showed James to the reception desk, John
turned his back on his brother and went into the office.
Marcus followed, prepared for an argument.

'We've already shaken on the deal,' he pointed out,
before John had a chance to speak. 'If you wanted to
object, you should have done it there and then. This
politeness, John, it's always been your downfall.'

'I wouldn't embarrass you in front of a guest,' John
retorted heatedly. 'We don't offer rooms at half price.'

'And that is policy?'

'It is.'

'Then if it is policy, this should be a formal discussion with all members of the board present.'

'Fine, I'll fetch Sarah. And you can tell reception
that the booking is not confirmed.'

Clive was sitting in the alcove where the staff took

their breaks, leisurely polishing an array of silver teapots, when Mrs Harvey came bustling down the corridor, shepherding half a dozen girls in front of her.

'Now get your dinner, and be quick about it,' she ordered brusquely.

'I bet it's soup again,' Lynne griped.

'It's very good soup.'

'Yes, Mrs Harvey, but it's always the same. A very good soup, every day.'

'My mother makes a nice soup,' Brenda sighed wistfully.

'She steals it from the Salvation Army,' Lynne mocked.

'Clive, dinner?' Mrs Harvey prompted.

'Coming.' He waited until the housekeeper and the girls had disappeared into the staff dining room. Checking to make sure no one else was in the corridor, he pulled a paper napkin from his pocket, unfolded it and took out half a sandwich. Opening the back door, he knelt down and whistled. 'Here boy!'

A filthy stray dog advanced warily across the yard. It growled when it saw Clive holding out the sandwich.

'Don't have a go at me. Here.' Clive tore the bread in two and threw half of it towards the dog. It approached cautiously, eyeing him as it wolfed it down.

'Good boy.' Clive ripped off a second piece.

Kate and Monica charged into the service area behind him. Throwing a pile of soiled sheets into the bins, they sent the enamel lids clattering.

'And we're late . . .' Kate started in surprise when she heard the dog barking.

'Oy, shut it. Stop your noise,' Clive shouted.

'Got yourself a friend?' Kate asked.

Katherine Hardy

'That's not allowed,' Monica preached sanctimoniously. 'It says in the book. "No friends".'

'Monica get your dinner.'

'It's not dinner, it's lunch.' She flounced off as Kate walked over to Clive.

'What's his name then?' she asked as she crouched down beside him.

'Dunno. We always had dogs when I was a kid. Me dad kept them in the yard. Called them guard dogs, but they were like kittens. They've all gone now. He's too old to look after them.'

'This one could do with a bath.' Kate moved towards the mongrel and held out her hand. 'Good boy.'

The dog barked all the louder.

'Oh, bugger off then.' Clive threw the last of the sandwich across the yard. The dog ran after it, still barking. 'Daft mutt.'

'Not my day is it? Everyone snapping at me.'

'Don't say anything.' Clive closed the outside door. 'Mrs Harvey would give me a bashing.'

'No, I won't say a word,' Kate agreed caustically. 'Not me. "Good old Kate". Housemaids can trust me. Management trusts me, so where do I end up? Stuck in the middle.'

'The situation we're in is all my fault.' Marcus was taking the blame squarely on his own shoulders as he faced John and Sarah across the office. 'I promised that the rooms would be full with custom from the theatres, but they're cutting back now that the cinema is taking over. So the rooms are empty. And better that they're filled at half price than not filled at all.'

'Can't you see the damage it does?' John argued vehemently. 'The Grand survives on its prestige.'

'You're just repeating everything Father told you. We

292

may as well hold a seance and ask him what he thinks, direct.'

'Rooms at half price set a precedent, Marcus. It starts to devalue the entire hotel.'

'Well it's obvious we'll never agree. Which means it's down to you, Sarah.' Both men turned to face her.

'As a policy it's wrong,' Sarah began cautiously.

'Thank you.' John smiled.

'But as a short-term measure it makes sense and it makes money. It's September, John. In three months' time the Grand will have been reopened for one whole year. We need to show the bank we're a success. Then we can move on and do all the things you've planned.'

'So you're voting with Marcus?'

'Yes,' she agreed reluctantly.

'God bless democracy.' Marcus grinned.

'I've told you it's not policy, Marcus. The half-price rate is only for those ten rooms for one month, then it ends.'

'Fine,' Marcus agreed.

'In that case I'd better tell reception.' John rose to his feet.

'John, I'm sorry.'

'Don't be, Sarah. That's procedure, clear and simple,' he replied stiffly, unable to hide his resentment. He left the office.

'Thank you . . .' Marcus began. Before he could say another word, Sarah went to the door. He didn't stop her from going. Left to himself he smiled, wallowing in the wonder of his success.

The maids were dashing around the service area, working at top speed to clear what had to be done before their break, when Mrs Harvey left her office and handed Lynne a call card.

Katherine Hardy

'Get that done.' Spotting another maid further down the corridor, she hurried after her. 'You there, Jane, Jenny, what's your name – take that ring off. You know the rules. No jewellery allowed.'

'There's always some bugger who needs something, just when I'm about to have me break,' Lynne complained.

'What is it?' Brenda asked.

'Bath, room sixteen.'

Monica took the card from Lynne. 'Give it here. I'll do it. I'm taking sheets up anyway.'

'I know her,' Lynne muttered as Monica ran off. 'Does me a favour, two days later wants it back. Well she can go whistle.'

Monica's hand shook as she tipped the jug of hot water into the slipper bath in James Cornell's room. She mopped up the splashes with the hem of her apron, and then took a deep breath before returning to the bedroom. Relieved that James had got no further with undressing than removing his tie, she went to the door.

'If there's nothing else, sir?'

'You must think I'm mad,' James commented as he pushed the pile of documents he'd been reading to one side.

'No. Why should I?'

'I take a bath more often than is healthy. It's this city. The air's full of smoke.'

'Is there anything else, sir?' she asked, nervous, now she was actually alone with him.

'Oh, I booked that restaurant,' he said almost as an afterthought. 'Will you be there? With your lady friend, I mean?'

'No, sir, I'm staying in tonight.'

'Right. Still, the table's booked, and if you know your way round the menu . . .' He hesitated, obviously waiting for her to pick up the hint.

'I couldn't, sir.'

'No. I shouldn't have asked.'

She laid her hand on the door knob. 'Shame though, you on your own.'

'Look I shouldn't have sprung it on you like this. Think about it. There's plenty of time. The only table they had left was for ten o'clock.'

'Oh then I can't, sir. We've got to be in by half past ten.'

'Right.'

'Pity.'

'I don't suppose . . . I mean there is a restaurant here?'

'Mr Cornell, I'm one of the maids.' She pulled at the apron and striped blue cotton dress she was wearing. 'I don't wear this out of choice.'

'No, I didn't think you did. But they serve meals in the room, don't they? Would you like that? I mean it's just a bit of company, that's all I want. Nothing else.' He laughed to hide his embarrassment. 'I wouldn't dare.'

'I'd like that, sir. I'd like that very much.' She returned a smile that was every bit as uncertain as his own.

Esme delved into her wardrobe and pulled out one of the dresses she had bought for Monica.

'It's going to be quite a night for both of us. I've had the most charming letter from a Mr Anthony Crozier, the son of an old client, Edward Crozier.' She held up the dress and scrutinised it. 'This one, perhaps . . . no I don't think so.' She continued to search in the wardrobe. 'Edward's by far and away one of my favourites. A true gentleman. This often happens. A father will send me his son for a little . . . education.'

Monica clapped her hand over her mouth. 'You don't mean you're going to—'

'With the boy?' Esme laughed, amused by the suggestion. 'Oh, Monica, I hardly think so.' She took out another dress. 'That's the one. Just right for your colouring. But if young Anthony needs educating in the ways of the world, I can point him in the right direction. Give the sort of advice a parent can't. And, if he's inherited his father's looks, it will be a pleasure to spend the evening in the company of a handsome man. As you'll soon find out.'

'I won't know what to do or say.'

'Just let him do the talking. And remember, if you get to his room at nine, make sure you're gone by eleven. Men can't tolerate more than two hours of talk. And if he makes the slightest move towards you, leave immediately, and with dignity. Tonight, Monica, you're a lady.'

'I should have told him no. I'll open me gob and make an idiot of meself.'

'If that happens just remember: there's a name for men like James Cornell.'

'What's that?' Monica asked innocently.

Esme leaned in close and whispered, 'Practice.'

'You brought this on yourself, John,' Mary rebuked her eldest son, as they sat together in the Bannermans' private living room. 'It's ridiculous, a woman being part of the Grand's management, even if she is your wife.'

'It's not that Sarah's done anything wrong . . .'

'No?' Mary asked bluntly, shaking her head in

disapproval. 'Look at you. Powerless in your own building. There's only one solution. Take the vote off her.'

'She's worked hard to make this place a success.'

'As did I,' Mary asserted. 'Then I saw it as my duty to step back.'

'I can't remove her. I don't want to.'

'Then make her side with you. A husband has a right to expect his wife's devotion.'

'Thank you, Mother. I knew talking it through with you would help, and now I'm decided. Sarah did the right thing.'

'That's right, John,' Mary commented sourly as he left his chair. 'Keep saying it. Eventually you might even convince yourself.'

Clive waited until the service area was empty of staff before attempting to offer the dog any more food.

'Where's your gratitude?' he complained when the dog growled at him as soon as he opened the door. 'It's half me supper, this.' He tried to tempt the animal closer with a piece of cheese.

Shrieks of laughter filled the corridor as Lynne chased Brenda, flicking her with a wet tea towel as they both ran towards him.

'Gerroff!' Brenda shouted.

'Exercise, that's what you need,' Lynne cackled.

The dog darted past Clive. Running towards the girls, it barked ferociously.

'Oh, my God!' Brenda jumped back against the wall.

'Clive, get it out,' Lynne screeched.

'You've scared him. Come here, boy.' He held out another piece of cheese. The dog snapped, catching Clive's finger as well as the cheese.

'Ow!'

'Get it out!' Lynne's screams mounted into hysteria. She picked up the nearest thing to hand, which happened to be a tin of polish, and threw it at the animal.

'Oh thanks, Lynne,' Clive yelled caustically as it ran off into the building.

The dog continued to race headlong along the staff corridor, alternately barking and growling, sending maids scattering in all directions.

'Out of me way,' Clive shouted as he ran after it.

The stray dived into an empty storeroom. Clive followed. Realising it was trapped, the dog turned on him.

'You'll get me sacked, you will.' Clive moved slowly towards the animal. The dog began barking even louder than before. Terrified that either Mr Collins or the housekeeper would hear the racket, Clive backed off.

'Shush. It's all right. Shush now . . .'

'Clive,' Mr Collins bellowed from the corridor. 'It's almost six. The bar's standing empty. What are you doing?'

'On me way, sir.'

'Then come on.'

Clive waited until Collins's footsteps echoed back down the passageway. He backed cautiously out of the storeroom, moving slowly and steadily, careful not to upset the dog any more than it already was. As he closed the door behind him the dog growled and hurled itself at the panels, which shuddered as Clive turned the key in the lock.

'Keep it shut, you little sod. I'll come back later.' He sucked his bleeding finger and wrapped his handkerchief around it before hurrying off.

*   *   *

The Grand

John walked into the office to find Marcus working on the books, and Sarah sitting at the desk opposite him, busy with the kitchen accounts.

'They've agreed the booking,' she informed him quietly. 'They even sent a telegram, so it must be important to them. That should do the Grand's name some good in London.'

'If we want to be advertised as a cut-price boarding house.' He lightened his tone before she had a chance to object. 'Still, Mrs Harvey wanted to take on an extra girl, now she can. I'll go and tell her.'

'Marcus, you know this shipping company,' Sarah said after John left. 'Perhaps we can reach some sort of compromise.'

'Why? Because John's upset?'

'He does have a point.'

'It's no wonder he's still angry. He's been reporting back to Mother.'

'When?'

'Just now, upstairs.'

'I can imagine what she said.' She bent her head over the accounts again.

'What sort of a compromise did you have in mind?'

'It doesn't matter,' she said coldly as she scribbled a note in the margin with her pencil.

'What do you mean going out?' Kate demanded of Monica, as they made their way towards the storeroom with their arms full of sheets.

'Just to see me mam. I'll be in by half past ten.'

'I thought you hated going back there. That's the first time in months.' Balancing the sheets precariously on one arm, Kate struggled to turn the key with the other. The dog leapt towards her as her as soon as she opened the door.

Startled by its barking, she jumped back as it hurtled past her. Brenda screamed, dropping the linen she was carrying. She dashed back towards Mrs Harvey's office, and safety.

'What on earth . . . I do apologise, Mr Bannerman.' Mrs Harvey left her desk and opened her door. John followed as she charged off, following the direction of the screams. Wild-eyed, cap off, hair loose, Brenda came running to meet them.

'Brenda, for goodness' sake—'

'It's hunting me, Mrs Harvey,' the terrified girl gibbered. 'It's got the scent of me blood.'

'What has?' John asked.

'Bleeding great dog, sir. Down there.'

John rushed down the corridor, leaving the hysterical maid to the housekeeper.

Alerted by the frenzy of barking and screaming that reached the foyer, Clive sprinted into the servants' corridor just as Kate managed to shut the door on the dog.

'What have you done?'

'It's your dog.'

'How did it get in?' John asked as he ran towards them.

'It's my fault, sir,' Clive admitted.

'Then why are you standing about? Get rid of it.'

Despite the order he'd given the barman, John pushed Clive aside and opened the storeroom door himself. The dog shrank back growling.

John crouched down, holding out the flat of his hand. 'Come on. Come here. You've caused enough trouble.' Before he could do anything to protect himself, the dog pounced, sinking its teeth into his hand.

Shocked, he jumped back, swearing. Kate and Clive screeched at the animal as it retreated, still snarling into a corner.

Quicker than the others, Mrs Harvey grabbed a broom from the service bay. She returned just as the dog was about to make another lunge. Delivering it a mighty whack to the head with the handle of her brush, she sent it flying back into the storeroom. Kate slammed the door and locked it. The dog went wild, barking and scrabbling at the door, shaking it in its frame.

'Mr Bannerman, are you all right, sir?' Mrs Harvey asked.

'No,' John snapped.

'What's happened?' Collins asked, dashing towards them. He glared at the assembled staff. 'Why aren't you at your jobs?'

'It's my fault, Mr Collins,' Clive volunteered before anyone else could be blamed. 'The dog ran past me.'

'Back to work now. And, Clive, I'll have a word once this shift is done.'

'I'm all right,' John protested as Mrs Harvey examined his hand.

'It's bleeding. I'll get some ointment.'

'Just a bite. Nothing to worry about.' John leaned against the wall as a sick feeling crept up from the pit of his stomach.

'Begging your pardon, sir,' said Collins, 'but that might not be the case. You'll need a doctor straight away.'

John looked at the concierge and paled, furious with himself for not thinking of the risk he'd run before he'd confronted the animal.

'It's not rabies,' Adele declared decisively as she left her bedroom to join John and Sarah in the corridor of their private apartment. 'People don't catch rabies, not in Manchester.'

'It needs a proper bandage, Adele,' Sarah said. 'Look in my bedroom.'

Adele turned, almost bumping into Collins who came out of the lift.

'She's right, though. It's a bite that's all,' John insisted. 'In a week's time there'll be nothing to show.'

'Mr Collins? Have you seen the dog?' Sarah asked urgently.

'Yes, ma'am. It's locked in the linen room. We thought it best to leave it there until the doctor arrives.'

Adele's voice drifted out of John and Sarah's bedroom. 'Where do you keep them?'

'The top drawer,' Sarah called back.

Marcus strode down the corridor.

'We're making a fuss over nothing. It's just a stray.'

'And stray dogs carry rabies, John,' Marcus said pointedly. 'For God's sake, sit down.' He led the way into the living room, where Stephen and Mary were sitting poised on the edge of their seats.

'Where's the dog now?' Stephen asked.

'Downstairs, sir,' Collins answered.

'Stop worrying, all of you. It'll be all right,' John insisted.

'And if it's not, Dad? Things don't just come right because you say they will.'

'They should put it down,' Adele advised as she came in with the bandages.

'Who let the dog in?' Marcus asked.

'Clive Evans, sir,' Collins revealed. 'It ran past him.'

'Sack him.'

The Grand

'You'll do no such thing, Jacob,' John intervened.

'He put your life in danger,' said Marcus indignantly.

'I won't have that boy dismissed, Marcus. Do you hear? What would that make me? Some sort of despot, sacking a boy because I've had an accident? He stays, and for once my decision's final.'

'I'll go back to the foyer, sir. The doctor is expected any minute and we've had to call the police. That's procedure in case the animal is infected.' Collins closed the door as he left the room.

'What happens with rabies?' Adele asked uneasily, looking from one face to another.

'It's not rabies,' John countered firmly.

'I pray it isn't, John,' Mary said fervently. 'But there were all those cases last year in Devon, and even closer in North Wales.'

'What cases?' Stephen queried.

'It was the soldiers,' Sarah said without thinking. 'Ignoring the quarantine laws, bringing dogs home from France.'

Stephen paled at the mention of soldiers, but everyone was too busy looking at John to concern themselves with him.

'They should have known better,' Mary asserted scathingly. 'Any fool knows the danger.'

'That was last year,' John stressed, 'and they were just scare stories.'

'But they weren't,' Sarah contradicted. 'They were actual cases.'

Stephen abandoned the glass of whisky he'd been nursing and walked out.

'Please, all of you,' John pleaded, 'will you stop panicking? I'm the one that's been bitten, and I'm fine. Look at me.'

*   *   *

303

Stephen tore into his room. He wrenched open his chest of drawers and searched frantically through his clothes. He found what he was looking for beneath a pile of socks. Having taken his gun and a handful of bullets, he left his room. He was functioning automatically, just as he'd done in the trenches, as he slotted bullets into the chamber and walked down the corridor towards the storeroom.

'Mr Bannerman!' Alarmed by the expression on his face, Kate left the service area and went after him.

'Oh my God!' Brenda wailed. 'He's got a gun. Mrs Harvey! Mrs Harvey . . .'

Kate ran after Stephen as he approached the storeroom. Judging by the banging coming from inside, the dog was still throwing itself against the door.

'Stephen, what are you going to do?' Kate asked apprehensively.

Without stopping to answer her, he unlocked the door and flung it open.

The dog was crouching in the middle of the storeroom floor, eyes wild, foaming at the mouth. It raised itself on its haunches preparing to spring. Stephen lifted the gun and fired.

Chapter Eighteen

Stephen strode into his parents' crowded living room.

'There's no point in standing around,' he snapped impatiently to the two policemen standing behind the doctor. 'The dog's body is waiting downstairs. For God's sake, take it away and do your tests.'

'Stephen, wait a minute,' John called as he walked out.

'Mr Bannerman,' the doctor remonstrated. 'I haven't finished. This wound needs proper cleansing.'

'Excuse me, but if I'm infected, then it's too late, and this is more important. I'm sorry, Dr Kenyon.'

'What happens now?' Marcus asked the doctor after John left.

'We need to remove what little remains of the dog's head for examination. Rabies would show up as dark spots on the brain tissue.'

'How long will that take?'

'I'm not sure. A couple of days.'

Marcus took out his wallet and slipped a wad of notes into Kenyon's hand. 'Tomorrow,' he contradicted.

'Why have you kept your gun?' John asked as he followed Stephen into his bedroom.

'Everyone seemed to agree that it was the soldiers' fault, so I dealt with it the military way.'

'Stephen, give it to me. I don't want you to have it.'

'I'm sorry. On behalf of us all, can I say sorry? Never mind that we fought a war. Maybe found a friend out there in the mud, some stupid dog, just as scared as us.' He wiped away his tears with the back of his hand. 'You can't die. I fought a war for you. You can't die . . . not now . . .'

John stepped closer to his son. He longed to hug him, but he was reluctant to make the first move, and, blinded by tears, Stephen remained oblivious of his father's intentions. Ashamed of breaking down, he bolted from the room.

John went to the bed. Stephen's gun lay on the centre of the counterpane. He picked it up, holding it out at arm's length, trembling at the thought of the dog – and all the men his son had been forced to kill.

The maids fled in advance of the stern-faced procession that wound its way through the servants' quarters. A man with an enormous beer gut carrying a toolbox headed the column. Behind him came a policeman carrying the dead dog wrapped in a tarpaulin that didn't quite cover the tail and legs. Bringing up the rear was Dr Kenyon accompanied by an exasperated Mrs Harvey.

'You can't do that in here,' the housekeeper challenged. 'Kate – you lot clear out right now,' she shouted at the hapless maids. They dutifully scurried away at her command, but not as far as she would have liked.

'We need a clean surface.' Dr Kenyon swept a cloth from the table the staff used for their breaks. 'Unless you'd rather we used the kitchen . . .'

The Grand

Mrs Harvey stood back helplessly as the policeman dropped the dog on to the newly scrubbed table top.

'What are they going to do?' Kate asked fearfully, looking from the bloodied tarpaulin to Mrs Harvey.

'Out!' Mrs Harvey vented her wrath on the girls. 'Go.' She turned to the doctor. 'You could let me put some sheets down. I don't want dog blood on this floor.'

'Mr Beasley?' Dr Kenyon signalled to the man with the toolbox. 'You know what to do?'

Beasley opened his box and pulled out a saw. After testing the edge, he set to work.

Mrs Harvey glanced at the serrated blade, imagined it cutting into the dog's neck, and scuttled back to her office.

'I was going to chuck the dog out, Mr Collins,' Clive explained, 'but you called me away.'

'That's enough!' The concierge cut him short. 'You don't answer back. You've broken enough rules. Broken the whole damned lot. If it was my choice you'd be out.'

'Oh, sorry, Mr Collins.' Kate and the other maids retreated back up the corridor.

'No, stop,' Collins ordered. 'You're all part of this. Did you know that animal was there, Kate?'

'No, sir. I saw the dog earlier but—'

'Night and day you get taught the rules,' he lectured, 'all of you. And I've heard you, laughing behind my back. Now you see what happens? The man who employs you, the man who treats his staff with the utmost respect, finds his life endangered as a result of your stupidity. You should all be ashamed.'

'But Mr Bannerman gets looked after, doesn't he?' Clive carped. 'Never mind us.'

'Clive, not one more word.'

The concierge's warning provoked Clive all the more. 'I got bitten. Look.' He held up his fingers. 'I got bitten too. And I hope to God Mr Bannerman's not ill, sir, I really do, but he's upstairs with his doctors and his family, and they're all looking after him, and what do I get? Nothing. I'm just staff.'

'You should have said earlier, boy. We'll get the doctor to take a look at you.'

'And if it *is* rabies? What happens then? Oh *then* I'm sacked, because if you're staff, and you're sick, no one looks after you. One week's wages and you're out through the door. I am sorry, Mr Collins,' he murmured remorsefully. 'For all the good it does.'

Lynne heard the sound of sawing as she rounded the corner in the corridor, but she assumed it was one of the porters breaking up packing cases. Expecting to find the girls, she called out, 'I've been scrubbing that enamel for two hours. What's all this noi—' She stopped dead at the sight of the headless dog laid out on the table.

She screamed just once, before the world turned black.

'They've got everything they need and they've promised results by the morning,' Marcus announced as he returned to the living room.

Mary pulled on her gloves. 'Adele, you come home with me,' she ordered gruffly.

'I want to stay.'

'Your father needs some peace and quiet. I'll bring you back first thing.'

'No, I'm not going. Every time something happens I'm bundled out of the way, but not this time. I'm staying.'

'It's all right, Mother,' said John. 'Adele, you can stay with me.'

'Very well. I'll see you in the morning, John.' Mary dropped a kiss on to his forehead as she passed. 'And everything will be fine.' She touched her son's face, hoping that the fear that was eating into her wasn't apparent on her own. 'I promise.'

'I'll walk you to the door.'

'I must remember that,' Marcus reflected after they left. 'Get bitten by a dog. Stop Mother talking.'

The explosion of laughter that greeted his remark was more a brittle release of tension than an expression of mirth.

'Marcus, you said half past seven,' Ruth raged from the open doorway. 'I've been waiting half an hour. I warn you, one day you'll find me gone. I've got better things to do with my time than wait around for you. And what's the matter with your mother? She didn't even have the grace to say "Good evening". You'd think someone had died.'

The silence that followed her remark was broken by John's laughter.

'What?' Ruth turned back to the corridor and stared at him.

'We must improve security in this place,' Marcus drawled, 'before any more mad dogs wander in and out of the building.'

Monica had changed out of her uniform into her ordinary walking-out dress by the time Kate had finished her shift and returned to their room. She picked up her toothbrush, dipped it into a saucer of salt and set about cleaning her teeth.

'Look at you,' Kate teased. 'You've washed your hair and it's not a Sunday,' Kate fingered one of the strands to check if it was still damp. 'What are you doing? Asking your mother for money?'

Monica rinsed her mouth and spat the water out into the slop bucket. 'I would if she had it. Money to buy me out of this place. Clive's right: we're treated like dirt.'

'Don't listen to him. The poor lad's in a state.'

'Maybe I want better things, but if I do, it's not so I can be posh.' Monica pushed her toothbrush back into the cracked glass on the rough wooden washstand. 'It's not the money. It's to stay alive. Because down here they don't care if we live or die.'

Clive sat on one the chairs in the alcove in the staff corridor. The area looked peculiar, almost naked, without the table. Collins appeared in front of him holding a bottle of whisky and two glasses.

'You don't have to sit with me, sir.' The concierge poured out the whisky and handed Clive a glass.

'It's like waiting for a death sentence.' Clive drained his glass. He was too upset to realise the significance of what he'd said, but Jacob Collins couldn't help equating the situation with the execution of his son. He tried to put it out of his mind as he stared at the empty space in front of them.

'What's happened to the table, Clive?'

'I think Mrs Harvey burnt it, sir.' They both looked up as Stephen walked in on them.

'Room for one more?'

'I'll fetch you a glass, sir,' Clive offered.

'I'll get it.' Stephen went to the cupboard where they were kept.

'I think your father was looking for you,' Collins said.

Stephen merely nodded, as he filled his glass and sat next to them.

*　　*　　*

The Grand

'You're worn out,' John said to Adele. 'Time for bed.'

'I want to stay with you.'

'Come on, young lady, nothing's going to happen. I'll tuck you in.'

'And read me a story?'

'Thank God those days are gone. Those books used to bore me to tears.'

'And me, that's why I went to sleep.' She left her seat and kissed her mother, before leaving with John.

As soon as Sarah was alone with Marcus and Ruth, she relaxed, allowing the strain to show on her face.

'It's the worst death,' she muttered.

'It won't happen,' Marcus reassured.

'My father treated a man once. He'd seen all sorts of death, but he said rabies was the worst. You become an animal. A mad thing, unable to breathe, to swallow – your own body turns against you, kills you.' The silence pressed in around her, intense, shattering. 'And if he was gone, Marcus, what would I do without him?'

He left his seat and crossed to the sofa she was sitting on. 'John won't die.'

'He could, and I'd be left here with his work all around me. Without him.'

'I'll be here.' There was genuine compassion in Marcus's voice but she didn't hear it.

She left her seat and paced restlessly to the fireplace. 'Marcus, don't,' she pleaded. 'Not now.'

'I'd be here for you. We all will.'

'*Please*! Dear God, John's life is in danger. Can't you leave me alone? Just this once.'

'Sarah, he didn't mean anything by that remark,' Ruth interceded.

Sarah found it easier to turn her temper on Ruth than Marcus.

'You can put up with it. God knows how. Sometimes I think you even welcome it. But I can't. John could be dying and the game keeps going, this pathetic seduction . . .'

'That's not fair,' Ruth protested. 'Marcus was only offering sympathy. I don't care what you think of him, Sarah, but he doesn't deserve this.'

'I've grown so used to it. I've even begun to listen to him. Siding with him when all the time . . . I'm sorry. Just leave me alone,' she begged as she retreated to her bedroom.

'Now hide your ordinary clothes in the service room in case I'm not back,' Esme warned Monica, as they stood in front of the cheval mirror in her room, both dressed for the evening ahead.

'Right,' Monica agreed nervously. 'I'd never have thought of that.'

'Years of experience. Now let me see.' Esme turned to face the maid, pulling out the ruffles of her dress. 'That's it, perfect. Teeth?'

Monica gave her a broad smile.

'Good. You look superb. I'm quite jealous.'

'Don't be daft. You look lovely.'

Esme checked her reflection one last time.

'I think it's fitting for Edward Crozier's son. Edward's a rare man. We were both quite young . . . and he didn't care about my profession. Not one jot. Remarkable man. If I'd met him earlier, before . . .' She snapped out of her reverie. 'Never mind. Monica, I think we're ready.'

'I'm not.'

'Of course you are. Off we go. And remember, out by eleven and not even the smallest kiss on the cheek, or he'll have to answer to me.'

* * *

The Grand

James sat alone in his room pretending to read a book. Every few seconds he turned a page and glanced across at the trolley standing in the corner. The light of the candles warming the chafing dishes flickered dully beside the silver ice bucket that held the wine bottle. Everything was ready. All he needed was his guest.

Just when he'd decided that Monica must have changed her mind, he heard a tap at the door. Setting aside the book, he rushed to open it. The sight of the maid, standing framed in the doorway in all her finery, took his breath away.

'Monica?' he asked faintly.

She smiled. Remembering his manners he stood back.

'Sorry, do come in.'

'Thank you.' She stepped inside, watching as he closed the door behind her.

The level in the concierge's whisky bottle had dropped considerably in half an hour of steady drinking, principally due to Stephen's efforts.

'I dunno, what's the point in them building a restaurant,' Stanley, one of the waiters, grumbled as he pushed a trolley load of dirty dishes down the corridor. 'Not that I'm complaining, Mr Bannerman, but I've been serving meals to the rooms, just like the old days.'

'Who's that, then?' Clive asked, feeling the need to talk about something – anything – other than the problem that was close to driving him insane.

'Room sixteen. Meal for two. Reckon he's got a woman in.'

Kate, who'd been working in the service bay, drew closer at the mention of sixteen.

'If you've got nothing else to do why don't you pull

313

up a chair?' Clive suggested to Stanley. 'Everyone's waiting for me to grow fangs and start howling at the moon. It's great fun.'

Marcus trod quietly down the corridor that housed the Bannermans' private rooms. Seeing John and Sarah's bedroom door slightly ajar, he stood still and listened. He could hear their voices, but their conversation was too quiet for him to pick up on what they were saying to each other.

Moving slightly, he caught a glimpse of them sitting on the bed. Sarah was gazing at John in a way Marcus would have given all he possessed to have her look at *him*. Sick with resentment and jealousy, he turned back to the living room. Ruth was still sitting there, alone.

'I envy my brother.' He paused waiting for one of her barbed responses, but for once, she merely looked at him. If he hadn't known better he might have even said there was something akin to love in her eyes. 'But I don't know if I envy him his wife, or just his marriage.'

'Because they're in love?' He nodded as he sat in the chair opposite hers.'I used to think that. When I was young I'd look at married couples and hope that one day I'd find the same thing that they shared. But then, as I grew older, I looked closer and saw how much they *needed* one another. As though apart, they lacked something. Most people cling to their other half because they can't manage on their own. And if that's love, if love does exist, then it's a weakness.'

'Then you could never love me?'

'As if you'd want it.'

'Perhaps you're right.' He looked at her again, and wondered why he didn't love her. She was beautiful,

witty, independent – all the qualities he would have
wished for in a wife. 'Perhaps love doesn't exist,' he
said finally. 'I've certainly never found it.'

'Then we're stronger than all those others.'

'And yet' – he gave a small, deprecating laugh – 'that
makes us perfectly matched. Would you ever marry me,
Ruth? If I asked, one day?'

'We don't need it . . . although it would only be a
marriage. And they don't have to last. These days we
could be together for a few years, then move on.'

'With no need for love?'

'We enjoy one another's company, Marcus, that's
enough.' She rose from her chair. 'I should go.'

'You can stay if you want.'

'Do you want me to?' He shrugged his shoulders. 'I'll
go. I'm not part of the family. Goodnight, Marcus.'

'Goodnight.' Reaching for his cigars, he watched
her leave.

Anthony Crozier glanced around apprehensively as he
walked through the doors of the Grand. The only hotels
he had visited during his eighteen years had been in
the company of his father, and he was overawed by
the prospect of having to deal with the staff himself.
Pushing his spectacles further up his nose, he looked to
the reception desk, but before he reached it, a woman
laid a hand on his arm.

'Anthony Crozier? You've the same profile as your
father,' she purred in a seductive voice. 'It's a pleasure
to meet you.'

'Miss Harkness.' He glanced away uneasily. He
hadn't expected her to look so elegant, or attractive.
'Sorry I'm late,' he apologised as he moved away
from her.

'And that is just like your father too. I've reserved a

table in the Reading Room. This way.' A footman was waiting. He showed them to their table, pulling out chairs for both of them.

'Now tell me at once, how is your father? Since I moved to this city I'm starved of news from London.'

'Miss Harkness.' A harsh note crept into Anthony's voice at the mention of his father's name. 'I'm sorry to tell you. My father passed away in July.' Stunned by the news, Esme closed her eyes against the pain wrought by the news. 'It was tuberculosis.'

'I'm so sorry, Anthony. He was a very special man . . .'

'That's the reason I've come. He left you some money. It's not much. Two hundred pounds. I have it here.'

'Oh, there was no need. He was the kindest of men, bless him.'

'And that's the point really. That is the point, Miss Harkness. He didn't name you in the will, of course. He wouldn't — you being what you are. He made a separate settlement. But there was a mistake, just a mistake. The solicitor sent the documentation to my mother. He sent it to my *mother*,' he repeated, emphasising the last word. 'She read it, and she knew your name, your reputation and what you do for a living. She read the document and she discovered that her husband, the husband she'd just lost, had been sleeping with a whore, and not just sleeping with her, but leaving her money. Can you imagine how she felt? Can you, Miss Harkness?'

'Anthony . . . I'm sorry . . .'

'All of us, my sisters, my mother, me, we thought we knew him. And now, when he's dead we discover what sort of man he really was. So I've come to give you the money, Miss Harkness, and I hope you're proud.' He slapped an envelope down in front of her. Pushing back his chair, he left the table.

'I don't want the money,' Esme protested, shattered by his revelation – and his bitterness.

'It's my father's final payment. To his whore. And I wish the bastard was still alive so he could see what he's done. What both of you have done.'

Esme stared after him, feeling as though her whole life had been torn into ragged, worthless shreds.

'My father's terribly impressed by my job,' James revealed as Monica concentrated on the arrangement of cutlery and wineglasses in front of her. 'He thinks I've moved above him, which is ridiculous. I was just lucky to get a good education, and find a lucrative position.' He looked at her plate. 'I should have ordered seconds.'

Monica looked up horrified. 'No . . .'

'But you've finished everything.'

'Only because it was nice.'

'I'm glad you're enjoying your food.'

Monica stared down at her plate in dismay. 'You must think I'm an idiot. "Don't rush your food," she said. "Don't rush your food." And look at what I've done. Do you want me to go?'

'Why should I want you to do that?'

'Because I'm pretending. I don't know what I'm doing here. I was taught all this.'

'By your lady friend.'

'Yes,' she admitted in a small voice.

'I did think . . .' He hesitated for a moment, not wanting to be rude. 'I mean you haven't been quite yourself. This morning you were chatting away quite naturally, and tonight you've hardly said a word. So maybe this friend of yours has taught you the wrong things. I thought you were quiet because of me, rabbiting on the way I do.'

'No, James, really you've not done that.'

'Well, that's a relief. And to think I was feeling out of my depth.'

'You?'

'When you arrived you looked . . . I don't want this to sound . . . oh hell, you looked sensational. God, my mother's always trying to introduce me to girls. "Ladies of society", she says, and they're all stiff and starched; they frighten me to death.'

Monica laughed.

'What's so funny?'

'You.'

'Really?'

'And I was dying, honestly I was, because I used the wrong glass. I picked up that one and I thought you'd seen me.'

'What does it matter, Monica? They're just glasses, they hold wine, they're all the same.'

'She makes me practise, my lady friend. You should see me, deportment and everything.'

'What on earth does that involve?'

'Book on me head, don't laugh, it does . . .'

Outside the door Kate cringed when she recognised the girlish giggles accompanying James's deeper laughter. She turned and walked quickly down the corridor. She was furious with Monica, but she couldn't help feeling just a sneaking streak of admiration as well. After all, Monica now knew what it felt like to be on the receiving end of the Grand's lavish hospitality, even if only for one evening.

'You can't leave me on my own,' Stephen challenged

as he struggled to pull the cork from another bottle of whisky.

'Duty in the morning, sir,' Collins reminded him, as he drew Clive out into the corridor with him.

'Am I working, sir?' Clive asked.

'You can leave the first shift. See what the doctor says.'

'And if it's bad news, I'll bite him,' Clive muttered gloomily.

'Goodnight, Mr Bannerman, Kate,' Collins called out as she walked down the corridor towards them.

Kate kept her distance as Stephen opened the bottle and filled his glass. Only when she was sure that Mr Collins and Clive were no longer in earshot did she murmur, 'Stephen?'

He turned around. 'Have some?' He offered her the whisky bottle.

'Remember you helped me that one time?' He nodded. 'Well, you're the only one I can tell.'

Even his drink-fuddled mind recognised that the maid was troubled. Pointing at the seat Collins had vacated, he topped up his glass to the limit while she sat next to him.

'There's this girlfriend of mine and this man,' she began. 'She's got these ideas, but it's her own fault . . .'

He moved his chair closer to hers and put his arm around her.

'I don't know what to do, Stephen.'

Leaning towards her, he kissed her full on the mouth. Horrified, she pushed him away. He gave her a crooked smile. 'Come on,' he mocked, '"friend of mine".'

Too angry and humiliated to answer, she stormed out, leaving him to his bottle.

'It's been three years' hard at work tied to the job, nothing else.' James smiled at Monica, who left the table, and sat at the opposite end of the sofa to him. 'So you see, I'm not the man of the world I appear to be. I must be a disappointment to you.'

'No you're not. You're a bloody miracle, sir.'

'Sir?'

Unable to meet his gaze, she looked down at her hands. The evening had sent her world tumbling around her ears. She'd played at being the lady with Esme, but this was different. This evening she had pretended to be a guest within the confines of the rooms she cleaned, scrubbed and dusted. And tomorrow, when her dress was hanging once again in Esme's wardrobe, she'd have to do it all over again.

He slipped his fingers beneath her chin and tilted her face to his.

'I've got to go, James.'

'Right.'

'I can't stay.'

'That's all right.'

'James,' she whispered uneasily. 'I've not — I've never done it.'

'Neither have I.'

'You must have!'

'Absolutely, genuinely, no.'

'I believe you.' She left the sofa. 'I've got to go,' she repeated, looking back at him just once before opening the door.

'I can't think when we last spent so many hours in the bedroom.' John reached for Sarah's hand as they sat together on their bed. 'Our honeymoon, I suppose. I've wasted so much time. Time that I could have spent with you.'

'We've plenty of time left.'

'Like this morning, sulking after the vote on the

cut-price rooms. I'm sorry. I've allowed the hotel to take over my life. I've meant to apologise a hundred times, but the moment always slips away. I'm too cautious. It comes of years of being told what to do by my father. He even told me to marry you.'

'Did he?'

'There I was, as cautious as ever, and do you know, I look back now and I can't believe it. But when I married you, I didn't love you. It was madness.'

John's confession stunned Sarah. Withdrawing her hand from his, she stared at him, not wanting to believe what he'd said. Oblivious of the pain he'd caused, he carried on talking.

'Oh, I thought you were wonderful, but I couldn't fall in love with you. I wouldn't let myself.'

'I see . . .'

'No you don't. Let me explain. I was scared.'

'So your father told you—'

'I know you never liked him, Sarah. But you should thank him for that. Of course, he wanted us to marry for all the wrong reasons. Your father was a doctor, and although we might have owned this place, Dad always felt that he was a tradesman at heart. "It would be a good marriage," he said. So I married you. And Marcus threatened that if I didn't hurry up he'd beat me to it. God, I was so young, and then I grew up. That's what you did for me.'

'That story, the one you tell the children? How you fell in love the moment you saw me?'

'It feels like it's true, now.'

'So when did you fall in love with me?'

'It just happened. It was always going to happen. There was no one moment, it just sort of . . . became.'

'That's fortunate for you,' she said drily. 'I loved you on our wedding day.'

'I promise, no more wasting time.'

He heard someone stumbling down the corridor outside. 'Stephen,' he sighed, going to the door. Sarah followed like a sleepwalker. In the space of a few minutes her whole world had irrevocably changed and she felt that nothing would ever be the same again.

Stephen collided with the wall. He stood back, trying to focus on John as he struggled to straighten himself to his full height. 'I'm not drunk,' he slurred, bracing himself for a lecture.

'And I'm not telling you that you are,' John murmured patiently. 'Let's get you to your room.'

'How are you? How's your hand?'

'Still on the end of my arm. This way.'

Sarah remained in the corridor as John led Stephen to his bedroom. Seeing the light on in the living room, she walked in. Marcus rose to his feet as she entered, eyeing her warily. He waited for another outburst. When it didn't come he broke the silence.

'What I said earlier. I didn't mean anything . . . I'm very sorry, Sarah.'

She eyed him coldly, calmly, then suddenly she kissed him. A hard, passionate embrace that took him completely by surprise. 'Now, get out,' she demanded as she stepped back.

'Sarah?' He gazed at her in bewilderment as she continued to stare at him.

When she refused to answer, he turned on his heel and left.

Chapter Nineteen

Terrified of being discovered decked out in all her finery in a guest corridor, Monica crept along quietly, jumping into the shadows at the sound of every creak, every door opening and closing. Heaving a sigh of relief, she finally reached Esme's door without mishap. She turned the handle and slipped inside, starting at the sight of Esme sitting bolt upright in a chair facing the door. Her mentor was rigid and inert, as if she'd been carved from a block of marble. Only one of the lamps had been lit, but it was enough for Monica to see a near empty brandy bottle and a full glass set on the table beside her.

'Miss Harkness?' When Esme didn't answer her, Monica stole closer. 'Please, Miss Harkness, what's wrong?'

Esme raised her head and looked up at her through dull, lifeless eyes.

'I need your help, Miss Harkness. I don't know what to do. It's Mr Cornell. You should see him and hear the way he talks. He's not a bit like you said he would be. I told him he's a miracle. Honest he really is. You see, I could go back. What should I do?'

'What are you asking me for? Why the hell do you listen to me?'

'Because you know everything.'

'Whatever you do, you'll do better than me.' And she resumed her rigid silence.

When minutes had ticked past and Esme still hadn't said a word, Monica stole back into the corridor. Now she'd made up her mind what to do, her step was quicker, more certain.

The door to room sixteen was slightly ajar. She wondered if she had left it that way, or if James had opened it, hoping that she'd return. She eased it wide enough to walk through. He was sitting on the bed, a book lying unread beside him. She walked in and closed the door behind her.

Hearing the click, he looked up, saw her and dropped the book to the floor. He went to her and wrapped his arms around her shoulders. Then he did what he'd been longing to do all evening, and finally kissed her.

Marcus sat in the bar as a horde of cleaners descended on the foyer. He watched as they set to work, polishing, dusting and washing every surface. He stared at the untouched drink set on the bar in front of him. It was morning and he was still dressed in his evening suit. He rose stiffly to his feet. Sleep might have eluded him, but there was no way he could face the new day dressed in yesterday's clothes.

Wide awake, Sarah turned her head and gazed enviously at John, who was sleeping peacefully beside her. Closing her eyes briefly against the pain of his revelations of the night before, she folded back the bedclothes and climbed softly from the bed.

She put on her robe and tied the belt as she walked into the living room. The curtains had been drawn and the window opened. The familiar early-morning sounds of the city filtered up from the street below, sounds she had become so accustomed to that she rarely even noticed them. The clank of milk churns, the creaking of heavily laden carts, the protesting whinnies of dray horses, the cries of the newsboys as they set up their stands. Standing at the window, she looked down on the bustling scene. She couldn't help thinking that life would go on like this every morning, whether she and John were there to witness it or not. Turning, she saw Marcus at the door watching her.

'Last night,' she declared flatly. 'It was revenge, nothing to do with you.'

'Revenge for what?'

'Something that had nothing to do with you.'

'But it happened.' For the first time in his life Marcus felt vulnerable. What he wanted most in the world was within his grasp, but he was powerless to do any more to make it his. 'Sarah, it's not a game,' he urged earnestly. 'It's far more dangerous, because it's real between us. You know it is. I've given away everything for you. My entire future, all ploughed into the Grand, and it can burn down for all I care. I did it for you, because you're here, and because you asked me.'

'It's still a game. And yes: I started it; but now it's over, Marcus,' she said finally, turning away from him.

'What about tonight?' James asked Monica as they lay in his bed. 'We could finally get to that restaurant.'

'It's Thursday. Mrs Harvey gives us housecraft lessons on a Thursday.'

'It's always "Mrs Harvey". I'd love to meet her.'

'But you do want to see me again?' she prompted shyly.

'Of course I do.' He reached out to her, realising she was serious. 'Really I wouldn't . . . I swear it.'

'My lady friend says—'

'She doesn't know everything, Monica. On the other hand, maybe your friend is right. Most men are like that. I've always been jealous watching them, but I couldn't—'

'If I didn't have my job, we could go out all day, or just do nothing together.'

'I'd love that.'

'Maybe we could.' She looked at him. 'I'm late. I'd better go.' But as he stroked her face and kissed her again, she made no attempt to leave.

Kate finished dressing, emptied her washing water into the slop pail, and looked across at Monica's empty bed. Sick with concern, she left the room and joined the stream of maids making their way to the servants' hall.

'All night long, snoring your head off,' Lynne complained to Brenda. 'It's like sharing a room with an elephant.'

'Well, you talk in your sleep. You even sing sometimes.' Brenda giggled. '"Onward Christian Soldiers". Proper little Bible-basher.'

Clive sneaked up behind them and barked in Brenda's ear, sending her screaming and Lynne laughing. He bared his teeth as Kate turned her head. 'Raw steak – that's what I need.'

'You're mad, you are,' Brenda said gravely.

'Mad dog?' He growled to prove the point.

'That's enough, Clive Evans,' snapped Mrs Harvey's voice behind him. 'It's too early for trouble.' She closed the back door behind her. 'Now, anything happen last night?'

Before anyone had a chance to answer her, she walked straight past them into her office.

John made a face at Sarah, Adele and Marcus across the breakfast table.

'I wish everyone would stop staring at me.'

'I hope you don't mind,' Ruth said from the doorway. 'I thought I should be here, if I'm not in the way.'

'Of course not, Ruth, come in.' John pulled out a chair for her. 'You can sit here, just as long as you promise not to stare at me.'

'You shouldn't have left so early last night,' said Marcus, offering her the coffee pot. 'You missed all the action.'

'What? Has the doctor been?'

'No.'

'Then what?'

Marcus shot a glance at Sarah, who looked away. Ruth glanced uneasily from one to the other, and understood more than Sarah would have wanted her to.

Monica dashed into the bedroom she shared with Kate. She had changed out of her evening gown into her street clothes in the service bay, but with Esme's room out of bounds at that time of the morning she had no choice but to hide her evening dress in her own room. She had bundled it hastily into the corner and was pushing her hair into her cap when Kate walked in.

'I'm reporting you.'

'It was me mam,' Monica lied unconvincingly. 'She had this cough. I couldn't leave her, she was sick and I'll work extra tonight.'

'You were in room sixteen.' Monica blanched. 'If I tell Mrs Harvey, she'll sack you and maybe that's what you deserve. But I'm telling her you stayed out for the night without a pass. I'll say it was your mother. But that will get you trouble enough. You won't have time for more of your tricks. It's the only way you're going to learn.'

The clock was ticking loudly into the silence in the Bannermans' living room when Mary arrived.

'Good morning, Mother.'

'John, I met the most delightful gentleman in the foyer,' she said as she breezed in ahead of Dr Kenyon.

'It was distemper,' the doctor announced without any preliminaries. 'It's fine. You'll need to keep up the injections, Mr Bannerman, but it's nothing to worry about. No sign of rabies.'

'What did I say?' John hugged Sarah, burying his face in her shoulder to hide his relief.

'Thank God.' Sarah had difficulty seeing through her veil of tears.

'All back to normal.'

'Yes.' Sarah hugged him again.

'Thank you, thank you very much.' Marcus shook the doctor's hand.

'Not at all. It's not often people are so glad to see me.'

Adele threw her arms around her father and kissed him. 'Congratulations,' she cried emotionally.

'I don't think that's the right word, Adele. I've done nothing.'

'No, congratulations are in order,' Marcus said resolutely, looking to Sarah. 'I don't think it's too early for champagne. It seems to be the right moment since I've got more good news. I'd like to announce my engagement.'

'What?' John whirled around.

The Grand

'To whom?' Ruth enquired acidly.

'When did this happen?' Mary beamed. 'Ruth, I'm delighted. Come here. I never thought I'd see the day, and I did so want to see him settled before my time's up.'

John shook his brother's hand enthusiastically. 'Congratulations. Well done.'

Marcus continued to look to Sarah.

'I can be the bridesmaid,' Adele said brightly, already thinking of clothes.

'Marcus, you've been keeping this quiet.'

'Indeed, Sarah, he's even kept it from me,' Ruth said. 'Thank you for your good wishes, all of you, but if Marcus has asked for my hand I haven't accepted yet.'

'Then what do you say?'

'This seems to be a family affair.' She turned away from Marcus and looked to the others. 'What do the rest of you think?'

'It's excellent news,' John smiled.

'Sarah?'

'I think you're mad.' Sarah spoke lightly, treating Marcus's announcement as though it were a joke. But her eyes were serious as she met Ruth's steady gaze.

'Then I accept.'

'You're right, Marcus.' John went to the door. 'I'll fetch the champagne, and if the Grand falls about our ears for one day, what does it matter?'

Collins walked into the crowded servants' corridor. 'Clive,' he shouted, looking around for the barman, 'you know I said you could miss the first shift? Well get back to work. The doctor's given the all-clear.'

Katherine Hardy

'Great! Thank you, Mr Collins.' Clive sank weakly on to the nearest chair.

'And I was going to build you a kennel,' Stanley quipped.

'Come on, Brenda.' Clive grabbed her by the waist as she passed him. 'Don't I get a kiss?'

'If she started, she'd never stop,' Lynne cautioned.

'Monica Jones,' Mrs Harvey bellowed from her office doorway, 'I'm told you stayed out all night without a pass.'

Monica looked up to see a thunderous expression on the housekeeper's face, and Kate standing defiantly at her side.

'It was me mam, she was sick.'

'I'll be contacting her to make sure that's true. But you know the regulations, and it's not the first time you've been slack. I'm sick of telling you, so you'll be on night duty for the rest of the month.'

'Starting when?'

'Starting tonight, when do you think?'

'I can't tomorrow, Mrs Harvey. I'll do every other night, but I've got to meet my friend tomorrow night.'

'Out of the question.'

'But I can't let him down.'

'Oh yes, it would be a man. Well you can tell him it's cancelled. It'll be Christmas before you get another night off.'

'But I've got to—'

'Monica, that's enough,' Kate warned. 'Mrs Harvey's told you.'

'Please, Mrs Harvey, just one night.'

'Monica, shut up. Come with me.' Kate held out her hand.

'One more word out of you, Monica Jones, and I'll have your job.'

The Grand

All the frustrations of the last few weeks crowded in on the hapless maid. Feeling cornered, she glared at everyone around her, before finally erupting.

'Then you can have it! You can bloody well have it! You and your rules and your filth and your muck. You can have them because they're all you need, a dried-up old bitch like you.'

'Out!' Mrs Harvey screeched.

'And no, I wasn't at me mam's. Do you know where I was? I was in room sixteen. I was with Mr James Cornell. I was with one of the guests. I spent the night with him. In bed, if you know what that means.'

Appalled by the flagrant disclosure, the housekeeper slapped her across the face.

Monica slapped her back. Mr Collins stepped forward.

'Jones,' he snarled, 'leave this building right now. You won't work in this city again. Now get out.'

'Just watch me,' she raged. 'You watch me, Kate Morris.'

'I'll throw you out if I have to,' Collins threatened as he opened the back door.

'I'm going.' Monica tossed her head high in the air, 'but I'm not going that way. I'm going *up*.' She strode defiantly past them, and ran past the back door towards the guests' lift, leaving a stunned silence behind her.

James Cornell looked around to check that he had everything. He slipped on his jacket, picked up his room key and turned to the door just as it opened to reveal Monica, white-faced and red-eyed.

'What's wrong?'

'Lost me job,' she whispered hoarsely.

'Because of me?'

'No, not really.'

'What will you do?'

'Don't know, sir.'

'Monica, don't call me that.' He went to her and pulled her head down on to his shoulder. 'You can stay here.'

'I don't want charity.'

'I want you to stay. I do. You know what last night meant to me. You're not . . . just some girl. And we can be together.'

'Is that what you want?' she asked anxiously.

'Yes. Please, Monica. Stay here.'

He didn't have to ask again. She looked up at him, her eyes shining from more than just tears.

As soon as Jackson Tyler and his men arrived, Marcus, Ruth, Sarah and John went down to welcome them. Mr Collins was presiding over the chaos in the foyer, directing porters to clear the area of mounds of luggage, having to bellow to make himself heard above the sound of the Imperial Shipping men shouting boisterously to one another. The concierge approached John as he reached the foot of the stairs.

'Mrs Harvey would like a word, sir,' he murmured discreetly. 'It is rather urgent.'

'Right, soon as I can.'

Jackson slapped Marcus across the shoulders. 'So, start as we mean to go on: where's the bar?'

'It's over there, and my entire family might be joining you. We've been drinking champagne since eight o'clock.'

'What's the occasion?'

'Nothing special.' He smiled. 'Jackson Tyler, my brother, John Bannerman.'

'Pleasure,' said Tyler. 'Not a bad place you've got here. And quite a bargain. I've been spreading the word: best deal in England.' He hailed Collins. 'You there, does Mr Cornell know we've arrived?'

'He's on his way down, sir. If you'd care to give the porters your luggage.'

'Right. Hold on,' Jackson said, snatching a bag from a porter. 'I need that.'

'I warned you that they'd think it was a permanent offer,' John whispered in his brother's ear.

'That's right,' said Marcus, then, turning to Ruth: 'I didn't tell you. With all the events of last night it quite slipped my mind, but as my fiancée you should know all the facts. There's been a revolution in the Grand Hotel.'

'In what way?' she asked suspiciously.

'Sarah voted with me.' Dazzling both women with a smile, he turned to welcome another of the shipping men.

'I told you it would be trouble,' John complained to Sarah, before moving on to join Marcus.

'Here he is,' Jackson shouted. 'James?'

The Bannermans turned to see James stepping out of the lift with Monica.

'Jackson, may I introduce my friend, Miss Monica Jones?' James led her towards his boss.

'Delighted.' He gave James a sly grin. 'You've not been wasting your time.'

'Good journey?' James asked.

'Stopped over in Birmingham. Last time I do that.'

Dumbfounded at the sight of the maid clinging to James Cornell's arm, it was as much as John could do to mutter, 'Mr Cornell.'

'Good morning, John, Mrs Bannerman. My companion, Miss Monica Jones.'

John nodded to the girl.

'We've met,' Monica said smiling, caught up in a

wonderful, miraculous, fantasy-come-true that incorporated her every childhood dream.

Stephen searched the corridors of the servants' quarters until he found Kate.

'I just wanted to say sorry.' He coloured in embarrassment at the memory of what he'd done the night before. 'It was my father and everything. I hope I didn't upset you.'

'It's the least of what happened last night.' She smiled back at him. 'It's best forgotten.'

'Oh, you think so?'

Lynne barged in. 'Oh my God, come and see it. You won't bloody believe it.' She blushed when she saw Stephen. 'Excuse my language, sir, but you should see this too. She's done it. That little piece of nothing's only gone and done it.'

Maids crowded around the door that led from the servants' corridor into the foyer. Crammed against one another, they took turns to peer through the glass porthole into the hallway.

'That's silk, that is,' Brenda sighed enviously. 'Real silk.'

Kate forced her way through, Lynne close behind her.

'Who's she with?' she demanded. 'Is she with him? Let me through.' She elbowed her way to the front.

'Wait your turn,' Brenda shouted.

'Let me through!' Shoving Brenda aside, Kate looked through the glass to see her roommate standing next to James Cornell. Monica looked across and saw her. As they gazed at each other through the window, Kate was conscious of the gulf that now separated them. A gulf that couldn't be wider if Monica had been sacked.

Clive left the bar and joined Collins at the desk.

'Clive, don't stare,' Collins censured. 'From now on, Miss Jones is a guest at this hotel.'

'Good for her.' Clive winked at her when no one was looking.

The foyer began to empty as Jackson Tyler and his men gravitated towards the Reading Room where coffee was being served. Marcus and Ruth went with him.

'I always liked that girl,' Marcus murmured to Sarah as he passed.

'I knew I shouldn't have gone to sleep,' John grumbled. 'One night and the world turns on its head.'

'Mr Bannerman, will you join us?' Jackson called back.

Taking Sarah's arm into his own, John led her into the Reading Room, leaving James and Monica in the foyer.

'Do you want to join them?' James asked. 'I hope you're not getting bored.'

'No.' Monica smiled nervously. 'I couldn't.'

He offered her his arm. She took it.

Esme Harkness noticed them as she walked down the stairs. When she saw Monica dressed in silk, she stopped in her tracks.

Bursting with pride, Monica smiled at her mentor, before walking on into the Reading Room with James. Esme stared after her in horror, watching as Monica moved among the throng of Imperial Shipping men and Bannermans.

Monica looked up to see the wintry expression on Esme's face. In that one instant fear struck at the enormity of what she'd done, and she began to wonder if she had taken the first step down the same slippery road that had led Esme into prostitution.

Chapter Twenty

M onica opened her eyes to all the luxury she had
ever dreamed of or aspired to. An elegantly
decorated room, a warm fire blazing in the hearth
and, the ultimate indulgence of all, lying naked
between fine linen sheets beside the man she loved,
with plenty of time to enjoy every minute of her good
fortune. No Mrs Harvey to tell her what to do, and no
chamberpots or ash bins for her to empty this or any
future morning.

She smiled at James, who was still sleeping peacefully beside her. Smoothing his tousled hair away from
his face, she was interrupted by a quiet knock at the
door. Kate crept in, hauling a metal bin for the hot
ashes and a fully laden coal scuttle.

'Morning, miss.' Keeping her eyes averted from the
bed, Kate knelt before the hearth.

Hugging her knees, Monica sat up in the bed.

'How's Mrs Harvey?' She gave Kate a broad smile
that was wasted on her back.

'She's fine, miss.'

'What's the time?'

'Just gone eight, miss.'

Monica held up her arm. 'Two minutes past,' she
corrected, tapping the gleaming gold bracelet watch
fastened to her wrist. 'James bought it for me. It's from

The Grand

Switzerland. Kept me awake all night with its tick tick tick. Have a listen.'

'Very nice, miss.' Kate kept her head down as she raked out the ashes from beneath the fire basket.

'You don't have to call me, "miss".'

'Oh but I do.'

'There's no need to be like that, Kate.'

'Don't know what you mean, miss.'

'All right, if that's the way you want it,' Monica snapped, 'I'll tell Mrs Harvey I don't care for the chambermaid's tone of voice.'

James stirred as she raised her voice. He looked up at her and beamed. 'Not a moment's peace,' he grumbled good-naturedly.

'Morning.' Monica kissed him full on the lips. He reached up, unintentionally pushing back the bedclothes and baring her to the waist.

Kate gathered her buckets together. 'Sorry, I'll come back later,' she mumbled as she dashed out through the door.

Monica laughed with the sheer joy of living, loving and freedom from drudgery.

'What's so funny?' James pulled her closer, twining his naked body around hers.

'Everything.'

He kissed her again. As their tongues met, she rolled on top of him, stroking her fingertips over his cool, smooth skin, burning with the wonder of love, and a sexual appetite she'd never imagined she'd possessed.

'Come on! What did she say?' Lynne demanded as Kate emerged into the corridor.

'Was she naked?' Brenda asked, wide-eyed with the bawdiness of it all.

337

'What were they doing? Were they at it?'

'Bet it stinks, that room. All rancid.'

'Shut up!' Kate hissed as the maids crowded around her.

'Good morning, girls.' Esme smiled, as she passed them on her way to the lift.

Kate muttered, 'Morning.' Keeping her head down so she wouldn't have to look at Esme, she carried her buckets on to the next room.

'She's happy,' Lynne jeered, loud enough for Esme to hear. 'Made her bedroom into a factory. Turning out whores just like herself.'

Kate couldn't resist the temptation to turn back. Esme was standing outside the lift, her head held higher than the maid felt it had a right to be. Lynne was right. Monica's transition from maid to whore was down to Esme Harkness and no one else.

'Just here.' Ruth Manning ordered the taxi to pull up outside a substantial Manchester town house. She surveyed it critically, the smile on her face turning to a frown when she saw a 'For Sale' sign in the garden, with a 'Sold' notice pinned over it. A procession of workmen walked in and out of the open front door, hauling out boxes and loading them into a furniture van parked in the drive.

The taxi driver opened the car door for her. 'That will be one pound eight shillings, miss.' He held out his hand.

Ignoring him, Ruth ran to the men.

'What is this? Who are you?'

'What does it look like?' Panting for breath, the man she'd addressed hoisted the box he was holding to shoulder height, before sliding it on to the floor of the van.

The Grand

'Where are you taking these things?'

'The Grand Hotel.'

Ruth whirled round to see Marcus standing behind her. 'What on earth is the point? Why move house before we're married? You'll only have to move again, when we find a house of our own.'

'The marital home is ready and waiting.'

'You expect me to live in the Grand? Any fishmonger with half a crown in his pocket could find a bed there, I certainly won't.'

'Do what you like. That's where I'll be.'

'One pound eight shillings, miss,' the taxi driver repeated doggedly, following her up the drive.

'Pay the man off,' Marcus advised. 'Then you can travel in the van with the rest of my possessions.'

'Kate Morris?' Mrs Harvey interrupted the maid when she was taking her break. Dropping the bar of snowfire she'd been rubbing over her knuckles into her pocket, Kate turned to face the housekeeper.

'This is Olive Clegg.' Mrs Harvey pushed a very young, stolid-looking girl towards her. 'She's your new housemaid. And look after this one. I don't want any more trouble.'

'That's not fair, Mrs Harvey,' Kate protested.

'Just you listen to Kate.' Stung by the truth in Kate's words, Mrs Harvey covered her embarrassment by concentrating her attention on Olive. 'She knows her stuff. She'll do you proud.' She glared at the corner where Lynne and Brenda were gossiping instead of sorting through dusters, as she'd ordered them to do.

'. . . and Christine Lumb,' Lynne carried on, oblivious of the housekeeper's presence, 'the one that does the ironing, well, she saw Monica Jones in the street drinking from a bottle. A bottle, mark you!'

Katherine Hardy

'Lynne! Work! Now!' Mrs Harvey ordered gruffly before going into her office.

The last thing Kate felt like doing was training another girl, much less making friends with one. Sighing, she emptied her pocket of the snowfire and a list, and laid them on the table.

'If you sit here and look at this, Olive, you'll understand what we have to do,' she explained to the blank expression on the girl's face. 'Mrs Harvey gets a tally of all the occupied rooms in the building from the concierge, Mr Collins, who in turn gets it from reception. Then Mrs Harvey writes out a list like this, but it's a different list every morning. When we read it, we can see how many sheets and things we're going to need. Then we start cleaning the rooms at the top of the list and work our way down. Got that?'

'No.' Olive's face grew even more vacuous. 'What's that?' She poked at the tablet of snowfire.

'It's a wax you rub on your knuckles. It stops you from getting hands like an old woman. You just rub it in whenever you get the chance.'

'You're the new Monica, that's what you are, Olive,' said Lynne. 'She was just like you, a little piece of nothing.' She pushed the pile of dirty dusters into the sink and turned on the tap, while Brenda carried off the ones that were still usable.

'You get one block of snowfire wax a fortnight from Mrs Harvey.' Kate ignored Lynne's outburst in the hope that Olive wouldn't ask who – and what – Monica was. 'Any more and it comes out of your own wages.'

'Now she's sleeping with every man in trousers,' Lynne persisted, unabashed. 'I told her, I said you're a bad lot, Monica Jones . . .'

'For the last time,' said Mrs Harvey in exasperation as she charged furiously through the door of her office. 'Stop prattling on about that girl. Now do as I say.'

'And if I don't?' Lynne muttered rebelliously.

'What was that?'

'We have to do this . . . do that . . . then one girl throws it back in management's face, and what happens? She's rewarded. She's flouncing about up there, drinking champagne. So why *should* we do as we're told?'

'Get back to work.' Mrs Harvey turned white with anger, simply because she couldn't think of a single rational answer to Lynne's question.

'I'm doing me job.' Lynne tossed a block of washing soap on top of the dirty dusters. 'Look at me. Here I am doing it. I'm just asking, why should we?'

'Because you have to.'

'Mrs Harvey's saying that Monica's a guest now,' Kate interrupted, in an attempt to calm a situation that was rapidly escalating out of control. 'And we shouldn't talk about the guests, whoever they are.'

'Exactly,' Mrs Harvey concurred, wishing that she'd thought of the answer. 'Now get that finished, quick sharp.' She retreated into her office, and this time she closed the door.

'"Mrs Harvey says, fah fah fah",' Lynne mocked. 'You watch this one, Olive. She's a creep. Make one wrong move, and she'll go straight to management.'

'That's not true,' Kate contradicted, as Lynne turned her back on the dusters soaking in the sink, and walked away.

'What do you mean, wax?' Olive asked in a slow, stupid voice Kate was already beginning to hate.

Marcus led Ruth down the corridor of the top floor of the hotel. Walking past John and Sarah's private

Katherine Hardy

rooms, he opened a set of doors that led into a virtually identical suite to the one used by his brother's family. He continued to open door after door, showing her spacious rooms, furnished in a style that might have been considered fashionable half a century before.

Ruth's mouth hardened into grimmer lines with every new revelation. Knowing full well that a row with Marcus would only succeed in making him more determined to live in the hotel, she actually welcomed his niece's presence when Adele wandered in behind the removal men.

'And this leads through to our own dining room, which leads to the living room, which in turn leads to the study.' He opened the final door with a flourish.

'All laid out in a row, Marcus. Just like an army barracks.'

'Shame on you, Ruth,' he joked humourlessly. 'When have you been inside an army barracks?'

'It's the best news,' Adele said sincerely. 'We'll be able to see each other all the time.'

'And your mother's room is just two steps away.' Ruth spoke to Adele, but her words were directed at Marcus.

'And, if I should stumble home drunk one night and get in the wrong bed, what would it matter?'

'Uncle Marcus!'

'You see, Adele,' said Ruth. 'This is the company I keep. A filthy mind.'

'You there,' snapped Marcus suddenly, 'careful with that.' He left them to follow a man who was struggling with a crate of crystal.

'We can redecorate,' Adele suggested, misinterpreting the gloomy expression on Ruth's face. 'We can do it together. Pick out colours and everything. You've got ages until you get married.'

The Grand

'That will be little consolation when I wake up tomorrow morning staring at brown curtains and antique lace,' Ruth snapped, allowing her anger to surface now that Marcus was no longer with them.

'I thought this suite only had the one bedroom.'

'It has.'

'So where's uncle Marcus going to go?'

'What do you mean?'

'If you're going to wake up here, then where is he going to sleep?' Adele stared at Ruth, colouring in embarrassment as the full implication of Ruth and Marcus's relationship finally dawned on her. 'Oh I see.'

'Adele, for goodness' sake . . .'

'No, I mean of course you are — of course you do — I mean it's none of my business. I knew that. Of course I did.' Adele turned a bright shade of pink.

Ruth smiled, amused by Adele's naivety. It was the first time she had smiled since she had entered the Grand an hour before, and she hoped it wouldn't be the last.

Collins had retreated to his office to take his break. He was happily ensconced in the chair behind his desk, a cup of tea at his elbow, reading a newspaper, when Mrs Harvey knocked just once before barging in.

'Excuse me, Mr Collins. I just need a moment.' She closed the door and leaned against it. 'Monica bloody Jones!' she exclaimed bitterly. 'It's all I can hear from every single girl. Monica Jones . . . Monica Jones . . . Are the lads the same?'

'They're excitable, yes.'

'The whole world's turned on its head. Do you know

343

what I saw in the market this morning? Strawberries.
In October.'

'I've just been reading.' He pinpointed an article
in the newspaper. 'There's a meeting of vegetarians
in Manchester Town Hall tonight. These are curious
times indeed.'

'What are we going to do? This Monica business is
bringing the place to a standstill.'

'It might help if the staff had some reward for their
endeavour. We didn't have a summer outing this year,
and with all the cutbacks Marcus Bannerman has been
making, there's some money left in the household
budget. Enough for beer and wine.'

'Why, Mr Collins. Are you suggesting a party?'

'Yes.' He answered her smile with one of his own.
'I rather think I am.'

Dressed in one of the frocks James had bought her,
Monica glowed from a heady combination of delight
and satisfaction, as they left the lift and walked into
the foyer. Hardly aware of the stares of the porters
and bellboys, she only knew that she had never been
happier in her entire life.

'We could have coffee?'

'I'm already late.' James lifted his eyebrows. 'Thanks
to you.'

'Just the one,' she coaxed. 'They've got American
coffee – that's the one they give any old guest, but
they leave the tubs open all night so it gathers dust.
I've seen it. Ask for the African, that's the best.' He
looked into her face and, quite unexpectedly, broke
into a laugh. 'What?' she asked.

'I've never met anyone who knows so much about
everything. Most women don't say a word, and speak
only when they're spoken to.'

'I can be quiet. Just tell me.'

'No, it's wonderful, honestly. They should all be like you.'

'Then you'd fall in love with them instead.'

'No,' he murmured. 'No I wouldn't.' He reached for her hand. 'African it is.'

Standing in the doorway of what would soon be his living room, Marcus thoughtfully surveyed the apartment he'd earmarked for his own and Ruth's use. Seeing him there, John joined him.

'This used to be the library,' John said. 'Father used to sit over there, hidden away, in that wing-backed chair. Do you remember that time we crept in, to look in his desk?'

'To find his snuffbox. Forbidden territory.' Marcus laughed.

'You tasted it. I sniffed it, but you put it on your tongue.'

'I did not.'

'You drank whisky straight from the decanter to get rid of the taste. Then you drank Epsom Salts to get rid of the whisky.' Marcus's laughter joined John's as the memories came flooding back. 'Welcome home, brother.'

'Thank you.' He shook John's hand. 'This move, it's your fault.'

'In what way?'

'Money. The Grand's taken everything. I couldn't afford the town house any longer,' said Marcus as they moved into the corridor.

'You should have said . . .'

'What could you have done?'

'I'm sorry,' John murmured guiltily.

Sarah breezed down the corridor, her arms full of

345

files. 'Do you know what pleases me most? Another Bannerman on the roster. Every single night, John and I have to be on standby in case there's a problem. Now we can share the workload, starting tonight.' She pushed a file into Marcus's hands. 'The Board of Trade insists that we cut our electricity consumption by fifty per cent because of this coal strike, so you've got to check every single room after six p.m., then again at midnight, turning off the lights.'

'I don't suppose I can refuse?'

'Not a chance.'

The two men took one look at the serious expression on Sarah's face and burst out laughing, just as Ruth emerged from the lift.

'What's so funny?' she asked. 'Something I've done, Marcus?'

'Hardly.'

'I'll need my own staff,' said Ruth. 'I can't have hotel maids going through my things. I need at least one chambermaid, and two housemaids dedicated to these rooms.'

'We're not having private staff coming out of the hotel budget. It's out of the question,' Marcus stated flatly. 'Was there anything else?'

Ruth stared frostily at him before returning to the lift. Sarah and John looked uneasily at each other, both embarrassed by Marcus's treatment of the woman he was on the verge of marrying.

'You did consult Ruth about this?' John asked.

'Why should I?'

'She's your fiancée.'

'So?' Marcus demanded contentiously.

'So?' John repeated angrily. 'She's going to be your wife. For God's sake, the feudal system's long since gone. She isn't part of your chattels—'

The Grand

'John, he only does it for effect,' Sarah cut in brusquely. 'Come on, we've got work to do.'

Jackson Tyler led a boisterous crowd of men into the foyer.

'Never too early for a drink,' he announced blithely, rapping his silver-topped cane on the door of the bar.

'I don't know how you do it.' Stephen stood back, shaking his head in admiration as Jackson shouted his order to Clive.

'Start with a prairie oyster. Raw egg suspended in vinegar. Little trick I picked up in France.'

'And that's not all you picked up in France.' David, one of the engineers, sniggered.

'Came back riddled with clap,' Jackson informed Stephen cheerfully. 'More fun than getting a medal.'

'Good morning, Miss Jones, Mr Cornell,' Mr Collins greeted them as they walked out of the Reading Room.

'Good morning, Mr Collins,' Monica answered politely.

'Now enjoy yourself, go round the shops, I'll be back at seven.' James kissed her on the cheek.

'James! Join us?' Jackson shouted from the bar.

'Small matter of work, Jackson.'

'Rubbish. The strike's still on, the canals aren't moving, so let's spend the company's expenses.'

'Later. Seven o'clock,' James repeated to Monica. She kissed him on the lips. 'Six,' he amended. He went to the door.

'James, you'll need these.' David left the bar and handed him a pile of papers. 'And if you could look at this . . .'

'Bye.' Monica called back. Then, catching sight of

Katherine Hardy

Esme Harkness, she nodded, uncertain what reception she'd get. 'Miss Harkness,' she said. Esme had already tried to express her opinion on her relationship with James, only she had refused to listen.

'Monica,' Esme said, coming to a halt. 'I was wondering. Are you busy?'

Monica lifted her arm, and looked at her watch, hoping Esme would see that it was new and very expensive. 'I could spare a couple of minutes.'

'We could take tea, in my room.'

'If I can pay.'

'Certainly. Mr Collins?' Esme turned to the concierge. 'Could you order tea for two to be sent to my room, please?'

'I think I should apologise,' Esme began, after the footman had delivered the tray and left the room.

'No.' Monica smiled in relief. She'd been expecting a reproach not an apology. 'No, I should say sorry, I really should. Look.' She held up her arm and showed Esme the watch again. 'It's got a diamond in the middle, right there, and it's all thanks to you, Miss Harkness. You said that I could do it.'

Esme poured out the tea and handed Monica a cup, giving herself time to collect her thoughts before replying.

'I should apologise, Monica, because I made my life sound rather wonderful. I always have. Whenever I met girls of your age before, it was always with the aim of employing them, manufacturing them into prostitutes. But not you, Monica. You deserve better. You should know that a life of prostitution is very different.'

'I'm not a prostitute,' Monica countered vehemently.

'It gets you nothing,' Esme continued quietly. 'Look

348

at me. I've got money, and I've got nothing. But I did say, I did warn you, that you should never follow my example.'

'I'm not like you. James doesn't pay me.'

'Then what's that?' Esme pointed to the watch.

'It's a present.'

'And that's the logic of a whore.'

'James wouldn't sleep with a whore. He's a gentleman.'

'It's because of gentlemen that whores exist.'

'But not James,' Monica insisted. 'I'm the first girl he's slept with. He loves me. He said so.'

'And when does he say it?' Esme probed. 'In the middle of sex?'

'And other times. Plenty of times.'

'I've had it said to me a thousand times. Then twenty minutes later, they'd go home, still smelling of me, to tell their wives how much they love them.'

'You have to spoil it, don't you? Just because you've never met a James Cornell. You may have slept with a thousand men, but not one of them was like him. And if they didn't love you, it was *your* fault. Because every time a man took you in his arms you reached for his wallet.'

'Monica, please. Can't you see that I'm only trying to help? I wanted you to advance yourself, but properly . . .'

'It's sad, Miss Harkness, that's what it is.' Placing her cup on the table, Monica rose to her feet. 'Because you're old and you've missed your chance, you can't bear to see anyone else happy.'

'Just stop and think, girl. What about when he goes? What will you do then?'

'I'll go with him. To London and further. He's talked about going to Paris. Both of us, together. And you're getting left behind. Surrounded by nothing, which is all you deserve.' She opened the door and walked out into the corridor.

'Monica?'

She turned to see that Esme had followed her.

'Miss Harkness? You never did allow me to use your first name.'

'If you must ply my trade, then I should give you a little professional advice.'

'I'm not a prostitute.'

'Sort out pay and conditions in advance. If you need an abortion, make him pay, and make sure it's expensive. And keep yourself clean. Gentlemen insist on that. They like a girl to be clean.' She stepped back into her room, closing the door softly behind her.

'He's different,' Monica insisted, talking to the empty corridor.

'Mr Cornell.' Mr Collins stopped James just as he was walking through the door. 'A message for you, sir.'

'Thank you.' James took the note and opened it. After reading it, he went straight to reception and rang the bell to attract the attention of the clerk.

'I was booked in until the end of the month, but I've been called back to London. I need to close my deals in Manchester. I'll be back at six to settle up. Could you get the staff to pack my things?'

'Yes, sir.'

'Thank you.' He thought of Monica as he turned back towards the door. Glancing at his watch, he decided that he didn't have time to look for her now. Not when he had a meeting to go to.

Chapter Twenty-One

'If a party means that they'll stop talking about little Miss Jones for five minutes, Mrs Harvey, then fine.' John offered the housekeeper a seat in his living room. 'And I'm having dinner with my brother tonight, so we can turn a blind eye.'

'Is Ruth coming? Can I come?' Adele asked.

'You can do your school work, young lady,' John said firmly, as Ruth walked into the room.

Mrs Harvey rose to her feet. 'Very grateful, sir. Miss Manning, could I have a word? About the wedding arrangements?'

'Why?'

'Well, there's things to get done. I'll need the number of guests in advance.'

'This is rather presumptuous. Do you imagine my reception will be held at the Grand? We haven't even set a date.'

'But I was told December the first. By Mr Bannerman,' she added hurriedly. 'December the first. It's booked.'

Olive slowly emptied the chest of drawers and wardrobe in James Cornell's room, handing each garment to Kate for expert folding and packing. Kate worked quickly, the frown deepening on her forehead every time she thought of James's hurried return to London.

Katherine Hardy

When the door finally opened and Monica walked in with a pile of shopping bags, she looked up anxiously, monitoring her old roommate's reaction to the mess of clothes and suitcases.

'What are you doing?' Monica demanded. 'You can't touch our things. Put them back.'

'He's not told you?'

'Put them back,' Monica shouted furiously.

'We're doing this on Mr Cornell's instructions. He's going back to London,' Kate divulged awkwardly.

'Are we?' Monica asked, a little too brightly. 'About time too. Better than this place.'

'Olive, leave us alone,' Kate ordered.

Olive walked obediently to the door and went.

'Is that my replacement?'

'Yes. She's a bit stupid.'

'You'll soon teach her. She's lucky.'

'I can get you work,' Kate offered diffidently. 'I know the bloke who runs the Red Lion. He always needs girls to clean up. I'll write you a reference, I'll nick some notepaper—'

'Kate, I'm going to London with James.'

'Then where's your stuff going? You've got no cases, nothing. Pack *his* stuff, that's what I was told.'

'Put them in his case.'

'I can't do that, Monica, not without orders.'

'I'll get permission. Just wait here.'

'You've got family in Salford. Go to them. They won't know. Two days from now all the gossip will move on to someone else, and I'll get you that job.'

'There's no need, no need at all.' Monica smiled as she opened the door.

'I'm trying to help,' Kate pleaded.

'I know.'

'I'll put your things in my room,' Kate said finally.

'There's no need.'

Kate kicked the foot of the bed as Monica closed the door. Why couldn't the girl see what was staring her in the face?

Marcus came through the door and saw Ruth waiting for him in the foyer, a thunderous expression on her face.

'Ah.' He smiled, enjoying her outrage. 'I knew there was something else I meant to tell you.'

James walked in and went directly to the desk. Seeing him, Ruth took Marcus's arm and led him up the stairs. The sound of their voices echoed down from the mezzanine as James asked for his bill. He had just finished settling it when Monica entered the foyer.

'I've been looking everywhere for you,' he said, conscious of the porters and clerks listening to his every word.

'Have you?'

'I was getting worried. All that fog. The whole city's closing down,' he gabbled nervously, hoping she wouldn't make a scene. 'The rest of the country's had sunshine – I was on the telephone to London. There's not a cloud in the sky there.' He smiled apprehensively, summoning up the courage to say what he had to. 'I've got to go back. It's this coal war – there's no point in trading until it's over. They want me in the office.'

'Can I come?' she asked eagerly. 'I've never seen London. You said you'd show me the sights.'

'I'll come back soon,' he answered, neatly evading her question. 'I promise. I'll spend the weekend. We could go to Alderley Edge. You can show *me* the sights.'

'I'd rather go home. With you,' she added so there could be no mistaking her meaning.

He drew her to the side of the foyer, out of the earshot of the clerk, but unfortunately not out of the earshot of all the porters.

'I don't know what my parents would say about that.'

'No . . .'

'You'll be all right,' he insisted briskly, giving her no chance to say otherwise. 'There's your family. They've a nice little house and plenty of room. You've told me so often enough.'

She knew he hadn't believed a word she'd said about her family. 'I suppose,' she conceded reluctantly, finally having to acknowledge that he was intent on leaving her. '*Are* you coming back?' she asked, panic-stricken at the thought of never seeing him again.

'I promise. I'm only rushing off because they've cancelled half the trains.'

'Mr Cornell?' the concierge interrupted.

Monica looked up to see the porters wheeling his cases out to a car.

'Thank you, Mr Collins.' Relieved to have an excuse to put an end to his leave-taking, James turned to Monica for the last time. 'You will be all right, won't you?'

She realised it was a rhetorical question when he picked up his briefcase.

'Me? Yes. I *could* come though,' she added desperately, searching for a way, any way, that would enable her to stay with him, even now, when he was on the point of walking out through the door. 'I'd love it. I could stay in a hotel and see you every day. You could stay with me . . .'

'If only I was made of money,' he murmured.

'There's boarding houses, though. They don't cost . . .'

She looked at him and saw his embarrassment at her pleading. 'Never mind.'

He pulled out his wallet. 'Buy that necklace, the one you liked. Then you can think of me when you put it on.' He held out a wad of notes.

'Don't do that.'

'Treat yourself . . .'

'Please don't,' she begged, suddenly realising the truth of what Esme had been trying to tell her.

Seeing humiliation mirrored in her eyes, he put his money away.

'Well, I'll see you soon.'

'Bye.' She held up her face for him to kiss. Giving her one last smile, he walked out through the door. Monica looked after him, watching through the stained-glass panels as he tipped the porter, before climbing into the car. It drove away and she found herself staring at the empty street.

The porters returned to the foyer and she retreated. She had reached the staircase and had placed her foot on the bottom step before realising that she had no place to go. Not in the guest rooms, and after what she had done, not even in the basement.

Catching Mr Collins's eye, she saw compassion in the look he gave her. She stepped hesitantly towards him, just as the sound of Jackson Tyler's laughter bellowed from the bar. She faltered for a fraction of a second, then turned.

Clive was clearing a table behind the door when she walked in.

'What are you doing?' he hissed. 'You can't come in here on your own.'

Terrified, she looked past him to the crowd of men.

'Monica, for once in your life, listen,' he pleaded.

'Monica!' Jackson beckoned her forward. 'Drink for the lady,' he shouted to Clive.

'I'm with them.' She gave Clive a hollow smile as she passed.

Clive stood back, watching, as one of the men moved aside so she could join Jackson.

'Thank God you're here.' He put his arm around her shoulders. 'I'm tired of looking at these ugly faces. What's it to be?'

'No stamina, old Jim,' David leered. 'You're well rid of him.'

'Champagne!' Jackson shouted. 'Let's start as we mean to go on.'

Mr Collins and Mrs Harvey stood on the fringes of the milling mass of maids and porters, supervising the arrangements for the staff party from the safety of the office doorway. Roy and Alfred moved a piano into position, as Mr Collins kept an eagle eye on the cases of beer and wine that were being carried out of the cellars, just in case someone decided to divert one for personal use.

'Those on the nine-to-twelve shift can't have a drink until after midnight,' Mr Collins shouted, in an effort to make himself heard above their noise.

'Normal duties in the morning, mind,' Mrs Harvey warned. She glared at Roy. 'Come on, Jack Dempsey, get that piano pushed back out of the way. I'd be quicker doing it myself.'

'Fine by me,' Roy groused.

'Oooh, it's started,' Lynne cried as she ran into the room. 'Just you watch it, Brenda Potter, you've no head for drink. Vimto for this one,' she yelled at Alfred.

'You can shove off.' Brenda elbowed her in the ribs.

'And remember what I said,' Mr Collins bellowed.

'It's not just electricity: they're cutting the gas by fifty per cent. Any lights that aren't needed must be turned off. It's an order from the city council.'

'Are you staying, Mrs Harvey?' Lynne asked.

'You don't need me to get in the way. One drink and I'm off.'

'Here you are.' Stephen walked in with a case of bottles. 'These are courtesy of the Imperial Shipping Company, and myself.'

'Oh flipping heck, brandy!' Lynne lifted out a bottle.

'Two brandy, two whisky, two gin, and there's port and rum in there somewhere as well.'

'Are you sure that's wise, sir?' Mr Collins asked.

'Clive told us you were having a party, so that's with our good wishes.' He peered at the concierge through an alcoholic haze that was clouding his eyes as well as his mind. 'Cheers.'

Kate ran after him as he returned to the bar. 'Stephen, is it right what the girls are saying? That Monica is in the bar?'

'Yes, she's with us.'

'Do us a favour? Keep an eye on her and make sure she's all right.'

'Of course I will.'

'Thanks.'

He smiled at her before opening the door that led into the foyer.

By the time Kate returned to the party, Alfred was playing the piano, and Roy was opening the whisky. Bottles of beer and wine were already being passed round.

'Stephen . . . oh, Stephen . . .' Lynne mimicked.

'Shut it.' Kate smiled as she said it. Lynne smiled back. Parties were too rare an event below stairs to spoil by arguing.

Katherine Hardy

'Ever had whisky before?' Roy handed Olive a glass.

'No.' She took the glass and downed the contents in a single greedy gulp. Spurred on by the porters' cheers, she held it out to Roy. 'Any more?'

'Word of advice,' Marcus said quietly, waylaying Stephen before he reached Jackson. 'No more drinks on the house.'

'They're your friends.'

'They're colleagues. I booked them in to make a profit. And if you've got any sense, you'll find better things to do than get drunk with this lot.'

'One day in the Grand, and already you sound like my father.' He went to the bar. 'All right, my round.' He raised his voice for Marcus's benefit. 'And, Clive, this is cash, not account.'

'It's like a bear pit,' Ruth complained as she surveyed the hot, smoky room. 'And there's nowhere to sit.'

'Here we are.' Marcus pulled out two spare chairs from Jackson and Monica's table.

'Marcus . . .' Ruth protested, glancing disparagingly at Monica, as he sat next to the girl.

'Ah, the happy couple.' Jackson lifted his glass as Ruth reluctantly took a seat next to Marcus. 'Here, help yourselves.' He pushed a couple of bottles towards them. 'Miss Manning, I think your fiancé has been keeping us apart.'

'Jackson!' David Jeffries hailed him from the bar. 'Armitage has been talking religion. I caught him!'

'I did no such thing,' Armitage remonstrated. 'I was just saying—'

Jackson rose unsteadily to his feet. 'Sconce him!'

'What's sconce?' Ruth asked Marcus, as all the men

rose to their feet and began chanting, 'Sconce! Sconce! Sconce!'

'Forfeit,' he explained, as David handed Armitage a pint pot.

'Down in one,' David ordered.

'Miss Jones.' Marcus acknowledged Monica who, deserted by Jackson, was sitting slightly apart from the rest of the people at the table.

'Mr Bannerman, Miss Manning.' She smiled, grateful to Marcus for noticing her.

'Miss Jones.' Ruth turned to watch Armitage finish his drink. Deafened by the cheering that saluted his accomplishment, Monica bowed her head. She was out of place, and she sensed that everyone, even those who were unaware of her situation, knew it. But just exactly where could she go from here?

'We could join them?' Sarah suggested to John as they saw Marcus and Ruth sitting in the bar.

'Do you want to?'

'No.' Sarah reeled back as a particularly loud cheer burst from the room.

'Marcus knows that the table is booked. Let's go through. It's not often we get a chance to be on our own.' He offered her his arm and led her down the dimly lit corridor into the dining room, passing Mr Douglas, the relief concierge, who was following council orders by supervising the extinguishing of half the hotel lights.

'I mean, I love it. Just sitting here,' Monica babbled eagerly to Marcus, as he filled her glass from a bottle on the table. 'I can't imagine what it must be like to *own* the place.'

'It's hard work.'

'Go on, though. I've worked here too. It's more than just that. People come into the foyer just to look at the place. And you grew up here. You must love this building.'

'I suppose you're right. Yes I love it,' he conceded. Bending his head close to hers, he whispered, 'No one's supposed to know that.'

He looked up to see Ruth eyeing him with a new respect.

'At least you talk to me. The rest of your family just turn away. They don't like what I've become.' She hesitated, before blurting out, 'What *have* I become, sir?'

'Whatever you want,' he said easily.

'I wanted to be a lady.' She turned shyly to Ruth. 'Like you, miss.'

Ruth wasn't sure how to answer the girl, but she managed a sympathetic smile.

'It's not what I expected, but then, maybe I expected too much. It's been worth it. Not just the money, and the food and having drinks and that. You get . . . I dunno . . . respect. People say "hello", they don't just walk past you. It's like you're alive. That's all I want. Bit of life.'

'Excuse me, sir.' Marcus turned to see Douglas, the relief concierge. 'Mr and Mrs Bannerman are waiting in the restaurant.'

'If we must.' Ruth left the table.

'Will you be all right?' Marcus asked Monica. 'I don't want to leave you on your own.'

'I'm not.' She nodded to Jackson.

'Then good evening, Miss Jones. And take it from a man who loves this building, it becomes you.' He took her hand and kissed it. Glowing at the unexpected compliment, Monica beamed at him.

Ruth took his arm as they walked into the foyer.

Marcus's understanding and generosity to Monica had shown her a whole new side to his character. A side that made her love him all the more, and even offered the hope that one day she'd be able to tell him exactly how deeply she felt.

'Olive, you're wasting good stuff,' Roy complained as she topped up her glass from the whisky bottle, yet again. 'There's people still on duty who haven't had anything yet.'

'Oh, unbutton yourself, Roy,' she cackled. Reaching out, she pinched his bum – hard. He yelped as Lynne, Brenda and Kate giggled helplessly.

Mr Collins and Mrs Harvey stood in the open doorway of the housekeeper's office monitoring the proceedings through jaded eyes.

'Mr Harvey won't miss me.' Mrs Harvey pronounced her words slowly and correctly in an effort to counteract the effects of a couple of drinks too many. 'He's always got his head in a book these days. He's become quite the scholar.'

'And what does he study?' Mr Collins asked.

'Anatomy.'

'Anatomy?' the concierge repeated in surprise.

'Studies of the human form. Proper drawings. I've not seen them close up. He shuts the book as soon as I come in.'

They looked up as Alfred stopped playing the piano. Adele Bannerman was standing in the doorway.

'Don't mind me. Carry on,' she said nervously, conscious that everyone was staring at her.

'Can I help you, Miss Bannerman?' Mr Collins glared at Lynne and Brenda who were both snorting with laughter.

'I heard there was a party.'

361

'Do your parents know you're here?'

'Yes. Anyway it's my home as well. Everyone else seems to be celebrating. Why can't I?'

'You can sit here with me, miss,' Lynne offered slyly, making room for her on the bench. She held out a bottle. 'Have some of this. We'll look after you.'

Adele crossed over to her. As she joined the maids, she glanced boldly at Mr Collins.

'That's right, park yourself there.' Lynne smiled insincerely. 'You'll have to rinse a mug out. Brenda's spat in them all.'

All the staff burst out laughing, giving Adele the uncomfortable impression that she was the butt of their joke. Alfred began to play the piano again. Very much the worse for whisky, Olive climbed on the table and started to sing. Spurred on by the shouts of the boys, she hoisted her skirts and kicked her legs high in the air.

Sorry that she had even thought of venturing below stairs, Adele felt totally lost and out of place, but lacking the courage to leave, she continued to sit next to Lynne.

Kate saw her from across the room. She waved and smiled, and for the first time Adele felt that she had a real friend in the room.

Stephen downed a forfeit pint in the centre of a crowd of clapping, cheering, chanting men. The noise was absolutely deafening, giving Jackson an excuse to move closer to Monica.

'Don't worry about this lot,' he shouted in her ear. 'They're all noise. Never left the junior common room, half of them.'

'I might go,' she murmured anxiously.

'You don't have to. James told me to look after you.'

'Did he?' she asked, wanting to believe him.

'Good lad, James.'

'Yes. He's lovely. I really should go,' she repeated, making no attempt to move.

'You're mad. Have you seen the fog out there? It stinks of sulphur.'

'It's the factories.'

'Look, if you're in a spot, there's always my room.'

'No thank you,' she replied primly.

'All right.' He pulled his key from his top pocket and laid it on the table in front of her. 'Room thirty-five. It's there if you want it.'

'Jackson!' David roared from the other side of the bar. 'This man works for Collis Browne.'

'Does he indeed?' Jackson rose unsteadily from his chair. 'They owe me money, the sods.' He disappeared into the noisy crowd, leaving the key lying in front of Monica. She stared down at it, seeing it as a passport to her new life. A despised life of prostitution, like Esme Harkness's.

Could she turn back? Return to skivvying by taking the job Kate had offered her in the Red Lion? She turned to the door, staring at the corridor that led back to the staff quarters. A couple blocked her view. The woman was beautifully gowned and coiffed, glittering with gold and diamond jewellery, the embodiment of the lady she had always yearned to be.

The noise of shattering glass broke in on her reverie. Moments later Clive appeared with a dustpan and brush. Falling to his knees, he began to clear the mess. She looked from Clive back to the woman. Making her decision, she scooped the key from the table and left her seat. Jackson eyed her from the bar. She held up her hand, parting her fingers so he could see the key. He nodded and smiled.

She walked past the porters and clerks in the foyer and climbed the stairs. Checking the corridor to ensure no one was watching her, she ran to Jackson's room. She unlocked the door, stepped inside and switched on a side lamp. She looked at her watch, not to read the time, but to remind herself of the rewards her new life could bring. Sitting on the bed she stroked the satin coverlet, she didn't have to check the quality of the sheets, she had folded enough of them.

Desperately trying to convince herself that she had done the right thing, she hummed a little tune to herself – and waited.

'I'm telling you, miss,' Lynne was saying, lunging unsteadily towards Adele. 'There's this woman in Ancoats, Mrs Hooper. And if you're walking down the street, Mrs Hooper jumps out and throws her baby at you.'

'She does what?' Adele asked, confused by the story.

'Throws her baby, and you have to catch it. Then all the other Hooper children swarm over you. They rob your pockets and steal your purse and everything. And you can't do nothing because you're holding the baby.'

'I don't believe you.'

'Oh, and you've walked through Ancoats have you?' Lynne scoffed.

'Yes.'

'When?' the maid challenged. 'When's a girl like you ever walked through that part of the town? You don't even know where it is.'

'I do,' Adele protested in the face of the combined laughter of all the maids.

Mrs Harvey heard the laughter as Mr Collins escorted her to the back door.

The Grand

'It's a Godforsaken night. Winter's come early this year.' He peered through the window into the yard. 'I'm sure the Grand could pay for a cab, just this once.'

'All God's children must walk in the dark.' She kissed him on the cheek. 'Good night, Jacob.'

A chorus of oohs and aahs filled the air. She smiled at the porters and maids who'd been watching them. 'Up at six. The lot of you.'

Mr Collins bolted the door behind her, and called to Roy, 'It's time Mr Douglas had a drink. I'll take his place. Mind this lot don't make too much noise.'

'I'll do my best, sir.'

'I have to clean out your chamberpot, every morning,' Lynne said to Adele, raising her voice to make sure everyone heard her.

'Really.' Adele turned beetroot.

'I have to scour it, most mornings. I don't know what you're eating but it doesn't half cling.'

Kate pushed through the crowd of sniggering girls.

'Miss Bannerman? That friend of yours from school, Christina, is in the foyer asking for you. I told her to wait.'

'What's she doing here at this time of night?' She looked at Lynne and the other maids. 'Excuse me.'

Lynne mimicked excuse me as Adele walked down the corridor with Kate following in her wake.

'You should have sent her up to my room,' Adele said when they reached the door that separated the servants' quarters from the public rooms.

'She's not there, miss. I made it up because I thought you were getting bored.'

Adele was grateful that Kate had decided to save her from further embarrassment, but she was also conscious and ashamed of her behaviour to the maid when Maggie Rigby had been a guest in the hotel.

'No, not at all,' she answered, anxious to salvage what little dignity she had left. 'But it is rather late. Goodnight.'

'Night, miss.' Kate called out as she turned back to the party.

The tension at the Bannermans' table in the restaurant was palpable, escalating with every passing minute.

'All day I thought he was trying to make me cancel the wedding, by pushing me as far as he could,' Ruth complained to John and Sarah. 'But now I see that this is his way of showing affection. I mean he's forever complaining about the Grand, but he loves this place.' She flashed an affectionate look at Marcus. 'He said so. So I'll put up with his games, and in the meantime, I can find us a house of our own. We won't be staying here.'

'Then people would say I'm marrying you for your money.' Marcus flicked the ash from his cigar.

'Why are you marrying me?' she asked lightly.

He surveyed her coolly for a moment before answering, 'Because you'll do.'

Ruth looked down at her plate. John saw her biting her lips in an effort to contain her rage.

'Did I tell you about the *Manchester News*?' he asked, steering the conversation into what he hoped would prove calmer waters. 'They printed a bad review of the restaurant, all of it lies, so I went to see them . . .' His voice trailed as he saw tears fall from Ruth's eyes. 'Straight to the editor . . .' He broke off when Ruth pushed back her chair and fled the room. Sarah gave Marcus a contemptuous look before following Ruth out through the door.

John stayed, but the expression on his face as he stared at his brother was even more scornful than Sarah's.

Monica's wait for Jackson proved to be a long one. And all the while she sat, fully dressed and silent, on the bed, steeling herself for the night that was to come. When the door finally opened she forced a smile, glad at least that the suspense was finally over.

Jackson swayed on his feet as he made his way unsteadily into the room. Pushing the door wide open behind him, he motioned David Jeffries and Armitage in. All three men grinned at her as Armitage closed the door and turned the key in the lock.

Monica stared at them, refusing to believe what was happening. Not even when Jackson stumbled towards her and took off his jacket did she believe it. Terrified, she continued to sit and watch while Jackson undressed, and the other two men stood back, watching – and waiting.

Chapter Twenty-Two

Exhausted by the busiest shift he could remember, Clive made his way to the servants' quarters, hoping to find the party in full swing. Instead he found the last few stragglers sitting amongst a mess of empty bottles and upturned chairs.

'Oh, thanks very much,' he complained bitterly. 'I've been working all night and no one thought to leave me anything.'

'You can share mine.' Olive waved a mug under his nose.

'Don't, Clive,' Kate warned. 'She's been sick twice.'

'Me mam's given up drinking,' Brenda related solemnly. 'Doesn't touch a drop these days.'

'That's because she's in prison,' Lynne slurred.

'There's some in here.' Roy held up an almost full bottle of wine. Clive nodded and followed him out of the room.

'I've had enough,' Kate said, and went to the door.

'Oh, off she goes. The next Mrs Harvey, Lenin's wife,' Lynne sneered.

Kate wandered down the dimly lit corridor, almost falling over a maid and footman who were kissing outside her bedroom door.

'Rosie, don't eat him.' Pushing past, she went into her room and sank wearily on to her bed.

*　　*　　*

The Grand

Monica lay slumped in a chair at the side of Jackson's bed. Bruised, battered, used and humiliated more than she would have believed possible, she clung to the edges of a tear that had split her frock in two, desperately trying to cover her nakedness.

Armitage finished buttoning his trousers and pulled on his jacket. He stood by the door waiting for Jeffries to buckle his belt.

Jackson looked at the two men as they opened the door. 'Night,' he called.

Neither David nor Armitage could bring himself to look Jackson in the eye. As they closed the door behind them, Jackson fell back on the bed. Oblivious to his presence, Monica continued to sit in the chair, staring blankly at the wall in front of her while her hands scrabbled at the edges of her ripped and bloodied frock.

'I'm perfectly fine,' Ruth lied as Sarah followed her into their private living room.

'So am I.'

'You think I'm an idiot for agreeing to marry that man?'

'Yes,' Sarah replied with more honesty than tact. 'Marcus is a bastard. And you – you're pretty, you're intelligent, you could do so much better.'

Ruth smiled at Sarah's reflection in the glass. 'You think so?'

Sarah smiled back, feeling a sudden surge of warmth for her soon-to-be sister-in-law. 'Yes, and you're rich. That must help.'

'Sounds like you want to get rid of me. On the very day Marcus moves into your home.'

'Ruth, don't. I had no choice in the matter. I don't get consulted in everything. I might have shares in the business, but when it comes to family, I'm just the wife.'

'Good Lord, is that a criticism of John? What a night this is turning out to be. No wonder you find Marcus so fascinating.'

'Yes,' Sarah replied thoughtfully, 'to be truthful he does fascinate me. He makes me laugh. He's excellent company, and he's clever. He might even be a genius. But he's cultivated that image at great expense. He's made himself attractive, but as a husband . . .' She shook her head doubtfully.

'Then you'd rather John's company?'

'I know you think John's a dull man. And don't tell me he lives in the shadow of his father – I know it only too well. And he's not the best father in the world. He tries, but not enough. He's still a Victorian.'

'So you find Marcus fascinating, and describe your husband as dull?'

'No . . . well, yes. That's my point. John gives me all the comfort and love I could possibly need. You won't get that from Marcus.'

'So you've chosen safety?'

'If you like.'

'I'd never choose such a thing.' Ruth pulled a gold compact from her evening purse and dabbed powder on to her nose. 'The way you describe your marriage, it seems like a small death. At least there's life in Marcus, even if it hurts. It's interesting, Mrs Bannerman. You came to talk sense into me, but I could swear you're the one who's confused.'

'I envied you.' John looked at his brother across the table. 'I really did. I'd look at you and think, that's the life. Sharp as any knife in business. Friends with any man you could name. And a different woman on your arm every night. The man about town.'

'Thank you,' Marcus replied drily.

'But it doesn't last. The older you get, the less impressive it becomes. You'll find yourself at sixty, still living that life, still with the endless parade of women. Except *they* won't get any older. And then, Marcus, then you become a joke. It's a very small step from being admired to being ridiculed.'

'Oh, then I should settle down? Become like you? An imitation of our father.'

'You think marriage is shameful. A defeat. But it's better than the other option. Playing the eternal butt of music hall jokes, the ageing roué. And I thought with Ruth, you'd found your chance.'

'Don't tell me you like her all of a sudden.'

'No. I can't stand her.' Marcus's laughter was as loud as his. 'But I'm not very fond of you, either, which makes you a perfect pair. I actually thought: At last he's found a woman as clever as him, as fast as him, and as cold.'

'As I said, I should marry her because she'll do.'

'If you're looking for the perfect woman, you'll wait a long time.'

'You found her.' Marcus looked his brother directly in the eye.

'Yes, thank God,' John said gratefully, oblivious of the envy in Marcus's voice.

'Ruth isn't Sarah. Never could be.'

'Well, Sarah's taken.'

'Then why should I settle for second best?'

'I must tell Sarah you said this.' John laughed.

'She knows.'

Still insensible to his brother's innuendo, John carried on blithely, 'I think you have found the perfect woman, and you can't bear it. You think it's a weakness, so you torment her.'

'Is this Ruth or Sarah?'

'Ruth,' John said in exasperation, seeing Marcus's question as an inane joke. 'Look, I can't make you fall in love with her, but maybe the fact that she'll do is enough. It kept Mother and Father together.'

'John! You cynic.'

'Because you're not just finding a wife,' John expounded seriously. 'God willing, you're starting a family. And if you don't understand how important that is, I don't know if I can begin to tell you. But your children, Marcus, they become yourself. They become your marriage. Then you find yourself at sixty, and your reputation, your standing, your pride, it's all in them.'

'Even a son who spends every night getting blind drunk?'

'So did we at his age, and we didn't have the excuse of a war.' John pretended to study his wineglass. 'Truth is, it breaks my heart to see him like this,' he admitted ruefully. 'I don't know if I should talk to him or leave him alone. But I'll tell you this. I'd rather be broken by him than have my latest chorus girl run off with someone else. You've got a chance to start a family of your own, Marcus. Don't waste it.' He dropped his glass back on to the table and sat back in his chair, waiting for Marcus to say something.

'If your example's so perfect, I should use the exact model. Sarah. You've had her for long enough.'

'Now that *would* break my heart.'

'Would it?'

John reached for the bottle and refilled both their glasses. Marcus watched him, and if John hadn't known better, he might have said that his brother was truly unhappy.

Jackson woke with a start. Looking to the corner of the room, he saw Monica slumped in the chair in the exact position she had adopted when they had finished using her. Rolling heavily off the bed he went to her.

'Come on. Get to bed.' When she didn't move, he stepped closer. 'Come on. I told James I'd look after you. I promised, and the bed's paid for. My treat.' He touched her shoulder. The warmth of his hand on her bare skin sent an explosion of hatred and loathing hurtling through her veins.

'*Get off me!*' Seeing his silver-topped cane lying on the dressing table, she jumped from the chair, snatched it up and brought it down viciously on his head. Jackson tumbled back. Catching his temple on the headboard, he fell to the floor.

Monica stared down at him shaking uncontrollably. He moved slightly, opened his eyes and groaned a single word.

'Bitch!'

Slowly, deliberately, with terrible precision she lifted the cane and hit him on the head. Taking a deep breath, she did it again . . . and again . . . and again . . . wanting to hurt and destroy him every bit as much as he had hurt and destroyed her.

Only when his head was a bloody, mashed pulp did she stop. The cane fell from her hands as she stumbled backwards into the chair staring in disbelief at what she'd done.

John and Marcus left the restaurant just as Ruth and Sarah walked down the stairs. Marcus held up the two glasses and bottle of wine he was carrying, and nodded in the direction of the Reading Room. Ruth turned and walked in ahead of him. Marcus smiled remorsefully at John and Sarah before following her.

'What did you say to her?' John asked.

'I'm not sure,' Sarah answered evasively.

'Goodnight, Mr Collins,' John called as the concierge walked into the foyer. 'Good party?'

'I dread to think, sir.'

Sarah laughed as they headed for the stairs, and the concierge took up his customary position.

Monica sat and stared at Jackson's corpse until she realised that she couldn't stay in the room. Tomorrow the maid would come, open the door, draw the curtains, see what was left of Jackson's body, and then the whole world would know what she'd done. She'd murdered a man. An important man. And they hung murderers.

She dived off the chair and scrabbled in Jackson's jacket searching for his wallet. It was empty. Frustrated, she threw it aside and kicked the corpse, then looked around the room, frantically trying to think. She ran into the bathroom and stared at her face in the mirror. An ugly purple bruise covered one side of her face from her cheekbone to her jaw. Pulling her hair across to hide it, she turned her attention to her dress. When she'd done what little she could to tidy herself, she stepped over Jackson's body, out through the door and into the corridor.

Listening hard for footsteps other than her own, she walked the full length of it. Then, on reaching the end, she quickened her pace and ran down the next corridor, stopping outside Esme's room and knocking as loudly as she dared.

'Miss Harkness,' she whispered fiercely. 'Miss Harkness . . .'

There was no reply. The town clock chimed midnight. She sank back into the shadows of the service bay, desperately trying to think out her next move.

'Mr Collins, it's an atrocious night out there.' Esme greeted the concierge as she walked into the foyer escorted by a dapper, middle-aged gentleman. 'Every place is closed. I don't suppose there's any chance of a light supper for myself and Mr Daniels?'

'It is rather late.'

'Are you the hall porter?' Mr Daniels demanded.

'Yes, sir.'

'Then do your job. Supper.'

Collins nodded. Esme gave him a small smile of apology as Mr Daniels led her into the restaurant.

'I'm sorry. All right?' Marcus looked at Ruth as he refilled their glasses.

'Liar.'

'I won't change. You agreed to marry me as I am, and I won't change.'

'I will.' Ruth eyed him coolly. 'I won't put up with your tricks. If I have to shout and scream in public, then I will. You won't get a picture-book wife, seen but not heard.'

'Good.'

'I've only one apology for you.' Masochistic to the last, Ruth couldn't resist bringing up the one subject that hurt her most. 'I thought you were inventing your tales of Sarah Bannerman. But she does like you. Very much. She told me.'

'Really?'

'Surprised?'

'Not at all,' he said carelessly, lifting his glass to conceal his shock.

As she crossed the threshold that marked the division between the guest corridors and servants' quarters, Monica heard voices. Keeping to the shadows created by the dimmed lighting, she crept up to the room where the party had been held. She peeped through the half-open door and saw Lynne sitting with Brenda and Olive. The new girl was upending a bottle into her mouth.

'Lick the label off, won't you?' Lynne sniped.

Seeing her chance, Monica darted past and on to the dormitory corridor.

'I don't even know Mrs Harvey's first name.' After licking the top, Olive abandoned the bottle on the floor.

'Sylvie.'

'Sylvie. Sounds like a hand cream.' Olive kicked the bottle and it rolled into the corridor. 'Put some Sylvie on your hands, stops them from chapping.'

'It was Mrs Ball before her.' Lynne stifled a yawn. 'I loved Mrs Ball. She had an ulcerated leg. Life of pain that woman. Killed herself with salts of lemon.'

'Has that door always been there?' Olive asked dully.

A shaft of light fell across Kate's bed as the door opened and closed. She stirred sleepily.

'You'll be sorry in the morning, Olive. We're up at six. Did Lynne have a go at you? She doesn't stop once she's off.' She opened her eyes. 'You all right?' She looked across and saw Monica sitting on her old bed.

'Oh, I thought you were Olive.' Sitting up, she swung her legs out of the bed. 'I've kept your things. They're in that bag over there. I thought you'd come back. But you can't stay. That's Olive's bed. You'll have to go home. Monica?'

'How much money have you got?'

'What?'

'Dunno what it costs. Dover. That's where you get the boats, Dover. It's not that far is it? Won't cost much to get to Dover?'

'What are you on about?'

'Boats cost. I'll need money for the boat. Miss Harkness, she's got money, she'll pay. There are thousands of people in France. They won't notice me.'

Monica's voice sounded odd, somehow strange. Kate reached for the candle and matches that were kept on the bedside table and lit the wick, gasping in horror when she saw the state of Monica's face.

'Oh bloody hell, what's happened? How did you do that?'

'I can't wait for Miss Harkness, not looking like this. But you could.'

'Who did that to you?'

'She always comes back. Never stays out. That's one of her rules. Always comes back to her own bed. And she's got money. She owes me.'

'You should bathe it. Here, let me bathe it.' As soon as Kate's fingers touched Monica's skin, the girl flinched violently away from her.

'*Don't!*'

'Monica. Tell me what happened.'

'Doesn't matter.'

'Tell me. Someone's hurt you. Who was it? It wasn't James.'

'Not James.' Tears fell from Monica's eyes as she shook her head. 'He wouldn't hurt me. He's a gentleman.' Pulling herself together she murmured, 'It doesn't matter.'

'Who did it?' Kate persisted.

'A man called Tyler. Jackson Tyler. Doesn't matter, he's dead.'

'Don't be so silly.'

'He's in room thirty-five. He's dead,' Monica repeated numbly. 'He deserved it. Who'd have thought? Little thing like me killing a man like that.' She began to cry again. 'There were three of them. I said no. I told them no, but they wouldn't let me go. They all took turns. With me. And it's not like they paid. Not one of them *paid* . . . I'm bleeding . . .'

'Where?'

Kate turned away as Monica stared at her.

'Oh, Monica,' she cried. 'He's not, though. He's not really dead. He can't be.'

'Have you seen the fog that's covering the whole town? They wouldn't find me in that. I'd get out of Manchester. People don't notice girls like us. I'll pay for a boat. There's tons of boats. I'll get to Paris on me own.'

'Monica, what have you done?'

'She'll come back. Miss Harkness always comes back. Go and wait.'

'I can't . . .'

'Then they'll find me here. With you. What'll they say then? We'll both get the blame,' she threatened viciously.

'But it was your fault. He attacked you.'

'You were in charge of me. My chambermaid. I was just a housemaid. You were supposed to look after me, but you didn't. Please help me, Kate,' she begged. 'Please, just go to Miss Harkness, that's all I want. She'll do the rest.'

Confused and bewildered, Kate couldn't even think clearly.

'Kate, I killed him. They'll hang me.'

Terrified by the mention of hanging, Kate put the candle down on the table. Wrapping a shawl over her nightgown she went to the door and opened it, but when she reached the main corridor she didn't head for Esme's room.

'Sir, sir . . .'

Stephen stirred sluggishly, realising that yet again he'd fallen asleep on top of his bed before undressing. Opening his eyes he saw Kate standing in the darkness next to him.

'Kate?' He reached out for her. 'This is nice,' he babbled drunkenly.

She moved back to the door. A shaft of light fell on to her face from the corridor and he saw her tears.

'You said you'd look after her. You promised. Why didn't you look after her?'

Monica sat on her old bed in Kate's room and waited, just as she had done all night. First for Jackson, now for Kate and Esme. Seeing the dress Esme had bought her bundled into the corner, she picked it up and hugged it close. Gradually, she became aware of a noise. Tick tick tick. It built up – louder and louder – until there was only the tick tick tick in the room. Tick tick tick!

Looking down, she realised the ticking was emanating from the watch James had bought her. Violently, she tore it from her wrist and threw it across the room. Tick tick tick! Tick tick tick! The din continued to grow louder and louder. Dropping the dress, she ran and stamped on the watch, shattering it into myriads of shining fragments.

She fell to her knees, scrabbling for the pieces. To her surprise they were wet. Reaching up, she felt a tear fall from her eye. Then she collapsed in a heap and began to sob. Harsh, rasping sobs torn from the depths of her pain and despair.

'I'm sorry,' she cried out to no one in particular. 'I'm sorry . . .'

'You can't do that, you can't!' Kate grabbed Stephen's coat, and pulled him away from the telephone.

'For God's sake, Kate. She's killed him!' Stephen struggled to extricate himself from her grip. 'Don't you see? We *have* to call the police.'

'You *can't*!'

'What do you expect me to do?'

'I don't know. I thought you could help. Money or something. You know what they'll do to her. Please, Stephen, for me. *Please* . . .'

'Stephen? Kate? What's going on?' John walked in on them in his pyjamas and dressing gown.

Kate stared at her employer in horror, realising that there was no hope of escape for Monica, not now. The police would have to be called.

'Spend the night here?' Marcus suggested to Ruth. 'Our first time in the Grand Hotel?'

'You'll have to beg.'

'Mr Bannerman,' Collins interrupted gravely.

'Oh, for God's sake don't tell me that I'm still on duty.'

'Your brother telephoned down, sir. There's a situation.'

'Jackson Tyler was in room thirty-five?' John looked to Stephen for confirmation as Sarah joined them in her nightdress.

'We don't know that he's dead,' Sarah said, slipping on her robe. 'We should look.'

The Grand

'The police said to leave everything alone.'

Kate backed quietly out of the room. Once she reached the end of the corridor she began to run as though her life depended on it.

'We don't know how much of this the girl has made up,' Sarah insisted.

Stephen looked around. 'Where's Kate?' Realising where she'd gone, he tore out of the room after her.

Monica was still on her knees crying over the watch when Kate burst in.

'You've got to get out,' Kate screamed hysterically. 'They're coming, they've called the police.'

'You told them?'

'It's not my fault. I'm sorry. Look, here's two quid. It's all I've got, Monica. Get out.'

'Two quid? What am I going to do with two quid?' Monica demanded scathingly.

'Monica, they're coming to get you. Just get out. I'm sorry, but you've got to *get out*!'

Finally realising the importance of what Kate was saying, Monica charged out into the corridor. She looked up to see Stephen blocking her path.

'Monica!' He grabbed hold of her but she fought back like a wildcat. Hearing Monica's screams, Kate ran out of the room and launched herself at Stephen, hammering on his arms with her fists in an attempt to make him release his hold on her old roommate.

'Get off her!' she shrieked, kicking his shins.

As Stephen moved back to protect himself, Monica finally broke free. Tearing down the corridor, she ran past the maids still talking in the rest area. Collins appeared at the door, with Clive and Roy in tow. Both porters were half dressed as though the concierge had just hauled them from their beds.

'Clive, clear out those girls as fast as you can,' Collins ordered as Monica hurtled past.

Olive stood in her way. Monica shoved the girl aside and kept on running.

'Monica?' Mr Collins called, realising only after she'd gone who had just torn past him.

'It's her, back in steerage,' Lynne jeered. 'Monica Jones.' She grinned at Brenda and Olive. All three of them began to chant, 'Mon-i-ca . . . Mon-i-ca . . .'

Spurred on by their taunts, Monica ran on up the stairs, into the corridor that led to the foyer. She burst into reception as a doorman opened the door to two policemen. She swung round. John and Sarah were hurrying down the stairs. Marcus stood at the entrance to the Reading Room, Ruth, impassive as ever, behind him. Collins appeared at the entrance to the office corridor with Stephen and Kate behind him. Backing away like a cornered animal, she whirled around again, frantically searching for an escape route.

Marcus held up his hand to stop the police from moving in on the terrified girl.

'It's all right,' he murmured gently. 'Come here.' He held out his hand to her.

'I'm a *guest*,' she ranted. 'You can't do this. I'm a guest in this hotel. You've got to treat me proper. You've got to. That's the rules.'

'It's all right,' Marcus repeated.

'That's the *rules*.'

Marcus drew alongside her. Petrified, she retreated into the corridor between the Reading Room and the bar. Esme Harkness and Mr Daniels were walking towards her. Esme stopped, realising that something was very wrong.

'Miss Harkness?' Monica began to cry at the sight of

her old mentor. 'I'm not clean . . . I didn't keep myself clean . . .'

Esme simply stood and stared at her. Marcus walked up to Monica and put his arm around her shoulders. The police moved in. Taking her from him, they bundled her hands roughly behind her back.

'There's no need for that,' Marcus protested. 'I said there's no need,' he repeated as they turned their backs on him and handcuffed her.

'Marcus, leave them.' John stepped forward, Sarah at his side. Monica looked back at Kate, who was standing crying next to Stephen. She called out, 'Sorry,' as the police dragged her to the door.

Stephen laid his arm around Kate's shoulders to comfort her. She pulled away. Sobbing, she ran back down the servants' corridor. As Collins turned wearily to the foyer he saw Lynne, Clive and Roy pushing past Kate. Holding up his hand, he turned his back on them.

John and Sarah went to Marcus and Ruth.

'What the devil's going on?' Mr Daniels demanded of Esme in a loud voice.

Struggling to keep her composure, Esme clung to his arm.

'She was one of the maids,' she said quietly. 'Just one of the maids,' she repeated, desperately wanting to believe it.

Chapter Twenty-Three

Kate stepped through an iron door set in a grey stone wall. A grim-faced female warder was waiting for her. She nodded briefly and led her down a stone-lined corridor to the accompaniment of locks being turned and bolts ramming home. Halting before another locked, bolted and barred gateway, the guard pulled a ring of keys from her belt, opened the door and ushered Kate into a high-walled yard.

Only too familiar with the route they were taking, Kate halted in front of a desk set behind yet another door. She opened her bag and handed it over so the guard manning the area could search it. While the warder rifled through her things, Kate signed her name in the visitors' book.

A few minutes later she was allowed to pass on into the corridor that housed the death cells. Unlike the normal cells, they consisted of suites of two rooms, one for day use, one for night. The warder led her to a door on the right-hand side of the passageway. Trying not to think what the door facing her led into, Kate stood back while the guard opened the door. Another warder rose to her feet as she entered the cold, comfortless chamber, with its stone walls and floor.

Monica was sitting at a plain deal table. Looking younger and more exhausted than Kate had ever seen her before, she smiled when she saw her visitor. Kate returned the smile as she took the empty chair the warder had placed for her on the other side of the table.

'You wouldn't believe what they're doing for this wedding,' Kate began awkwardly, glancing at the warder behind her. 'They're even whitewashing the back yard in case some guest wanders out there by mistake. You'd think it was a royal occasion.'

'What happened to the petition to get them to change the date?' Monica asked.

'They gave it to Miss Manning, and she said it was too late. All the invites had gone out and nothing could be done about it. Mr Bannerman would have listened. That's Mr *Marcus* Bannerman – he's been asking after you.' Kate took a deep breath. 'Winter wedding suits a cold-hearted woman like Miss Manning.' Not wanting to think about what was going to happen to Monica in the morning, she changed the subject. 'Has your mam been?'

'They're sending a letter to the Home Secretary. Did I tell you? Imagine that, the Home Secretary reading my name. It's not even going to Parliament: it's going to his house. My solicitor was in here. He sat in that seat you're sitting in now, and he said it might work. He promised, and he's the best. He's a Sir. I knew Miss Harkness wouldn't let me down.'

'You don't know it was Miss Harkness who paid his bill.'

'Who else has got that sort of money? Solicitors like that cost a fortune.'

'She hasn't been in to visit you?'

'No.' Monica smiled as she shook her head. 'But she said she'd look after me, and she has. She's my friend. All the way through the trial I had the very best, that's how she works – the very best of everything. And she can't visit. There's all those men from the press outside. They'd plaster her name over the papers. She can't come.'

'I suppose you're right.' Kate looked around the cell, playing for time while she thought of something else to say. 'Clive Evans took me out for a drink last week. I think he's a bit keen.'

'He's nice, Clive.'

'Yes. Mrs Harvey only gave me an hour.'

'Go on then. You don't want to lose your job.'

Kate hesitated, realising that this would probably be the last time she'd see Monica. 'What are you having for your tea?'

'Lamb and potatoes. I asked for it. I could have had whatever I wanted. I could have had something posh, but I couldn't think of anything else.'

'I'll be off then.' Too numb for tears, Kate pushed back her chair.

'I'll see you next week.'

Monica's outwardly casual remark sent the cell spinning. Kate grabbed the back of the chair to steady herself. Silence pressed down, oppressive, terrifying, as she struggled against the sick sensation in her stomach. Feeling the need to prepare Monica for the worst, she murmured, 'You might not.'

'They're sending a letter to the Home Secretary. To his house.'

'Right.' She picked up her bag. 'Bye, then.' She went to the door. The warder rose to open it for her. She turned back, 'Monica—'

'If you see me mam, tell her I'm all right,' Monica interrupted cheerfully, sensing what Kate was going to say and not wanting to hear it. 'I've got books and everything. I wish we'd been better friends.'

'We are.'

'We could have been best friends if I'd listened. But I never listened, did I? Well, it's too late now. Bye, Kate.'

'Bye.'

The door opened and Kate stepped outside, feeling as though her heart was breaking.

Mrs Harvey lifted the lid on a large box that held oblong wooden slats. Picking up the first pair, she checked that the string threaded through each side of the slats was still strong. Then she took up position in the downstairs service area and called the maids, waiting until they had lined up in front of her before handing out the slats, two to a girl. As soon as each maid had been given her set, she sat on the bench behind the housekeeper and tied them on to the soles of her shoes.

After she had handed out the last pair, Mrs Harvey shouted, 'Ready!'

They rose to their feet. The housekeeper blew on a whistle, and the girls started moving around, clattering noisily over the flagstones on their wooden blocks.

'There's one.' Jumping into a corner, Lynne slammed one of her slats down on a cockroach.

'There's another!' Brenda chased it into the corridor.

'I've got it.' Lynne lifted a pile of sacks. Sitting, staring up at her through small, black, beady eyes was a rat. She screamed, and the girls came running. 'It's a rat,' she cried as soon as she found her voice.

'Mrs Harvey,' Brenda cried. 'Mrs Harvey!'

'It's a bloody great big rat. It's got teeth,' Lynne shrieked, as the housekeeper came running.

*   *   *

Ruth picked her way elegantly through the chaos of tables, chairs and flower garlands that littered the foyer.

'Your lilies have arrived, miss.' Mrs Harvey pointed to a pile of long white boxes.

'Good.' Ruth removed three packets from her handbag. 'Zinc oxide, lithopone and ultramarine.' She handed the envelopes to the housekeeper. 'You divide the flowers into three batches, one for each colour, then let them stand in the dye for twelve hours so the colours come up through the stem and into the petals. Is that clear enough? Or should I write it down?'

'No, that's fine, miss.'

'Then what are you standing about for? Get it done.'

Mrs Harvey called to a porter to carry the boxes as Ruth walked away. Marcus met her at the foot of the stairs.

'We should have hired staff in for the day,' she complained. 'It's written all over their faces. Insolence. But if we'd cancelled because of that girl's hanging, it would have been an admission of guilt. As if the Grand were somehow to blame. And, as you keep telling me, the Grand comes before everything.'

'Ruth, calm down.' He folded his arms around her. 'Let me take you to lunch.'

'Excuse me, Mr Bannerman, Miss Manning,' Mr Collins interrupted. 'It's a tradition that the staff hold a collection when a member of the family gets married . . .'

'Judging by their mood you might raise all of two shillings,' Marcus commented drily.

'Obviously, it won't be a great sum. I was wondering if you'd like to choose something?'

'Tell them to keep their money,' Ruth snapped.

'It is tradition,' Mr Collins insisted politely.

'But it's not a traditional wedding, is it? I mean a present from the staff – it supposes some great romance, as if bride and groom are going to spend the rest of their lives together and Marcus and I have made it clear that we're under no such illusion. It's more of an experiment. Nothing to do with love, or any of that nonsense. It's just a wedding, that's all. Just a wedding.' She stopped, realising that she'd said far more than she'd intended. 'If you'll excuse me.' She ran on into the Reading Room.

'Have you seen John, Marcus?' Sarah asked as she walked down the stairs.

'In the office. And I'm fine, thanks for asking,' Marcus called after her.

'Sorry.' She turned back. 'How are you?'

'Excellent. Just think – this time tomorrow I'll be married. I'll be . . . safe.'

He wandered away, seemingly happier than Sarah had seen him in months.

John replaced the telephone receiver as Sarah walked in on him.

'You won't believe this. We've got people asking to book into the murder suite.'

'Stephen didn't come home again last night.'

'I'll speak to him—'

'When you've got the time,' she broke in acidly.

'It's not my fault. Ever since this story hit the headlines, takings have been down. I've got to find some way of recovering the profits before the year's end. Perhaps the murder suite is not such a bad idea.'

'Twelve months ago, we worked every hour God sent to get this place open. If I'd known it would mean this — not seeing one another from one day to the next . . .'

'If I can just reach the New Year.'

'You said that last year.'

'It will get better. Once Monica's gone, and everyone stops talking about her . . .'

'John, you make the poor girl sound like an inconvenience.'

'I didn't mean—'

'Think of where she is now.'

'Yes.' He reached for the telephone. 'I've got to make some calls.'

'All right. Are you going out for this drink with Marcus tonight?'

'I better had. I'm his best man.'

'I thought you would. Marcus gets everyone's time. I wish I had that talent.'

John looked after her as she went. More than anything, he wanted to spend time with her — a few more weeks. That's all he needed — a few more weeks. Reluctantly, he dialled for the operator and lifted the receiver to his ear.

Lynne and Brenda wheeled a trolley full of flowers and vases past the painters whitewashing the corridors, into the service bay.

'That bloke in the papers last week,' Brenda whispered in an awed voice. 'You know, that lad down the mines. Awful way to die, much worse than hanging.'

Too preoccupied to take in what Brenda was saying, Lynne picked up one of the packets Ruth had given to Mrs Harvey. Squinting at the directions on the back, she read, '"Verboten". That's German that is! Miss-high-and-mighty-Manning has gone and bought German pigment. I'm not touching that.'

The Grand

'His mates were larking about,' Brenda continued, still trying to gain Lynne's attention. 'They pulled his trousers down and put an air hose up his bum. An air-pressure hose. Forty pounds a square inch. Straight up him. He blew up dead. Hanging's a luxury compared to that.'

'What are you talking about?' Mrs Harvey thundered from the doorway.

'Nothing,' Lynne bit back defiantly.

'I've told you I don't want Monica Jones mentioned. Not once. Not ever! Understood? Think of those soldiers killed in Dublin! Save your sympathy for them, not that little whore.'

The back door opened, and Kate walked in. Unpinning her hat, the maid looked at the housekeeper to let her know she'd heard what she'd called Monica. She turned and walked on down to her room.

Dropping the sachet on to the trolley, Lynne went to follow her.

'Where are you going?' Mrs Harvey demanded imperiously.

'To see if she's all right.'

'Back to work.'

Glaring at the housekeeper, Lynne flounced back to the trolley.

Clive left the bottle bay, where he'd been stacking crates, and headed for the staff dormitories. He stared at the housekeeper as he turned the corner, daring her to stop him.

Taking note of the set expression on his face, Mrs Harvey thought better of the idea. Instead, she vented the anger she would like to have expended on Clive on the maids.

'Do your jobs, all of you!' she barked.

Lynne watched her retreat into her office. Studying

the bottles ranged under the sink, she quite deliberately picked up the largest, unscrewed the top and began pouring the contents into the vases.

'That's disinfectant, that is.'

'And if they were hanging a lady, oh then we'd have to stop, Brenda.' She replaced the bottle under the sink, opened the boxes of lilies and began shoving them into the disinfectant-filled vases. 'We'd have to show respect then.'

'You never liked Monica Jones.'

'Still don't. But I don't like what they're doing to her, either. You with me?'

Brenda reached for another box of lilies. Tearing it open, she joined Lynne in pushing them into the disinfectant.

Kate walked into her room, tossed her bag on to her bed and looked around. She picked up her pillow and punched it soundly with her closed fist before throwing it down in frustration.

'You all right, Kate?' Clive asked through the open doorway.

'I wish I'd done it. They don't search you, not properly, and you can take food in. I should have done it.'

'What?'

'Poison. That stuff we use in the sluice, microlene, that's poison. I could have baked it in bread or something. Put her out of her misery.'

'Only one more day . . .'

'Oh that's supposed to help is it?'

He walked into the room and sat on her bed. 'Come here.' She looked at him before sitting next to him. 'How was she?' He hugged her close.

'She looked about twelve.'

The Grand

Stephen looked in through the door. Seeing them together, he stepped back. 'Sorry.'

Kate moved away from Clive and went to the chest of drawers. 'Excuse me, I've got to work.'

'I've only just got in,' Stephen explained. 'I meant to see you before you went. How was she?'

'You can read it in the papers. Now if you don't mind, I've got to get into me uniform. You can pay half a crown and watch, or get out.'

Clive waited for Stephen to make the first move. Kate closed the door behind him.

'She doesn't need bothering,' Clive said resolutely as he followed Stephen down the corridor.

'Then what were you doing?'

Clive didn't answer. Ignoring Stephen, he darted past him, back towards the cellars.

Adele squinted down, trying to see her reflection in the sideboard mirror as she stood to attention in her bridesmaid's dress. Sarah knelt before her, pinning the hem up another inch.

'I should have thought,' Adele moaned. 'Little girls dress up as bridesmaids. I'm going to look ridiculous.'

'It's more of a cocktail dress,' Mary criticised from the depths of the armchair next to the fire. 'I'm not sure it's suitable for church.'

'If you'd like to get on your knees and alter it, I've got plenty of other things I could be doing,' Sarah griped, beginning to wonder if Mary ever approved of anything.

'Is Marcus around?' Stephen asked from the corridor.

Sarah looked at him in despair. 'Stephen, have you slept in those clothes?'

'I spent the night at George's. I'll clean up in a minute. Uncle Marcus?'

'He's in the study, why?'

'Nothing. Someone was looking for him, that's all.'

'You'd be far more worried if your son spent every night at home without any friends,' Mary declared as Stephen left.

Sarah averted her eyes from her mother-in-law, and looked back at the dress. Jabbing a pin into the hem, she only wished she could push it into a delicate part of Mary's anatomy.

Marcus was on the telephone when Stephen broke in on him. He quickly wrapped up the conversation.

'Right, get it done by the end of the day.' Replacing the receiver, he looked questioningly at his nephew.

'Could I have a word?' Marcus sat back and waited for Stephen to begin. 'At the year's end, Dad gets all the statements from the bank. Not just the monthly accounts, everything. And I had that account, the money Grandfather left me. Four hundred pounds . . .' His voice trailed in embarrassment.

'And you've spent it.' It wasn't a question.

'Yes. It's my account. It should be confidential. But that's what happens when the bank manager's a friend of the family. Dad gets told.'

'What's this got to do with me?'

'If I could borrow some money . . .'

'Four hundred pounds.'

'Or part of it. I'll pay you back.'

Marcus left his chair and loomed over his nephew. Stephen backed away.

'He was my father as well. He worked all his life to save that money, then you throw it away . . .'

'I'll pay it back.'

The Grand

Pushing his fingers into Stephen's chest, Marcus shoved him against the wall. 'How?'

'I will,' Stephen protested uneasily.

'How?' Marcus repeated, shoving him again.

'Get off . . .'

'Four hundred pounds.' He pushed him again as though to emphasise the amount. 'Wasted!' He shoved him again. 'Am I supposed to find that funny?' He forced Stephen into a corner. 'Am I supposed to tolerate that, just like my brother?'

'Get off me.' Stephen finally pushed back.

'That's more like it. That's the first thing you've done for yourself since you returned from the war.'

'Look, if the answer's no, just say so.'

'As from tomorrow, I'm a married man, living here, more a part of this family than I ever intended. And if you think I'm happy to live with a drunk and a liar, you're quite mistaken. Your father puts up with it. He's spineless – he doesn't dare say anything that might upset you. I'm not like him.'

'I'll find the money somewhere else.'

'Ask him. Go on, ask your father.'

'I can't.'

Marcus sat back in his chair, pressed his fingertips together and looked at him. 'If I give you the money, there's something you'll have to do in return.'

'What?'

'Are you coming for a drink tonight?'

'If you want.'

'I'll show you then. But remember: I'm not doing it for you. Nor for John. It's for your mother. Call it a wedding present. I'll see you tonight, eight o'clock.'

'Thank you,' Stephen replied apprehensively, as he left the room.

* * *

'Harkness,' Olive whispered theatrically to Kate, Lynne and Brenda as they sorted linen in the service bay in the guest corridor.

Esme walked past a few moments later, quieter, more subdued than she had been when she had first arrived at the Grand.

'Good afternoon, girls.'

Lynne and Brenda mumbled 'afternoon' after she'd passed by.

'She's worn that dress three times now,' Olive hissed.

'So?' Brenda threw a sheet into the soiled-linen bin.

'So, it's cost her, paying for Monica.'

'Loose change to her,' Lynne said scathingly.

'You might not like her, but fair dos, she's the only one in this hotel that's done Monica proud,' Brenda said defensively.

Kate looked up and saw Esme walk into her room. Convinced that Esme had waited, just to hear what the maids were saying about her, Kate slammed down the pile of linen she was holding and ran furiously up to her door.

'Kate, we've got the coal to shift . . .'

Ignoring Olive, she opened Esme's door and walked straight into the room.

'Kate.' Esme smiled as though she'd been expecting a social call from the maid. 'Have you been to see Monica? I didn't like to ask in front of the girls. How is she?'

'Praising you to the stars. Since you paid for her defence, and keep paying, even now, the day before she's hanged.'

'No one knows who paid.'

'But you let us think it's you, don't you? You heard

the girls just then, and you loved it. Holding your head up high, all proud and wounded, like you've done your best.'

'Someone had to pay. The poor girl had nothing . . .'

'*It wasn't you!*' Kate screamed at the top of her voice.

'No one knows . . .'

'I know. I know who bloody well paid, and it wasn't you, Miss Harkness.'

'Then who was it?'

'I wouldn't tell you. You led her there. You led her to the gallows. You, with your talk of ladies and gentlemen and the finer things in life. But when she needs help, you weren't there, not with one penny.'

'I would have. I couldn't afford . . . I did try . . . I swear I did . . .'

'You haven't even visited her. Not once,' Kate continued to rage. 'She's dying tomorrow, Miss Harkness. She's swinging by the neck, but you can't dirty yourself by going to her cell.'

Esme broke down. Her sobs were genuine, but mixed in with her remorse was the hope that the sight of her tears might silence Kate.

'I can't. It is my fault. Do you think I don't know that? If I'd been here that night – if she'd listened – listened to the things I'd said, instead of hearing what she wanted to hear . . .'

'Oh, so it's her fault now?'

'No.'

'I know why you can't go. The same reason you ran away from London.'

'What do you know,' Esme shouted angrily. 'You're nothing. You're a servant, you'll stay a servant all your life. At least Monica could think . . .'

'But it keeps catching up with you, Miss Harkness.'

Kate's voice was ominously soft. 'It keeps happening because you make it happen.'

'Get out of my room.'

'Killing your kids, that's part of a prostitute's job. Having one abortion after another. How many children did you have ripped out and burnt? No wonder you left London. Every back street and alley must be like a graveyard. And now there's another one. The girl you dressed up as a daughter, as if she could replace them, now she's dying, the same as all your kids. And you killed them, you killed them all.' Trembling, exhausted by anger, Kate finally ran out, dashing past Lynne, Brenda and Olive, who'd been eavesdropping outside the door.

Lynne looked into the room. Esme was standing next to the bed, crying. She looked up and saw the girls.

'Leave me *alone*!' She strode to the door and slammed it in their faces. Sinking down on to the bed, she struggled to draw breath, but she couldn't help wondering if there was anything left in her life to make the effort worthwhile.

Chapter Twenty-Four

'The Grand Hotel has no comment to make,' Marcus said flatly down the telephone as Sarah walked into the study. 'Whatever our thoughts on the execution, it's business as usual.' He hung up the receiver and looked at her.

'The wine's arrived for the reception.'

'This is the last time I get married,' he quipped. He knew that he should go and check the delivery, but he sensed that Sarah wanted to talk.

'You were both alike in some ways. You and Monica.'

'What? Both condemned to a terrible fate tomorrow morning?' he suggested glibly.

'Both ambitious and dangerous.'

'I had the advantage. If she'd been a man she would have got everything she wanted.'

'I think that's a bit romantic.'

'I'm a very romantic man.'

'Marcus, did you pay for her defence?' she asked outright.

'What on earth makes you think that?'

'You did that favour for Mr Collins.'

'You're not supposed to know about that.'

'Why? Because it's bad for your image?'

He laughed. 'Some charity must have paid for Monica's defence. The Fabians, or the Bolsheviks.'

'But they'd want to advertise their cause.'

'True. But it wasn't me. First and foremost, I'm a businessman. The Grand has suffered enough scandal. If the press discovered that a member of the Bannerman family helped that girl, we'd be closed within days.'

'A lot of people supported her.'

'Not the sort of people who stay here.'

'All the more reason to keep it secret.'

'You're determined to prove your point. If it had been me, I'd have succeeded.'

'You might yet. There's still the chance of a reprieve.' She looked earnestly into his eyes. 'It shouldn't be a secret. Whoever paid for Monica's defence deserves to be thanked.'

'It's enough that you think me capable of such an act. I had no idea that you thought so well of me.'

'It's a surprise to me, too.'

Taking her hand and kissing it, he finally went to the door.

Kate was sitting alone in her room when Collins knocked and opened her door.

'Kate, Mr Bannerman would like to see you.'

'Tell him to sod off.'

'He deserves to know how she is after all he's done.'

'Not now. Not today. I hate it, Mr Collins. Going upstairs to report back like I'm a spy. I went to see Monica because I *wanted* to see her. Not for him.' For the first time since she'd left the cell she started to cry. 'What can I tell him? She's seventeen . . .'

'All right.' Collins put his arm around her, allowing her to bury her head in his shoulder so she wouldn't see his own tears. 'It's all right, Kate.'

'They're killing her, Mr Collins. Killing her dead.

The Grand

Tomorrow morning at eight o'clock. And she's only seventeen years old.'

'Of course, you're new,' Olive crowed to a young girl, airing her few weeks' experience. 'You weren't here when it happened. I was Monica's replacement, I was. I'm sleeping in her bed. And I was told that when you get hanged all your guts fall out.'

'Right,' Mrs Harvey's voice barked angrily from the doorway. 'That's it! I've told you a hundred times, that girl's name is not to be mentioned. Not in fit company.'

'It's not just me, Mrs Harvey. They're singing songs about her in the music halls.'

'Get your room cleared by six, then come for your wages. You're out.'

'Mrs Harvey.' Collins walked out of the cellar where he'd been supervising the barmen. 'She didn't mean any harm . . .'

'I'm in charge of the girls, Mr Collins.'

'Mrs Harvey,' he repeated in a sterner tone.

Taking a deep breath, she walked ahead of him into her office, watching as he closed the door, but both of them knew that the staff would be listening outside.

'My decision stands. She's out. You don't have authority over me.'

'You're in charge of the household, I'm in charge of the entire hotel. We've never made a proper distinction between our jobs, perhaps it's time we did.'

'Mr Collins, I give my life to this hotel. And when the day comes for me to retire, what will people remember? All my hard work? No, just one name, one girl. Monica Jones.'

'Oh, for God's sake, Sylvie, if only you'd stop and think. You knew the girl. Have some pity.'

'She was a murderous little slut.'

'She was raped, woman. She was defending herself.'

'She knew what she was doing. She went to that room of her own free will.'

'It wasn't just intercourse. They did things. Things they couldn't print in the paper. They . . . ripped her. It was butchery.'

'Did she murder Jackson Tyler?' she demanded coldly.

'No girl could expect to—'

'Did she kill him?'

'Yes,' he conceded grudgingly.

'Then she deserves it. And if you'll pardon my saying, Mr Collins, you're not without bias. You've had one of your own family put to death, and I'm sorry for that. I'm sorry, but it doesn't make the sentence wrong, not for everyone. Now either Olive Clegg is out, or I'm going, and if you want to go upstairs and tell the family that the housekeeper has walked out the day before the wedding, you're very welcome. Now which is it to be?'

Taking his silence as a token of her victory, Mrs Harvey went to the door, opened it and looked at Olive, who was sitting on a bench being comforted by Lynne and Brenda.

'Pack your things,' she ordered abruptly before striding away.

Collins walked out of the office behind her. Straightening his back, he looked at the assembled staff, but he reserved his most sympathetic look for Olive.

'You did what you could, sir,' Clive acknowledged gratefully.

The concierge nodded, before following Mrs Harvey into the foyer.

*　　*　　*

The Grand

'Stephen can lead the way,' Marcus shouted to the crowd of men assembled in the bar. 'He knows every pub within a ten-mile radius, and owes money in all of them.'

'I'll see you tomorrow, I hope.' Ruth gave Marcus a tight, brittle smile.

'Stay here tonight with me?' He put his arm around her. 'Surely you don't believe all that superstition about not meeting in the morning?'

'Best not to tempt fate. We've got all the bad luck we need already.'

Wishing she would stop tormenting herself, he kissed her goodbye and turned to the men.

'Come on, you pack of scroungers. Stephen, where's your father?'

'I don't know. Busy?'

'Busy, busy, busy . . .' Marcus shook his head as he led the way into the foyer.

Esme Harkness stood back as the warder unlocked the door for her. Motioning her through, the guard waited while she gathered what was left of her courage and stepped inside.

'Place your bag on the table, miss.'

Esme reluctantly handed it over, resenting the indignity of having her personal possessions rifled through by a stranger. The warder pushed the visitors' book towards her and she signed her name. Gathering up her bag, Esme followed the warder down a long, stone-lined corridor, feeling as though she'd stumbled into hell.

Miss Roberts, the senior warder in charge of the death cells, met her at the next door.

'I'm afraid someone's just going in now. If you'd care to wait, Miss . . . ?'

'Harkness. Miss Harkness,' Esme repeated. She glanced into the stone-lined waiting room Miss Roberts was showing her into. 'I'm sorry. I'm really very sorry. Don't . . . don't tell her I was here.'

She turned and ran. Tears fell from her eyes, hot, blinding, as she fled back towards the area where her bag had been searched.

Monica was sitting at the table in her day room playing cards with one of the warders. She looked up expectantly as the door opened. Miss Roberts walked in.

'You've got a visitor.' She glanced out into the corridor.

Monica sat and waited while the warder cleared the cards from the table, and vacated the chair.

'Is it me solicitor?' Monica asked impatiently. 'Is it good news?'

'I've heard nothing yet. The governor will let us know.' Miss Roberts moved aside as John Bannerman walked into the cell.

'Mr Bannerman,' Monica cried out in surprise.

'Hello, Monica.' He sat in the chair opposite hers.

Motioning to the third guard in the room, Miss Roberts left them with only one warder.

'It was you, wasn't it? You paid for my defence,' Monica said suddenly.

'It was my hotel. You were my guest, my staff. I've devoted everything to the Grand. I have to accept responsibility. Even for this.'

'It wasn't your fault, sir.'

'It's my hotel.' He looked at her intently. 'I haven't told anyone, not even my wife. So, if it is discovered, I can take the blame on my own. The Grand could carry on with Sarah and my brother. They'd manage without me.'

'So why have you come now, sir?' One look at his face was enough to tell her why. 'It hasn't worked, has it? The letter.'

'We've tried everything,' he conceded wretchedly.

'They're going to hang me.'

'All day I've been trying think of something else we can do.'

'It's all right, sir. There's nothing to say.'

The door opened and Miss Roberts walked back into the cell, quietly taking her place by the door.

'I know what you wanted, Monica. Your ambitions. And if it helps – if it gives you, I don't know, comfort, I suppose – the Grand Hotel is one of the finest buildings in one of the greatest cities on God's earth. You were a part of it. Only a few precious days above stairs, but that's more than most girls have in their whole life. You made it.'

'Did I?'

'For the rest of my days, I'll remember how you looked. A lady.'

'I wasn't. I was pretending.'

'Monica, they're all pretending. And when all those other women are gone and forgotten, you'll be remembered. Not in the way you wanted, but you will be remembered.'

Tears fell from her eyes, hitting the unvarnished surface of the table and bouncing like raindrops. 'I'm going to die.' The magnitude of her statement sank in. She stared at him in horror. 'Oh God! Oh my God!'

John left his chair and moved around to her side of the table. He held her in the way he had held Catherine, Stephen and Adele when they had been children.

'I don't want to die.'

'I'm sorry, sir.' Miss Roberts stepped forwards. 'You have to stay in your chair . . .'

John didn't even look at her. Shaking her head, Miss Roberts withdrew, every bit as distressed as he was, but far more practised at concealing her emotions.

'Can't you do anything, sir?' Monica begged.

'I tried. I did try.'

'Please, sir. *Please*.'

He did the only thing left to him. He continued to hold her.

'This isn't a bad place,' Marcus commented to Stephen as he looked around the nightclub. Furnished in a more up-to-the-minute, fashionable style than the Grand, a style that wouldn't wear more than a season or two, it boasted white-jacketed waiters, palm trees, and non-stop music. 'They make fifty quid at the bar on a good night. But it could do better.'

'You know a lot about it.'

'I should. It's mine. I own it, and it needs a manager. What do you think? It's hard work. I want the profits doubled. Let me down and I'll sack you.'

'I . . . I don't know.' The offer took Stephen completely by surprise.

'Right, I'll find someone else.'

'No. It's just . . . not what I imagined myself doing.'

'Your father certainly wouldn't like it. Mind you, he disapproves of everything. He hasn't even turned up tonight in case it's a bit too wild. But he thinks you'll find your way back to the Grand like a lost dog. Perhaps he's right.'

The picture Marcus painted of his future in the hotel had the desired effect.

'I'll do it.'

'Don't give me an answer now.'

The Grand

'I'll do it. I will. Thank you.'
Marcus held out his hand and they shook on it.

Clive walked down the dormitory corridor. Stopping outside Kate's room, he looked through the open doorway. Kate was standing next to the bed, still dressed.

'You all right?' he asked tentatively.

'Yes.'

Her abrupt answer put an end to any thoughts Clive had of walking in. He smiled at her, a smile she didn't even see, then left.

Sinking down on to her bed, Kate reached beneath it and pulled out Monica's dress. She held it close, wrapped her arms around it and lay back on her pillow.

She lay there all night, holding the dress, watching and waiting for the dawn. When morning came she was still awake, staring up at the skylight, hugging the dress. Looking down she stroked it, and continued to wait.

Monica sat at her table, ready, dressed. She looked up as the door opened. Miss Roberts walked in followed by the governor, a white-coated doctor, the prison chaplain and two male warders.

Panicking, knowing why they'd come, Monica pushed back her chair. It scraped noisily over the flagstones.

'It's not yet,' she pleaded. 'It's not eight o'clock. It's not yet, it's not . . .'

No one said a word. One of the warders walked behind her chair. Helping her to her feet, he swiftly tied her hands together behind her back. She made no attempt to fight him, only repeated, 'It's not yet . . .' as the doctor walked up. Standing alongside the warder behind her, he rolled up her sleeve and injected her with morphine. She barely felt the needle.

The chaplain came closer, and for the first time Monica was aware that he was reciting the burial service.

'I am the resurrection and the life, saith the Lord; he that believeth in me, though he were dead, yet shall he live; and whosoever liveth and believeth in me shall never die. I know that my redeemer liveth and that he shall stand at the latter day upon the earth . . .'

Miss Roberts opened the door, then both she and the governor went out into the corridor. The two warders placed Monica between them and followed, the doctor and the chaplain bringing up the rear.

Monica stared at the back of Miss Roberts's dress as they walked towards the door at the end of the corridor. It was cut from a coarse, woollen cloth, so very different from the silks she had loved. She could feel tears rolling down her cheeks, but she couldn't even reach up to wipe them away. The chaplain's voice continued to drone behind her, '. . . thou hast set our misdeeds before thee, and secret sins in the light of thy countenance. For when thou art angry, all our days are gone; we bring our years to an end, as it were a tale that is told . . .'

The door opened, Miss Roberts and the governor walked through.

'Turn thee again, O Lord, at the last, and be gracious unto thy servants. Oh satisfy us with thy mercy, and that soon; so shall we rejoice and be glad; all the days of our life . . .'

The warders gently laid their hands on her bound arms and helped her through the doorway. She looked up and saw the gallows above her, fashioned from strong, planed wood. Not at all what she had expected.

The Grand

Her tears became sobs.

'I'm sorry,' she cried. 'I'm sorry . . .'

The warders tightened their grip on her arms, giving her all the help she needed to keep walking, slowly, inexorably, towards the gallows. Still not wanting to believe what was happening, she didn't struggle, or try to fight them. Her eyes filled with tears again, blinding her as they reached the wooden steps.

'. . . now I say this brethren, that flesh and blood cannot inherit the kingdom of God; neither doth corruption inherit incorruption. Behold, I show you a mystery. We shall not all sleep, but we shall all be changed, in a moment, in the twinkling of an eye, at the last trump; for the trumpet shall sound, and the dead shall be raised incorruptible, and we shall be changed . . .'

Paralysed with terror, Monica stood stock still when she reached the platform. The executioner pulled a hood over her face. She felt the noose slipping over the cloth . . . she felt him adjusting the knot below her left ear . . .

As the hands on the clock in the servants' hall moved towards eight o'clock, the bustle in the staff quarters slowed to a snail's pace. Lynne, Brenda and Clive stood silently in front of the table, watching the seconds tick away. As the other maids walked into the service area they laid down their things and joined them. Mrs Harvey saw what was happening; choosing not to interfere, she went to her office.

Brenda murmured a prayer, an old childhood one that they all knew. But no one joined in. They only bowed their heads and waited.

Mrs Harvey sat behind her desk and looked at her

watch. Staring straight ahead, she remembered the girl, but denied her any sympathy, telling herself that no decent woman could possibly feel any compassion for a murderer and a whore.

Mr Collins had dressed for duty, but he lingered in his room. Sitting on his bed he stared at his watch, holding vigil and waiting, his thoughts not only with Monica, but also his son.

Alone in her room, Esme cried bitterly. Distraught with guilt, remorse and misery, she had never felt so totally isolated and abandoned in her life. But her tears were more for herself than Monica.

John left his bedroom in his dressing gown. He went to the window in the living room and stared at the town clock. As the hands crept towards eight he became aware of Sarah standing at his side. She looked at him as the first chime struck, amazed to see that he was crying.

She held him close. She felt that she had never known him less than she did at this moment.

The clock struck the second chime.

'She's at rest now, John,' she murmured.

Miss Roberts stepped back as the sound of the lever being pulled filled the air. The floor disappeared beneath the slight, slender, hooded figure.

Monica's body swung like a pendulum over the drop.

'Man that is born of woman hath but a short time to live, and is full of misery. He cometh up, and is cut down, like a flower; he fleeth as it were a shadow, and never continueth in one stay.' The last chimes

The Grand

of the clock echoed into the chamber as the doctor
pulled out his stethoscope and moved towards the
corpse.

Chapter Twenty-Five

As soon as the first cars were sighted, the staff were ordered into the foyer and lined up by Mrs Harvey and Mr Collins, ready to greet the bridal couple. The maids had been provided with new black uniforms, white aprons and caps for the occasion. Holding small envelopes of confetti issued by the housekeeper – one to each girl – they waited until Marcus and Ruth walked in through the doors, before showering them with multicoloured paper petals.

They made it clear by the miserable expressions on their faces that none of them wanted to be there, and it wasn't only Lynne and Brenda who took care to see that most of their confetti ended up wasted on the floor.

As the guests filed in through the doors behind them, Marcus took Ruth in his arms and kissed her. With the sound of applause ringing in her ears, Ruth moved back. Chilled by the impassive expression on Marcus's face, she trembled, suddenly afraid. Sarah had warned her, everyone who knew Marcus well had warned her. So why had she agreed to marry the man?

Collins shepherded the staff into the bar, ordering them to pick up their trays of champagne. For the first time in the history of the hotel, the maids worked

The Grand

alongside the footmen in handing out drinks to the guests. The light, melodic sound of a waltz drifted out of the ballroom as guests queued to offer Marcus their congratulations.

'How was it, sir?' the concierge asked John.

'The perfect wedding, Jacob. A sadist marrying a masochist.'

'And how are you?'

'I'm all right. Thank you.'

'No, sir. Thank you.'

Ruth cornered Mrs Harvey in the Reading Room. 'I thought I told you, no confetti. When a barrow boy marries a milkmaid, that's when you throw confetti.'

'Your husband told me,' the housekeeper replied defensively.

Ruth saw the flowers for the first time. White with anger, she pointed to them. 'Roses?' she questioned icily.

'I found the lilies dead this morning. I went to the market, first thing—'

'I suppose it's bloody useless to even try.' Turning, she saw a guest watching her. 'Elizabeth.' She smiled graciously, acting the happy bride for all she was worth. 'When did you arrive? Father would love to see you.'

Taking care to avoid Ruth, Lynne and Brenda wove their way through the crowd, conscientiously guarding their trays of champagne against the movements of the guests.

'It's cruelty,' Lynne complained. 'Where's the League of Nations when you need it? We should be in mourning, Brenda.'

'We're wearing black.'

'And you know why we're here, don't you? Why we're allowed in the foyer? It's that Miss Manning . . .'

'Mrs Bannerman,' Brenda corrected.

'Whatever, it's her. Because she thinks we're dirt. Having a bit of dirt around makes her look posh.'

Mary found Ruth in the crowd and kissed her on the cheek.

'Congratulations. Strange little service, rather modern I thought. Certainly not in my translation of the Bible.'

'Have you seen what uncle Marcus has bought Ruth?' Adele asked. 'It's a car. It's parked outside. It's amazing.'

'It almost didn't arrive,' Marcus said, smiling absently and putting his arm around Ruth. 'I spent yesterday on the phone tracking it down.'

'It's for both of us,' Ruth explained to Mary and Adele. 'And I can't drive.'

Kate stole into the foyer from the servants' corridor. Dressed in the same black uniform as the rest of the maids, she kept her head down as she collected empty glasses and stacked them on to a tray.

'What are you doing here?' Lynne asked.

'Mrs Harvey said.'

'I'll tell her, frosty bitch.'

'Lynne, don't,' Kate begged. 'At least this gives me something to do.'

Lynne went to the bar, where Clive was filling up Brenda's tray.

'They've only got Kate Morris back in shackles,' she fumed. 'I could heave. I really could.'

'Take these over there.' Clive laid a couple of glasses

on to her tray. 'The woman in blue, Mr and Mrs Rattigan.'

'Oh aye, I'll give them their drinks.' Turning to the bar so no guest could see what she was up to, she spat in both glasses.

'Lynne!' Brenda gazed at her in disbelief.

'They're all frothy. They won't see. They're dancing on Monica's grave. All of them.'

'Go on, then,' Clive said, smiling broadly, just as angry about Kate as her. 'I'm not stopping you.'

'Spit and polish, that's all they want from us. Well I've polished the floor. Now they can have the spit.' She waltzed out of the bar, smirking. 'Mr and Mrs Rattigan?' she stood before their table. 'Your drinks.'

As they took them, Lynne turned and gave Clive and Brenda a triumphant thumbs-up sign.

'I don't know what's so different about a nightclub,' John protested to Stephen. 'You might as well work here.'

'It's a better job. More freedom.'

'Freedom from what?'

'The Grand Hotel,' Stephen replied cuttingly, looking his father directly in the eye.

'It might be just what he needs,' Sarah said smoothly, coming to Stephen's defence as she took John's arm.

'Perhaps.' Surrendering to Sarah's attempts at peacekeeping, John kept his voice low. 'But I wish you'd talked it through with me first.'

'I will. I'll make an appointment,' Stephen retorted tartly, wanting to hurt his father.

'What have I done?' John turned helplessly to Sarah, as Stephen joined Marcus and Ruth. 'He can't talk to me without biting my head off.'

'I've told you often enough,' she murmured patiently.

'If you devoted some time to him instead of the Grand . . .'

'Oh for God's sake. He's a grown man.'

'Yes, and he grew up on the front line.' She looked at Stephen as he stood next to Marcus, and her heart went out to him.

'Just as you'd expect, he's livid,' Stephen griped to Marcus. 'And I know him: give him two days and he moves on to "disappointment". I can't wait.'

Lynne appeared at his side. Without even looking at her, he dumped his empty glass on her tray and took a full one.

'I didn't know you owned a club,' Ruth commented as Marcus exchanged both their glasses.

'Well, that's marriage: a voyage of discovery. Enjoy it. Cheers.'

They all raised their glasses and took a sip. Moving behind their backs Lynne gave another thumbs-up sign to Clive and Brenda. Mrs Harvey swooped down on her.

'Take that grin off your face.'

'Sorry, Mrs Harvey, just enjoying meself. Do you want one?' Lynne offered her the last full glass on her tray.'

'I'm not allowed.'

'Shame. You deserve it.'

'Kate, you shouldn't be working,' Stephen sympathised, when he saw her taking coats from some late arrivals.

'I'm all right.'

'Don't be ridiculous. Take the afternoon off. Tell them I gave you permission.'

'You're not management.'

'All the same . . .'

'Could you leave me alone please?' she requested testily. 'I've got a job to do.'

'Kate, don't be like that.'

'Excuse me, Mr Bannerman.' Clive stepped between Stephen and Kate. 'I think Kate wants to be left alone.'

'Thank you, Clive. I can fight my own battles.' Aware that Mrs Harvey was watching her, Kate took the coats and went to the cloakroom.

'Go on, then. Get me a drink,' Stephen ordered Clive.

'Don't know if that's wise, sir.' Clive managed to make the last word sound like an insult.

'What do you mean?'

'Judging by past experience, you can't handle it.' The barman turned on his heel.

'Don't walk away from me . . .' Furious, Stephen ran after him into the corridor, his anger blinding him to the fact that Clive was deliberately leading him away from the crowd.

'Don't turn your back on me,' he shouted.

'What's that? An order?' Clive squared up to him.

'If you like.'

'Make up your mind. One minute you're our friend, the next minute you're in charge.'

'You're so bloody smart, aren't you? No wonder you came back without a scratch. Sitting there, safe at your post, laughing and joking, while the rest of us fought.'

'I did my duty . . .'

'What, in the Gunners? Don't make me laugh. We lost a dozen men when we came under fire. From British shells. That's how well you did your job.'

It was one taunt too many. Clive lunged at him.

Stephen was ready and waiting. Grabbing the barman, he pushed him back through the door into the foyer.

The crowd scattered as the two men exchanged punches. Collins and John pushed their way through the crowd to break up the fight.

'Your family?' Ruth looked to Marcus.

'Obviously,' Marcus replied, 'they understand the spirit of this wedding very well indeed.' And he smiled coldly.

Thrusting Stephen and Clive apart, Collins and John led them away from the guests, towards the office.

'Calm down,' John ordered abruptly, as his son leaned against the wall.

'It was my fault,' Stephen said flatly, still glaring at Clive.

'Clive, go downstairs,' Collins directed.

'I started it. Not him,' Stephen protested.

'Get the wine ready for the meal,' Collins ordered in a marginally friendlier tone. 'Just get out of sight.'

'Sorry, sir.' Clive scowled at Stephen before opening the door that led to the servants' corridor.

'Stephen, what happened?' Sarah asked as she joined them.

'Nothing. Absolutely nothing.' He gave her a strained smile. 'I'm having the time of my life,' he lied unconvincingly, as he returned to the party.

Kate had picked up her tray to collect more glasses when Mrs Harvey confronted her.

'Go on, get to your room.'

'What have I done?'

'They were fighting over you, and you know it. Go on.'

418

Biting her lip, Kate did as she was told.

Lynne ran to Brenda.

'Did you see that? Kate's got the blame! It's a bleeding liberty the way we're treated . . .'

'We shouldn't put up with it. I'm that upset . . .'

Seeing Kate heading for the lift, Stephen pushed past the people crossing the foyer.

'Kate . . .'

She cut him dead as she stepped inside. He followed. The doors closed on them.

'I'm sorry,' he apologised contritely as soon as they were alone.

'I wouldn't recognise you without a drink in your hand,' she retorted caustically.

He threw the glass he was holding to the floor, smashing it.

'Oh, that's impressive.'

'I thought . . . I thought we were friends.'

'I don't mind friends. I can cope with friends. But you want more than that.'

'And what if I do?' he asked seriously.

The lift arrived at the basement. Kate yanked the door open. The one time she would have welcomed the presence of other people the downstairs area was deserted. She went straight to her room. To her dismay, Stephen followed.

'What's wrong with wanting more?' he pressed.

'What's *wrong*?' She turned on him furiously. 'You've seen what happens when a girl gets above herself. She was hanged this morning.'

'That's not fair.'

'No, it wasn't fair. She was me friend . . . could have been,' she amended despondently.

'I wouldn't treat you the way she was treated.'

'You only like me because I'm staff. Because I'm

below you. You don't have to try. I'm just . . . *here*.
And I like it,' she asserted defiantly. 'I like washing
and scrubbing. That's all I'm good for. I'll stay here
until the day I die. I know that's all I can ever expect
from life, and I don't want anything else. I don't want
the trouble.' She opened the door to her room and
walked inside.

'I'm not asking you to change.'

'But I'd have to. One step towards you and I'd have
to.' Trapped, with nowhere else to go, she finally faced
him. 'You can do better. Find yourself a lady, Stephen.
I'm stopping here. I'm well off, I am. Good job. Good
hotel. Working for your dad. I couldn't do better.'

'Oh, yes? John Bannerman? You worship him?'

'He's a good man.'

'He's an idiot.'

'He is not . . .'

'I know him better than you.'

'You don't.'

Stephen paced furiously around the room. 'It was
his fault. All his fault that I went out there. He was
so bloody proud that I was going to do my duty and
uphold the family name.'

'He was worried sick every day that you were
gone.'

'Anyone can worry. All he does is worry. If I'd
refused to go . . . what would he have said then?'

Silence stole in from the servants' quarters, thick,
unnerving.

'Stephen, I was here. You wanted to go. It wasn't
him.'

His anger turned to tears. Turning his head so she
couldn't see him, he began to cry. Kate watched for a
moment, but as he sank to the floor, she knelt beside
him, reaching out to offer what comfort she could.

The Grand

'It's over. Why don't you let it end?'

He looked into her face. 'Don't you see? Don't you understand? It was *better* out there. It made sense. I want to go back.'

This time he made no attempt to hide his tears. Hugging him, she wished she could do more to help. Then, suddenly, she realised there was something she could do after all.

Sarah sat in the office listening to the distant clamour of the party echoing along the corridor. The sounds of merriment only made her feel all the more despondent when she thought of the estrangement between her husband and her son, and, even worse, the estrangement between John and herself.

'Enjoying yourself?' she asked, as Marcus pushed the door open.

'Very much.'

'It looks wonderful, doesn't it?' She gazed through the glass panel set in the wall in front of her. 'The girls look smart. I don't know why we've got that rule, not allowing them in the foyer.'

'Then change it. You've the power.'

She smiled. Encouraged, he sat beside her.

'Yes, I think I will change it.'

'That's the first decision concerning the Grand Hotel you've made yourself. Congratulations.'

She smiled again, brushing aside a tear as she did so.

'I'm sorry, long day.'

'What's wrong?'

'Nothing. Stephen.'

'And John?'

She didn't answer him, but neither did she deny it.

'It's all right. From now on everything is going to be all right. I've made myself safe, for you.'

She looked at him in bewilderment.

'I'm a married man. I know you'd never leave John, you'd never take the risk. And I won't leave Ruth, I swear it. I'll keep her. So you and I can be together. Safe.'

She stared at him incredulously as Ruth walked in.

'People are asking where you are, though I could have told them. It's hardly a surprise.'

'Get out,' Marcus ordered.

'Not crying, Sarah?' Ruth sniped. 'That's guaranteed to attract him.'

'Ruth, leave us alone.'

'I will not, Marcus.'

'I've married you. What more do you want? Now get out.'

'I think you'll find, now that we're husband and wife, I'm not prepared to put up with this.'

'You've got the ring. You've got the marriage lines. I've done enough. You've got everything you need.'

'And it seems you need me, Marcus . . .'

'I need you for just one thing. You can bear my children. You're good stock. A good investment. And don't you dare complain. You knew the terms of this marriage. You created them. You wanted me, you've got me, it's done. Don't expect anything else.'

Shattered, Ruth stood before both of them, lost for words. Terrified of breaking down in front of Marcus, she finally turned and walked out. Horrified, Sarah pushed past her brother-in-law and fled up the stairs.

Ruth returned to the party. Pushing her way through the crowd, she nodded and smiled at the guests, concealing her pain beneath a veneer of bridal happiness as gossamer thin as her veil, all the while knowing that Marcus was right. She had no one else to blame for her pain other than herself. She had set the terms of their marriage. And now she was caught in a trap of her own making.

Marcus looked after both women as he left the office. There was no choice for him to make: he followed Sarah.

At the top of the stairs, he passed Esme Harkness. Immaculately gowned and jewelled, she slowly descended to the foyer, the barbed comments of the guests meeting her halfway as one or two of them recognised her and passed on her history to their neighbours.

She crossed Lynne and Brenda's path when she reached the ground floor. Both maids stopped and stared. Ignoring them, she headed directly for John. Seeing her coming, he waited.

'Mr Bannerman, am I welcome?' she asked quietly.

He nodded. 'Miss Harkness.'

Esme smiled. Taking a glass of champagne she joined the throng. Head high, she moved among them, desperately trying to lose herself in the crowd.

'It was all her fault,' Lynne declared flatly to Brenda, as she stared after her. 'She led Monica on. And they let her. They *let* her.'

'My mother says we might be in service,' Brenda responded, 'but we've got our rights. They're no better than us. Just richer.'

'She's right. Your mother is right.' Lynne slammed her tray down on the nearest table. 'Come on. We're going.'

As they made their way to the servants' corridor, heads turned to follow their progress. The maid who had been standing closest to them whispered to a footman, who in turn repeated her words to a porter. Slowly, one by one, all the staff laid down their trays and headed for the door.

Mrs Harvey tried to stop Lynne from leaving, but Lynne heaved the door open, and walked on down the corridor. The rest of the staff followed her lead.

'Brenda Potter,' Mrs Harvey hissed, keeping her voice down lest she be heard by the guests. 'Rosie, Janet Birdsall, you just . . . Lucy! Lucy Jenkins! Sidney . . .'

Ignoring her, they all continued walking.

'Mr Collins, have you hired the staff out to another wedding?' Adele asked innocently. 'They all seem to be going.'

'So I'd noticed.'

He continued to watch the proceedings from a distance, making no effort to go to Mrs Harvey's assistance.

Ruth waited until she was alone in the ladies' room. She stared at her reflection in the mirror while carefully teasing out a thick strand of hair. Curling it around her finger, she played with it for while, before grabbing and pulling at it with all her might.

Tears of anguish started into her eyes as she continued to heave on it. Her eyes grew round with pain, she bared her teeth in determination.

Suddenly, without warning the clump fell free. Light-hearted with relief, she continued to stare at her reflection. Finally, smiling, she threw the hair into the bin as she walked to the door.

'Get back upstairs, all of you, right this minute!' White with rage, Mrs Harvey stood in the downstairs area, glaring at the mutinous staff. They held their ground. A few, including Lynne, Brenda and Clive,

The Grand

who had joined them from the cellar, stared back at the housekeeper, unabashed by the seriousness of what they'd done.

'One more chance,' she yelled imperiously, working herself into a frenzy. 'Get up those stairs. You've got until the count of three: one . . . two . . . three. That's it, you're sacked. Every last one of you, get out,' she screamed at their implacable, hostile faces. 'I said get out. *Get out!* Do you hear me? I said *get out!*'

No one moved. The housekeeper began to shake uncontrollably.

Quietly, calmly, Mr Collins stepped out from the corridor where he'd been monitoring the proceedings, and stood in front of Mrs Harvey. He looked at the staff, waiting a full minute before speaking.

'You've made your point. Now back to work.'

Clive nodded, acknowledging the concierge's authority, before moving. One by one, the staff followed him, filing back up the stairs without a word.

Mrs Harvey looked at Collins. He returned her gaze, before joining the rest of the staff and walking away.

Sarah strode into the living room, Marcus close on her heels.

'She's your wife. You made her your wife, then you treat her like that?'

'It's what she wants. You might not believe it, but it's true.'

'You bastard!'

'I have to be, to get what I want.'

'You can't *have* what you want.'

'I can. I always have. Except for one thing. One woman.' He stood in front of her. 'The woman my brother brought home, the woman my brother married.

Then I had to stand back and watch, watch him, and you, together, Sarah. He gives you nothing.'

'He loves me.'

'I love you. The proof's all around you. This hotel. Your job. Your son's future. What do you want me to do? Take it away, destroy it? Because I would.'

'Don't threaten me.'

'That's how far I'd go. What would John do for you?'

'I love him.'

'Then protect him. Stop me. I'll hurt him – I won't stop.'

Intimidated by his threats, she turned away. He touched her shoulder. She shrugged him off. He touched her hair, she grabbed his jacket intending to push him away, but instead she found herself gazing into his eyes.

They moved at the same time. There was no free will: they were drawn to one another like magnets. Their lips met in a kiss, light, gentle, but it soon became savage, voracious.

Light-headed, Sarah reeled away from him to see Collins standing in the doorway. She paled, horrified at what she'd done – all she'd risked.

'Mr Collins . . .'

Lowering his eyes, he said what he'd come to say, and no more. 'Excuse me. They're about to start the dance. You're expected to lead, sir.'

'Jacob it's not—' Sarah began.

'Excuse me, Mrs Bannerman.'

'Jacob, wait a minute,'

'Excuse me.'

Sarah looked at Marcus before tearing after the concierge.

*   *   *

The Grand

John sat with his mother and Adele.

'Of course, half of them are staying the night. It's the first time the hotel's been full since October . . .'

'Mr Bannerman?'

John looked up to see Kate and Stephen standing in front of him.

'I'm sorry, sir.' Aware of the people listening to her, Kate was deliberately vague. 'But I had to, sir. I had to tell him what you did for . . . my friend.'

Struggling with his emotions, Stephen stepped towards his father, and opened his arms. John looked up warily. Frightened by the strength of his own feelings, he went to his son and hugged him.

The lift opened and Collins walked out. Sarah ran down the stairs, Marcus a few steps behind her.

'Mr Collins . . .' she called.

Pretending he hadn't heard her, he crossed the room briskly, and went to the band.

'He's here, you can start. Go.'

They began playing the bridal waltz. Sarah still tried to get to Collins, but he joined the staff.

'Alfred, get those chairs moved back,' he ordered.

The crowd moved to the side of the room, clearing a space for the dancing to begin. Marcus went after Sarah but his mother intercepted him.

'There you are. You're supposed to start the dance. Everyone's waiting.'

'I seem to have lost my wife.'

Ruth left the crowd and walked towards him.

'I'm still here,' she said calmly.

Cupping her face in his hands, he looked down at her, feeling sorry for her, sorry for what she'd made herself. Holding out his hand, he led her on to the floor waiting for the beat before spiralling her around into the centre of the room. John walked up to Sarah and took her hand.

'Come on.'

'It's their dance.'

'I don't care.'

As they danced, he slowly became aware of both Marcus and Ruth staring at his wife. Sarah glanced back at Marcus. The smile on his face faltered, as he sensed the ever-expanding distance between him and the wife he so passionately adored.

Collins watched the proceedings impassively as Stephen went to Kate and held out his hand.

'I can't.' She stood back shaking her head.

'Monica would. Prove her right, Kate.'

Tears started into Kate's eyes at the mention of Monica's name, but she took his hand and they joined the dance.

Disgusted by the sight of Kate in Stephen's arms, Clive walked out, but Lynne and Brenda smiled, delighted by the turn of events, and their delight turned to laughter when they saw the furious expression on Mrs Harvey's face.

Esme took one last look at the dance floor before turning away. She was waylaid by a gentleman who offered her his hand. Hesitating for barely a second, she took it and allowed him to lead her on to the floor.

More and more couples joined those on the floor. The music played on, soft, lilting, and Mary sat back in her chair, contented if not happy. Her husband's and her own life's work was safe. The Grand Hotel still shone, the brightest and finest jewel in Manchester.